AUDEN AND ISHERWOOD: THE BERLIN YEARS

Auden and Isherwood
The Berlin Years

Norman Page

St. Martin's Press
New York

St. Martin's Press, Scholarly and Reference Division,
175 Fifth Avenue, New York, N.Y. 10010

First published in the United States of America in 1998

This book is printed on paper suitable for recycling and
made from fully managed and sustained forest sources.

Printed in Great Britain

ISBN 0–312–21173–2

Library of Congress Cataloging-in-Publication Data
Page, Norman.
Auden and Isherwood : the Berlin years / Norman Page.
p.   cm.
Includes bibliographical references (p.   ) and index.
ISBN 0–312–21173–2 (cloth)
1. Auden, W. H. (Wystan Hugh), 1907–1973—Homes and haunts–
–Germany—Berlin.   2. Isherwood, Christopher, 1904–   —Homes and
haunts—Germany—Berlin.   3. Auden, W. H. (Wystan Hugh), 1907–1973–
–Friends and associates.   4. Isherwood, Christopher, 1904–   –
–Friends and associates.   5. Berlin (Germany)—Intellectual
life—20th century.   6. British—Travel—Germany—History—20th
century.   7. Authors, English—20th century—Biography.   8. Berlin
(Germany)—History—1918–1945.   9. Berlin (Germany)—Biography.
I. Title.
PR6001.U4Z765 1997
820.9'00912—dc21
[b]   97–35010
                                                                      CIP

For Kamal

Contents

Contents

List of Plates

Acknowledgements

For advice and assistance of many kinds I am grateful to the following: Don Bachardy, Neville Braybrooke, Sally Brown (British Library), Katherine Bucknell, Mrs Mireille Burton, Jane Callander (BBC), Humphrey Carpenter, Mrs Alethea Constable-Maxwell (née Turville-Petre), A. T. Cornwell (Hon. Obituarist, Oratory Society), Ralf Dose (Magnus Hirschfeld Gesellschaft, Berlin), Loren Driscoll, Wayne Furman (New York Public Library), Robert Golding (Free University, Berlin), Rainer Herrn (Magnus Hirschfeld Gesellschaft, Berlin), David Luke (Christ Church, Oxford), J. R. Maddicott (Librarian and Archivist, Exeter College, Oxford), Francis O. Mattson (Curator, Berg Collection), Luke McKernan (British Film Institute), Professor Edward Mendelson (Literary Executor, the Estate of W. H. Auden), Mr and Mrs Konrad Muthesius, Peter Parker, Renata Stepanek (née Muthesius), A. J. Tinkel (Archivist, Oratory School), Professor Thorlac Turville-Petre, Edward Upward, Rick Wandel (National Museum and Archive of Lesbian and Gay History, New York).

The Leverhulme Trust generously granted me an Emeritus Fellowship for research on the subject of this book.

Quotations from W. H. Auden's 'Berlin Journal' are copyright by the Estate of W. H. Auden and reproduced here by kind permission of Professor Edward Mendelson and the Henry W. and Albert A. Berg Collection, the New York Public Library, Astor, Lenox and Tilden Foundations.

Prologue:
Looking for Berlin

Like many of us, this book originated in chance and accident rather than forethought and planning. Not long after the *Wende*, the coming down of the Wall, I happened to be in Berlin, and, as I wandered through the newly open city, it struck me (as it doubtless struck many others at that time) that after some sixty years – roughly the span of my own lifetime – Berlin had returned to a state it had not known since the Nazis came to power. This brought to mind the group of English writers who had, briefly or not so briefly, made Berlin their home in the last years of the Weimar Republic, and I wondered idly how much in a merely material sense had survived two generations of destruction and rebuilding, partition and reunification: how far the physical fabric of the Berlin that Wystan Auden, Christopher Isherwood, Stephen Spender and others had lived in and written about could be, historically or sentimentally, recovered or rediscovered.

So I went home and did a little biographical and topographical research and, the next time I was there, wandered the streets again, only this time with a 1930 map of Berlin in one hand and a modern map in the other. Not surprisingly, I found that a lot had disappeared. I found, for instance, that the neat lawns of a public park now cover the site of the busy, fashionable, dignified neighbourhood of tall houses, theatres and restaurants where Isherwood stayed when he first settled in the city, and the tenement where he lived briefly but (from a literary point of view) productively with the family of his working-class lover has likewise vanished. But I also discovered that an unexpected amount has survived. The two houses where Auden lived in 1928–9, one in a smart suburb, the other in a former working-class district, still stand, and while there is no trace of the various lodgings that Isherwood occupied during the earlier part of his time in Berlin, the more celebrated house which provided him with the primary setting for his Berlin stories remains intact, its interior not much changed since that time. Of all these sites only one is commemorated by an official plaque – bearing, as it happens, erroneous information.

1

Particular bars, cafés, dance-halls and cabarets have long ceased to exist: many of them, indeed, barely outlived the Weimar Republic itself. Notorious squares, streets and alleys have become respectable when they have not been entirely swept away. Of 'the Passage', the alley off the Friedrichstrasse frequented by homosexual pick-ups and widely celebrated in fact and fiction, not a trace remains. A once famous political theatre, after being for a time a 'porno' cinema, is now a disco hall and a venue for rock concerts. But the shape and pattern of the city, the streets that are perambulated in getting from one place to another, even the street names, have changed surprisingly little. The hidden skeleton of the U-Bahn or subway and the visible one of its elevated counterpart the S-Bahn are still there to convey us on the same trips that Auden and his friends made. Landmarks like the Zoo Station and the Kaiser Wilhelm Memorial Church still stand, though the latter only part-ially, its stately spire snapped off like a broken tooth and officially transformed, like the bombed Coventry Cathedral and the deva-stated dome in the centre of Hiroshima, into a faintly self-conscious symbol.

When a city is smashed to pieces by natural or unnatural disas-ter, there are two options open to the rebuilders. They can take the opportunity to plan and build a new city. Or they can rebuild the old one so that what they end up with is very like what has disappeared – sometimes so like it that the ignorant visitor may be seduced into according the modern structure a deference appro-priate only to the antique. Just as some of the baroque churches of Munich were scrupulously restored down to the last lick of gold paint, the new Berlin rose in the postwar years along familiar lines, and the spatial feel of the present-day city, when due allowance has been made for new buildings and changes in traffic flow, may not be so very different from what it was around 1930. Certainly, one can still, for instance, walk the route that Spender took when he stepped out of his lodgings and went to visit Isherwood in his, or the even shorter route that led Auden from *his* room to the famous Cosy Corner bar. One can also, if so disposed, in the spirit of the literary pilgrim exploring Dickens's London or Hardy's Wessex, tread in the footsteps of Sally Bowles, Mr Norris and other fictional or semi-fictional characters whose literary lives are largely confined to this city.

My interest growing, I moved on from topography to less tan-gible aspects of the past, asking myself what had taken these young

Englishmen to Berlin and what they had found to fascinate and detain them there, making Auden, for instance, feel 'homesick' for the city after he was obliged to return to England to earn his keep, and a little later impelling him to write poems in bad German to express his nostalgia and longing to return. The biographer's trade nourishes any natural tendency that already exists towards scepticism, and I was not prepared to take at face value the well-publicised boasts by both Auden and Isherwood that they had gone there purely and simply – well, simply – for sex. Berlin around 1930 was not just an enticing destination for sex holidays or fieldwork in the study of decadence. It was the most exciting city in Europe, perhaps in the world, for anyone sympathetic to experiment and innovation in a wide variety of art forms, high and popular, pure and applied: a vital city that in a surprisingly short time had become a magnet for gifted young artists and artistes.

When Auden, in the last line of one of the best known of his early poems (written, incidentally, in the first month of his stay in Berlin), expressed a wish for 'New styles of architecture, a change of heart', he may have had the Bauhaus specifically in mind but was surely not speaking only of architecture. The line expresses the mood of a whole generation for whom Berlin seemed to offer the promise of artistic and social tolerance. The tragedy, it goes without saying, is that the heyday passed so quickly – was, indeed, already under serious threat at the point at which this book begins, though many of those with whom it is concerned came to recognise this grim reality only with the passing of time.

The number of talented Berliners had been swollen by others who, like Bertolt Brecht and Kurt Weill, had come from other parts of Germany, as well as by an international crowd of writers and others, actual or aspiring, who headed for the German capital just as, a few years earlier, their slightly older counterparts had headed for Paris. To read the biographies, autobiographies, letters, journals and memoirs of those who were young or youngish during that period is to encounter many accounts of expeditions to and periods of residence in the city – by, for example, Paul Bowles and Aaron Copland, Francis Bacon and Aleister Crowley, William Plomer and Harold Nicolson, Robert McAlmon and John Lehmann. Auden and Isherwood differed from these, however, both in staying longer and in absorbing their Berlin experiences more thoroughly into their lives and their art.

This book begins with an account of the time spent by these two young writers in Berlin, its boundaries being the arrival of Auden, aged 21 and a brand-new Oxford graduate, in October 1928, and Isherwood's final departure a few weeks after Hitler came to power early in 1933. Its immediate chronological span is thus about four and a half years, though Isherwood was not the only English visitor who went on writing about Berlin long after he had left the city for good. The second chapter looks at the city they found when they stepped off the train: its history and its contemporary ethos; its historic landmarks and newly erected public buildings; its places of entertainment and also certain private dwellings, usually notable only because they were once the homes of writers; its social life by day and night; and some representative creative talents who were active in the city during the period with which we are concerned.

Chapter 3 presents portraits of a number of figures who seem to me to be interesting in two respects. All of them impinged in one way or another on the lives of one or both of the writers in question, and in addition they help to exemplify the kind of personalities and life-styles to which Berlin at this time was hospitable. Not all of them are Germans, but some would be hard to parallel in, say, London or New York at the same period, and since they tend to flit like shadows through other biographies of Auden and Isherwood (understand-ably enough, given the much larger scope of these undertakings), it has seemed worthwhile to try to recreate them in as much detail as possible, especially since most of them are remarkable individuals in their own right and by any standards. A conspicuous absentee from the list is Jean Ross, the prototype of Isherwood's best-known char-acter, Sally Bowles, who has been so exhaustively investigated by other writers as to leave little or nothing to be added to the record. In Chapter 4 the cinema, an art-form that flourished in the Weimar period and has a special bearing on the work of Isherwood, is given separate treatment. Finally, since the reason for investigating the lives of the young men who stand at the centre of this study is that they were writers, there is a chapter that considers the literary out-come of their Berlin experiences: the poems, plays, autobiographies and fictions that exploited and transformed (often more than is read-ily realised) elements from the lives they had lived there, the places they knew and the people they met.

Among other things, this book may also, in its small way, lay claim to being an experiment in biography. At a time when fiction and most other literary genres have been radically 'made new' by a century of innovation, all but a very few biographies still resolutely follow the nineteenth-century model by offering a chronological birth-to-death narrative of a single life. Not a few, indeed, seem, technically speaking, to represent little advance on the annalistic method of the Roman historians, conducting the reader through the subject's life (and the author's files) in the unshakeable belief that what gives shape and meaning to experience is the fact that Monday is followed by Tuesday and February comes after January. Sometimes, though, there may be a case for limiting the focus to a crucial or formative phase of a life, as (to cite two rare exceptions to the general rule) James L. Clifford does in his *Young Samuel Johnson* and H. C. Robbins Landon in his *Mozart's Last Year*. But in any case we do not live alone but very largely through our relationships, so that sometimes lives, including the lives of writers, need to be seen not monolithically but in juxtaposition to each other.

Though many other figures are introduced, the emphasis in this book is on two writers, Auden and Isherwood, who not only talked, ate, wrote and slept together but between them spent the last four and a half years of the Weimar Republic in Berlin. It may therefore be thought of as an attempt to write a biography, or microbiography, of two men and a city during a period which, though brief, was of considerable, even crucial, importance in the lives of all three. That Berlin, and Germany, could never be the same again after the Nazis came to power will hardly be disputed. That going to and living in Berlin involved far-reaching choices for Auden and Isherwood, affecting the course of their future life and work, may be less immediately obvious but is, I believe, fully borne out by the evidence.

1

Two Young Englishmen

In the summer of 1928, Wystan Hugh Auden, aged 21, left Oxford with a third-class degree in English literature, a considerable quantity of poems, and a nearly finished play, *Paid on Both Sides*. His Oxford had been, among other things, the Oxford of Evelyn Waugh (four years older than he), Harold Acton (three years), Henry Yorke, who became the novelist Henry Green (two years), Brian Howard, later a friend of both Auden and Isherwood (two years), and John Betjeman, who entered the university in the same term as Auden himself. The young men of this generation had been schoolboys during the Great War, in which the fathers of many of them had fought and, not infrequently, died.

In the immediate postwar years the atmosphere of Oxford had had an unmistakably military flavour. As Christopher Hollis points out in his memoir of the period, the majority of undergraduates came from military service and some took shortened courses: 'Military life was still the life they thought of as normal and they referred to Hall as the Mess' (*In the Twenties*, p. 17). By the time Auden got there, however, efforts to revive the carefree and hedonistic glories of prewar days and to combine them with the new freedoms of the Jazz Age were well under way. As Martin Green has shown at considerable length in *Children of the Sun*, mid-1920s Oxford witnessed the glittering rise of the New Dandies, and though the group that formed around Auden was 'entirely separate from [Harold] Acton's and quite hostile' (p. 333), regarding Acton and his poetry as frivolous, Auden himself developed a personal brand of non-Etonian aestheticism. As Green aptly says, he cultivated the 'eccentricities of dandyism' and became 'a phenomenon of self-stylisation' (p. 334), and this was a personal style that was to last, with modifications, for the rest of his life.

It was, says Betjeman's biographer, Bevis Hillier, 'the Oxford of plus fours, verandah suits, violet hair cream, batik or Charvet silk ties and open sports cars' (p. 130), and of more or less illicit visits to the London theatres and nightclubs by the train familiarly known as the Flying Fornicator. More sourly, Henry Green recalls in his not unsnobbish autobiography *Pack My Bag* that on entering Oxford he and his contemporaries were 'either to become money snobs or too sensitive to the difference money makes...I was to court the rich while doubting whether there should be great inequalities between incomes...We played at being gentlemen' (p. 195).

This wasn't, however, entirely Auden's style, sartorially or otherwise. During the General Strike he had driven a car in London for the Trades Union Congress ('out of sheer contrariness', as he later said), and the resolve to be unfashionable and nonconformist, which later in life developed into an instinctive and comprehensive eccentricity, is revealing. His first publication, the *Poems* of 1928 (privately printed by Stephen Spender), had been an altogether more serious affair than that of his fellow member of Christ Church, Harold Acton, who was proud to be thought of as an aesthete and who as a schoolboy had brought out, with Brian Howard, a pink-bound volume titled *The Eton Candle* and quickly dubbed *The Eton Scandal*. Auden was not averse to schoolboyish high jinks or to flying his sexual colours from the mast: the private mythologies or fantasy worlds shared with Isherwood and prominent in his early poems and plays suggest a nostalgia for a pre-adolescent, private-school world of privileged irresponsibility. But the camp glamour of the Harold Acton set, which sought to perpetuate in the postwar years the vanished world of Wilde and the Decadents, and perhaps even the earlier blue-china atmosphere of Wilde and Pater's Oxford, did not seduce him. Industrial archaeology and the Icelandic sagas were more to his taste than Japanese prints or 'the Hellenic ideal', and his vision looked to the bracing north rather than the relaxing south.

Born in York in 1907, he was the youngest of the three sons of George Auden, MD, who in the following year became school medical officer for Birmingham. Dr Auden had interests in Greek, Latin and psychology, while his wife, a trained nurse and a High Anglican, had an enthusiasm for music. Long before his Oxford days Wystan had made up his mind to be not just a poet but a great poet, which necessarily meant an original poet. Poetry, though, is a vocation rather than a profession, and sooner or later he had to earn a living. A year after leaving Oxford, he was to imitate another Oxford contemporary, Paul Pennyfeather in Evelyn Waugh's *Decline and Fall*, by drifting into that traditional refuge of the highly educated and totally unqualified, private-schoolmastering. But

first, with what seems like extraordinary generosity, his father
offered him a year on the Continent. During the summer he fell
ill, and in August spent three weeks recuperating at the Belgian
resort of Spa; it may have been there that he had some sessions of
psychoanalysis. But by October he was fit enough to travel to
Berlin, where he remained, with some interruptions, until the
summer of the following year.

Why Berlin? It was a time when many British writers and artists,
still following the eighteenth-century tradition of the Grand Tour
as modified by Byron and by such Victorian escapees from intolerance and repression as John Addington Symonds, instinctively
turned south, especially towards the Mediterranean regions. It was
a fashion that had recently received a boost from the great popularity of Norman Douglas's *South Wind* (1917). But Auden was
proud of his Icelandic name and looks, and took delight in unfash-
ionably preferring the north. A more practical consideration was
that, being extremely fair-skinned, he burned easily and painfully
when exposed to the hot sun. Isherwood came to share and perhaps imitate his refusal to conform: indeed, he held out much
longer, since while Auden later in life made a home in Ischia,
Isherwood had turned fifty before he even set foot in Italy.

Paris, since the late nineteenth century the inevitable destination
for many aspiring artists and writers, and in the 1920s a refuge for
Prohibition-fleeing Americans, was by now past its palmiest days
even for those less inclined than Auden to Francophobia. Berlin,
moreover, was the place where some of the most progressive
movements in painting and theatre, architecture and cinema, and
other pure and applied arts were located. Even more enticingly, it
had a richly deserved reputation for sexual permissiveness and for
the diversity of its sexual underworld. A joke current in Berlin at
the time said that, if a lion were sitting outside the Reichstag and a
virgin walked past, the lion would roar. Stephen Spender recalls
the joke in his introduction to Thomas Friedrich's pictorial history
of Weimar Berlin, and was probably also recalling it when he made
the character based on Isherwood in *The Temple*, his *roman à clef*
partly set in late-1920s Berlin, declare solemnly that it was ' "a city
with no virgins. Not even the puppies and kittens are virgins" '
(p. 185).

Thanks to this dual reputation, the city was attracting an international crowd of artists and writers as well as tourists, as a
sentence from Robert McAlmon's memoirs makes clear:

I went to Berlin, and there, or soon to be there, were Thelma Wood (sculptor), Marsden Hartley (painter), Djuna Barnes (writer), Berenice Abbott (photographer), Harriet Marsden (dancer), two musicians whose names I have forgotten, Isadora Duncan, and quantities of others....

Even though these are not now names to conjure with, the mood of excitement created by these incessant international comings and goings is unmistakable, and the 'quantities of others' might have included, for instance, Francis Bacon, Paul Bowles, Aaron Copland, Aleister Crowley, William Plomer, and Beatrix and John Lehmann, of all of whom something will later be said.

Moreover, and not least important for a young man living on an allowance from his father, the exchange rate was such that for anyone with sterling or dollars to spend it was a cheap place in which to live. As McAlmon puts it, 'No one knew from one day to the next what the dollar would bring in marks, but everybody knew that, whatever happened, the dollar bought in Berlin as much as ten or twenty dollars would buy elsewhere.'

Of the ten months between his departure for Berlin and his reluctant return to England and job-hunting, Auden spent a total of only about seven in the city: the rest of his time was passed in other parts of Germany and in short visits home. But it was to be in many ways a decisive choice: nothing less than a turning-point in his life, which might have turned out entirely differently if, say, he had got a better degree and remained at Oxford. He was to write some of his finest early poems in Berlin and to embark on his first collaboration with Isherwood. He was also to recognise and come to terms with – indeed, eagerly embrace – his own sexual identity: before Berlin he had been engaged to a Birmingham girl who was training to be a nurse and had cheerfully described himself as 'ambidextrous'. A letter of this period tells how he went to a wedding, got 'decently drunk', and fell in love with one of the bridesmaids. There appears, however, to have been nothing bisexual about his adventures in Germany, and one of his first acts after returning to England was to break off his engagement. A note in his journal at this time makes the fervent promise to himself that he will never commit such a folly again. He also developed a bohemian mode of existence and acquired a taste for living outside England both of which were to persist for most of his life thereafter. And he became so much of a Germanophile that, when he later came to look around for a place in which to settle, one of the requirements was that the German language should be spoken there. Later he was to make the request that his friends should play the music of Wagner on the day of his funeral.

At first he lodged well away from the centre of Berlin, with a distinguished middle-class family who had probably been found through personal contacts; they were remarkable people, and they and their home will be described a little later. During these weeks he worked on his German, which eventually became fluent but far from accurate, and also on the revised version of his 'charade' *Paid on Both Sides*, which was completed by the end of the year and dispatched on New Year's Eve to T. S. Eliot, editor of the *Criterion*. In December he also wrote the poem that begins 'We made all possible preparations', at first untitled but later given the title 'Let History Be My Judge'. It is one of those mildly obfuscatory poems that Auden liked to write at this stage of his career, suggesting a world of political conspiracy and revolutionary action, of broken promises and betrayed ideals, as if Franz Kafka had engaged in a collaboration with John Buchan.

He went back to England to spend Christmas with his family in Birmingham, and presumably saw something of his fiancée at this time. Certainly he saw his friend Christopher Isherwood, whom he had met three years earlier during the Christmas vacation following his first term at Oxford. Oddly enough, they had been at the same preparatory school and appear in the same group photograph taken there, but the age difference had meant that they had hardly known each other. Isherwood, who was three years older, had left Cambridge without a degree at the same time that Auden left school, and was now a medical student in London, a less than half-hearted venture that lasted only two terms.

Isherwood himself had paid his first visit to Germany the previous May, when an elderly cousin who was British Consul in Bremen had invited him for a holiday. A letter sent from Bremen to his Repton and Cambridge friend Edward Upward conveys the authentic flavour of the trip. Written from Elsassestrasse 42, Bremen, it is dated only 'Wednesday', bears no salutation, and is signed 'Marco Polo' – self-mockingly, or perhaps enviously, for it expresses the desire 'never to remain more than a week in any country' and declares: 'Yes, after all, our later days must be spent in travel.' The envy is more unambiguous in the comment that 'The whole town is full of boys. In their silver-braided forage-caps, mackintosh tunics and green (word illegible) lace-up shirts.' Like his description of the tramp-steamer on which he had sailed, with its Chinese cook, Welsh cabin-boy and drunken captain, this is premonitory of the observing eye of the fictional style he was later to adopt.

This brief visit, though apparently barren of sexual escapades, was of considerable significance in that Isherwood fell under the spell of Germany and received a vision of it as a Promised Land of liberation and fulfilment, a spiritual homeland. (This last word is used in *Christopher and his Kind* (p. 17) when he suggests that, entering Germany in 1929 and asked by an immigration official the purpose of his visit, he 'could have truthfully replied "I'm looking for my homeland and I've come to find out if this is it."') The subsequent literary treatment or non-treatment of the brief Bremen trip is instructive. In *Lions and Shadows*, the early autobiography where it chronologically belongs, it is unmentioned, but nearly a quarter of a century later it forms the basis of a whole section ('Mr Lancaster') of a heavily autobiographical work of fiction, *Down There on a Visit*. The author's subsequent judgement (*Christopher and his Kind*, p. 10) is that this version contains 'too much fiction and too little frankness'. In the late autobiography *Christopher and his Kind* the Bremen episode, which might easily have been accorded a colourful page or two, receives just four sentences.

It is not difficult to guess that one of the non-literary topics of conversation during Auden and Isherwood's brief Christmas reunion in England must have been the availability of boys (not necessarily attired in the Bremen style) in the bars of Berlin. It was a subject on which Auden had already made himself an expert, and it calls for no imaginative leap to surmise that Isherwood must have felt and expressed a strong desire to see things for himself. Auden's explorations of the rent-bars that abounded in the city were already well under way, and his wish to have them more conveniently to hand must have been the principal motive for his change of lodgings very soon after his return to Berlin in January 1929.

The cover story was promulgated that his middle-class hosts insisted on practising their English on him instead of allowing him to learn German – which was, after all, his official reason for being in Berlin – and there is no reason to doubt the truth of this. But the truth is not always the whole truth, and other, more urgent

motives were at work. A letter written at this time declares that
'The German proletariat are fine, but I dont [*sic*] like the others very
much....', 'proletariat' here having sexual as well as social connotations. From all points of view a room much nearer the city centre,
and one to which he could take back a 'friend' without awkward-
ness, was infinitely more satisfactory than being the paying guest
of a socially well-placed family in a posh suburb. There was also the
excitement of doing something unconventional, a motive detect-
able in his statement to an English correspondent that from the first
of the month he was going 'to live in a slum'. It was an act of
modest daring that Isherwood was later to imitate. At any rate
Auden liked his new location well enough to remain there until
the end of his sojourn in Berlin.

In his 1987 preface to *The Temple*, a version of the novel he had
written nearly sixty years earlier, Stephen Spender identifies 1929,
a shade facilely, as the last gasp of a dying order, 'just before the
Thirties, when everything became politics'. Auden was to become
increasingly aware of political issues as the year wore on, but at its
outset he seems to have been totally immersed in more subjective
and hedonistic matters. And after the evasions and subterfuges and
disapprovals of England, it was not surprising that the atmosphere
of late Weimar Berlin should have gone to his head.

A glimpse of what the city had to offer during this period to
visiting English homosexuals is provided by the experiences of the
painter (though not then a painter) Francis Bacon, who spent about
three months there in the winter of 1927–8, shortly before Auden's
arrival. (Bacon's biographers suggest different dates for this escap-
ade, but the one given here seems the more likely.) Bacon, who was
about 18 at the time, in later years provided conflicting versions of
the circumstances in which he had been taken off to Berlin by an
older man. At one time it was a 'sporting uncle', a friend of his
father's who had been charged with the task of making a man of
him; on another occasion, the person on whom this ill-defined duty
devolved was an old army friend of his father's in London, who
promptly fell in love with the lad and took him to Germany.
Andrew Sinclair has plausibly and intriguingly identified this latter
individual as Sir Percy Loraine, who had married Bacon's grandmother (a marriage that lasted only briefly) but was known to be
fond of young men. Loraine was a distinguished career diplomat
who soon afterwards became High Commissioner for Egypt and
the Sudan and finished his career as Ambassador to Rome; he

earns, or at any rate receives, an entry in the *Dictionary of National Biography*.

At any rate, Loraine, or someone equally obliging, carried the young Bacon off to Berlin – a choice of destination that says much for its contemporary reputation in England – and they installed themselves at the luxurious Adlon Hotel, where a waiter would wheel in a trolley ornamented with curving swans' necks at the corners and imperturbably serve breakfast to them in their huge double bed. In the evenings they toured the bars, nightclubs and cabarets, including the Eldorado, the famous transvestite bar that Otto Dix had painted in 1927. Bacon detected in the city, at least in retrospect, 'an atmosphere of tension and unease'; Berlin was, he said near the end of his life, 'a very violent place – emotionally violent, not physically – and that certainly had its effect on me'. Such an atmosphere, decadent, edgy and unstable, is certainly palpable in works as different as the drawings of Georg Grosz and the Berlin novels (for instance, *Laughter in the Dark* (Russian version, 1932)) of Vladimir Nabokov, a resident of the city from 1922 to 1937 and one of a large number of Russian émigrés who helped to enrich Berlin's cultural life in the interwar period. It is an atmosphere brilliantly and unsettlingly conveyed in Fassbinder's film version of another early Nabokov novel, *Despair*.

Auden's new base in Furbringerstrasse was good for poetry as well as sex, for it was there that he wrote a number of poems that were to remain in the canon of his work, including 'From scars where kestrels hover', 'Love by ambition', 'Before this loved one', 'The strings' excitement', 'A Free One', and the first section of '1929' beginning 'It was Easter as I walked in the public gardens'. In February he was briefly back in England to celebrate his 22nd birthday (on the 21st of the month) and to dash up to Scotland to visit his friend Cecil Day-Lewis, now teaching in Helensburgh. Then, in the following month, under the stimulus of their Christmas conversations and no doubt also encouraged by Auden's letters, Isherwood arrived in Berlin for a short visit. It was his first sight of the city in which he was to spend most of the next five years.

At about this time Auden had formed a romantic attachment to a young sailor from Hamburg called Gerhart Meyer, who is mentioned by name, commended for 'Absence from fear . . . From the sea', and hailed as 'the truly strong man' in his poem '1929'. Though brief and one-sided, the affair was, as we shall see, intense. His first reaction to the boys of the Berlin bars, readily available

and remarkably cheap, had been an understandable euphoria, and
in one letter written at this time he confessed – sexual and social
liberation proceeding hand in hand – that he was spending 'most
of my time with Juvenile Delinquents' and described the city as
'the buggers daydream'.

The same letter adds, probably with some exaggeration, that
there were 170 male brothels under police supervision. The figure,
presumably derived from gossip rather than published statistics,
may be slightly exaggerated, though another account (see p. 63
below) gives a figure not much smaller. Auden also states that he
has learned a good many German obscenities; and that his current
boy is 'a cross between a rugger hearty and Josephine Baker. We
should make D. H. Lawrence look rather blue. I am a mass of
bruises'. The wish to shock is transparent, the more especially
since the recipient of these confidences was a woman, the fiancée
of his friend Bill McElwee. But the hinted taste for masochistic
pleasure is confirmed by his friend John Layard, who claims to
have witnessed a sexual session between Auden and one of his
boys which started with a pillow-fight and proceeded to blows as
the prologue to serious sexual activity. 'Wystan liked being beaten
up a bit,' observed Layard thoughtfully. When Auden said of A. E.
Housman, in his 1938 sonnet, that his 'private lust' was 'Something
to do with violence and the poor', he knew what he was talking
about – knew about masochism at the hands of rough trade, that is,
if not about Housman.

That pillow-fight suggests a reversion to childhood or early
adolescence on the part of the young Oxford graduate: one thinks
of the apple-pie beds that, in a more decorous and more timid age,
Housman and his chums would occasionally make for each other
on the occasion of their reunions. Auden's own comment at this
time that he was 'having the sort of friendships I ought to have had
at 16 and didnt [sic]' suggests a conscious – and, as he ruefully
added, 'expensive' – attempt on his part to make good the missed
opportunities of his boarding-school days, when many of his peer
group would have passed through a phase of homosexual experimentation and in this way, as the saying goes, 'got it out of their
system'. The note already cited is enigmatically phrased but seems
to indicate that during his early weeks in Berlin Auden still
thought of himself as working his way, doggedly though with
considerable gusto, through a necessary stage on the road to heterosexuality, respectability and marriage. A letter to Day-Lewis at

this time revealingly compares Gerhart's predecessor, his first boy-friend Pieps ('the most elemental thing I have yet met'), to his fiancée. It is clear that as far as Auden was concerned his engagement to the student nurse identified by Humphrey Carpenter as Sheilah Richardson was at this stage still a reality.

The turbulence of his sexual and emotional life gave Auden little leisure to acquire knowledge of the wider and deeper realities of the society in which he was now living, and perhaps at this stage he had little desire to do so. As I shall be arguing later, however, his first impressions of Berlin as 'the buggers daydream' was itself something of a daydream. It was an entirely natural response to his liberation that nevertheless ignored both the grim social and economic realities (there was a vast army of the unemployed in Germany at this time) and the sinister political rumblings as expressions and demonstrations of Nazi ideology, including its intolerance of homosexuals and other minority groups, became more blatant and more strident.

If, during his first few months in Berlin, Auden was overwhelmed by the unprecedented freedoms now placed at his disposal, what is really extraordinary is the speed with which he passed from the immaturity of his initial responses to an articulated self-awareness and self-knowledge. Reading the journal (still largely unpublished) that he kept during the spring of 1929, I found myself repeatedly struck by his mature grasp of the situations in which he and his friends found themselves, his evident desire to understand his own nature and behaviour, and his ability (sometimes, admittedly, a little over-exercised) to extrapolate general truths from individual experience. Studying his laconic but penetrating analyses, it is easy to forget that this was a young man of barely 22 who had only just stepped off the class-driven conveyor belt of public school and ancient university.

The turning-point at which Auden definitively recognised his own sexual identity and chose his own future may have come around Easter 1929, just after Isherwood's short visit. Isherwood left England on 14 March and recalled long afterwards that the visit had lasted 'a week or ten days'; but he makes an appearance in the first six entries in Auden's journal, and if (as is usually supposed) the journal was begun on 23 March his visit must have lasted a fortnight. (The journal entries give only the days of the week, not the dates, and were clearly written retrospectively.) Quite possibly, however, the first journal entry (headed 'Saturday') refers to 16

March, which would fit in with Isherwood's arrival, possibly on
the previous day. It is preceded by the statement that 'Christopher's visit will serve as well as any thing else as the introduction
to this journal. Wherever one starts there will be loose threads.'

On the Saturday (16 or 23 March) they visited Magnus Hirschfeld's Institute of Sexology, where Isherwood was later to make his
home, then went to a restaurant with Auden's English friend, John
Layard, and from there to Auden's favourite *Jugendsbar* (boy-bar),
the Cosy Corner – an establishment that was to acquire a status in
accounts of Auden and Isherwood's Berlin comparable to that of
the Café Royal in 1890s London. Layard joined them again the
following evening, after which they went (in Auden's habitual
phrase) brothel-crawling. No doubt the Cosy Corner, which by
something more than a happy coincidence was a stone's throw
from Auden's lodgings, was again on their itinerary.

Almost fifty years later Isherwood recalled his first crossing of
the Cosy Corner's threshold in terms that present it as a rite of
passage, ceremony of initiation or ritual of spiritual rebirth. In the
autobiographical *Christopher and his Kind*, which significantly takes
1929 as the starting-point of its narrative, he writes: 'I can still make
myself faintly feel the delicious nausea of initiation terror which
Christopher felt as Wystan pushed back the heavy leather door-
curtain of a boy bar called the Cosy Corner and led the way inside'
(pp. 10–11). Like Auden, though prepared to be promiscuous and
to enjoy it thoroughly, Isherwood was really in quest of romantic
love, of the Ideal Friend. It did not take him long to discover, and
feel 'instant infatuation' for, a youth named Berthold Szczesny who
hailed from the German-speaking part of Czechoslovakia and was
nicknamed 'Bubi' (Baby). 'To be infatuated,' he observed in *Christopher and his Kind*, 'was what [Christopher] had come to Berlin for.
Bubi was the first presentable candidate who appeared to claim the
leading role in Christopher's love-myth' (p. 11), and one wonders
whether the apparent candour of old age was not actually substituting another, more cynical 'love-myth' for the romantic one here
discredited. For all the retrospective self-mockery, the infatuation
did not wear off quickly, for four months later Isherwood was still
in pursuit of Bubi. The boy is the subject of Auden's poem 'Before
this loved one', written in March in response to his friend's 'instant
infatuation'. It was a subject on which they were both experts.

The Cosy Corner makes frequent appearances in recollections of
this period, and in the mythical Berlin that was created by Auden,

Isherwood and others it looms considerably larger than the Brandenburg Gate or the Kaiser Wilhelm Memorial Church. In due
course Isherwood, by then an habitué rather than a candidate for
initiation, was able to introduce John Lehmann to the sexual free-
masonry of the Cosy Corner, and long afterwards Lehmann too
recalled the seismic effect of the experience in a very thinly fictionalised account in which Isherwood appears as 'William' (actually
one of his real names):

> One of the first things William did to further my education, was
> to take me on a tour of the homosexual bars and night-clubs. We
> started with one of the most popular non-smart *Lokals*, the 'Cosy
> Corner'. This *Lokal* was a sensational experience for me, a kind of
> emotional earthquake, and I think William was right to throw me
> in at the deep end. Things unimagined by me in all my previous
> fantasies went on there. The place was filled with attractive boys
> of any age between sixteen and twenty-one, some fair and curly-
> haired, some dark and often blue-eyed, and nearly all dressed in
> extremely short lederhosen which showed off their smooth and
> sun-burnt thighs to delectable advantage....
> The lavatory had no cubicles. I was followed in by several
> boys, who, as if by chance, ranged themselves on either side of
> me and pulled out their cocks rather to show them off than to
> relieve nature as I was doing. I don't think a drop fell into the
> gutter from any of them; but many sly grins were cast in my
> direction. I returned to our bench, shaken by this exhibition into
> a turbulence of anticipation. William said to me 'Any you fancy?'
> (*In the Purely Pagan Sense*, p. 44)

Lehmann's drooling mixture of incredulity and self-congratulation,
we can be fairly sure, had also been both Auden's and Isherwood's
at a slightly earlier date.

But by the time of Isherwood's arrival, Auden had plainly qualified himself as a knowledgeable guide, and his journal names a
number of other bars, some of them more than once, occasionally
indicating their particular ambience or clientele. The Hollandais,
for instance, seems to have been a high-class and relatively decorous establishment: an advertisement in the gay newspaper *Die
Freundschaft* refers to its music, its international flavour and its
Sunday tea-dances. Auden's reaction to its denizens was, interestingly, one of moral disgust, and his preference was unmistakably

for what he more than once refers to as 'rough stuff'. On 24 April 1929, after an unsatisfying visit to the Hollandais, he went on to the Café Hallesches Tor in the working-class area where he lived, and clearly felt more comfortable for the move.

The Hollandais was in Bülowstrasse, where, picturesquely situated under the arches of the overhead railway and felicitously located at number 69, it was only one of a number of gay and lesbian bars and similar establishments in this busy thoroughfare. Among others, there were the Continental Club at number 2, the Nationalhof (37), the Bülow Casino (41), the Conti-Casino (47), the Dorian Gray (57), the Dede (91), the Hohenzollern Lounge (101) and the Pan Lounge (105). Another neighbourhood patronised by Auden was the Alte Jakobstrasse, not far from his home in Hallesches Tor. (The street still exists, but scarcely a building survived the wartime bombing.) Here, at number 49, was an establishment where, on that momentous Easter Sunday of 1929, Auden met Gerhart Meyer, while at number 60 was the celebrated Eldorado Lounge, much frequented by transvestites. Also near Hallesches Tor, and leading from Alte Jakobstrasse into Kreuzberg, was Skalitzerstrasse, and on one occasion recorded in his journal Auden visited a bar at number 7 and picked up a boy whose name he either never learned or subsequently forgot.

Isherwood made the most of his brief first visit to Berlin and, once discovered, Bubi quickly assumed a central role in his life. The third entry in Auden's journal announces Monday as 'The great Bubi day' and continues:

> Pimping for someone on whom one has a transference creates the most curious feelings. Chiefly I remember Christopher and Bubi playing ping-pong. The sense of bare flesh, the blue sky through the glass and the general sexy atmosphere made me feel like a participant in a fertility rite. . . . In the pine wood I felt the third baboon and a public school one, Sunday walks to be back in time for chapel. In the train all was gloom, reviving a little at tea and later in bed.

As with much else in the journal, there are some obscurities here, but they are not quite impenetrable. 'Having a transference', a recurring phrase, seems to mean having formed a strong emotional bond, though not necessarily being in love. Why 'all was gloom' in the train is not clear: perhaps Bubi had left them by then, or perhaps Auden had had enough of his lover's love, for it certainly seems to have been Wystan and Christopher who were 'later in bed' together.

The course of Isherwood's infatuation did not run altogether smooth, and two days later he and Bubi quarrelled. The subject of their quarrel can be inferred from a scrap of German dialogue reproduced without comment in the journal. Isherwood was evidently anxious to convince the youth that the relationship he desired was that of lovers and friends rather than hustler and client; he felt possessive and was jealous of Bubi's professional contacts with other men, and the next day set off to resume his attempt to transform the rent boy into the Ideal Friend. Coached by Auden, whose conversational German was a good deal better than his own at this stage, he delivered a carefully prepared speech; he had, however, overlooked the Great Phrase-book Fallacy, and was quite unable to understand Bubi's reply. Isherwood's time in Berlin soon came to an end, but Bubi's magnetism, not to mention Auden's friendship and the wider lure of Germany, was strong enough to bring him back again before long.

Auden's reaction to Isherwood's brief visit was an interesting one and is the occasion for a long entry in the journal. Perhaps infected by his friend's excitement, he embarked on a series of sexual encounters: first with his regular boy friend Pieps, then in brothel-crawling and in a visit to the notorious 'Passage' where, after an initial failure of nerve, he made an assignation with one of the boys frequenting that neighbourhood. By the time he came to write the journal entry, self-awareness and self-mockery had been brought to bear on the episode:

> I overcame my fear enough to march up to the boy in the Passage when I saw him again and say, 'Bist Du frei nexte [*sic*] Donnerstag?' ['Are you free next Wednesday?'] He stared coldly at me as [if?] he couldnt hear what I said. I repeated it as he lowered his eyes. 'Ja.' 'Gut, um 4 uhr dann' ('Yes.' 'Good, at 4 o'clock then') and swept off brandishing my cigar picturing myself as the Baron de Charlus [in Proust's *A la Recherche ...*]. Actually I was a middle class rabbit. . . .

Isherwood's visit had, however, not merely whetted Auden's sexual appetite but had filled him with a spirit of emulation, and it was only a matter of days before he had found an equivalent to

Bubi. This was Gerhart Meyer, the most important of Auden's lovers during his time in Berlin. The splendours and miseries of his brief affair with Gerhart form the heart of the Berlin journal: his former lover, Pieps, is gradually cast off, though he continues to make frequent appearances, and Auden continued to feel affection for and even to have sex with him. Only near the end, after Gerhart's defection, is another boyfriend, Herbert, taken on. As in an Olympic medal ceremony, Pieps and Herbert stand in the journal as significant but inferior figures on either side of the golden Gerhart, to whom, after more than one promise, attention must now be turned.

First, though, a word on Auden's reputation for promiscuity will be in order. Although his reaction to his new-found freedom and independence was a certain amount of promiscuity and sexual experimentation – and after all he had, only a few months earlier, been *in statu pupillari* at Oxford, with home and family nearby in Birmingham – the scale of his known sexual adventures has been somewhat exaggerated. This sensationalising of his Berlin sex-life can have seriously misleading implications, for Auden was at heart a devout believer in romantic love with a strong desire for a stable love-relationship and for domesticity. In later years he more than once expressed a wish to father a child, and seems even to have considered marriage as a means to this end. The tragedy of his subsequent personal life is that, even when he seemed to have formed a monogamous partnership, it turned out to be a delusion. But in any case the scale of his predatory descents upon the Berlin bars was less sensational than has sometimes been suggested.

The main source here is a notorious entry in the journal he kept at this time. This oft-quoted memorandum, which appears right at the end of the journal and thus constitutes a final reckoning, is headed 'Boys had, Germany 1928–29' and lists nine individuals. Five are identified by Christian names – Pieps, Cully, Gerhart, Herbert and Otto – while the rest are designated 'Unknown', with some brief indication added (presumably as an aid to memory) to record where they were encountered. Of this latter group, one had been met in 'the Passage': as other entries in the journal make clear, Auden often visited this spot but was sometimes too nervous to proceed beyond voyeurism. Two other boys had been met in bars, and the fourth had been picked up in Cologne during a tour of Germany in May; though ugly, this last had, it seems, given satisfaction.

Of the named boys, 'Pieps' has already been referred to. He had been encountered in a Berlin bar quite soon after Auden's arrival in the city, and is briskly mentioned in a letter to his friend John Layard: 'I like sex and Pieps likes money: it's a good exchange'. There is, perhaps, a pinch of affectation in this no-nonsense cynicism. More revealingly, at his first meeting with Layard he had rejected the latter's sexual advances with the remark that 'I've got a boy named Pieps.' 'Gerhart' must be Gerhart Meyer. (Isherwood later used the names Pieps and Gerhart, the latter spelt Gerhardt, in *Goodbye to Berlin*.) 'Cully' has been plausibly identified by Humphrey Carpenter as Kurt Groote, also named in '1929' and the subject of another poem, 'Love by ambition'. 'Herbert', already mentioned, is known to have been Auden's travelling companion during the tour of Germany in May. And 'Otto' was Otto Küsel, who, as we shall see, accompanied Auden to the Harz Mountains early in the summer and is associated with two other poems, 'Upon this line between adventure' and 'Sentries against inner and outer'. Otto, it seems, was a genuine Juvenile Delinquent, having escaped from a reformatory. Elsewhere in the journal three other boys – Franz, Heins and Paul – are named, and it is clear that Isherwood had a brief affair with the last of these; the absence of their names from the list presumably indicates that so far as Auden was concerned they were no more than acquaintances, though Franz and Heins were on familiar enough terms to visit him at his lodgings and were involved in a highly dramatic episode involving Layard that took place there. Auden saw both of them frequently and on at least one occasion went swimming with Franz.

There is a curiously scrupulous note appended to the list in which Auden puts on record his 'regret' at having associated with one of the anonymous boys picked up in a bar: 'He was not nice and was very dirty; ie Pure lust on my part. All the others were nice.' This repudiation of lust and emphasis on 'niceness' is surely revealing, but is seriously at odds with, for instance, Dorothy J. Farnan's description of Auden as 'engaging in frenetic sexual activity' in Berlin and showing evidence of a 'voracious' sexual appetite (*Auden in Love*, p. 35). The tally of nine partners in as many months, even when those who were not 'boys' but friends of his own class like Isherwood and Layard are added, is perhaps not everyone's notion of the frenetic and the voracious, and hardly qualifies Auden as a Don Giovanni of the boy-bars. (To emulate Auden's scupulousness, it should be said that there is just possibly, but far from certainly, a question mark at the head of the list, and if it is not just a fancy of this bleary-eyed researcher it may point to one or more shadowy pre-Pieps encounters, the memory of which had, several months later, faded almost to vanishing point.)

The really significant point, however, is that with five of the individuals listed something more than a one-night stand was involved. Carpenter is surely right to insist that while 'the length of the list might suggest that Auden was in the habit of "cruising"…he much preferred to have a steady relationship'. The journal indeed reveals that cruising was very much against his nature (which is not of course the same thing as saying against his wishes), for he writes there: 'Feeblesness is a problem. I have often thought I would go brothel-crawling but I can't do it. I become attached to someone, and enter on a relationship at once. Which means of course that I dont want to be free. Complete lechery as Christopher remarked is the end of all pleasure.' Evidently he and Isherwood had discussed the theory and practice of the subject during the latter's March visit. What Auden refers to as his 'feebleness' is clearly a temperamental inability, despite occasional forays, to espouse the kind of large-scale promiscuity represented in his experience by, among others, Francis Turville-Petre.

David Luke has recently suggested that Auden's brief affair with Gerhart in April 1929 was 'more emotionally involving than any of the others' and that the decision to keep a journal coincided with his meeting and falling in love with the young sailor. Although the dated entries begin in March (and continue to 26 April), the cover of the journal bears the inscription 'April 1929', and there is other evidence suggesting that the early entries at least were made retrospectively. If so, Auden may have been enough of a romantic at the time to have selected this means of marking his association with Gerhart as the beginning of a new era, for he had met the youth on Easter Sunday, 31 March, and their first assignation (in Auden's lodgings) had been on 1 April. (With life supplying symbolic dates so lavishly, one hardly needs literature.) As Luke points out, it is Gerhart who dominates nearly twenty pages of the journal, the entries from 31 March to 16 April.

Auden's excitement, emotional as well as sexual, during the first few days of his brief love-affair with Gerhart leaps from the pages of the little book he preserved and carried from place to place for the rest of his life. Meeting Gerhart was something that nearly didn't happen. On that Easter Sunday Auden had wanted to go to the UFA cinema in Alexanderplatz, to see a new film, Joe May's *Asphalt*, but it was sold out by the time he got there. So, at a loose end, he dropped into a gay bar at 49 Alte Jakobstrasse that enjoyed a solid petty-bourgeois clientele and had been recommended by a friend as currently offering a good deal of action. (It became a favourite haunt and is referred to in the diary simply as '49'.) Gerhart walked in, and was introduced with the recommendation that he spoke English. In accordance with time-honoured protocol, Gerhart suggested that the Englishman should buy him a glass of beer, and followed this up with the offer to sleep with him for ten marks. Auden pointed out that he had no ready cash, and that the banks did not open until Tuesday, but Gerhart, perhaps a little unconventionally for his kind, declared himself willing to grant credit. In the event an assignation was made for the next day and duly took place, the youth arriving late and leaving as soon as they had finished in order to look for another customer.

So far, one might think, so commonplace, if not sordid. But the transaction produced in Auden a state of euphoria, and his reaction to it was a curious one, for on the Tuesday (2 April) he called on Layard – ostensibly to tell him about Gerhart, but subconsciously aware that his excitement would stimulate Layard's desire to share the boy's favours. In the journal this subconscious wish has been brought to the surface, and its motives are analysed: altruism (he wants to do his friend a good turn) but also 'sex-snobbery' (he wants his friend to approve of his choice and envy his good fortune sufficiently to want the boy for himself). Perhaps also he wished to revive the curious sensation he had experienced in 'pimping' for Isherwood, though the case now was crucially different. For whereas he had not cared for Bubi he was well on the way to falling in love with Gerhart, and he spent a restless night. It was not the last that Gerhart was to cause him.

Nor was it a night of bliss for Layard, who the following day attempted to commit suicide. Layard's own bizarre story, however, is best reserved for a later chapter rather than being allowed to interrupt the considerable momentum of Auden's affair with Gerhart. On Thursday, while they were having tea together, Gerhart suggested to Auden that they should go to Hamburg, his home town, and Auden agreed to do so that very evening. Dashing back to his lodgings, he left an excuse for Pieps, who was to have visited him that evening, borrowed money from his obliging landlady, and made hasty preparations to set off for the station. The journal

catches the excitement of the occasion with its rapid transitions
from epigrammatic generalisation and literary self-consciousness
to a self-mocking snapshot of Berlin low-life:

> Few things are better than a hurried meal when one is packing to
> go off to a lover. I wondered what books one takes on these
> occasions. I took Donne, the Sonnets, and Lear. In the tube I had
> an encounter with a whore. I stared at her feeling "I'm king of
> Berlin." She promptly came and stood beside me till I got out. I
> wanted to make her an 18th century bow and say "Enshuldigen
> [*sic*] sie, Madame, aber ich bin schwul [Forgive me, Madame, but
> I am gay]."

In the waiting room at the Zoo Station, where he had arranged
to meet Gerhart, Auden thought briefly of Layard, by now in a
Berlin hospital, and told himself that he could feel for his friend's
misery even in the middle of his own happiness. The journal,
however, has no truck with such insincerities and insists that the
knowledge of Layard's plight was no more than a sauce to his own
pleasure.

In the train Gerhart quickly began to flirt with a girl, and the
journal, always eager to swing from the particular to the general,
offers a brief analysis of the categories of jealousy. But the most
vivid sentences evoke the magic of his lover's physical presence:

> He has the most extraordinary power I have met in any one. He
> laid his hand on my knee and switched on the current, an
> amazing sensation. What is odd is that when he could have
> any woman he liked from the Queen of England upwards, he
> chooses whores and not the prettiest ones either. I am so jealous
> with him that I am frightened when he goes to the lavatory that
> he won't come back....

It needs no special insight to see little prospect here of a happy and
stable relationship, and not coming back was to be a regular feature
of Gerhart's behaviour. Even before they reached the hotel in
Hamburg he had told Auden that he wanted to visit a 'friend'
and could not put it off until the next day since the friend was
going away. Auden was not deceived by this palpable fiction,
though at this stage he was still prepared to believe Gerhart's
promise that he would soon return.

He did not, of course, and a long journal entry for 5 April traces the stages of Auden's expectation, anger and anxiety during that largely sleepless night spent alone in the Hamburg hotel bedroom that had been the anticipated scene of bliss. The diarist's hindsight permits a distanced self-mockery that was surely not available at the time: 'First I posture before the glass, trying to persuade myself but in vain that I am up to his physical level. Then I read the Sonnets to prove my superiority in sensibility. Every time I hear a taxi I go to the window but it's only a whore returning....'

By 5 a.m. he had made up his mind that Gerhart had absconded with his money: how he came to be acting as purse-bearer is not clear. A few hours later Auden made his way to the British Consulate to report that he had been robbed. An impulse to telephone the hospitals to see whether Gerhart had been run over was resisted, and before long he turned up, having got drunk the night before. Kisses and reproaches were followed by lunch, a pub and a visit to the harbour, where Gerhart was sick, and a second visit to the Consul, where, a little puzzlingly, Auden collected his money. (Possibly they had simply cashed a cheque for him.) Gerhart, with his streetwise promptness to turn a situation to his own advantage, was dramatically wounded by the disclosure that his friend thought he had robbed him, and declared it was something he would never, never forget.

Later, for the second time that day, and probably not accidentally, they ran into Rosa, a girlfriend of Gerhart's, and the three of them went to the cinema, where Rosa was understandably upset when the two young men embarked on some heavy petting in the semi-darkness; at any rate she moved to a seat at some distance, from which her sobs were clearly audible. Gerhart, in a symbolic expression of his wish to have his cake and eat it, embraced both of them simultaneously. What the rest of the audience made, or thought, of this off-screen drama is not on record.

When they left the cinema a tearful Rosa continued to pursue them into a restaurant until Gerhart got rid of her and then proceeded to flirt with the waitress and a couple of housewives. When they moved on to a beer-house, Gerhart asked his curiously unsuspicious friend and paymaster to wait outside: getting tired at last of cooling his heels, Auden entered and found him chatting with a girl. At first Auden put on a fair imitation of nonchalance, strolling up to the bar and ignoring the pair, but once outside in the street he and Gerhart had a row: he had, Auden told him bitterly, spent 170 marks on the trip – probably adding that he had precious little to show for it. Gerhart, turning nasty, informed him that, whether he liked it or not, he was going home with the girl, but would be back in an hour and a half. Auden, who by now was learning fast, knew better than to believe him – a scepticism that turned out to be fully justified, for, once again, Gerhart did not return. The next day Auden took the train back to Berlin.

The graphically picaresque recital of the day's events in Hamburg runs to only a few hundred words but conveys not only the rapid swings between joy and exasperation in Auden's love affair with Gerhart but also a process of learning that involved disillusion and a growing awareness of his own nature. In the streets, bars, restaurants, cinemas and cheap hotels, through passion, jealousy, excitement, frustration, anger and self-mockery, Auden was qualifying himself as a great love poet, and the copy of Shakespeare's sonnets he had packed for the trip suggests that such a purpose may not have been far from his own mind.

Two days later Gerhart turned up in Berlin and a reconciliation took place. The journal makes little of this event, which Auden was probably able by now to view with instant as well as retrospective irony, but there is a striking vein of coarseness in his entry for the next day (9 April). In a bar in Alexanderplatz evidently frequented by what Auden elsewhere refers to as 'rough stuff', they inspected the female whores, for whom Gerhart had a taste that was far from fastidious; among the assembled company there were also bargain-price boys and a peroxide blonde who sought in vain to enlist Gerhart's sexual services. (So far from being flattered or tempted, he seems to have given her a black eye.) Auden notes that one of the whores accompanied her highly explicit solicitation by raising her leg like a dog making water. It could all be a description of one of Georg Grosz's more lurid caricatures, and might be supposed to reflect a mood of disgust were it not that the lovemaking with Gerhart that followed earns high marks, and the experience of having breakfast together the next morning even higher. For Auden, even at 22, it was this kind of domesticity (illusory though it turned out to be) that really satisfied.

The cosy breakfast scene was repeated a couple of days later, but it would have taken a larger stock of self-deception than Auden possessed not to recognise that the relationship remained almost wholly one-sided, and there were moments that must have been painful. The night before, for instance, during a tour of the bars,

Gerhart had announced that he was going off to see a client, and was only dissuaded from doing so when Auden promised to compensate him for his loss of earnings. Perhaps there was some consolation in Gerhart's insistence that the only thing that particular client was interested in was being thrashed within an inch of his life.

The journal preserves some vivid scraps of their conversation that morning. First Gerhart asked whether there was any truth in rumours that the Prince of Wales (later Edward VIII) was homosexual, and Auden expressed the opinion that he was not. His comment that everyone is bisexual prompted Gerhart to declare that, being a sailor and therefore 'hot', he liked both men and women – perhaps as close as he ever came to tact and conciliation, though still not very close. Less tactfully, he went on to suggest that they take a woman to Auden's room and both have sex with her – or, if this was not in Auden's line, he could watch while Gerhart performed. It is hard to be sure in what spirit the proposal was made, but in any case it does not seem to have been one that was acted upon.

Thereafter the references to Gerhart become more disillusioned. On the 13th Auden noted that he no longer felt the magic of Gerhart as he had done in Hamburg (only eight days earlier); he might have added that the King of Berlin had lost his throne. There was also an ugly moment when he realised that Layard's revolver, which he had been looking after since the suicide attempt, was missing, and that Gerhart had taken it. Later in the day, perhaps sensing that time was running out, Gerhart asked for a new pair of shoes and a cap, which led to another quarrel. The next day they went window-shopping in Friedrichstrasse, Auden told Gerhart that he could have the cap or the shoes but not both, and Gerhart sulked. After the shoes had been bought Auden was 'ashamed' of himself for spending so much money on his lover: infatuation had yielded place to a sober assessment of the situation, and by the next day he was prepared to admit to his journal that Gerhart's conversation bored him.

For his part Gerhart, having got his shoes, seems to have gone out of his way to be difficult and even hurtful. He told Auden that he used to be a pimp for a female prostitute and enquired whether Auden would like to pimp for him. The wish to hurt is as palpable as the sense that this is a relationship that was very near the end of the road. When Auden, perhaps in a last-ditch attempt to rescue their collapsing relationship, suggested they go to the mountains together, Gerhart retorted that he only liked seaports. Auden's comment at this point, though a shade melodramatic and posture-striking, is impressive in its mature self-awareness: 'This is the revolt of the symbol. The disobedience of the day-dream. From that moment I love him less.'

After yet another argument about money, Gerhart decamped in the middle of the night. As Auden was going out the next morning he met Gerhart on the stairs and was informed that he was going to sleep until two o'clock; according to the landlady's subsequent testimony, however, he was only in the room for five minutes before signalling to a friend from the window and making off. As well as Layard's revolver he took with him Auden's dressing-gown, leaving in exchange a note giving the address in Hamburg to which he was returning.

Auden's summing up of the affair thus concluded is scrupulously and characteristically even-handed:

> In viewing this little history I feel that it is too easy to say "He's a bad egg. I made a mistake." If a person does one an injury one is always half to blame. My dissatisfaction with him during the last few days inevitable though it may have been means that I havent treated him right and this is the result....

But the note of depression later in this entry is understandable. The affair had lasted, from start to finish, little more than two weeks – not long by ordinary reckoning, but long enough for Auden to experience the whole cycle of infatuation and disillusion. The prominence given to Gerhart in the journal implies that it was an experience of great intensity: no other two-week period from either Auden's or Isherwood's time in Berlin is known to us in such intimate and graphic detail. Loutish and exploitative though he was (and though Auden came to know him to be), the handsome sailor exerted a spell beside which the attractions of Pieps and Herbert were superficial. Perhaps his secret was to have come along at precisely the right moment. Conceivably, somewhere, he is still alive, a hale octogenarian.

All we know of Auden's relationship with Gerhart, not to mention Pieps and others, makes nonsense of Farnan's claim that most of Auden's sexual adventures in Berlin involved 'merely an appetite, for his many encounters were usually with boys of the street whom he paid, rather than with equals for whom he felt a romantic passion' (p. 35). Auden himself would hardly have endorsed the facile categorisation implied here: sex with the proletariat for money is mere lust, real love being confined to one's own class. He might also have been surprised by Carpenter's verdict on the affair with Gerhart: 'Auden seems to have obtained some happiness from the affair, though he recorded their sexual encounters in his journal with coolness and a lack of excitement' (p. 98). This both fails to catch the flavour of a peculiarly intense fortnight and to allow for the long-term effect of an episode through which Auden discovered much about his own capacity for loving, including his propensity towards relationships involving unequal affections and pain for himself. One relationship commonly involving unequal affections is that of parent and child, and although Auden seems sometimes to have been seeking an elder brother (he observed with interest his own gratification when Gerhart took charge of buying the tickets for Hamburg), he is more often looking for a son. One of the most striking statements in the entire journal is to precisely that effect: 'With boys I understand what a parent feels. Otto going off in the car. Writing for money.'

Even before Gerhart's departure, when the situation had clearly begun to deteriorate, Auden sought to console himself by reflecting in his journal that, beside an unrequited homosexual attachment, reciprocated heterosexual love was flavourless ('tame and easy'). The 'attraction of buggery', on the other hand, was 'partly its difficulty and torments'. (Like others of his generation Auden consistently uses the term 'buggery' as a synonym for 'homosexuality' rather than as designating a specific physical act.) His conclusions are both general and personal: 'There is something in reciprocity that is despair. How one likes to suffer.'

Once again, in these oddly confused but deeply revealing statements, the potential of heterosexual love as a source of 'difficulties and torments' seems to go unrecognised. In less abstract terms, the comparison was between the still-present Gerhart and Auden's distant fiancée. Uncharacteristically, Auden doesn't seem to have considered the further logical alternative of unrequited heterosexual love being superior to homosexual reciprocation, or indeed the very possibility of a requited homosexual passion. The idea of unequal loving anticipates a fine poem, 'The More Loving One', written almost thirty years later, and the impressive persistence of the idea suggests that this became a permanent element in Auden's attitude towards love. David Luke may be right in seeing these reflections as evidence of Auden's 'romantic emotional masochism', though they might also be viewed as coming from a man anxious to preserve his self-respect and make the best of a bad job. The 'mass of bruises' boast quoted earlier may suggest that the masochistic leanings were not only emotional.

In late April, a few days after Gerhart's disappearance, Auden's brother John arrived in Berlin to spend a few days there en route for Vienna. He was a geologist by profession and had recently seen service in India. Auden's notes on the time they spent together are very brief and indicate that they did not go in for an exchange of confidences, but there is an interesting summary note later in the journal in which he characteristically reflects on the origins of his own sexual orientation and then extends his personal reflections to some sweeping and facile psychological generalisations:

If [John] was not my brother I could do much more. As it is there is always Joseph and Esau. The interesting question is our different reactions to the same environment and the same mother. Why should one go whoring and the other for boys.

Both are a criticism of the mother. Buggery seems an [*sic*] near unconscious criticism of the mother as a love-object. Whorer a more conscious reaction against her sexual teaching. The bugger presumably though finds his mother more satisfying (she loves me better than John) – ie the bugger gets too much mother love, so shuns off women altogether, the whorer too little, so must always have another.

On the evening of the 26th he saw his brother off at the Anhalter Station. He had spent the afternoon boy-hunting, or at least boy-watching, in the Passage, but this was one of the many things that he was unable to speak about.

Caught up in the rapid twists and turns of Auden's sexual and emotional life, it is easy to forget that he was always a poet, disciplined with regard to his writing if towards nothing else, and during these turbulent weeks the writing went on. A new play, *The Enemies of a Bishop*, was also begun at just about the time that Gerhart and the dressing-gown disappeared in the direction of Hamburg. And since this was Berlin and the year was 1930, with sex and poetry went politics. At the beginning of May there occurred, not far from his lodgings, a confrontation between

Communists and police that led to several days of street-fighting and left 23 dead and some 150 injured. These events are reflected in the second section of '1929', written at about this time:

> All this time was anxiety at night,
> Shooting and barricade in street.
> Walking home late I listened to a friend
> Talking excitedly of final war
> Of proletariat against police....

Perhaps it was these disturbances and this 'anxiety', and perhaps also the wish for a change after the end of his affair with Gerhart, that led Auden, in the middle of May, to leave Berlin for a week or so on a trip that took him to half a dozen German cities. The tour seems to have been decided on at a moment's notice, though the earlier (and ungraciously rejected) invitation to Gerhart suggests that he had already entertained the wish to visit the mountains. His itinerary included Magdeburg (a medieval and baroque city until it was smashed to pieces on a January night in 1945), Kassel, Marburg, Cologne (where he met one of the anonymous boys listed in his journal) and Essen, and he was accompanied throughout by a young man called Herbert (also on the list) as well as an unidentified Dutchman named Dan who evidently shared his sexual tastes. (Dan may perhaps be identified with the D. van Lannep to whom Auden sent a copy of his *Poems* of 1928, though van Lannep remains equally a mystery.)

Herbert had been picked up on 26 April in a well-known homosexual bar, the Adonis Diele, whither Auden had proceeded after seeing off his brother's train to Vienna, and the boy had presumably helped to fill the vacuum recently created by Gerhart's departure. On the occasion of their first meeting, Auden had taken him back to his lodgings and had felt a pang of social conscience when the youth, inspecting the contents of the wardrobe, remarked wistfully, or perhaps with calculation, that he wished he possessed something similar. The relationship lasted long enough for Herbert to be taken along on the six-day excursion, but not much longer, and the journal records the point of no return:

> Köln to Essen. Herbert irritating and I irritated and superior. His behaviour a reaction against my snobbishness.... Herbert's impatience in the train. Odd in someone who must have to put

up with so much.... My relations with Herbert never recovered after Essen. I must never have anyone to live with me again. It doesnt work.

It was not a resolution that he was to adhere to, but the self-awareness, like the careful apportioning of blame, is characteristic.

One of the many places they passed through was the village of Rotehütte-Königshof in the Harz Mountains, and Auden took such a fancy to this spot that within a short time he was back there, this time accompanied by a brand-new boyfriend, Otto Küsel. It was now June, and he liked the mountain village well enough to stay there for some weeks – and, presumably, to sing its praises in a letter to Isherwood, who arrived from England early in July and recalled the spot long afterwards as 'surrounded by forests. The air smelled of resin and echoed romantically with jangling cow-bells.... the whole place could have been a setting for one of Grimm's fairy tales, except that it had a railway station' (*Christopher and his Kind*, p. 14). Auden quickly acquired a large circle of acquaintances among the local people, a dozen of whom are named, with brief descriptive tags, in his journal, and his unconventional behaviour seems to have provoked interest but not scandal. He is known to have written several poems there, and possibly he and Isherwood worked together on *The Enemies of a Bishop*.

Soon, however, real drama invaded their idyllic retreat. Isherwood naturally wanted Bubi's company in Rotehütte and before leaving England had asked Auden to telephone the boy in Berlin and invite him to join them. Bubi, however, failed to show up, whereupon Isherwood dashed off to Berlin in search of him. At Auden's suggestion, in his tour of the bars in quest of information about Bubi he was assisted by Francis Turville-Petre. Francis was an English resident in Berlin and a colourful character of whom Isherwood was later to see much more. For the moment Francis was useful as an interpreter as well as possessing a profound knowledge of the bars and the boys. It turned out that Bubi was wanted by the police and had prudently vanished, so there was nothing for Isherwood to do but return 'mournfully' to his empty bed in the mountain village.

Shortly afterwards, having got wind of Isherwood's quest and suspecting that Bubi might be with him, the police turned up. And while they were pursuing *their* inquiries, with a remarkable sense of timing, a letter from Bubi was delivered and read by Isherwood 'under their very noses'. Bubi was in Amsterdam, about to 'ship out as a deck-hand on a boat to South America', and would be glad of a loan. At this point in Isherwood's account in *Christopher and his Kind* there occurs a striking passage that is, in its emotional stance and even in its language, reminiscent of the cloak-and-dagger world of some of Auden's early poems: 'The letter thrilled Christopher unspeakably. As he read, he began to feel that he himself had become an honorary member of the criminal class. Now he must be worthy of the occasion.' That last phrase, so redolent of Isherwood's class and background, of a world of exhortatory headmasters and speech-days, has been subverted by a 'thrilling' act of class-betrayal, like Auden showing solidarity with the workers during the General Strike. Though Bubi was not to be found, the police had not entirely wasted their time, however, for they discovered that Otto was an escapee from a reformatory and took him away with them. Auden, it seems, had not lost his taste for juvenile delinquents.

The quest, that favourite heroic motif of Auden's early writing, was now about to be translated into action, for Auden and Isherwood decided to set off post-haste for Amsterdam. It was a decision in the spirit of the urgent, peremptory concluding line of one of Auden's early poems: 'Leave for Cape Wrath tonight'. With their departure the village must suddenly have seemed much duller, for Auden in particular, whether thumping out Anglican hymns on a piano in the railway station buffet or wrestling naked with Otto in a meadow, had been a source of considerable interest to the local community. The innkeeper, tolerant despite the invasion of his premises by the police, had the last word, observing that he expected ' "a lot of things happen in Berlin which we wouldn't understand" '.

In Amsterdam Bubi was quickly found and duly seen off for South America. Almost exactly twenty years later (one wonders whether some unconscious anniversary-marking was at work) there was a curious coda to Isherwood's love affair with Bubi. In his travel book *The Condor and the Cows* (1949) he describes their reunion in Buenos Aires on 16 February 1949. Bubi, at last publicly identified as Berthold Szczesny, had settled in South America in the 1930s, had prospered, and, on the threshold of middle age, was engaged to be married. The book observes with notable discretion that at an earlier epoch 'The Cosy Corner was...much frequented by Berthold, Auden and myself'. Well, yes: but then 1949 was still much too early for Isherwood to be candid about, and take retro-spective pride in, his Berlin adventures.

Meanwhile, back in Amsterdam in that summer of 1929, the two Englishmen enjoyed a day's sightseeing before Isherwood returned to England. By the end of July, Auden too was back home, his 'year' in Berlin (actually somewhat less) now over. Almost at once he was writing to Layard that he was 'homesick for Germany', also that he was breaking off his engagement. The latter was an experi-ment that had failed and one that, with the greatly increased self-knowledge that Germany had given him, he did not intend to repeat.

It was not a good time to be looking for employment: 'Do you by any chance,' Auden wrote to Naomi Mitchison, 'know of a job for me? Anything from nursing to burglary...' (*You May Well Ask*, p. 117). He was to spend the next year as a private tutor, then five years as a schoolmaster, followed by employment with the GPO Film Unit and the Group Theatre, journeys to Spain and China, and, in the last year of the 'low dishonest decade' for which he became the principal British spokesman, to go to New York and there to meet the great love of his life, Chester Kallmann. He was, however, back in Berlin, as we shall see, in the summer of 1930, but from this point the main emphasis of this narrative must shift to Isherwood, whose own, considerably longer period of residence in the city began later in 1929.

During the late summer of that year the two Berlinophiles saw a certain amount of each other in London, where Isherwood was now living, strictly from motives of economy, with his mother. Auden, too, was short of money, and soon had to migrate north, where he could live rent-free in a cottage in the Lake District owned by his family; a little later he returned to the family home in Birmingham. On the occasions when the two friends managed to meet, reminiscences and expectations of Germany must have loomed large in their conversations, and it was to Bubi and Otto that they dedicated the play that they worked on together at this time, *The Enemies of a Bishop*, which was reported, probably in August, as 'nearly finished'. These were also prolific months for Auden as a poet, and among other poems known to have been written at this time are 'On Sunday walks', 'The silly fool' and the third section of '1929' (in August), 'Will you turn a deaf ear' (in September), 'Sir, no man's enemy', 'Which of you waking early' and the final section of '1929' (in October), and 'It's no use raising a shout', 'To have found a place' and 'Since you are going to begin to-day' (in November).

Their conversations and letters must have kept alive Isherwood's enthusiasm for the city he had so far seen only on a couple of tantalisingly brief visits, and must have confirmed his wish to return for a longer stay. So, on 29 November, he set out once more for Berlin. It was to remain his base until May 1933, a period of almost three and a half years, though his numerous absences during that time add up to about 12 months. Still, it was long enough, and it occurred at the right stage of his career as a writer to prove a crucially important chapter in his life, as it had already done in Auden's, and for him to annex Berlin as fictional territory.

Again, why Berlin? The answer is more obvious but at the same time more complex than in the case of Auden, partly because Isherwood himself did his best to falsify the record. He had seen enough of the city, and heard enough about it from Auden, to be excited by the opportunities it offered for sexual adventures, and in *Christopher and his Kind* he declares that his statement in the much earlier autobiographical volume *Lions and Shadows* that he went to Berlin primarily to meet John Layard was 'avoiding the truth', and that so far as he was concerned 'Berlin meant Boys'. A similar motive is self-imputed in a review Isherwood wrote of Gerald Hamilton's *Mr Norris and I*:

> When I came to Germany in 1929 I was twenty-four years old and in many respects very immature for my age. One of my chief motives for wanting to visit Berlin was that an elderly relative had warned me against it, saying that it was the vilest place since Sodom. For months I had been day-dreaming of it as unrealistic-ally as a child dreams of the jungle; he hopes to meet tigers and pythons there, but doesn't expect them to hurt him.
>
> (The elderly relative was a cousin, Basil Fry.)

None of this, however, will quite suffice as an explanation, and it certainly does less than justice to his seriousness as an artist. Writing of his Berlin years in the later autobiography *Christopher and his Kind*, he is plainly exhilarated by his own new-found candour concerning his sexual nature: parodying Lawrence, he seems to be declaring to anyone who cared to listen, 'Look! I have come out!' But the old man's candour may be as oversimplifying and misleading as the caginess of the young author of *Lions and Shadows*, and ought to be treated with a similar scepticism.

As far as sex was concerned, his psychological predicament was more complex than the cheerful equating of Berlin and Boys suggests. In the later book he confesses, or claims, that 'he couldn't relax sexually with a member of his own class or nation. He needed a working-class foreigner'. A similar point was made in an interview with Carolyn G. Heilbrun shortly before the publication of *Christopher and his Kind*, where he refers to the 'sexual colonialism' of his early years and admits that the class question certainly entered into the matter. Spender, perhaps partly under Isherwood's influence, took a similar view, suggesting that a homosexual relationship 'would have been almost impossible between two Englishmen of our class.... Men of the same class just didn't; it would have been impossible, or at least very unlikely'. There is some overstatement, and some disingenuousness, here (it would have been surprising, for instance, if Spender had not known that Auden and Isherwood had been lovers), but the implied power of the class taboo is striking.

In the Berlin bars, several kinds of barrier simultaneously collapsed. To make love to a German who almost certainly spoke no English was to simplify the transaction enormously by placing it outside the nexus of class, education and language from which any encounter with an English lover was inseparable, while the commercial nature of the transaction, often reinforced by the age difference, conferred a power that would not obtain with a lover of one's own age and class. Moreover, frankness, both in emotional declarations and in sexual explicitness, comes much more easily to the inhibited when a foreign tongue is being spoken, provided that knowledge of the language is sufficiently rudimentary – as Isherwood's German certainly was at this stage.

In a 1987 interview Spender also pointed to another dimension, remarking that 'sex with the working-class of course had political connotations. It was a way in which people with left-wing sympathies could feel they were really getting in contact with the working class'. A sceptical or snide reaction to this claim comes too trippingly off the tongue: earlier generations had given the poorer classes soup and tracts, or WEA lectures, but the liberated postwar generation could demonstrate their solidarity less patronisingly by sleeping with them. Perhaps E. M. Forster, one of Isherwood's heroes, was the great exemplar here, for had he not, even before the War, made Helen Schlegel sleep with Leonard Bast? Purchased sex could even be viewed as a kind of charitable donation. There is a curious moment in Auden's journal when he deplores the boasting of an American met in one of the bars that he often obtained sex without paying for it: it's so nice, says Auden, to know that you can give a present to someone who needs it ('present' in this context usually meaning, of course, payment in money or goods for sexual services). More seriously, it may be questioned whether the chicken-and-egg question should not be answered the other way round. Quoting Spender's remark in his biography of William Plomer, Peter F. Alexander has commented that 'for writers like Auden, Spender and Isherwood, left-wing politics offered the chance to get close to the working-class that so attracted them sexually' (p. 180).

There were, though, at least two reasons apart from sex that took Isherwood to Berlin. A novelist, unlike a poet, needs a lot of hard information: it is difficult to write good fiction without actually knowing a considerable amount about the external world, and this is especially true if the writer's powers of invention are weak, as Isherwood's certainly were. His experience of life so far had been largely constrained by the rituals of his class: shaped by home, family, public school, university, he had seen little that a thousand other aspiring novelists had not also seen. His early books are, inevitably, autobiographical, and it was a mode that persisted throughout his career (a fact of which he made no secret): his forte was always to be the role of an observer rather than an inventor, the celebrated plainness of his prose indicating among other things the limits of his imagination, and even a late book like *Down There on a Visit* is in effect a sequence of fictionalised memoirs rather than a novel. His invention, it seems, only came into play in the manipulation of material already supplied by life, and that manipulation may have been to some extent unconscious or forced upon him by considerations of prudence.

In Berlin he was to seek, and to find, material for the books that, however lightly he claimed to regard them in his later years, have remained his most widely read. As he moved from one bar or one lodging to another, he was not just answering the call of desire or economic necessity, but seeing life – and filling notebooks and diaries, which was always an important part of his method of work:

I've always kept diaries extensively [he said in 1961], and they give me a great sense of security, because I feel at least this part is factual. Having, however, built on these little islands of fact, I think one goes back and reconstructs everything and changes everything and interferes with everything.

(*London Magazine*, n.s. 1, June 1961, p. 42)

Perhaps at some level even his homosexuality was explored and expressed as part of his qualifications for the novelist's trade. In his old age he told an interviewer that 'Being gay has given me an oblique angle of vision on the world. Without it, I might never have been a writer' (Scobie, 1975), and the photographic or cinematic metaphor is revealing: angles of vision can be chosen and exploited. Auden had supported the 1926 strikers out of 'contrariness', and there was something of a willed and defiant quality about his friend's sexual role. As he said in another interview at about the same time, 'as long as nearly all the poets, and nearly everybody are going to harp on heterosexuality, I think "No, I won't, I absolutely won't"' (Heilbrun, 1976). It was a perceptive friend who once remarked to him that if the rest of the world was homosexual, Christopher would make a point of being heterosexual.

There was also a secondary practical and professional reason for a young novelist in the late 1920s to wish to dissociate himself from England and the English literary scene. In the wake of the uproar and legal proceedings that followed the publication of Radclyffe Hall's lesbian novel *The Well of Loneliness* in 1928, British publishers were edgy about the fictional treatment of homosexuality, and in the year that Isherwood settled in Berlin Forster had been impelled to make a discreet plea for tolerance in his contribution to a symposium on 'The Censorship of Books'. Observing that homosexuality 'exists as a fact among the many other facts of life', Forster added that he did not see 'why writers who desire to treat it should be debarred from doing so – always providing that there is nothing pornographic in their treatment' (*The Nineteenth Century and After*, 1929, p. 445). It was not, however, an argument that was quickly to prevail, and in his introduction to *The Temple* Spender goes so far as to say that 'In the late Twenties young English writers were more concerned with censorship than with politics.'

According to Spender's retrospective diagnosis of the mood of his generation, the natural reaction to this repressive ethos was to go to Germany, which offered freedom from censorship along with many other kinds of freedom:

> For many of my friends and for myself, Germany seemed a paradise where there was no censorship and young Germans enjoyed extraordinary freedom in their lives....
>
> Censorship, more than anything else, created in the minds of young English writers an image of their country as one to get away from....
>
> Another result of censorship was to make us wish to write precisely about those subjects which were most likely to result in our books being banned....

'Paradise', like 'daydream', is a word that revealingly recurs in such contexts, but the grim irony of history ensured that the paradise would soon be lost and Germany subjected to a censorship, and even a burning of books, that went far beyond anything known in England. In the event Isherwood, like Spender and others, was to publish his books in England, with all the restraints and limitations that this for a long time implied.

Isherwood's rejection of the values and conventions of his class extended beyond his sexuality and was considerably more complex and deeply rooted than mere cussedness. Near the end of *Kathleen and Frank* (1971), the book about his parents that he wrote in his sixties, is a very interesting page that recalls his return to school, wearing a black armband, after the death of his father in the Battle of the Somme in 1916. He was acutely aware of being cast in the role of 'Orphan of a Dead Hero', a role that carried the full endorsement of Crown, Church and Press; soon, though, he discovered that 'being a Sacred Orphan had grave disadvantages', was even 'a kind of curse which was going to be upon him, seemingly, for the rest of his life'. He began to identify all those who enforced this sense of obligation – 'people he actually met, and disembodied voices from pulpits, newspapers, books' – as 'The Others', and to react against the sense of guilt they imposed upon him.

From rejecting the Hero-Father, he proceeded to a rejection of 'the authority of the Flag, the Old School Tie, the Unknown Soldier, The Land That Bore You and the God of Battles'. Also, he might have added, the sexual orientation expected of a healthy English male, and the marital and dynastic ambitions demanded of a member of the English landed gentry. But ancestor-worship was not, as his revered Forster might have put it, Isherwood's ticket: as he says, not unhistrionically, in *Down There on a Visit*, he had 'vowed to disappoint, disgrace, and disown his ancestors'.

The apron-strings that he so decisively cut were not only tied tightly but double-knotted by obligations to the dead, and in going to Berlin he was both rejecting the past, with its burden of responsibility, and making a gesture of defiance at England and the family. For Germany was not just Abroad but for many English people in the 1920s, especially of the older generation, was still the Enemy. What could emphasise more startlingly and unambiguously his refusal to accept, however metaphorically, the mantle of the avenging son than to go and live among those who had slain his father? By a route that may have begun in his early years, when his adored but somewhat suffocating mother impressed upon him the pride he should feel in the history of his family, and that led through the Flanders mud, he headed for Berlin and a very literal and liberal practice of the precept to love one's enemies.

What 'The Others' had in common was that they were older, representatives of the Past, and the flight to Berlin became a flight from the past as well as from a country perceived as still unrepentantly repressive and intolerant. In Spender's *The Temple*, the hero (based on the author) goes to visit his friend William Bradshaw (based on Isherwood) at his London home,

> his mother's small early Victorian stucco house in a quiet garden-like square in Bayswater. As he was walking up the front steps the door was opened by a lady soberly dressed in the style – though it was ten years since the Peace – of a war widow. She looked at him through eyes as large and watchful as William's but, as it were, in a minor key of sadness and resignation, looking back on the past, where his were in the major key of the future....
>   (p. 15)

This is echoed in *Kathleen and Frank*, where Isherwood writes that he 'revolted early and passionately against the cult of the Past'.

The refusal to accede to the demands – the moral blackmail – of his country and class informs much of Isherwood's early writing. His first published novel, *All the Conspirators*, completed in November 1927 and published in 1929, had rejected the values of the upper-middle-class family, while *The Memorial*, the novel that he worked on in Berlin and that was published during his residence there, extends the indictment to the British ruling class in general. It was clearly now time to extend his little fictional empire, as E. M. Forster, always a role-model, had done before him. Boys were all very well in their place, but, whatever his claims to the contrary, Isherwood went to Berlin primarily to work, and one of the most revealing moments in *Christopher and his Kind* depicts him leaving his English companion after an evening in the bars in order to get to bed and be fresh for writing the next morning. His comment on this disclosure ('Seldom have wild oats been sown so prudently' (p. 29)) goes far towards subverting the more colourful and more widely repeated claim that 'Berlin meant Boys'.

His English companion was Francis Turville-Petre, who had assisted in the fruitless search for Bubi four or five months earlier, and it was Francis's door that Isherwood knocked on when he arrived in Berlin at the end of November. Francis was the only Englishman he knew in Berlin, and though they were different in many ways they shared, and had both rejected, a similar back-ground and similar expectations on the part of family and class. Francis, though not a Sacred Orphan, was another scion of the landed gentry, another first-born, another soldier's son. At any rate they got on well enough for Isherwood to accept Francis's suggestion that he take a room in the same house, and Isherwood found it congenial enough to remain there after Francis left Berlin. He stayed, in fact, for about ten months, working on the third draft of *The Memorial*.

So far as his social life was concerned, one of his great advant-ages was knowing very little German. For turning his back on England had set him free not only from family and background but from language and culture. In using a language in which he was still inexpert and in which words were stripped of nuances, implications, connotations and indications of class he felt 'a mar-vellous freedom'. The phrase is his own:

Christopher's relations with many of the boys soon became easy and intimate. Perhaps they recognised and were drawn to the boyishness in him. He felt a marvellous freedom in their com-pany. He, who had hinted and stammered in English, could now ask straight out in German for what he wanted. His limited knowledge of the language forced him to be blunt and he wasn't embarrassed to utter the foreign sex words, since they had no associations with his life in England.

(*Christopher and his Kind*, p. 30)

Revealingly, when he was reunited with Bubi in Berlin some three years after their Amsterdam farewells, he 'found it very odd to be able to chatter away to him in German – odd and a little saddening, because the collapse of their language-barrier had buried the magic image of The German Boy'.

There are also certain advantages for a writer in being in an alien linguistic environment, so that the language of his art remains aloof from the language of banal quotidian experience. It is no accident that many of the most brilliant modern stylists (Joyce, Beckett, Nabokov and Stein among them) have worked under these conditions, and the effect on Isherwood was to endow his English prose with a purity and directness that may owe something to his being distanced from its everyday use. Gertrude Stein's observations in *The Autobiography of Alice B. Toklas* on being an American writer in Paris are to the point:

> One of the things that I have liked all these years is to be surrounded by people who know no english. It has left me more intensely alone with my eyes and my english. I do not know if it would have been possible to have english be so all in all to me otherwise.... I like living with so very many people and being all alone with english and myself.

As a teacher of English, too, he would have had constantly to simplify his use of the language, stripping it free from obscurities, ostentation and modishness. German, on the other hand, was for him not only the language of the daily life of street, market and café, but also the language of sex: as he observes in an entertaining passage in *Christopher and his Kind* (p. 23), whereas a table was 'the dining-table in his mother's house', *ein Tisch* was the shabbier article of furniture to be found in the Cosy Corner.

Isherwood kept a diary in Berlin but seems to have subsequently destroyed it for prudential reasons after the Berlin books had been written, perhaps when he went to America in 1939. It is clear, though, that he quickly made a circle of friends and acquaintances, or rather two circles. One, formed initially through his relationship with Francis, was drawn from the bars and their population of regulars, including young male prostitutes, full-time and part-time, professional and amateur. The other was formed through his friendship with Karl Giese, the assistant and lover of Dr Magnus Hirschfeld, in the premises of whose celebrated Institute Isherwood's room, like Francis's, was located. This was an altogether more sedate world of what Isherwood later called 'middle-class queens', and their characteristic ambience was not the bar or the brothel but the tea-party or the strictly run club where homosexuals could drink and dance together. Through Karl he met a Communist ex-army gymnastics instructor called Erwin Hansen who was to remain a friend for some years and eventually leave Germany with him in 1933.

Residents of the Institute were in the habit of meeting for tea each day in Giese's room, and this was only one item in an often rather formal community life that Isherwood seems to have come to share. Hirschfeld himself was getting on in years, had sober habits and went to bed early, but when he was away the younger residents would organise dinners and parties with dancing. When the master of the house was present, social life would be more serious: lectures were arranged by the Scientific-Humanitarian Committee with social gatherings to follow, and there were also musical evenings and recitations from Goethe and other writers. There is every reason to suppose that, especially as his German improved, Isherwood took part in some of these formal and informal activities, and he must have had a strong sense of belonging to an enlightened community of a kind that could hardly have been paralleled in England, or perhaps anywhere else in the world, at that time.

One aspect of the enlightenment was a capacity for startling unconventionality – startling, at any rate, to one recently arrived from England. It seems that Isherwood took many of his meals at the common table of the Institute, and in a 1977 interview he recalled that 'We all sat down to lunch with extreme politeness and discourse [perhaps a transcription error for 'discretion' or 'decorum']. The only thing was a number of us were in drag, which was never mentioned'. Neither at the time nor some half-century later, it seems, was Isherwood unaware of the comic potential of such scenes, but the novelist-autobiographer's nose for bizarre copy was only the more superficial part of his reaction to the Institute and its inmates. At a deeper level his time there was an education in the open acceptance of sexual identity, the

possibility of community and the need for action. As he told the
same interviewer, Don Douglas:

> It was then that Isherwood got his first insight into what had
> seemed to be a purely private affair. 'I never recognized that I
> belonged to a tribe. Before that I just thought that I had some
> friends who liked boys like I did and others who liked girls. It
> never seemed to be that we were battling against anybody.'

The table-talk at the Institute opened his eyes, transforming secrecy
into community and private tastes into public issues.

His residence in Berlin was interrupted after only two or three
months when, in February 1930, he returned to England for family
reasons. But by May he was back again, and soon afterwards met a
boy who became the prototype of Otto Novak in *Goodbye to Berlin*.
(His real name is unknown and he should not be confused with
Auden's Otto Küsel). It was to be a long-term relationship, for,
despite his initial enthusiasm for the pick-up bars, Isherwood, like
Auden, was attracted by the idea of a stable, loyal and affectionate
partnership. Otto's family came from the Polish Corridor, the area
ceded by Germany to Poland under the terms of the Versailles
Treaty, and, like so many other migrant families then and later,
had settled in Berlin: he was 16 or 17, had Slav rather than German
looks and was not conventionally handsome, was heterosexual,
and cajoled Isherwood into spending more on him than he could
afford.

At the end of June, Auden, who was now a schoolmaster,
returned to Berlin for a two-week visit. It was a great success,
and he left with reluctance, describing himself after his return as
'much too miserable at having to leave Berlin to write a decent
letter', and boasting to his correspondent, Naomi Mitchison, that he
could 'probably exhaust and shock you with Berlin confessions'
(*You May Well Ask*, p. 118). More enigmatically, he told his brother:
'I had a wonderful fortnight.... As usual my heart broke up like a
treacle tart.' Auden, it goes without saying, was introduced to Otto
and in turn introduced him into a poem written for Isherwood's
birthday the following year. Back at his job in Scotland, he wrote
and sent to Isherwood half-a-dozen poems written in German; they
are not precisely dated but seem to have been written in or around
September 1930, and all but one express the pain of his withdrawal
symptoms. One poem makes a promise to return to Berlin in four

months' time – that is, in the Christmas holidays – but however fervently intended the promise was not kept. (More will be said about these poems in Chapter 5.)

Isherwood received visits from two other English friends during the summer of 1930. During August he met Stephen Spender in Bamburg, and in the last week of that month Edward Upward visited him in Berlin (the first of two visits paid by Upward). A year older than Isherwood, Upward had been at both Repton and Cambridge with him and, as Allen Chalmers, is prominent in *Lions and Shadows*. In *Christopher and his Kind* he is accorded the accolade of 'Christopher's closest heterosexual male friend' (p. 42); he was also a fellow novelist and a Marxist, though not yet a member of the Communist Party. Politics must have featured prominently in their conversations, for Isherwood dates from this visit an increased awareness of the political realities of the city he had made his home:

> Here was the seething brew of history in the making – a brew which would test the truth of all the political theories, just as actual cooking tests the cookery books. The Berlin brew seethed with unemployment, malnutrition, stock market panic, hatred of the Versailles Treaty and other potent ingredients.
>
> (*Christopher and his Kind*, p. 43)

His 'political awakening' was an important stage in his development that made possible the Berlin stories with their depiction of the intersection of private lives and public events. Within a few weeks, as if to reinforce the lesson he had learned, the Nazis greatly strengthened their position as a result of the Reichstag elections and had to be recognised as 'a major political party'.

Spender, who was soon to join him in Berlin, had been born in 1909 and was hence a little younger than either Isherwood or Auden. He had made his way to Germany partly through Isherwood's example and encouragement. In the preface to his *Letters to Christopher* (1980), Spender states that he 'first met Christopher Isherwood in Auden's rooms at Christ Church, Oxford in 1928'. Auden introduced Isherwood to him as 'The Novelist of the Future', and Spender seems quickly to have fallen under the spell of his personality. More than half a century later he wrote:

Wherever [Isherwood] was seemed to me to be the trenches. When he asked me to join him in Berlin it was as though some admired commander had asked me to be his adjutant, and it was in this spirit that I joined him for months at a time through freezing Berlin winters and once or twice [twice, actually] through Baltic summers on the island of Sellin.

(*Letters to Christopher*, p. 9)

In his autobiography Spender recalled that, at later meetings in London, Isherwood

simplified all the problems which entangled me, merely by describing his own life and his own attitudes towards these things.... The whole [Oxford and Cambridge] system was to him one which denied affection: and which was based largely on fear of sex. His hatred extended, though, beyond Oxford. It was for English middle-class life. He spoke of Germany as the country where all the obstructions and complexities of this life were cut through.

(*World within World*, pp. 102, 104)

However, a much more recent declaration by Spender that what 'really' drew him to Berlin was 'the hypnotic fascination of Christopher Isherwood's life' there (*Observer*, 28 November 1993) suggests that it may have been his friend's lifestyle as much as his personality or his convictions that exerted such a powerful magnetic force. As often, different stages of life and different confessional climates seem to have elicited different myths or versions of the truth from the same source.

Spender did not proceed straight to the German capital, which Isherwood had not yet made his home, but initially exchanged Oxford for Hamburg, writing a shade melodramatically on the opening page of a journal he kept at the time, under the date 22 July 1929, 'Now I shall begin to live.' According to Hugh David, Spender stated towards the end of his life that he went to Hamburg because Auden and Isherwood had already annexed or colonised Berlin (*Stephen Spender: A Portrait with Background*, p. 120). If so, the wish to escape from under their shadow was a natural one, though it was not in the event to be entirely accomplished. In Hamburg he experienced 'a tremendous sense of relief, of having got away from Oxford and home'.

As with Isherwood's early weeks in Berlin, the sense of what has been left behind seems almost stronger than the awareness of what it has been exchanged for. If Isherwood's idealised Germany is reminiscent of Forster's idealised Italy ('the beautiful country where they say "yes"'), it is because both were to a large extent lands of fantasy and wish-fulfilment, and Isherwood's great admiration for Forster is once more to the point here. But Isherwood, of course, came to know Berlin much better than Forster ever knew Italy: to know the reality that badly dented, if it did not wholly destroy, the fantasy.

In the fullness of time, Isherwood turned Berlin itself into a literary construct, and before the end of 1930 he had moved to the neighbourhood that was to become Isherwood Country. At the end of August he wrote to Spender, 'My financial troubles are worse than ever before': Otto's demands had proved a decided strain on the modest allowance made by his capricious Uncle Henry, and he needed to find cheaper accommodation. This intermittently generous relative, who had made Isherwood his heir, is presumably the model for the elderly, lisping globe-trotter and boy-chaser in Auden's poem 'Uncle Henry', written in about 1931.

Henry Bradshaw-Isherwood-Bagshawe, to grant him the full splendour of the name he adopted after his ill-starred and short-lived marriage, is a figure who seems to have stepped straight from the pages of the early Evelyn Waugh. The elder brother of Frank, Christopher's father, he was Christopher's godfather, held the family purse-strings, took a fellow homosexual's interest in his nephew's adventures, which he liked to have recounted to him in detail over a tête-à-tête dinner, and caused consternation in the family by his late and unexpected marriage, which fortunately proved without issue.

Impecuniosity was, at least, Isherwood's cover story, though it is not difficult to guess that there might have been other motives, both sexual and literary, for his initial move, in October, to the slum tenement where Otto's family lived. Auden, in exchanging the rather grand house where he first stayed for lodgings near the Cosy Corner, had told a correspondent that he was going to live in a slum, and now Isherwood was following his example. Like George Orwell's more celebrated descent upon Wigan, this episode was actually of very brief duration, but the leaky roof, the toilet shared with three other families (if you were too fastidious to resort to the bucket in the kitchen), and the washing facilities in the kitchen sink (unless you made the trek to the public baths) must have been a revelation to a young man brought up in an English country house. *Goodbye to Berlin* was, needless to say, to exploit this material.

Very soon Isherwood moved out, briefly to Admiralstrasse, then in December to Nollendorfstrasse, where he was to remain until his time in Berlin was terminated by public events. There, in the apartment presided over by Fräulein Thurau, one of his fellow lodgers was an English girl, Jean Ross, who became the model for Sally Bowles. Spender had arrived in Berlin in September 'in order to see a girl whom I hope perhaps to marry': this was Gisa Soloweitschik, a 17-year-old Lithuanian, who provided Isherwood with a model for Natalia Landauer in *Goodbye to Berlin*. Spender took a room in Motzstrasse, a short walk from Isherwood's lodgings, and during this winter the two met regularly. From Berlin Spender wrote to John Lehmann:

> There are four or five friends who work together, although they are not all known to each other. They are W. H. Auden, Christopher Isherwood, Edward Upward and I.... Whatever one of us does in writing or travelling or taking jobs, it is a kind of exploration which may be taken up by the other two or three.
>
> (*Christopher Isherwood: A Personal Memoir*, pp. 8–9)

There was some truth in this, though possibly not very much, and in quoting the passage long afterwards Lehmann commented that Spender 'was a great maker of legends' and that this 'may have been largely (his) fantasy'.

One visitor to Berlin at this time was Paul Bowles, the American composer and writer, who became acquainted with both Isherwood and Spender. Bowles arrived from Paris with his friend, the composer Aaron Copland, and was unimpressed by the transition, finding Berlin visually and socially unattractive: 'It was,' he wrote later, 'like a film of Fritz Lang's. The "haves" were going hog-wild while the "have-nots" seethed with hatred. There was a black cloud of hatred over the whole east end of the city.' Bowles had been given a letter of introduction to Jean Ross, who introduced him to Isherwood, who in turn introduced him to Spender. Bowles, younger than either of the two Englishmen, found them 'overwhelmingly British, two members of a secret society constantly making reference to esoteric data not available to outsiders'.

(This and the previous quotation are taken from Christopher Sawyer-Laucanno's biography of Bowles, pp. 100–1.) The outsider/insider polarity is prominent in the early work of Auden and Isherwood, and Bowles's comment suggests the ways in which the closed worlds of an upper-middle-class upbringing, including the mandatory private and public schools and ancient universities, could collude with a sense of sexual difference that must to some extent remain covert to generate this 'secret society' atmosphere. Bowles added, with some acuteness, that Isherwood alone was a very different man from Isherwood in Spender's company.

Despite his disapproval and resentment – he objected, for instance, to Spender's 'Byronesque' habit of wearing his shirt open to his chest as being an excessively crass announcement of his status as a poet – Bowles saw a good deal of them while he remained in Berlin. In his autobiography, *Stepping Out*, he describes how they would meet daily on the terrace of the Café des Westens, often joined by Jean Ross and Aaron Copland. But Berlin remained for him 'a strange, ugly, vaguely sinister city', architecturally hideous, and he quitted it without regrets. He did carry away with him, however, and in due course put on record, one vivid picture of the young Spender, blonde and sunburnt, standing in the middle of his room at the top of the house in Motzstrasse with the setting sun streaming through the window, and looking 'as though he were on fire'. Bowles's unintended parting gift to Isherwood was his surname, later appropriated for the latter's most famous fictional character.

Auden, meanwhile, was languishing in a Scottish schoolroom – though, to be fair, he seems to have enjoyed teaching, and was in any case still writing. During the summer holidays he had begun a play, *The Fronny*, which obviously bore some relationship to his Berlin experiences, for its title was the name given to Francis Turville-Petre in the private mythology shared by Auden and Isherwood (it adapts 'Der Franni', the nickname given to Francis by the Berlin rent-boys). The first act was finished by September, and portions were sent from time to time to Isherwood for comment. On 8 December Auden sent the complete play to T. S. Eliot of Faber & Faber, who rejected it, but nine months later asked to see it again, agreed to publish it, and then changed his mind. It was also turned down by the Hogarth Press. Subsequently the manuscript disappeared, the work surviving only in a very fragmentary form. Isherwood, too, had been busy, and by the end of 1930 his novel

The Memorial was finished, though getting it published was to take up much of his time in the following year, and it was not to appear until early in 1932.

With *The Memorial* completed, Isherwood worked during 1931 on the first draft of *Lions and Shadows*, an autobiographical work that makes frontier-crossings into fiction in the same way that his fiction constantly strays into autobiography or history. He also began to ponder a vast and never-to-be-completed fictional enterprise, an epic (or at any rate a very long) novel to be called *The Lost*. In March, during the first of three absences from Berlin during this year, he spent about ten days in London, hoping to persuade the publishing firm of Jonathan Cape to accept *The Memorial*. He was unsuccessful, but six months later it was accepted by the Hogarth Press.

He was back in England at the beginning of October on a short visit to his mother, and found himself exchanging one country in a state of turmoil for another. On 21 September Britain had abandoned the gold standard, causing a fall in the value of sterling that was bad news for anyone who was, like Isherwood, living abroad on a small income derived from England. A little earlier in the same month, the British government's attempts to deal with the economic crisis had produced riots in London and Glasgow and a naval mutiny at Invergordon. Aware of the collapse, in the previous July, of the German Danatbank and the ensuing closure of all German banks for some three weeks, Isherwood must have had an unpleasant sense of *déjà vu*.

In July, however, his absence from Berlin had taken him not to England but to the village of Sellin on the Baltic island of Rügen (usually spelt Ruegen by Isherwood). The island had long been a popular resort and is briefly mentioned as such in Forster's *Howards End*. Isherwood had gone there with Otto and Spender, and they had been joined – unenthusiastically, for beaches were not his cup of tea – by Auden. It was this holiday that produced what is perhaps the most familiar icon of British writing in the 1930s: a photograph of the three young men, apparently so remarkably unequal in physical stature that Spender looks like a giant and Isherwood (as he later said) gives the impression of standing in a hole, but all grinning boyishly. The picture was taken by Spender, at this period a shutter-happy enthusiast, with what he called 'a masturbatory camera designed for narcissists'. A less familiar photograph from the same holiday shows Isherwood gazing thoughtfully, even soulfully, at the naked upper torso of Otto, who has his own eyes modestly cast down and appears to be strumming, or at least contemplating, a guitar.

Twelve months later Isherwood and Spender were back on Rügen (which provided a chapter in *Goodbye to Berlin*), though by that time Otto belonged to the past. Isherwood's Jewish friend Wilfrid Israel was with them during this 1932 holiday and duly makes an important appearance in *Goodbye to Berlin*, though not in the section on Rügen.

Looking at these photographic records, it is necessary to remind oneself rather sharply that these were three young writers of promise, or more than promise. For the atmosphere of adolescent high jinks is strong, and in some of the retrospective accounts the idealisation seems remarkably transparent and distinctly naive. In Spender's *The Temple*, for example, his autobiographical protagonist returns to England in a state of gloom:

> London and Oxford towards which he now knew himself being hurled seemed to spell out unutterable grey blankness, a permanent fog. The summer he was leaving seemed more than happiness. It was a revelation. For a moment he thought he had been insane ever to leave Joachim and Heinrich. He should have gone on walking with them down the Rhine for ever .... (p. 132)

Taken all round, the coastal climate of North Germany is not markedly superior to that of London or Oxford, and walking down the Rhine in the winter months could be guaranteed to dampen romantic enthusiasm. This symbolic and subjective use of weather, clumsily introduced into a realistic narrative, points to a more widespread immaturity or irresponsibility. In some of its manifestations it is probably influenced by the emphasis placed on youth, sunshine, scenery and the body beautiful in a tradition of gay sensibility and gay writing that goes back at least to Walt Whitman and Edward Carpenter. In Spender's case one suspects, too, that climate has become a convenient metaphor for sexual permissiveness.

To be fair, it must be added that Spender's journal contains an entry showing that, even on the Baltic beaches and in the copulatory pinewoods, politics could make themselves unignorably felt. There were many young Nazis on the island, enjoying themselves with an earnestness that carried more than a hint of menace:

...the Nazis were doing exercises every evening in the woods....when they sunbathed they would build little forts for themselves on the beach, set up a flagpost, hoist a Nazi flag on it and gaze up in reverence. Whilst they were lounging round listening to the music, they seemed always to be waiting for a patriotic air and when one was played they would stand to attention.

This is paralleled in one of Isherwood's letters written from Rügen to Upward, which first evokes idealised memories of English seaside holidays and then introduces the brutal contemporary images of uniformed, 'hog-necked' Nazis. Before his fictionalised account of the Rügen idyll had been published, the National Socialist Party had opened on the island a vast holiday camp for its members. But by that time Isherwood was far away and felt no obligation to allow his memories to be contaminated by contemporary realities.

In 1932 *Lions and Shadows*, which was not to be published until 1938, was temporarily abandoned, and Isherwood turned his attention to *The Lost*. His vacillation suggests some lack of creative pressure, or at least of a clear sense of direction, and he was not in fact a fertile writer even in his youth: four years elapsed between the appearance of his first two novels, three years between his second and third, even though all of them are short. In August, though, he began the first draft of what became the Berlin stories, and the long-awaited appearance of *The Memorial* in February must have boosted his confidence.

A number of new friendships belong to this period. In the previous year he had met Gerald Hamilton, the prototype of his Mr Norris, and during a visit to England in August 1931, as well as seeing Auden and Upward, he met John Lehmann, who was then working for the Woolfs at the Hogarth Press but was soon to go to Vienna. Other new acquaintances were Gerald Heard and William Plomer. In his autobiography Plomer praises Isherwood as a conversationalist: ' "Amazing" was one of his favourite words, and his capacity to be amazed by the behaviour of the human species, so recklessly displayed everywhere, made him a most entertaining talker' (p. 298). Plomer introduced him in September to E. M. Forster, who had read and admired *The Memorial*; later Forster and Isherwood became close friends, corresponding often, and Isherwood was one of the early readers of *Maurice*. Soon after their first meeting Isherwood wrote to Forster that he was occupied with 'an indecent bumptious stupid sort of novel about Berlin'.

Lehmann's memoir of Isherwood, published after the latter's death, recalls that at this first meeting he was attracted by 'the quality which appealed to me so much in *The Memorial*, an exact feeling for the deeper moods of our generation with its delayed war-shock and conviction of the futility of the old pattern of social life and convention' (p. 11). After Lehmann had moved to Vienna later in the year – for he was anxious to concentrate on his writing rather than on publishing other men's books, and he shared the common urge to escape from England – he visited Isherwood in Berlin. Lehmann had the knack of being in Berlin at moments of crisis: he was there when Hindenburg nominated Hitler as Chancellor, and again when the Reichstag burned down. ('I was in a bar near the Zoo,' he writes, 'when a friend who had been spending the evening at a cinema came in and told us "The Reichstag's on fire!"' (p. 14).) Some vivid pages of his autobiography are devoted to this latter visit, when, 'in the midst of the last agony of the Weimar Republic', he noticed around the city 'huge pictures of Hitler...displayed in the failing light in windows illuminated by devout candles': 'The crucial elections were approaching, and bloody conflicts between the Nazis, the Communists and the Social-Democrats were taking place almost every day in some part of the ice-bound city that was laid out like a patient about to undergo an operation without any anaesthetic at all' (*The Whispering Gallery*, p. 209).

Francis Turville-Petre, whose lifestyle was nomadic and unpredictable, had disappeared from Berlin soon after Isherwood's arrival but reappeared early in 1932. Soon, however, he became bored with the city and conceived a yearning for a rural retreat, settling (more or less arbitrarily, it seems) on a village named Mohrin some distance northeast of Berlin and not far from the Polish border (it is now in Poland and called Moryn). Francis now announced that he had formed great resolutions. He would live in the country, drink less and go to bed early, and he invited Isherwood to join him in this Thoreau-like enterprise.

The affair with Otto was in decline, Mohrin would be cheaper than Berlin, and it would be a good place to work, so Isherwood readily agreed. Francis had already engaged Erwin Hansen to keep house for them, and Erwin had recruited a young assistant called Heinz Neddermayer. On 13 March, shortly before they all set off,

Isherwood met Heinz, who was not only to become Otto's successor as the object of his affections but to share his life for much of the rest of the decade. Isherwood was to stay in Mohrin until late June, though there must have been at least one visit to Berlin during that period, for he was there in April to see Upward, who was on his way back to England after a visit to the Soviet Union. As for Francis, the new regime quickly and predictably palled and he soon began to slip off to Berlin with Erwin for weekends, bringing back with them one or more boys from the bars.

Such promiscuity was not really Isherwood's style, and he quickly fell in love with, and became deeply attached to, Heinz. He was a working-class youth of about 17, slim and with features that Isherwood later described as 'somewhat negroid' and that included a broken nose. He seems to have had no mother, brothers or sisters, saw little of his father and lived with his grandmother. Isherwood's account of their relationship gives an insight into his own emotional needs:

> Heinz had found his elder brother; Christopher had found someone emotionally innocent, entirely vulnerable and uncritical, whom he could protect and cherish as his very own. He was deeply touched and not in the least apprehensive. He wasn't yet aware that he was letting himself in for a relationship which would be far more serious than any he had had in his life.
>
> (*Christopher and his Kind*, p. 73)

Francis, who paid Heinz's wages, demanded that Isherwood should pay half when he learned that they were sleeping together. The relationship was not just a holiday romance, however: it lasted throughout the 1930s, and its centrality in Isherwood's early development is suggested by his remark to an interviewer, after *Christopher and his Kind* appeared in 1977, that the book was 'Basically ... the story of my relationship with my friend Heinz, his arrest and its aftermath, and the attitudes I developed as a result of that' (to W. I. Scobie, 1977).

Spender paid a short visit to Mohrin, then, in July, joined Isherwood again on Rügen for the second of the two summer periods already mentioned. This time there was no Otto, but Heinz was there, of course, also Spender's younger brother Humphrey, who later became a well-known film-maker. During this month Isherwood wrote to Lehmann about *The Lost*, his grandly conceived novel about Berlin: 'It is written entirely in the form of a diary, without any break in the narrative. It will have lots of characters and be full of "news" about Berlin.' This suggests an attempt to convey the drama of contemporary events, but as Brian Finney points out, 'This must have been a false start as he dictated a new draft outline of the entire novel to his brother Richard a month later' – that is, when he was staying with his family in London in August. In its recast and slimmed-down form, the book planned to make use of Otto's family and of Jean Ross, and can therefore be regarded as a very early version of the book published seven years later as *Goodbye to Berlin* – in Isherwood's words, 'the very first draft of his fiction about Berlin ... as crude as his first drafts always were'.

In August and September, as we have seen, he was in England, and towards the end of this visit he seems to have quarrelled with Spender, who decided not to return to Germany. On the last day of September Isherwood left London to return to Berlin, and to a Germany in which public events were moving towards a crisis that had its origins much earlier. In the introduction to *The Temple*, a reworking (in 1986–7) of the novel he wrote in 1929 about the summer he had spent in Hamburg, Spender observes that '1929 can be looked at as the last pre-war, because pre-Hitler, summer, bearing the same relation to February 1933 as July 1918 does to August 1918'. The reality was, however, that those three and a half years – nearly the whole of the period with which this chapter is concerned – had to be lived through one day at a time, and the record of those times is one of gradually mounting tension, anxiety and violence. Behind the world of slum lodgings and rent-bars was a world of politics and power-struggles: behind the personal dramas of Isherwood's love affairs or his attempts to write, the Republic was slowly dying.

In his study of Weimar culture, Peter Gay labels the period from December 1923 to October 1929 'The Golden Twenties' (his terminal date confirming Spender's claim); that from October 1929 to May 1932 'The Beginning of the End'; and the months from June 1932 to January 1933 'Into Barbarism'. The elections of 14 September 1930, held at a time when Isherwood was in Berlin, had seen a campaign that 'plumbed new depths of demagogy and sheer violence' and one that resulted in a massive victory for the Nazis, whose number of seats in the Reichstag rose from 12 to 107 (the much more modest Communist increase was from 23 to 77). 'For many intellectuals,' writes Gay, 'September 14, 1930, marked the death of the Republic.' The world economic crisis, and an unemployment rate in Germany that by the beginning of 1932 exceeded six million, produced serious political instability as well as widespread misery and anger.

This situation was of course exploited by the National Socialists in every possible way. In February 1930, for instance, an obscure Nazis supporter named Horst Wessel had been murdered by the Communists. The son of a Protestant minister, Wessel had kicked over the traces with remarkable thoroughness, living with a prostitute, consorting with pimps and devoting himself to political action. The Nazi propaganda machine quickly turned him into a martyr and folk-hero, and a song he had composed became an anthem of the Nazi party.

Many of the activities of the National Socialists must have impinged directly on the experience of anyone living in the city at this time. Street violence was becoming commonplace, and by the end of 1930 there were signs that the rapidly growing private army of stormtroopers was 'getting out of hand'. The phrase is used by the American journalist and historian William Shirer, who was living in the city at that time and later wrote: 'Its members, even its leaders, apparently believed in a coming Nazi revolution by violence, and with increasing frequency they were taking to the streets to molest and murder their political opponents. No election, national, provincial or municipal, took place without savage battles in the gutters.'

Hitler's personal prestige and the power of his party continued to grow. In the presidential election held in March 1932 he polled over 11 million votes (an increase of some 86 per cent over the previous election), coming second to Hindenburg. Since Hindenburg had failed to gain an absolute majority, a further election was held in the following months, and Hitler again increased his vote substantially (by over two million); this time, however, Hindenburg obtained his majority. Though defeated, Hitler had doubled the Nazi vote in two years and strengthened his personal position immensely. As Shirer notes, a menacing background to these elections was the private army of Stormtroopers, now numbering some 400,000, who stood poised ready to seize power on Hitler's behalf when the time was ripe.

In the Reichstag or parliamentary elections in July, there was a sensational victory for the Nazis (230 seats out of 608), following a campaign 'marked by sanguinary clashes between Communists and Nazis, and Socialists and Nazis'; they were now the largest party in the Reichstag. When new elections were called for in November, the Nazis lost 34 seats but remained the strongest party. On 8 August, soon after the July elections, Goebbels wrote in his diary that Berlin was 'full of rumours', that the Nazis were 'ready to take over power' and that the Stormtroopers were 'leaving their places of work in order to make themselves ready' while the party leaders themselves were 'preparing for the great hour'. The next day he wrote that the stormtroopers were 'throwing an ever stronger ring around Berlin'.

Isherwood was in London at this time, and he had been on Rügen at the time of the July elections, but he spent enough of 1932 in Berlin itself to be well aware of what was going on, and he was back from England in time to witness the campaign leading up to the elections of 6 November, in which the Nazis lost two million votes and 34 seats in the Reichstag, while the Communists strengthened their position. Hitler's personal ascendancy seemed unstoppable, however, and Kurt von Schleicher, who became Chancellor on 2 December, was to hold office for only 57 days and to be the last Chancellor of the Weimar Republic.

On 30 January 1933 Hitler was made Chancellor, and five weeks later, in the elections of 5 March, the Nazis won 288 seats, giving them an outright majority in the Reichstag. Later in the same month an Enabling Law granted dictatorial powers to Hitler. But by then, for Isherwood, as for many others living in Germany who had not yet made their escape, it was time to go.

All of this was the background to the final phase of Isherwood's life in Germany, and sometimes more than the background. On 3 November 1932 he wrote to Spender about the transport strike that had begun that very day, and in *Christopher and his Kind* he recalls that this 'resulted in widespread public violence against strikebreakers and others'. He witnessed a street incident in which a young man was brutally attacked by a group of Nazis on their way back from a political rally, and later made use of it in *Goodbye to Berlin*.

It must be remembered, though, that daily life is not often lived at the fever-pitch attained by historical accounts or fictionalised versions of them, and in mid-January Isherwood was writing to Spender that the political situation was 'very dull':

I expect there is a great deal going on behind the scenes, but one is not aware of it. Papen visits Hindenburg, Hitler visits Papen, Hitler and Papen visit Schleicher, Hugenberg visits Hindenburg and finds he's out. And so forth. There is no longer that slightly exhilarating awareness of crisis in the gestures of beggars and tram-conductors.

(The eye of the professional novelist and the dedicated cinemagoer can be detected in those observed gestures.) When Hitler came to power, Isherwood wrote to Spender that 'we are having a new government, with Charlie Chaplin and Father Christmas in the ministry': it was the more politically aware Spender in England who responded to the situation by exclaiming that 'The news from Germany is awful.'

Even the sleazy paradise of the boy-bars had begun to be invaded by politics, the boys taking sides in arguments and joining one organisation or another. Real life provided one of its symbolic moments when, on 1 April, Isherwood went to make some token purchase at a Jewish department store as a gesture of protest and recognised, standing at the entrance in a stormtrooper's uniform, one of the youths from the Cosy Corner. The transformation of some of the young bar-haunting prostitutes into gleaming instruments of the new regime is presented, though not without tactful evasion, in *Goodbye to Berlin*.

Despite all this, work, love affairs and the comings and goings of friends were perhaps more real, and certainly more interesting, to Isherwood than the reported doings of politicians, though later he expressed regret at not having taken a closer professional interest in the psychology of the members of the Nazi High Command. Lehmann had visited him in October, on his way back to Vienna, and was in Berlin again in late January, just at the time Hitler became Chancellor, and yet again in late February, when the Reichstag was burned. Meanwhile, over Christmas, Auden paid a ten-day visit and discussed plans for his play *The Dance of Death*, not produced until 1934. At this period Isherwood was seeing a good deal of Beatrix Lehmann, John's sister and a well-known actress, who was visiting Berlin, and they spent New Year's Eve together.

Shortly after the mid-January letter to Spender, Hitler's accession to power made it impossible to complain of dullness, and many foreigners, Isherwood among them, either left Germany or began to make plans to do so. Even Aleister Crowley, the footloose poetaster, theosophist, diabolist and self-styled Beast from the Book of Revelation, who had been living in Berlin in 1932, deemed it prudent to depart – despite his claim to have presented the National Socialists with the idea of using the swastika as their symbol, and thereby having presumably earned their undying gratitude. Lehmann's memoir notes that after the Reichstag fire 'Hitler's triumph was complete...and the Nazi terror was unleashed against the Communists and all the known opponents of the new regime' (p. 14). Among the exhibits in present-day Berlin's grim and grimly named museum Topographie des Terrors is a dramatic photograph of police rounding up Communists in a large-scale operation on 22 January.

In addition to known opponents, minorities such as Jews and homosexuals were victimised. Lehmann adds that 'Foreigners who had no obvious affiliation were left alone, at any rate for the time being, but the frequenters of the boy-bars, many of which were being raided, passed some uneasy nights'. Demonstrations of Nazi power took theatrical as well as practical forms: another picture in the same museum shows a *Sportfest* in Berlin's Sportpalast on 17 March in which police with raised rifles were lined up in the shape of a swastika.

Early in April, just a few days after the first Nazi boycott of Jewish-owned businesses on the 1st, Isherwood left for England, taking with him a number of his belongings, including papers and manuscripts. During three weeks spent in London he saw, among others, Gerald Hamilton (whom he had helped to flee from Berlin), Edward Upward and Bubi. He also visited some friends of Forster's at Esher and met Joe Ackerley there: it was to turn out to be a valuable contact, for Ackerley was literary editor of *The Listener* and was later to put a good deal of reviewing work Isherwood's way. It was at this time that Forster lent Isherwood the typescript of *Maurice*, which Isherwood liked and praised.

Back in Berlin on the last day of April, he began to make preparations for a departure that would merely, and perhaps barely, anticipate an official request to leave the country. Francis had bought a small Greek island in the hope (to prove sadly vain) of resuming his career as an archaeologist, and he invited Isherwood to join him there, so to Greece he decided to go. The Berlin dream had turned into a nightmare: there was (as he wrote long afterwards) 'terror in the Berlin air'; and in the end he could not get away quickly enough. During his last two weeks in the city events moved rapidly. On 2 May the German trade unions were suppressed. Four days later Hirschfeld's Institute, with which Isherwood had been closely associated during his first year in Berlin, was invaded and ransacked.

So, on 13 May, he set off for Athens, accompanied by Heinz and Erwin. They took a week over the journey, travelling by train via Prague and Vienna to Budapest, then by river steamer to Belgrade, finally by train again to Athens, where Francis met them. Isherwood spent an uncomfortable three and a half months on Francis's island, St Nicholas, then, still accompanied by Heinz, began the wanderings that were to occupy most of the next seven years. (The Greek episode was put to good account in *Down There on a Visit*.) As for Berlin, the city with which most of those who know his name most readily associate him, it was a long time before he saw it again and he was never again to make it his home.

The relationship of the two writers, and the literary results of their love affair with Berlin (more interesting, after all, than their other love affairs), survived their departure. During the 1930s they collaborated on several enterprises: the plays *The Dog Beneath the Skin*, *The Ascent of F6* and *On the Frontier*, and the travel book *Journey to a War*, based on their visit to China. Isherwood's Berlin fiction also came later in the decade, *Mr Norris Changes Trains* in 1935 and *Goodbye to Berlin* in 1939, so that what had started as a diary ended almost as a historical study. In a later chapter (Chapter 5) we shall consider the ways in which, over a period much longer than that of their actual residence, the experiences of the years 1928 to 1933 were transformed into art.

2

Berlin: Places

Although its origins go back to the Middle Ages, and although in 1871 it was promoted from the chief city in Prussia to the imperial capital, Berlin retained until near the end of the nineteenth century an air of provinciality. Like London and other European cities, however, it had been growing dramatically during that century: its population quadrupled between 1800 and 1871, and was already over half a million (521,933) at the time of the first official census in 1861. The symbolic million mark was passed in 1877, and it reached two million by 1905. By this time it had already become recognised as a major international city with a markedly modern flavour: in 1898 it had been nicknamed 'Chicago on the Spree', presumably on account of the number of new buildings that were rising. Later, a 1915 guide described it as 'the most American city in continental Europe'. It also had its share of the problems of modern urban civilisation, including extensive slums and a serious housing shortage. At the same time it was a green city, with nearly twenty per cent of the area within the municipal boundaries consisting of woodland.

The 1931 census, conducted during Isherwood's period of residence, showed a population of 4,288,700, making it the world's third city (after London and New York). It was the most important railway centre in Europe, and already a rapidly developing focus for the new age of air travel, nearly fifty thousand passengers passing through Tempelhof Airport in 1930. Nor was its importance merely a matter of size and economic growth, for after the turn of the century it had begun to compete with Munich as a cultural and artistic centre for Germany, and by the end of the 1920s it had become a serious rival to Paris as a laboratory for creative experiment and innovation.

In a matter of some fifty years, then, from the 1870s to the 1920s, the old Prussian capital had transformed itself into a cosmopolitan city, and as such it had begun to attract a heavy tourist trade.

Auden and Isherwood were not the only non-Germans in Berlin,
for of the one and a quarter million visitors to the city who registered with the police in 1930 one-fifth were foreigners. Many, of
course, came on business, but others were lured by the city's
reputation as a centre of the sex industry with a bizarrely and
perhaps uniquely varied nightlife. A 1927 guide describes the
Eldorado, the transvestite nightclub in Motzstrasse already
referred to, which was very close to the quarter that Isherwood
was a little later to make his own:

> There is a secret about the place that belongs to the Berlin night.
> This place, one of Berlin's most popular, recruits its patrons
> mainly from circles where the arithmetic of love is not without
> its mistakes. Here men do not only dance with women but with
> men. And women dance with women. And the nice gentleman
> from Saxony, who dances with the blond singer, doesn't have the
> slightest idea that his blond lady is a man....
> (Eugen Szatman, *Das Buch von Berlin*, quoted in von Eckardt and
> Gilman, *Bertolt Brecht's Berlin*, p. 31)

But this, the guide teasingly continues, is all good clean fun compared with 'the bars that one *really* doesn't talk about...they are
known only to the initiated' – a group among whom Auden and
Isherwood unquestionably came to be numbered.

William Plomer, a year older than Isherwood and later a friend,
was in Berlin in 1930 and detected a more complex, even paradoxical flavour. He refers in his autobiography to 'the then notorious
night-life', adding that 'Blatant impudicity on such a scale was
certainly exciting to youthful senses, but there was something
desperately sad about it – and at times something grotesquely
funny' (p. 274). On a more respectable level, the city had an 'air
of modernity, open-mindedness and vitality', so that in 1929
Harold Nicolson, who was presumably not thinking on this
occasion of the kind of establishments 'known only to the initiated',
could speak of 'the charm of Berlin'.

Gerald Hamilton, the 'original' of Isherwood's Mr Norris, found
Berlin 'more agreeably mixed and international than London' (*Mr
Norris and I*, p. 128). What he meant by 'mixed' is spelled out:

> During the last years of the decrepit Weimar Republic, Berlin
> outvied Paris with its night life. But though it was supposed to

be gay, there was a sordid element about it which was very noticeable. There were alleged to be no less than 132 homosexual cafés registered as such with the tolerant police. Some of them were used only by ladies as a rendezvous for their Lesbian friends. Others were exclusively for *Transvestiten*, men and boys who like to dress up as women. The rest were patronized by the usual kind of homosexuals who hoped to meet their destiny at such places. There were weekly homosexual papers, such as the famous *Freundschaft* which published the most fantastic advertisements I have ever seen in print. Then again there were some cafés which specialized in a particular attraction, such as having a genuine hermaphrodite on the premises. The height of decadence was reached on the so-called *strich* or avenue, where prostitutes offered themselves for sale. There were girls in men's clothes, often holding a whip, boys in girl's clothes, and the usual supply of men and women offering themselves to either sex in return for ample payment.

(pp. 129–30)

Hamilton's air of prim disapproval should not be taken seriously, since he was a practising homosexual who knew what he was talking about.

In *Christopher and his Kind* (p. 29), Isherwood suggests that Berlin's reputation for decadence and perversity may have been 'largely a commercial "line" which the Berliners had instinctively developed in their competition with Paris': since Paris had for generations exploited a reputation for easily available straight sex, it was natural for Berlin to compete by offering 'a masquerade of perversions'. The roots of the phenomenon seem, however, to lie more deeply in traditional cultural patterns. The intensely masculine ethos of Prussian militarism may have created behaviour patterns comparable to those generated by the single-sex schools and colleges attended by the ruling class in England, and the homosexual scandals at the highest levels that rocked German society in a period well before Berlin's international heyday suggest widespread and well-entrenched practices and lifestyles.

Moreover, the subcultures in question have evinced a remarkable knack of surviving. A whole generation after the years with which this book is concerned, when the middle-aged Auden returned to live in Berlin for a time in the 1960s, he would have found, among so much change and so much eradication of landmarks, places to enter which was to step back into the earlier epoch. His lines written in February 1965 and titled 'Economics', make the point succinctly:

> In the Hungry Thirties
> boys used to sell their bodies
> for a square meal.
>
> In the Affluent Sixties
> they still did:
> to meet Hire-Purchase Payments.

Loren Driscoll, who knew Auden well and who himself lived in Berlin at this time, has described to me one institution that flourished in Berlin in the 'Affluent Sixties':

I recall going into Elly's Bier Bar one evening. There, sitting prominently at the bar, was Grandma – actually Grandpa, who had been carefully dressed up by his wife before setting out and was there every Saturday night. Then there was a massive truck-driver, heavily tattooed, with his little boy-friend, and a nice young couple embracing, only a toothless old man had his hand on the young man's crotch. As I entered, the boy looked at me, raised his eyebrows, shrugged his shoulders, and went on kissing his girl. Elly herself was an institution: a lesbian who wore Cary Grant suits and George Raft hats and permitted no hanky-panky in her establishment while she stood there chewing her Havana.

The world of Georg Grosz was still alive and well, it seems, at least in microcosm. And even today, a further generation on, though Berlin has yielded to cheaper and more climatically favoured spots as a venue for the sex-vacation market, by no means every link with the past has been severed, and there is said to be at least one tiny, crowded and smoke-filled 24-hour bar in the neighbourhood of Isherwood's Nollendorfplatz that in decor and clientele bears a strong resemblance to the long-defunct but historic Cosy Corner.

As with many expanding cities, Berlin's centre had not remained constant, but as a result of the upheavals of the last half-century we need to make a double effort of the historical imagination in order to gain a sense of where the hub of the city was situated at various points in its history. Even today, perhaps, for those who have got to know Berlin it is necessary first to think of it as it was before the building of the Wall (the demolition of which has not stopped its citizens from speaking of their city as divided into East and West) to grasp the changes that took place during the period of rapid expansion from about 1924 to 1929: the period near the end of which Auden and Isherwood saw it for the first time.

A glance at a map of Central Berlin in the early 1920s shows the east–west axis of Unter den Linden dividing the area into two roughly equal parts. Near its west end stood the Brandenburg Gate, with the Reichstag nearby, while towards the east were the Cathedral, the Imperial Palace, the Stock Exchange, the National Gallery, Opera, museums and other public buildings. This picture already has an air of looking-glass unfamiliarity to anyone who has known 'West Berlin' in recent decades and for whom the Brandenburg Gate, for instance, has been thought of as lying well to the *east* of the centre.

During the 1920s, however, the centre had begun to shift to the west, rather in the way that, at a less feverish pace, the centre of London had shifted in the early nineteenth century. What had been the 'west end', the area around the Tiergarten, became the 'old west end' as a 'new west end' established itself around the Kurfür-stendamm and the Kaiser Wilhelm Memorial Church (built in 1895 and standing, as its gaunt ruins still do, at the meeting point of six busy streets). The central area now extended itself as far west as the Schloss Charlottenburg, and the Kurfürstendamm ('Ku'damm') developed from a residential street to the brightly lit string of smart shops, cafés, restaurants, cinemas and theatres that it still is. The Zoo Bahnhof (main railway station opposite the Zoological Gardens) became and has remained a favourite centre for rendez-vous and sexual encounters as well as arrivals from and departures to distant cities.

Legislation at the beginning of the decade had created a brand-new municipality of Greater Berlin by adding to the old city seven towns, 52 rural communities and 27 landed estates, and the second half of the 1920s saw the city assuming a new status, and to some extent a new identity, through building and entrepreneurial and technological activity on an unprecedented scale. It quickly became, for instance, an international conference and exhibition centre, with a major radio exhibition in 1924 and an agricultural exhibition in 1926. The Radio Tower, operational from 1926, was described by an official guide in a striking piece of self-conscious symbol-making as 'a masterpiece of modern technology and the symbol of New Berlin'. With the extensive construction of docks during the same period, Berlin became Germany's second largest river port, while the Rummelsberg Power Station, built in the mid-1920s, was the most modern in Europe. The city's largest department store, the Karstadt in Hermannplatz (destroyed in the Second World War), opened its doors in 1929.

Public, commercial and private buildings reflected (and some surviving specimens still reflect) Berlin's growing reputation as the centre of the modern movement in architecture, and thanks to the work of Gropius, Häring, Mendelsohn and others it became 'the uncontested centre of all the most progressive developments in contemporary architecture'. The chronic housing shortage was tackled with the building of new estates and the provision of parks and sports facilities: in 1930 alone, 44,000 new homes were constructed. In 1929 Walter Gropius designed apartment blocks on innovative lines for Siemenstadt, an estate housing employees of the giant Siemens electrical firm.

Martin Wagner, who was in charge of the city's planning department, was responsible for the Wannsee resort, where Auden and Isherwood used to swim and sunbathe. In *Christopher and his Kind* (p. 39) Isherwood relates that he and his lover Otto went to swim in 'the great lake at Wannsee'. This lakeside resort had been established in 1907 and became very popular after its beach was artificially extended in 1929–30. A photograph taken in 1932 shows a large and crowded terrace café with the beach and lake edge full of bathers beyond it, and a view of pine-woods and low hills on the opposite side of the lake. They also visited Luna Park, which is mentioned in both Auden's journal and Isherwood's autobiography. This was a huge and popular leisure complex on the Halensee, on the edge of the Grunewald. Dating from 1904, it had become Berlin's largest amusement park, with attractions that ranged from Expressionist sculptures to a swimming pool with artificial waves. During a visit there on 26 April 1929, Auden was greatly struck by the nonchalance of a eunuch in the showers; it seemed to him an instance of genuine courage that he contrasted with the show-off antics of some of the swimmers.

The public transport system, coordinated by the formation of the Berlin Transport Joint-Stock Company in 1929, was of a high standard. By the mid-1920s the city's rail network covered

53 kilometres, and there was about the same amount of U-Bahn and S-Bahn (roughly, subway and overhead railway) lines, as well as some seventy tramlines and twenty bus routes. Like W. P. Frith celebrating in oils the nineteenth-century railway boom, German artists of the period turned their attention to what the Victorians liked to call the romance of transport. Among the paintings in the Berlin Museum are Jakob Steinhardt's 'Joachimsthaler Strasse und Bahnhof Zoo' (1925) and Albert Birkle's 'S-Bahnhof Berlin-Tiergarten' (1926–7) – the equivalent, say, of titling a painting 'Euston Road and King's Cross' or 'Green Park Underground Station'. All of this implies a busy, bustling city, and Berliners, like Londoners and New Yorkers, had the reputation of being brash, aggressive, dynamic and no respecters of persons.

In the autumn of 1928, at precisely the time of Auden's arrival in Berlin, the electricity companies launched a campaign to turn the city into a *ville lumière* or city of lights that would rival Paris, and Bertolt Brecht and Kurt Weill were commissioned to write a song to publicise this endeavour. According to John Willett's valuable study *The Theatre of the Weimar Republic*, 'the capital now saw an influx of major talents.... the attraction of Berlin for composers and conductors was perhaps stronger than for any other class of artist, for it was above all else the city's musical life that most felt the effects of the boom'. Arnold Schönberg had arrived in 1926, Paul Hindemith came soon afterwards, while from 1925 Igor Stravinsky (later one of Auden's operatic collaborators) had made it the principal location for performances of his works. A photograph of 1930 shows five great conductors – Bruno Walter, Arturo Toscanini, Josef Kleiber, Otto Klemperer and Wilhelm Furtwängler – and few cities in the world at that time can have been capable of bringing together such an array of interpretative talent and fame.

Willett's account makes it clear that the theatre, too, flourished on all levels, from productions of German and international classics in the numerous state and private theatres (in 1931 there were 36 theatres with a seating capacity of 43,000) to shows aimed partly at the tourist trade with titles like *Get Undressed* and *Donnerwetter – 1000 Women*. On 7 July 1926 the *Berliner Tageblatt* had reported that nine theatres were devoted to revues and attracted nightly audiences of some 11,000. In the month in which Auden arrived, Max Reinhardt's production of Shakespeare's *Romeo and Juliet* opened, as did Stravinsky's *Histoire du Soldat*, and in the next few months anyone living in Berlin could have seen, among much else, plays by Sophocles, Goethe, Shaw, Maugham, O'Neill and Cocteau. Diaghilev's ballet paid the city a visit in June 1929.

This was the age of Hermann Hesse, Thomas Mann and Rainer Maria Rilke; of Georg Grosz and Otto Dix; of Kurt Weill's collaborations with Brecht and Kaiser; of *The Blue Angel, All Quiet on the Western Front* and *The Threepenny Opera*. Klemperer was musical director of the Staatsoper and Einstein ran the Kaiser Wilhelm Institute for Physics. As some of the dates already cited indicate, the two young Englishmen came to Berlin when many of the visible symbols of its modernity and prosperity still had the gloss of newness upon them, though the brief period of boom was already past, and the economic crisis at the end of the decade and the political developments that quickly followed were soon to inaugurate a darker era.

HOMES AND HAUNTS

The temporary homes occupied by Auden and Isherwood during their residence in Berlin took them to several parts of the city, ranging from affluent bourgeois graciousness to working-class slum, for periods that varied from a few weeks to more than two years. Auden's first lodging was in the Potsdamer Chaussée, in the suburb of Nikolassee, situated in the beautiful area of lakes and woodland in southwest Berlin. It lies at the southeast end of the long, narrow Havel lake and is handy for the Wannsee Strandbad, a very popular sandy beach a kilometre long whose popularity has already been mentioned. This was both the least central and by far the grandest Berlin house that either of them was to live in – so grand, indeed, that some such genteelism as 'paying guest' seems to be required. For Auden found himself in the imposing home of a prominent and gifted family, and an account of Anna Muthesius, her husband and the house he designed for his family will be given in the next chapter. It was, however, not quite what Auden had come to Berlin to find, and he stayed there for only a few weeks.

From there he moved, at the very beginning of 1929, geographically centrewards and socially downwards, to 8 Furbringerstrasse in the working-class district of Hallesches Tor. This neighbourhood lies at the south end of the major north–south route of the Friedrichstrasse, and in Auden's day there stood, just to the northwest, the magnificent pile of the Anhalter Bahnhof, a mainline station completed in 1870, spared by bombs in the Second World War, but a victim to postwar speculators. It was blown up, for its bricks, in 1952, though its evocative ruins can still be seen across a car park. Auden went there on at least one occasion, to see his brother John off for Vienna after he had briefly visited him in Berlin; as we have seen already, it was an occasion memorable for the words not spoken, the opportunities missed.

Though the neighbourhood of Hallesches Tor has changed much more drastically than the affluent and carefully preserved *rus in urbe* of the Nikolassee, this house too still stands. It lies in the West Kreuzberg district, in what was then the southwest quarter of the central area of the city, and was remembered by Stephen Spender as 'an area of slum tenements'. A stroll round the neighbourhood today, beginning from the U-Bahn station that Auden must often have used, shows that it has gone up in the world and become busier and noisier in the process. The canal and the overhead railway now divide a six-lane throughway with thundering traffic, and around the station, instead of slum tenements, there are modern highrises surrounding public gardens, a public library and other municipal buildings, together with the cosmopolitan and polyglot trappings (a coiffeur, a pizzeria) of affluent modern life.

Just to the east of the station stands the unignorable landmark of a domed red-brick church resembling a Congregational chapel that has got out of hand, and from this point Zossenerstrasse runs south. This too is now a busy traffic route, but to turn left into Furbringerstrasse, where Auden lived, is to be at once in a quieter world. Number 8, on the right, is a five-storey apartment building that, like most of the houses in the street, has been refaced, but number 28, exactly opposite, has its original facade and conveys a very good impression of what the whole street must have looked like in 1929. Despite the chipped and broken, pitted and scarred stonework, as ravaged and discoloured by time as Auden's own face later became, there are still vestiges of the original baroque splendour in the balustrades and the pediments over the tall windows, and the huge wooden doors are elaborately carved. The faded letters of the word 'Kurzwaren' (haberdashery) can still be read above the ground-floor windows, a reminder that the old Berlin houses characteristically had shops or workshops on the street-level and apartments or *pensions* above. If he cared to, or was in a condition to, raise his head, Auden must have seen this facade every time he left his lodgings during the months he lived in Furbringerstrasse.

Returning to Zossenerstrasse and crossing the now busy street, one finds these days a group of commercial premises with (according to custom) the shared number 7: a *Zahnärztin* or lady dentist, a unisex hairdresser, an agency specialising in 'alternative' bus tours and, on the corner, a boutique stocking obviously expensive ladies' wear. Here, in the days when the entire neighbourhood was considerably scruffier, stood the Cosy Corner. This was the rent-bar that assumes almost mythological status in *Christopher and his Kind*, where Isherwood's account (already cited) of his first visit in March 1929 takes on the air of an excursion to the underworld with Auden as his Virgil, and his pushing aside of the heavy leather curtain across the door seems to enact some arcane and hazardous ritual of rebirth. Oddly enough, the opposite side of the street has not shared its partner's transformation: a working-class café-bar, a tiny second-hand bookshop with stock tumbled into the window, a junk shop with the castoffs of other people's lives heaped in laundry baskets and dumped on the pavement – all these, in complete contrast to the modish establishments across the street, seem still to belong to the world in which Auden lived.

The Cosy Corner was no more than a minute's walk from the door of the house where he lodged, a convenient distance in bad weather, or late at night, or with a companion for whom time was money (and money was also money), or when remaining vertical presented difficulties. Presided over by Auden's tolerant landlady, Frau Günther (listed, with her husband, in a directory of the period), the lodging-house in Furbringerstrasse was also a location vastly more suited to his requirements than the handsome suburban home of the Muthesius family. It remained his base until he left Berlin. From his room it was no more than a few minutes' walk, past a graveyard and across the canal, to the U-Bahn station that gave him access to other parts of the city. I was there on a winter morning when, after an overnight snowfall, workmen were scattering sand on the paths by the canal just as they no doubt did in the early months of 1929 – for, although the most familiar images, verbal and photographic, of Auden and Isherwood's Germany are of a land permanently bathed in sunshine in which the normal costume was a swimming costume, Berlin can have a ferociously cold winter.

Where Isherwood stayed on that first visit to Berlin in March 1929 is not known, but it seems likely that he shared Auden's room (they were at any rate intermittent lovers), or perhaps found another room in the same house. By the time he returned to the city in November, Auden had gone home, and Isherwood's first step was to contact the only Englishman he knew in Berlin, Francis Turville-Petre, whose strange life and career will shortly be recounted. Francis's rooms were in 9A In den Zelten, a fashionable street lying between the northeastern corner of the Tiergarten (then a little less extensive at that end than it is today) and the banks of the River Spree, and not far from the Reichstag and the Brandenburg Gate. Although there is still a street bearing the name In den Zelten, not the slightest trace remains of what must once have been a busy and prosperous area, partly residential, partly commercial. Instead, lawns and trees surround an earnest-looking new complex of buildings dedicated to the official promotion of culture.

The neighbourhood had traditionally been a place to which Berliners could escape for relaxation and a breath of fresh air – the name means 'In the Tents', presumably with reference to stalls originally providing food, drink and entertainment – and in the 1920s it still contained many restaurants and an opera house that was to accommodate the German parliament after the burning of the Reichstag in 1933. In *Christopher and his Kind* (p. 32) Isherwood describes a Christmas ball held at 'one of the dance-halls' in the street, a fancy-dress occasion exclusively for men, some of whom wore female attire. In those days the street lay just outside the green and wooded spaces of the Tiergarten, which was extended during the 1950s after the wartime bombing of adjacent built-up areas. As well as being a pleasure-resort, In den Zelten seems in the 1920s to have become something of a writers' and artists' colony. Two expatriate American writers who lived there were Robert McAlmon at number 18 and Djuna Barnes next door.

Possibly, indeed, it had had this reputation even in the nineteenth century, for the famous Hungarian violinist Joseph Joachim, director of the Berlin Conservatory and a friend of Brahms, had lived at number 10. Long before Isherwood's arrival, Magnus Hirschfeld (see next chapter) had established his Institute for Sexual Research in Joachim's former home, a large house on the corner of In den Zelten and Beethovenstrasse. Hirschfeld had also acquired the neighbouring property (9A), had had communicating doors built between the two houses, and had turned the ground floor of 9A into a lecture hall. On the floor immediately above were apartments for the resident medical staff; above that were guest rooms, in which Christopher and Francis lived; and on the top floor were rooms or cells for the accommodation or confinement of those awaiting trial for alleged sexual offences. For it seems that among the Institute's many roles was that of a kind of refuge or sanctuary for offenders of this kind, the police permitting Hirschfeld to assume responsibility for them while they lived under his roof. Contemporary photographs and drawings show Hirschfeld's premises to have been very extensive: the main house is a splendid mansion on a corner site, while 9A, with its five main floors, attics and semi-basement, was on a smaller scale though slightly taller.

Isherwood's room, looking down into a courtyard, was 'dark and cheap'; Francis, who was not short of money, had two rooms that afforded a view of the park. Isherwood spent nearly a year in In den Zelten; although visits to his favourite working-class bars must have involved a journey, it was a good spot for a writer, far from dull but away from the hurly-burly of the city centre. It was there that he worked on the third draft of *The Memorial*, there that he made love to 'Otto', and perhaps there that Auden stayed when he visited his friend in June and July 1930. It may have been their conversations about Francis at this time that led Auden to begin his play *The Fronny* very soon after returning from Berlin.

After leaving the Hirschfeld establishment, possibly for financial reasons, in October 1930, Isherwood occupied two lodgings in quick succession, each for only a few weeks, for by December he was installed in Nollendorfstrasse, where he was to remain until the time came for him to leave Berlin. The two working-class neighbourhoods in which he briefly dwelt have both been swept away by the destruction and rebuilding of the last sixty years. Simeonstrasse, where he lodged at number 4 with the family of his lover Otto, was in the Hallesches Tor district, like Auden's second home in Berlin, but seems to have vanished without trace. In *Goodbye to Berlin* it is renamed Wassertorstrasse, a name that means Watergate Street and was rather surprisingly deemed by its inventor to sound 'more romantic' (*Christopher and his Kind*, p. 43). Admiralstrasse, in the Kottbusser Tor district, where he stayed briefly in November, still exists but has been wholly reconstructed, and there seems to be no sign of number 38.

The Nollendorfstrasse house, however, not only stands but is the only one of the buildings associated with Auden or Isherwood to have received official recognition. Outside number 17, on the north side of the street, is a plaque recording, with more enthusiasm than reliability, that Isherwood lived there from March 1929 to January/February 1933, and identifying him (probably not much to the gratification of his ghost) as the author of the Berlin stories and the inspirer of the musical *Cabaret*. (His residence there began, of course, nearly two years later than stated.) The pre-1914 house itself, on which the corresponding building in the Berlin stories was closely modelled, has a reconstructed facade, though the exterior of number 16 next door gives a better impression of what it must once have looked like. Inside, however, it retains a good deal of the atmosphere it must have possessed when Isherwood pushed open the very heavy doors and climbed the wide staircase, with its massive wooden handrails and banisters and its stained-glass windows on the landings. The rooms have wide doors and high ceilings with elaborate plasterwork; the apartment I was able to visit still possesses a massive tiled stove in one corner, just as in the description of Fräulein Schroeder's flat at the beginning of *Goodbye to Berlin*.

The street, less narrow today than the description at the beginning of *Goodbye to Berlin* leads one to expect, and now tree-lined, has been extensively rebuilt. Like so many other streets and neighbourhoods, it seems to have gone up in the world, and the epithet 'sordid', which Spender applies to it in a rather obscure passage of his autobiography, is now far from applicable to this street of neat small businesses and middle-class homes. In any case, however, Spender's memory may have been at fault and the epithet never have been merited, for Isherwood describes his move there as a move from a working-class to a middle-class neighbourhood: though 'neither elegant nor in good repair', the street was 'middle-class-shabby' rather than 'slum-shabby'. In an earlier generation, the houses, again, followed the traditional pattern of devoting their semi-basements to shops or workrooms (Isherwood refers to them as 'cellar-shops'). Number 17 has five storeys above its semi-basement, the top two of which apparently comprised the *pension* run by Fräulein Thurau, the 'original' of Fräulein Schroeder. If one walks east to the end of the street and crosses the busy Moetzenstrasse to the street opposite, what is now a pedestrian precinct gives a better idea of how the house fronts of the neighbourhood, tall and elegant (and these days generously spray-painted), must formerly have appeared.

Nollendorfstrasse is only a couple of minutes' walk from Nollendorfplatz, the hub of the main routes in that part of the city and
the centre of Isherwood's fictional microcosm. Spender describes it
in his autobiography as having been 'a grand-shabby square
dominated by a station of the overhead railway'. It is today neither
shabby nor grand, merely unremarkable. What must have been,
especially at night, a very animated scene – it was a favourite resort
for homosexuals, and there are said to have been some forty gay
bars in the immediate neighbourhood – is now decorously quiet to
the point of featurelessness. The cleaning-up of Nollendorfplatz,
however, which began as soon as the Nazis came to power,
invoked the usual Law of Minimum Displacement of Offending
Entities. For in the course of more than sixty years the centre of
activity appears to have moved no more than a block or two west –
a remarkable testimony to the vitality and continuity of a subculture and the deep attachment it can form to a particular neighbourhood.

Two large-scale reminders of the period have survived these
changes. The overhead railway mentioned by Spender still bisects
the square. He and Isherwood would have been familiar too with
the station entrance beneath it, now a good deal the worse for wear
but fresh and bright when Isherwood lived nearby, for it had been
built in 1925–6. And on the south side, turning its massive back on
the more modest rears of the Nollendorfstrasse houses and presenting a bold, greyish-white, architecturally eclectic front to the
square, is the Metropol, though that has not always been its
name. Built in 1906, within recent memory a 'porno kino' and
now a venue for discos and rock concerts, this was one of the
most important of Berlin's theatres in the period with which we
are concerned. (In *Christopher and his Kind* Isherwood seems by an
odd lapse of memory to refer to it as a cinema.) It opened as the
Theater am Nollendorfplatz in 1921, and, as a plaque informs us,
Erwin Piscator was Regisseur and Theaterdeiter there in 1927–31.
Piscator attracted a constellation of talents to his theatre, and under
his direction it played an important role in the development of
political and documentary theatre. Asked in a 1961 interview
whether Weimar theatre was politically aware, Isherwood replied
that it was 'intensely aware' and added that the Theater am Nollendorfplatz was *'entirely* political'.

There is also a third and much less obtrusive reminder of the
past in the shape of a small triangular plaque of pink, or at least

reddish, marble. This was placed in Nollendorfplatz a few years ago in memory of the victims of the Nazi persecution of homosexuals. Its siting is a reminder of the reputation enjoyed by that neighbourhood in the years before 1933, and a no doubt less conscious acknowledgement of a still vital subculture in the nearby streets. Mounted on a wall near the entrance to the U-Bahn station, just beneath the raised tracks that Spender recalled, its shape and colour allude to the 'Rosa Winkel' or pink triangle that homosexuals imprisoned in the concentration camps were compelled to wear as a stigmatising badge, and its inscription declares laconically:

> Tot Geschlagen
> Tot Geschwiegen
> den
> Homosexuelle Opfern
> des
> Nationalsozializmus
> (Murdered and silenced, the homosexual victims of
> National Socialism).

Beneath, a plaque states that it was in January 1933 that the Nazis began to shut down the gay bars in the square. That was, of course, just two or three months before Isherwood began his own preparations to move out of his home nearby, out of Berlin, out of Germany.

The neighbourhood of Nollendorfplatz has never been the centre of the city, but in Isherwood's fiction it is the point where excursions to other parts of Berlin begin and end. It is perfectly true, though, that it was conveniently situated as a base, lying as it does roughly halfway between the West End and Kurfürstendamm area to the west and the Unter den Linden and Friedrichstrasse area to the east. If one walked northwest from the Platz, one quickly reached (as one still does) the vast expanse of Wittenbergplatz, with the imitation Greek temple (1911–13) that is the entrance to its subway station, and, on the corner, the huge KaDeWe department store (1906–7, rebuilt 1950). From the north side of Wittenbergplatz there was in Isherwood's time a fine view along the broad Tauentzienstrasse, with tramlines down the middle and motor traffic on either side, towards the Memorial Church, looking in contemporary photographs strangely intact to anyone familiar with the present-day ruin. The Lady Windermere, the smartish bar where Jean Ross worked, was just off the Tauentzienstrasse. Another ten minutes' walk brought one to the Zoo Station, so often mentioned in writings of the period by Isherwood and others.

Motzstrasse, which ran and runs southwest from Nollendorf-platz, was where Spender lived while he was in Berlin, and his autobiography contains an evocative description of his short journey to visit Isherwood. He would, he recalls,

> walk past... grey houses whose facades seemed out of moulds made for pressing enormous concrete biscuits. Then I would come to the Nollendorfplatz, an eyrie of concrete eagles, with verandas like breasts shedding stony flakes of whatever glory they once had into the grime of soot which caked this part of Berlin....   (*World Within World*, p. 121)

Spender's retrospective account makes the whole neighbourhood seem considerably less attractive than it appears in Isherwood's fiction: grubbier, smellier, slipping below the faint line that distinguishes respectable poverty from slum-dwelling. One is left with the choice of believing the fiction that is much closer to the event or the non-fiction that may reflect the process of slow revision to which memory subjects experience, and my own inclination is to believe Isherwood.

All cities, Isherwood's or Spender's Berlin as much as Defoe's or Dickens's or Virginia Woolf's London, are reinvented when they are appropriated by writers, and when the writer is a visitor, like Hemingway or Orwell in Paris, invention is made so much the simpler. Entire facets of the real city can be disregarded, while selected sites can assume symbolic or mythological status. A nice example of this occurs in Spender's autobiography, in which the third chapter begins: 'At the side of a lake there is a city...' The fact is that Hamburg has two dominant physical features, a river and a lake, but it suits Spender, in his account of the time he spent there, to ignore the Elbe and turn the Alster into the symbolic heart of the city. The river, with its docks and adjacent working-class neighbourhoods, represents labour, economic life, domesticity and responsibility, while the Alster is a lotus-eaters' land of swimming, sunbathing and sexual opportunity – or at least it suited Spender to pretend so. Rivers remind us that they have come from elsewhere and are moving on to yet other places, carrying people and objects with them; lakes leave us in peace as if time had ceased to exist. So

Spender's redrawing of the map of Hamburg serves an obvious purpose, but his Hamburg is a subjective city that we can visit only in the text that enshrines it.

Much more than Hamburg, and more than most cities, Berlin seems always to have lent itself readily to conversion into symbol. Apart from the writings with which this study is centrally concerned, it has generated a large number of works in literary and other media that have a topographical starting-point. In our immediate period, for instance, there are the films *Berlin, die Symphonie einer Grosstadt* (*Berlin, the Symphony of a Great City*, 1927), a dawn-to-dusk evocation of the life of the capital; *Asphalt* (1929), which appeared while Auden was living in the city and which he had intended to see on the day he met Gerhart; and *Berlin – Alexanderplatz* (1931), based on the 1929 novel by Alfred Döblin. A painterly analogue to these 'city' films is Otto Dix's triptych *Big City* (1927–8).

Individual sites and buildings acquired and sometimes retained symbolic potency. Very soon, the arson attack on the Reichstag was to be seen as an attempt to destroy not just a building but German parliamentary democracy, and the ruined Reichstag was turned into a symbol of great propagandist power – and not only by the Nazis, for in 1945, as the Russians advanced on Berlin, their objective was the Reichstag, a ruin since 1933, furnishing an extraordinary instance of a vast military machine directed at a symbol. One of the most potent photographic records of the period shows a Soviet soldier attaching a flag to one of its towers, thereby proclaiming the fall of Berlin. Today, or rather tomorrow, the rebuilding of the Reichstag (to designs by a British architect), following Berlin's regaining of its capital status, will render it, according to *The Times* (6 December 1994), 'a symbol of democracy rather than German power'. Nearby, in the postwar years, the Wall, Checkpoint Charlie and the Brandenburg Gate became part of the mental landscape of millions who had never visited the city, and not the least potent element in the worldwide reaction to the coming down of the Wall was the fact that a symbol was being dismantled before our very eyes. But symbols are not lightly discarded by a symbol-haunted generation, and a Checkpoint Charlie Museum now stands on the site of the former crossing from East to West.

Another piece of official symbol-making, launched into the world by the postcards of a million tourists, is the ruined Kaiser Wilhelm Memorial Church in the very heart of Berlin, its snapped-off spire as evocative of past splendour and violent destruction as the 'bare ruined choirs' of an English abbey. And as I was collecting material for this book the continuing political power of a symbol was demonstrated by the suggestion (*The Times*, 30 August 1993) that one of the reasons why Berlin would fail to win the 2000 Olympic Games (as, despite a vigorous and costly campaign, it did) was the existence in a northwestern suburb of the 1936 Stadium – or, more precisely, the association of that building and that event with the Nazis. To visit the Stadium today – so massive, silent and ghost-ridden – would be like visiting a grave-yard no longer open for business, were it not that for anyone who has ever seen Leni Riefenstahl's *Olympia* (1938), given its première on Hitler's birthday, the place is forever inseparable from the images created by that work. In such ways do topography, history and art collaborate.

In his Berlin stories, Isherwood is a topographical as well as a historical novelist. Place-names abound, and it is as easy to trace the movements of his characters on a contemporary map of the city as it is to trace Moll Flanders' wanderings on a map of early eighteenth-century London. In *Mr Norris Changes Trains*, for instance, Norris's flat is in Courbierestrasse, only a short walk from Nollendorfplatz, and the narrator meets him 'by appointment in a small restaurant near the Memorial Church'. Bayer's flat is in Zimmerstrasse, which cuts across Friedrichstrasse and was later the site of Checkpoint Charlie, and his office is in Wilhelmstrasse. The Communist meeting that Norris addresses is held in the district of Neukölln, and a Nazi *Lokal* is placed in Kreuzberg, now very largely occupied by Turkish and other immigrants but then a working-class district where Auden had lodged. After the narrator has first met Norris on a train journey they part on arrival at the Zoo Station, and when he later leaves for England Norris is seen off from the same station, from where Kuno later vainly tries to make his escape. Returning from England, Norris rides in a taxi along 'the dear old Tauentzienstrasse' to his lodgings in Nollendorf-strasse.

Yet this is, after all, the art of the illusionist, and the Berlin that finds embodiment in the work of Isherwood and others is a very personal construct, a carefully modified version of the city they lived in. Certain places, people and events are given prominence, sometimes a symbolic prominence, while others find no place on the maps they draw or in the semi-documentary accounts they give

– for this is true not just of topography but of all aspects of the city's life and history. At the outset, Isherwood and his friends brought with them an image of Berlin that bore only a limited relationship to reality: already there was a darker and grimmer side to the city that seemed to them to extend the bright promise of enlightened tolerance and unrestricted freedom. To cite only a single, though a major, instance: unemployment in Berlin was in 1927 already running twice as high as in the country as a whole, and matters rapidly got worse, so that by the winter of 1929–30, during which Isherwood took up residence, unemployment and hardship were widespread. Many of the 'boys' who were so readily and delightfully available in the Cosy Corner formed part of the statistics, and one of the interests offered by Isherwood's fiction is the balance it strikes, and the compromises and evasions it effects, between a romantic and sentimental *Bildungsroman* and a historically grounded reflection of realities that it became daily harder to ignore.

CULTURES AND SUBCULTURES

Periods of strife and turbulence, as Abraham Cowley pointed out long ago and Harry Lime more recently, are unpleasant to live through but do wonders for the creative arts – and not only the arts. The Weimar Republic was no exception. Defeat, civil war, mass unemployment, stratospheric inflation, then, after a brief interval of prosperity, more economic troubles following the Wall Street Crash, and the tensions and bloodshed that accompanied the rise to power of the Nazis: any German who lived through this decade and a half might well have felt that he or she had supped full of horrors. It was, however, during the same years that Berlin became a centre of innovation and influence across a wide field of artistic, scientific and technological activity – from theatre to photography, from architecture to psychoanalysis, from sexology (Hirschfeld's researches anticipating the later endeavours of Kinsey and Masters and Johnson) to television (the first transmission was made in 1929).

It was as though the political, social and economic collapse that followed military defeat had a liberating effect on art and thought, long-established conventions in the pure and applied arts collapsing along with so much else, including fixed incomes and sexual mores. But the transformation, it goes without saying, was not complete: probably such transformations never are. The old imperial apparatus of power as personified by judges, civil servants and professors to a large extent survived in the new republic. Peter Gay has also argued in his *Weimar Culture: The Outsider as Insider* that although the prevailing tone of Imperial Germany had been conservative and anti-modernist, the modernist opposition – as exemplified, for example, by Expressionism – had in fact begun to flourish during that epoch, and to this extent what has come to be regarded as the Weimar style actually predates the Republic.

In the interwar period Berlin, as we have seen already, became a cosmopolitan city, and Weimar culture has in many of its manifestations the flavour of international modernism. Much of it, however, grew directly out of a highly specific social world at a particular moment of its history. That world and that moment are conveyed to us by some of the enduring cultural artefacts of the age: products, one would add, of high and low, serious and popular culture, if it were not in the nature of Weimar art to blur, challenge and override such traditional distinctions and hierarchies. An artist like Grosz, a dramatist like Brecht, a composer like Weill, all drew on popular sources as surely as media created by new technologies such as photojournalism and cinema offered their mass audiences authentic artworks.

Kurt Weill's career is in many respects paradigmatic. Born in Dessau in 1900, he came to Berlin in 1918 to study composition with Busoni. He was a precocious student whose early works were in the traditional forms: a string quartet (1919), a cello sonata (1920), a symphony (1921). But in 1922 he began to write for the theatre, and from 1926 his collaborations with the dramatists Kaiser and Brecht resulted in a prolific and brilliant seven-year period that ended when he fled from Nazi Germany (he was Jewish) early in 1933.

With Kaiser he produced a one-act opera *Der Protagonist* (1926) and, at the end of his Berlin period, *Der Silbersee* (1933). The latter, his last work for the German theatre, was written after a quarrel with Brecht, who dubbed him (with gross unfairness) 'a phony Richard Strauss'. But it is for his collaborations with Brecht that he is primarily remembered, and between them they were responsible for six works for the theatre, three cantatas and other works. Their greatest success was *Die Dreigroschenoper* (*The Threepenny Opera*, 1928), which was quickly translated into 18 languages, had over 10,000 performances in a period of five years and reached a still wider public through Pabst's 1931 film adaptation, which has become one of the classics of the German cinema. Other notable Brecht/Weill collaborations included *Happy End* (1929) and *Mahagonny* (1930).

After both Brecht and Weill had left Berlin and a few months after the Weimar Republic had ceased to exist, they were briefly reunited in Paris in the summer of 1933 and, their quarrel patched up, the two produced *Die Sieben Todsünden* (*The Seven Deadly Sins*). It was to be their last collaboration, for after settling in America Weill declined Brecht's invitations to work with him again: he himself began a new career, and a highly successful one, composing Broadway musicals. The music of this final period, terminated by his untimely death in 1950, is of a quality that matches the deft and sparkling lyrics of the carefully chosen writers who worked with him, including Ogden Nash and Ira Gershwin, though it substitutes a cheerful optimism for the indignation and protest of the Berlin years, a melodious sweetness for the uncompromisingly harsh, spiky, angular music he wrote to Brecht's words.

Die Sieben Todsünden received its first performance in June 1933 at the Théâtre des Champs-Elysées. Although not strictly a product of Weimar Berlin it is worth considering as a work impossible to fit into any accepted generic category but one of great musical and dramatic power. It was the outcome of a commission for a ballet; what resulted, however, was a mixture of ballet, opera, morality play and fairy tale. Brecht wrote the text, George Balanchine did the choreography and Caspar Neher the décor, while Tillie Losch was the prima ballerina (if that classical term is appropriate to this highly innovative work) and Lotte Lenya, the composer's wife, created the role of Anna.

Or the roles: for Anna is a pair of Siamese twins with the same name, sharing (as a line of Brecht's laconic and acidulous text points out) the same heart and the same savings-bank passbook. In the course of the work, they travel the length and breadth of America in quest of money to build a house in Louisiana (a third Anna/ana) where their family can live happily ever after, and in the course of their wanderings from city to city they encounter in contemporary American life a series of situations exemplifying the seven deadly sins.

The America is that of the earlier *Mahagonny*, half real, half mythical, and the two Annas represent two sides of female, or perhaps human, nature: one is serious, thoughtful and sensible, the other prettier, more impulsive and emotional. They react differently to the seven situations, the former expressing herself through song, the latter through dance. There is also a male vocal quartet representing their family.

Lotte Lenya's vocal style was highly distinctive and created a tradition, still very much alive (in, for example, the performances of Ute Lemper and Teresa Stratas), for the interpretation of Weill's work. The singing often turns momentarily into declamation, and the words are enunciated with great distinctness, in recognition of their parity of importance with the music, while that music incorporates a variety of popular styles ranging from jazz and the cabaret song to the Viennese waltz and the military march. Weill's aim to create a modern international folk music involved the use of popular forms, dance rhythms and instrumentation closer to that of the jazz band than the symphony orchestra. This was a style that had reached its maturity in the Berlin collaborations with Brecht but had already established itself before those collaborations began.

I have begun at the end of Weill's European career, but he was at the time a brand-new refugee and *Die Sieben Todsünden* represents a continuation not only of the partnership with Brecht but of the style defined during the brief brilliant Berlin years. This was a partnership of youth (Weill was only 27 when he met Brecht in the spring of 1927, Brecht only two years older), and one in which not only accepted forms but the very nature of theatrical experience were being questioned and subverted. Highly characteristic is the crossing of generic frontiers or merging of modes traditionally kept separate – by introducing, for instance, song into ballet or drama so as to create a popular opera form. Characteristic, too, is the use of the bizarre and the grotesque for purposes of social criticism: like some of the drawings of Grosz, *Die Sieben Todsünden* evokes a fantasy world that nevertheless bears a disturbing relationship to the real world, and in the process exposes the latter as ugly, greedy, mercenary, unjust and cruel.

Die Dreigroschenoper in particular has often been seen as having a representative quality, of embodying the Zeitgeist. It was the second of the Brecht/Weill collaborations (the first, the singspiel *Mahagonny*, later forming the basis of a full-scale opera). It opened on 31 August 1928 at the Theater am Schiffbauerdamm in Berlin, and was an immediate success with the public, though it was also, predictably, the target of savage critical attacks. Auden, who arrived in Berlin soon after its première, went to see it shortly afterwards. Its reworking of the eighteenth-century English *Beggar's Opera* meant that its origins were both popular and international, and recordings of early performances show how readily it absorbed the jazz idiom of its period while putting all these elements to the service of contemporary political satire. It is hard to believe that Auden did not remember his attendance at the first production of *Die Dreigroschenoper* when, a generation later, he collaborated with Stravinsky on *The Rake's Progress*.

In their youthfulness, their willingness to conduct experiments that involved a rejection of traditional forms and modes, and the collaborative nature of their art, Weill and Brecht were not only representative of Weimar art as a whole but suggestively similar to two other young collaborators, Auden and Isherwood. Auden's plays (three of them written in partnership with Isherwood) and the many poems that represent pastiches of ballads, cabaret songs or graffiti draw zestfully on popular sources in defiance of traditional hierarchies of the 'serious' and the 'light'. It comes as no surprise to learn that during the 1930s Auden not only edited the *Oxford Book of Light Verse* but co-edited (with John Garrett) a highly eclectic anthology of verse, *The Poet's Tongue*, in the introduction to which poetry is defined as 'memorable speech'. Weimar culture favoured the collaborative arts such as cinema and theatre, and it may be no coincidence that Isherwood's fiction was much influenced by the cinema or that Auden devoted much of his creative energy first to theatre and film and later to opera.

Like Weill, Brecht was not a Berliner by origin, having come to the city from Bavaria. Born in Augsburg in 1898, he had studied medicine in Munich, spent much time in Berlin from 1922, and settled there in 1924. *Die Dreigroschenoper* was his first major success, marking the transition from his early dramatic work to *Lehrstücke* or didactic plays, and since he left Germany in 1933 his Berlin heyday lasted barely five years. His biographer Klaus Völker has vividly described the chaotic and near-disastrous rehearsals for *Die Dreigroschenoper*. The première, however, was a huge success and the play ran for nearly a year in Berlin. The choice of Gay's *Beggar's Opera* as a starting-point was not as unikely as it sounds, since the English play had been very successfully revived at the Lyric Theatre in London earlier in the decade.

Brecht's attack on bourgeois ideology and morality has its visual counterpart in the work of Georg Grosz (1893–1959) and Otto

Dix (1891–1969). On a wall of Berlin's splendid Neue National-
galerie there hang today three paintings: two of Dix's portraits of
successful men, in a violent, almost brutal and Goya-like style,
and between them a satirical work by Grosz. The juxtaposition
shows very clearly the difference between Dix's harsh realism
and the more fantastic, even nightmarish vision of Grosz. The
cynicism and misanthropy of the latter, though sometimes recalling
Brecht in the exposure of the hollowness and sordidness of bourgeois civilisation, spring from more subjective and emotional
origins. Grosz's autobiography tells of a childhood experience
that reads like a grim parody of a Wordsworthian 'spot of time':
gratuitously pushed into the mud by an older boy, he was granted
a vision of 'ein tieferes Gesetz der Brutalität', a profound law of
brutality. He had discovered that hell lay about him in his infancy.
His depiction of drunkards, prostitutes and madmen owes its
force, as Martin Kane has pointed out, to a deeply and incurably
personal sense of human wickedness and degradation rather
than to any clearly formulated political philosophy. Although
he had joined the German Communist Party in December 1918,
Grosz was characteristically to speak, through his paintings and
drawings, from an individual sensibility rather than with a party
voice.

Born in Berlin, he had studied art and then served in the war,
suffering a nervous breakdown which led him to attack a hospital
orderly and to attempt to desert. He suffered the Dostoevskian
ordeal of being sentenced to death and then having the sentence
commuted, followed by a period in a mental institution. He had
never actually seen active service, hence his battlefield pictures are
based on imagination rather than experience. The drawings in the
series *Ecce Homo*, executed in 1920–2, evoke the 'brutal and
depraved eroticism' (Kane, p. 53) of the bourgeoisie in postwar
Germany and led to Grosz and his publisher being prosecuted for
obscenity, They were found guilty and fined, while the plates were
destroyed and unsold copies confiscated. In court Grosz declared
that 'It is clear that my whole view of the world is in complete
contrast to that of the State Prosecutor; it is radically more negative
and sceptical.... When I behold the greater part of mankind, I see
no beauties or delicate forms....' The Swiftian tone of his words is
unmistakable, and his work has as close an affinity to the fourth
book of *Gulliver's Travels* as *Die Dreigroschenoper* has to its eighteenth-century counterpart.

Grosz was in trouble again in 1928 for his collection of drawings *Hintergrund*, executed for Piscator's production of an adaptation of Hasek's novel *Der Gute Soldat Schweyk*. One of the drawings depicts a crucified Christ wearing army boots and a gas mask. After legal proceedings that dragged on for a couple of years, the charge of blasphemy was at last dropped, with costs being awarded to the defendants, and this outcome was hailed as a victory for the Left. By this date art had become inescapably political, and the trial was given wide publicity and regarded as a political rather than a moral or religious issue. Later Grosz, who fled Germany and reached New York a week before Hitler became Chancellor, found himself on the Nazi hit list. But the horror and revulsion so forcefully evident in his drawings remain very personal: like Swift, he is appalled not by systems but by humanity itself. He returned to Berlin from exile in 1959, just in time to drop dead in Savignyplatz.

What was true of artistic forms and conventions was also true of modes of thinking, feeling and behaving, and if Berlin was, in Robert McAlmon's phrase, 'a city of hyperbole', the life lived by some of its citizens and many of its visitors suggested at times a calculated effort to break with the past by casting off restraints – by going to extremes of personal conduct that matched both the extremes of creative innovation and the extremes of contemporary history.

As Von Eckardt and Gilman's survey of the period shows, the wild 'inflation' was not merely fiscal but extended to drink, dancing, drugs, sex and much else. Not everyone was willing or able to surrender themselves to a life of hedonism: there was large-scale poverty and misery, for this was a society that carried wretchedness as well as pleasure to extremes. As Klaus Mann puts it in his autobiography, for many people the years immediately following the defeat constituted a nightmare that caused violent shocks to their moral standards as well as their bank accounts – and Mann's grim zeugma seems the appropriate device to catch the spirit of the age.

Mann, who met Isherwood in 1931 and became a close friend (they later lived for a time in the same *pension* in Amsterdam), had arrived in Berlin in 1923, found it 'gorgeously corrupt', and 'had the time of my life'. Autobiographical hindsight, however, enabled him to do justice to the violent and absurd confusions of the postwar scene. Eating 'greasy borscht' in 'one of those Russian restaurants which then sprang up at every other corner', he reflects that the waitress could easily have been a Grand Duchess in exile, even 'a niece or cousin of the late Czarina', for Germany was not the only country to be living with the results of cataclysmic upheaval, Berlin was full of refugees, and in terms of the old social hierarchies chaos had come again. For Mann, Berlin was a place that absorbed and magnified whatever tendencies were scattered more thinly elsewhere, its hyperbolical wickedness a parodic equivalent to, and compensation for, Prussia's lost hyperbolical military might:

> Corruptible and always hankering for sensations, Berlin absorbed political and intellectual currents from everywhere. It was its function and force to organise whatever moods were floating throughout the land; to focus and dramatise the desires of a diffuse and inarticulate people. When the general vein was dashingly patriotic, the capital surpassed all other places in vociferous demonstrations. When the vogue was cynical-apocalyptic, Berlin did a great job in displaying misery and vices on a colossal scale.
>
> "Look at me!" blared the capital of the Reich. "I am Babel, the monster among cities! We had a formidable army: now we command the most riotously wicked night life. Don't miss our matchless show, ladies and gentlemen! It's Sodom and Gomorrah in a Prussian tempo. Don't miss the circus of perversities! Our department store of assorted vices! An all-out tale of brand new kinds of debauchery!"   (*The Turning-Point*, pp. 86–7)

For Mann, as for many others, economic disaster and moral collapse, inflation and debauchery, social confusion and sexual 'perversity', were all aspects of the same phenomenon.

One non-German in Berlin, Robert McAlmon, observed that the rate of exchange, so favourable to foreigners, attracted a horde of visitors and 'made for wildness':

> In spite of the poverty-stricken situation of the people there were several smart cafés and one futuristic dance place for tea dancing as well as for night encounters. Otherwise there were joints and dives of every order, and there was no telling whom one might encounter, anywhere. From Russia, Poland, the Balkan States, from Scandinavia, England, France, and South and North America, visitors flocked into Berlin, and even hardened

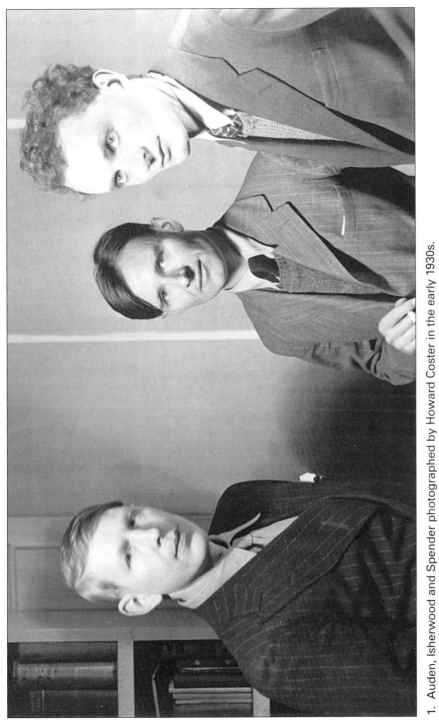

1. Auden, Isherwood and Spender photographed by Howard Coster in the early 1930s.

2. Auden and John Layard in Germany, 1929, probably at Rötehutte.

3. Auden, Spender and Isherwood on Rügen Island in 1931; a print
   given to Gabriel Carritt and signed by all three.

4. Isherwood and Otto on Rügen Island *c.* 1931.

5. The young Francis Turville-Petre with his sisters.

6. Tauentzienstrasse, Berlin, 1930.

7. Dr Magnus Hirschfeld at his desk in the Institute *c*. 1926.

8. Part of the interior of the Hirschfeld Institute, Berlin.

9. Wystan Hugh Auden, Cecil Day Lewis and Stephen Spender in Venice during the PEN Club

10. Marlene Dietrich in *The Blue Angel*.

11. Conrad Veidt in *The Student of Prague*.

Berlin night-lifers could not tell with certainty how the tone or quality of any night club might change from week to week. . . .

Dopes, mainly cocaine, were to be had in profusion at most night places. A deck of "snow", enough cocaine for quite too much excitement, cost the equivalent of ten cents. Poverty-stricken boys and girls of good German families sold it, and took it, as they congregated in the dreary night clubs for the warmth not available on the streets or in their homes, if they had homes. . . .

If this social and moral climate entailed much individual misery, it also nourished an intellectual and artistic culture that made Berlin, for many who came from abroad, the natural successor to Paris as the place where Pound's injunction to 'make it new' was being most strenuously implemented. Hence, for example, the Romanische Café, situated opposite the Kaiser Wilhelm Memorial Church and a ten-minute walk from Isherwood's Nollendorfplatz, was 'comparable to the Café de Dome in Paris and the Café Central in Vienna':

It was filled, almost around the clock, with painters and art dealers, writers and publishers, journalists and editors, radio entertainers and broadcasting officials, musicians and con-ductors, actors and producers, dancers and choreographers, psy-chiatrists and divorce lawyers, bohemians of all kinds, who seemed to be lost, girls of all ages who hoped to be found, and a lot of cigarette smoke and stale air.

This mingling of painters, radio personalities, actors and the rest illustrates the close contacts between the 'serious', popular and performing arts, the readiness to cross traditional boundaries of taste, so characteristic of Weimar Berlin. And if it also sounds like a natural setting for Mr Norris and Sally Bowles (herself a per-former), that may be a tribute to Isherwood's documentary skill.

Klaus Mann's first novel, *Der Fromme Tanz* (*The Pious Dance*, 1925), draws on his Berlin experiences at closer range than his autobiography. Its hero is a young artist, Andreas Magnus, who comes to the city from the provinces. He is both repelled and fascinated by the size and ugliness of the great capital, and des-cends into a grimy world of sordid lodgings as well as into the nightlife of cabarets and gay bars, hustlers and their well-dressed

clients, transvestites and cocaine addicts. The account of his nocturnal tour of such establishments with two companions has an
Orwell-like quality, if one can imagine Orwell having selected gay
bars instead of doss-houses for his sociological fieldwork:

> But how much bigger the city was by night, when it instantly
> enlarged into a gigantic blazing dream....
>   In the vicinity of the main streets, though at a decent remove,
> naturally, there was some of what they were seeking...: places
> where queerly heightened merriment prevailed and youths in
> alluring outfits tossed paper streamers into the air. With ladylike
> charm, the landlord, white, fat and heavily perfumed, would
> shout out a welcome to them. The young gentlemen would
> burst into shrill notes of rejoicing whenever such old acquaint-
> ances...dropped by the club: their hands made small darting
> movements as if they were tossing their dear guests flowers or
> little balls of silk; they would call 'Hello, sunshine! Just look, the
> three Graces!' – and shake like dancers on the high, uncomfor-
> table barstools they used as perches. But soon they would come
> over to the threesome's table, for they knew them to be well-
> disposed, first to joke a little, to make a great fuss over a silk train
> which, as the great ladies they were now, they pretended to
> wear, to get tipsy on the wine they were treated to. Then their
> eyes would suddenly grow earnest, their carefully painted faces
> would collapse beneath the layer of cosmetics, they would sit
> down, this time with very unaffected movements, and begin to
> talk about money.   (Part II, ch.5)

Subsequently the party, continuing its tour, visits a club, the 'Para-
diesgärtlein' (Little Garden of Eden), 'on the first floor of an elegant
house', then, after two or three in the morning, a considerably less
smart establishment, the 'Sankt-Margaretenkeller' (St Margaret's
Cellar), some distance from the city centre and much frequented
by *Transvestiten*.

  Not all the customers at the Romanische Café or establishments
like those described in Mann's novel were residents of the city.
Some who came to Berlin from other parts of Germany or from
other countries passed through quite briefly, and in the group
of writers with whom this book is concerned Spender, Lehmann
and Upward belong to this class. Others, Auden and Isherwood
among them, stayed longer – indeed, as long as they could.

Robert McAlmon, an incurable wanderer, paid several visits to Berlin in the early 1920s, quitting the city eventually because 'the innumerable beggars, paralytics, shell-shocked soldiers, and starving people of good family' depressed him. His 1925 volume *Distinguished Airs* contains three stories described as 'grim fairy tales' which take as their subject Berlin's celebrated nightlife. One of them, 'Miss Knight', was admired by James Joyce and Ezra Pound. In the title story the narrator is an American who takes a friend on a tour of the night spots, including a 'queer café'.

Much later, in his autobiographical *Being Geniuses Together 1920–1930*, McAlmon observes (with perhaps some of the facile hyperbole that belongs to an oft-told tale) that 'At nights along the Unter den Linden it was never possible to know whether it was a woman or a man in woman's clothes who accosted one'. (*Never*?) As in an earlier passage quoted, he mentions that cocaine and other drugs were widely available, and the picture of a flourishing drug culture is confirmed by other sources.

A more jaundiced, not to say apoplectic, foreign observer was Wyndham Lewis, whose *Hitler* (1931) goes in for Carlylean fulminations: 'No city,' he writes at the top of his voice, 'has anything on it as regards the stark suggestions of being the Hauptstadt [capital] of Vice, the Excelsior Eldorado of a bottom-wagging most arch Old Nick sunk in a succulent and costly rut.... ' That 'Eldorado', as Lewis must have known but many of his readers surely did not, was no metaphor but a real and notorious place. Interestingly, in locating the nightlife that has 'established itself overnight', Lewis specifies the neighbourhoods in which Isherwood and Spender had made their homes at this time: 'the Kurfürstendamm, Nollendorf Platz, Wittenberg Platz, Motzstrasse, Tauenzienstrasse'.

For Stefan Zweig, Berlin's cosmopolitanism made it 'das Babel der Welt', the Babel of the World, and a city in which

> all values were changed ... Bars, amusement parks, honky-tonks sprang up like mushrooms. ... Along the entire Kurfürstendamm powdered and rouged young men sauntered, and they were not all professionals; every high school boy wanted to earn some money and in the dimly-lit bars one might see government officials and men of the world of finance tenderly courting drunken sailors without any shame. Even the Rome of Suetonius had never known such orgies as the transvestite balls of Berlin, where hundreds of men costumed as women and hundreds of

women as men danced under the benevolent eyes of the police. In the collapse of all values a kind of madness gained hold, particularly in the bourgeois circles which until then had been unshakeable in their probity. But the most revolting thing about this pathetic eroticism was its spuriousness. At bottom the orgiastic period which broke out simultaneously in Germany with the inflation was nothing more than a feverish imitation.... Everywhere you looked it was plain that the whole nation, tired of war, actually longed only for calm and order.

There is (once again) surely some exaggeration here (*every* high school boy?), and conceivably less than justice is done to Tiberius and Caligula, but the portrayal of 'the collapse of all values' carries conviction. Many of Zweig's details, including the male prostitutes and the transvestite balls, are paralleled elsewhere as well as serving as glosses to the experiences of Auden and Isherwood. For while his comments refer to the early 1920s, it is clear that much of the ethos he evokes still persisted at the end of the decade. In the period of gross inflation some of those high school boys may have been driven onto the streets by hunger rather than greed – a point that does not seem to occur to Zweig – but even six or seven years later mass unemployment was still causing hardship and desperation that took many into establishments like Auden's Cosy Corner and its many competitors in different parts of Berlin, some of them referred to in his journal.

The emphasis in these passages on cross-dressing is striking, and reminds us that it was an acquaintance of Auden and Isherwood, Dr Magnus Hirschfeld, who gave the world the term 'transvestism'. A later chapter will have something to say on the prominence of this phenomenon in the cinema of the period, but manifestations of sexual ambiguity of differing kinds make an appearance in a great variety of contexts. For the moment, two tiny examples. Germany's most popular vocal group at this time was the Comedian Harmonists, a close-harmony group some of whose members sang in a tenor so light and so high in the register as almost to be a falsetto. Like listening to a counter-tenor (or, presumably, a castrato), the result, though charming, is slightly unsettling, seeming as it does to call into question ingrained expectations and assumptions about male singers. For an even more disconcerting opposite, we can turn to Weill's *Die Sieben Todsünden*, where the role of the mother is performed by a basso profundo whose vocal powers are given full scope by Weill's score.

A more sustained and sympathetic, and probably also a more realistic, account of the boys who took to or were driven to prostitution is given in the 1926 novel *Der Puppenjunge* (translated as *The Hustler*), by John Henry Mackay (1864–1933). Mackay's Scots father died when he was a baby and he was taken by his German mother back to Germany, eventually settling in Berlin and taking out German citizenship. After his mother's death in 1902 he threw himself into campaigning for 'boy love' under the curious pseudonym of 'Sagitta', his identity not being revealed until after his death (possibly by suicide) six days after the Nazis' 'burning of the books' on 10 May 1933. Mackay was a poet of sorts, one of whose effusions is well-known to many who have probably never heard his name, for Richard Strauss set it in his well-known song 'Morgen'. In its small way, 'Morgen' is thus, like Michelangelo's David in its greater, a widely unacknowledged example of homosexual art: just as that well-developed shepherd boy is, for most visitors to Florence, no more of a sexual object than the Ponte Vecchio, Strauss's song must have been sung and enjoyed by multitudes innocent of its disconcerting message. Like many covert homosexual texts, including some of Auden's own poems, the poem is couched in sufficiently vague terms to make it eligible for ready appropriation as an inoffensively 'ordinary' love song:

> ...stumm werden wir uns in die Augen schauen,
> und auf uns sinkt des Glückes stummes Schweigen....
> (silently we shall look into each other's eyes, and upon us
> falls the peace of quiet joy)

Not many of those who have sung or enjoyed Strauss's fine song will have identified it as a hymn, presumably unconscious on the composer's part, to boy-love. In its linking of pederastic sentimentality with a Romantic view of nature – sunshine, lakeside, woodland walks are all there in its eight lines – it is thoroughly characteristic not only of the *Naktkultur* (roughly, 'cult of nudity') of its period but of a persistent vein of pederastic art, widespread (as Brian Reade's *Sexual Heretics*, 1970, abundantly demonstrates) in Victorian England and far from unknown today.

Mackay also wrote novels, of which the first, *Der Schwimmer* (*The Swimmer*, 1901), is a very early example of the 'sports novel'

subgenre, glorifying physical activity. In recent years he seems to
have become something of a cult figure in specialised circles: a
biography of him by Thomas A. Riley was published in New York
in 1972, and a Mackay-Gesellschaft (Mackay Society) founded in
Germany in 1974, while some of his writings have been reissued.

Der Puppenjunge is really two stories in one, depicting male prostitution from different points of view, and in literary terms one of
them is greatly inferior to the other. About half of the book tells of a
young man's infatuation with a boy he meets in the street, and is
almost intolerably sentimental. The other half, depicting the boy's
experiences after he runs away from home and comes to Berlin, has
considerable dramatic power and documentary interest. It is, moreover, set in an urban jungle as precisely delineated as Defoe's or
Dickens's London: in its picture of 'the Passage', which by this time
needs no introduction to readers of the present book, Mackay's
novel recalls the 'street' films of the same period that rooted the
lives of their characters in a specific sordid neighbourhood.

As the boy reflects at one point, 'Everyone comes to Berlin some-
time', and his adventures blend the picaresque tradition with the
study of his corruption and degeneration. Unable to find employment, he is by slow degrees initiated into the precarious career of
hustler, is exploited by clients, fellow hustlers and landlords, and
in time learns to exploit others as the price of survival. He fre-
quents the Adonis Lounge, which serves as a kind of club enabling
the boys to meet each other as well as customers:

> He opened the door, threw back a curtain, and was in a small
> front room, bordered on the right by a large bar. In a corner,
> opposite the entrance, stood a tall stove. At several small tables
> were seated figures, hard to recognise in the dim light of the
> room, but apparently juveniles.... They were without exception
> young lads from sixteen to perhaps nineteen years old....

As the novel's translator, Hubert Kennedy, points out, there are
signs that the Adonis Lounge, like much else, is based on an actual
establishment. Elsewhere in the novel Mackay gives an address for
it, Novalisstrasse 20, which places it at the north end of Friedrichstrasse, beyond the railway station. Either it subsequently moved
or (perhaps more probably) Mackay was thinly disguising the real
location, for a 1930 guide refers to a spot of the same name but
places it at the other end of Friedrichstrasse:

Very promising is the name of a club in Alexandrinen Street near the Halle Gate. Here, where not only the more shady, but also the more disreputable element of Friedrich Street pours out, the evil alliances are more numerous than the good ones. From the white poison (cocaine) to love of all kinds, everything is traded here that can be exchanged for money. Adonis Lounge is the name of the place, in which nothing reminds one of the beautiful legendary figure.

Auden's Cosy Corner – to which, throwing back the curtain just like the boy entering the Adonis Lounge, he introduced Isherwood – may be supposed to have been similar in its set-up and its atmosphere, though located in another area of the city. Auden's journal indicates, however, that he also knew and visited an establishment referred to as the 'Adonis Diele' (Adonis Hall) – as already noted, it was there that he picked up Herbert, one of his boyfriends – and this may be assumed to be identical with the one described in the guidebook, and probably also with the one Mackay refers to.

Near the end of *Die Puppenjunge* Mackay puts into the mouth of his tedious and ineffectual hero an attack on Paragraph 175 of the existing legal code, which criminalised homosexual behaviour: ' "There are few human beings who have not become criminals against their fellow humans – not directly, but rather indirectly, in that they tolerate and advocate laws such as this one for example...".' Within a line or two this role-reversal – the real offenders are the persecutors and those who tacitly or otherwise tolerate persecution – turns into an indictment of all authority: '...what are all the crimes in the world compared with the ones carried out by those in gowns and vestments, robes and uniforms'.

In the section of *Goodbye to Berlin* titled 'The Nowaks', Isherwood introduces a boy named Pieps who, like Mackay's character, has run away from his home in the provinces to seek his fortune in Berlin. (Whether this character owes anything other than his name to Auden's first Berlin boyfriend, whom Isherwood would almost certainly have met in the spring of 1929, it is impossible to say.) There he lives by his wits and from hand to mouth, picking pockets 'in an amusement-hall in the Friedrichstrasse, not far from the Passage, which was full of detectives and getting too dangerous nowadays'. It is characteristic of Isherwood's caginess and willingness to make compromises with the known and observed reality that the boy should be depicted as a pickpocket rather than a prostitute and that the nature of the Passage's reputation should not be specified. The paragraph ends with a reference to the female prostitutes who plied their trade in the neighbourhood.

A similar protest becomes the central theme of another gay novel of the decade, Bruno Vogel's *Alf* (1929). As Michael Gilbert has said in his introduction to the recent translation, this short novel 'links the repression of gay sexuality to an entire network of oppression extending from the family, school and church (including religious instruction in the Gymnasium), to the judicial, political and military institutions of German society'. This is effected by tracing the hero's progress from home to school, where he falls in love with Felix, a fellow student, and eventually into the army. The second half of the book seems to represent a thematic shift from an attack on sexual intolerance to an exposure of the futility of war; what connects the two is the conviction that both proceed from an older generation of teachers and preachers who have betrayed the youth whose upbringing has been in their hands.

Vogel was born in 1898, the same year as his character Felix, and, like his other main character Alf, served in the war. Returning to Leipzig, he became a journalist and founder of a gay rights group, and in 1925 published a pacifist novel, *Es lebe der Krieg! Ein Brief* (*Long Live the War! A Letter*) which attracted considerable attention and led to his and his publisher's prosecution on charges of obscenity and blasphemy. Among those who successfully came to his defence were Thomas Mann and Magnus Hirschfeld, but when the book was reissued in 1926 and 1928 it was in bowdlerised form, the complete text not appearing again until 1978. Vogel left Germany before Hitler came to power and lived successively in Austria, Switzerland, Norway and South Africa, eventually settling in London where he died in 1983.

Vogel was clearly influenced by the teachings of Magnus Hirschfeld, who is mentioned in one of the letters written from the front by Alf to Felix. Like Hirschfeld, he wrote and worked towards the decriminalisation of homosexual behaviour, and a turning-point in his young hero's experience is the chance discovery, through a pamphlet he stumbles upon in a second-hand bookshop, that 'Paragraph 175 of the National Criminal Code would impose on their love for each other a prison term of up to five years'. As with Mackay, Vogel's disillusion with law and traditional morality, both of which call upon him to disavow his own nature, is extended to a comprehensive disillusion with authority:

They were all just beautiful, grand, empty words: the Law; the Fatherland; Christian culture: the sweet and honourable Death on the Field of Glory; the Best, which is what one's educators want for one, Chastity – oh, one could go on for pages listing such ideals! And how we all fell for the whole swindle – these pedagogical con artists understood perfectly how to dress these words so skilfully with a halo of sanctity so that nobody dared even to stop and think what all the speeches really might mean.

Parents, teachers, lawmakers are all in a conspiracy to entrap the young, and have woven 'the net which we got caught in'. The metaphor is that used by Joyce's Stephen Dedalus, and some of the sentiments are similar, though the ending of Vogel's *Bildungsroman* is bleaker – and his literary art, it hardly needs adding, incomparably cruder.

Outside the smoke-filled cafés, bars and nightclubs, and at a distance from the busy Berlin streets, the young found other ways of developing an alternative culture to that of an older generation tainted by apparent complicity in the war. That the photographs of Auden, Isherwood and Spender taken on Rügen Island and referred to a little earlier should commemorate semi-nudity and beach culture is not surprising, for this was the age of *Naktkultur*, another cultural manifestation in which Germany set the fashion. Valentine Cunningham has reminded us that 'The English varieties of nudism were consciously Germanic imports.... One of Britain's pioneer nudist colonies was actually called *Spielplatz*' (*British Writers of the Thirties*, p. 184). One of the lesser-known events in Anglo-German relations occurred in 1936, when the British government sent a team of observers to Germany to study and report on the Strength through Joy movement. As Auden and his friends must have very well known, *Naktkultur* was also a contemporary fashion with which Rügen seems to have been popularly associated.

Though its origins lay in Romantic nature-worship combined with modern scientific notions of bodily health, it was also a manifestation of the sexual revolution and of rejection of the values of urban and industrial society and the enclosed spaces of home and school. Perhaps it was this subversive, anti-authoritarian quality and its association with romantic individualism as much as its tendency to darken the ideally white northern skin that soon led it to incur the official disapproval of the Nazis. A passage in Spender's *World Within World* offers some suggestive juxtapositions in

the course of a discussion of the multifarious cultural manifestations of Weimar modernism. Remarking that

> Everything was 'new', deceptively so. There were buildings,
> with broad clean vertical lines crossed by strong horizontals,
> which drove into the sky like railroads. There were experiments
> in the theatre and opera, all in a style which expressed with
> facility the fusion of naked liberation with a kind of bitter pathos,
> which was characteristic of this Germany...

Spender proceeds to actualise the metaphor of 'naked liberation':

> Modernism in this Germany was (within certain limits of which I
> was not then aware) a popular mass-movement. Roofless houses,
> expressionist painting, atonal music, bars for homosexuals, nud-
> ism, sunbathing, camping, all were accepted.... (p. 108)

An early Spender poem, the Whitmanesque 'oh young men oh
young comrades', celebrates 'those fabulous possessions / which
begin with your body and your fiery soul', then proceeds to urge
the unconverted to uncover:

> Count your eyes as jewels and your valued sex
> then count the sun and the innumerable coined light
> sparkling on waves and spangled under trees....

Spender's *Journals*, published 34 years later than his autobiography,
make more explicit links between homosexuality and the cult of the
outdoors (the following passage is from a retrospective account
written in September 1939):

> I was 20 in those days, and I was caught up mostly with the idea
> of Friendship – *Freundschaft* – which was a very important part of
> the life of the Weimar Republic. This, if it was frank, was also
> very idealistic. It was not cynical, shamefaced, smart, snobbish,
> or stodgy, as so often in England. It was more like Walt
> Whitman's idea of camaraderie. I admit that I do not feel at
> all easy about this now, but I set it down for what it was.
> Two friends, young men, faced the world together: they
> camped, they travelled, they were happy in each other's
> company.... (p. 26)

The world of Forster's *Maurice* is not far away, with the English greenwood exchanged for a Baltic sand dune or a glade in the Black Forest: Edward Carpenter, 'the English Whitman', had been a significant influence on Forster, and very Forsterian too is the appropriation of an ordinary word, 'friendship', for a specialised and semi-private purpose (Spender must have known that *Freundschaft* was also the title of a leading Berlin gay newspaper).

In Spender's *The Temple*, Paul reflects that 'Nakedness...is the democracy of the new Germany, the Weimar Republic' (pp. 36–7). Later, he finds himself 'beginning to tire of the self-conscious insistence of the Germans on their bodies. They worshipped the body, as though it were a temple' (p. 113). In the meantime, Paul has been reading Lawrence's *Fantasia of the Unconscious*, a book that was as important to Layard and Auden as Forster's work was to Isherwood. (Lawrence, of course, had known both Forster and Carpenter, and had written on Whitman.) An entry that Paul makes in his notebook constitutes Spender's fullest endorsement of Weimar *Naktkultur*: '...I confess that till now, whatever I may have pretended to myself, I have always regarded my body as sinful, and my own physical being as something to be ashamed of and to be overcome by compensating and atoning spiritual qualities. Now I am beginning to feel that I may soon come to regard my body as a source of joy....' (p. 54).

Although English writers such as Forster and Lawrence might authenticate such impulses, it was clearly necessary to leave England (as Forster and Lawrence themselves had in different ways done) in order to undergo this conversion. In *World Within World* Spender acknowledges that on arriving in Hamburg he experienced 'a tremendous sense of release, of having got away from Oxford and home' (p. 109). What had been left behind was not only parents and tutors but post-Victorian morality and the prohibitions of English legal and social intolerance. As in Forster's fiction, this transition or release is expressed through contrasting metaphors of enclosed and open spaces, and to the young Spender it seemed that the 'life of the senses' lived by young Germans was 'a sunlit garden from which sin was excluded' (*World Within World*, p. 107). Auden might have claimed to have found his own sunlit and sin-free garden in the rent-bars and cruising grounds of Berlin, but Spender's role is that of an apologist for the outdoor life – a camp culture with a difference – and *The Temple* (a novel of remarkable badness but at the same time a document of considerable interest) is full of images of beaches and pine woods, haunted by bronzed bodies as eternally young and vigorous as the figures on Keats's Grecian urn.

DEATH OF A DAYDREAM

For all their aesthetic shortcomings, novels like *The Hustler* and *Alf* likewise have a documentary force, even at moments a tragic eloquence, that sheds a severe ironic light on the naive lusts of the young Auden and Isherwood. Isherwood had been excited rather than deterred by the warning that Berlin was 'the vilest place since Sodom', and Auden had eagerly inquired, on the eve of his departure, whether the city was 'very wicked'. Auden's boastful early description of it as a 'buggers daydream', like Isherwood's later claim that for him 'Berlin meant Boys', depict the city as a kind of northern equivalent of the Capri of Norman Douglas or the Taormina of Baron von Gloeden. The reality – as Mackay's account of prostitution as a desperate means of survival and Vogel's indictment of intolerance in their different ways make clear – was much grimmer. Or, more accurately, the grim reality lay just beneath the hedonistic surface. Moreover, during the Auden/Isherwood period, public persecution was on the increase, and any guileless joy at the outset at exchanging the prohibitions of England for the freedom of Berlin must have received some hard knocks from subsequent experience. As the American historian Richard Plant has shown in his graphic account of Nazi persecution of homosexuals, *The Pink Triangle*, their elimination was from an early date 'an important aspect of Nazi ideology and action'.

Prussia had a long tradition as the most homophobic of the German states, and various establishment-rocking scandals and sensational court cases did nothing to promote tolerance. But intolerance soon became organised, systematic and official, and Plant has shown that 'the sexual tolerance so often associated with the Weimar Republic began to disappear as rapidly as Germany's economy began to crumble.... The years from 1929 to the end of the Weimar Republic were years of mounting tension' (p. 27). Those are, of course, precisely the years with which the present study is concerned. It was during this period, too, that the Brown Shirts, under the command (by an extraordinary irony) of Ernst

Roehm, a known homosexual later murdered by Hitler, became 'even more brutal and more repressively efficient'.

Even before Auden's arrival a warning signal had been made, on 14 May 1928, in the shape of a Nazi response to a question about its attitude towards Paragraph 175:

> It is not necessary that you and I live, but it is necessary that the German people live. And it can only live if it can fight, for life means fighting. And it can only fight if it maintains its masculinity. It can only maintain its masculinity if it exercises discipline, especially in matters of love. Free love and deviance are undisciplined. Therefore, we reject you, as we reject anything that hurts our nation.

This inflexible reasoning led straight to the day less than five years later, and while Isherwoood was still in Berlin, when Hitler, only three weeks in office as Chancellor, banned gay rights organisations; it also led, not long afterwards, to the prison camps and the gas chambers. And it was as early as 1929, the year of Isherwood's arrival, that the official Nazi newspaper launched an attack on Hirschfeld, whose campaign against Paragraph 175 (described in the next chapter) appeared to be having some success:

> We congratulate you, Mr Hirschfeld, on the victory in committee. But don't think that we Germans will allow these laws to stand for a single day after we have come to power.... Among the many evil instincts that characterise the Jewish race, one that is especially pernicious has to do with sexual relationships. The Jews are forever trying to propagandise sexual relations between siblings, men and animals, and men and men. We National Socialists will soon unmask and condemn them by law....

Such threats were interpreted in some quarters as being directed exclusively at Jewish homosexuals – an optimism that subsequent events did not justify. Almost before Auden and Isherwood arrived in the city, the paradise – if it had ever been that – was beginning to go out of business, the daydream to turn sour, for anyone who cared to read the signs of the times.

3

Berlin: Faces

ANNA MUTHESIUS

As we have seen, Auden's first home in Berlin was with a family living at Potsdamer Chaussee 49, in the southwestern part of the city. How he was put in touch with them is not clear, but since he seems to have gone straight there after arriving in Berlin, and since they were hardly the sort of people to advertise for a lodger, some personal introduction must have been involved. Auden's biographers pass lightly over the Muthesius family (by one, indeed, they are not even named), merely characterising them as 'bourgeois'. They were in fact unusually interesting people, standing high in the social hierarchy of the capital, having among their friends some of the leaders of artistic and intellectual life, and owning one of the finest and most attractive private homes in the city.

When Auden arrived he found it presided over, in formidable style, by Anna Muthesius, who had been widowed in the previous year. Her husband, Hermann Muthesius (1861–1927), had been a distinguished architect who earned a place in the standard works of reference. He was keenly Anglophile: he had spent several years (1896–1903) in London as an attaché at the German Embassy, and he and his family paid frequent visits to England thereafter. Possibly on one of these visits they had met the Auden family or some of their friends.

Hermann's knowledge of English art and industry had led him, in the early years of the century, to play a leading role in establishing the Deutsche Werkbund, an association of artists, craftsmen and industrialists, with the aim of creating in Germany something analogous to the English arts and crafts movement inspired by Morris and Ruskin. The Werkbund subsequently proved influential in areas ranging from industrial design to architecture. Hermann's particular professional interest was in the English country house, and his book *Das moderne Landhaus* (1905) describes over three hundred examples of country house architecture drawn from England, Germany, Austria and Finland. In Germany, as well as designing estates of model homes for workers, he had built houses for the rich based on a modification of English country house styles. His own home, where Auden lived briefly, still stands and is very much in this style: spacious and imposing, it is set in a large garden with a deer meadow behind. Nearly seventy years after Auden's sojourn there, it remains remarkably dignified and tranquil, though no longer occupied by a single family.

Hermann had been killed in a street accident while inspecting progress on his latest commission: stepping out of a car driven by his son, he had been knocked down by a tram. (The street where it happened now bears his name.) It was thus his widow who became Auden's landlady, though the latter term seems wildly inappropriate for a figure as gifted and dynamic as Anna Muthesius. Born in 1870, she had married Hermann in 1897 and had had five children, of whom one had died in infancy. The remaining three boys and a girl were all living at home when Auden moved in; the youngest of the boys was 24, while Renate, the baby of the family, was 14. The only survivor, she now lives in Munich.

Before her marriage Anna had been a professional soprano, and although she seems to have given up her career she retained her musical interests as well as involving herself in a wide range of social and artistic activities. At the age of 90 (she lived until 1961) she was, according to a newspaper article published to commemorate her birthday, still entertaining her guests by singing to her own piano accompaniment. Accounts of Anna suggest a very energetic individual, perhaps even a little overbearing, with something of the Ibsenite heroine and the 1890s 'new woman' about her. She designed her own clothes as well as window-displays for Berlin department stores. Her feminist convictions led her to write articles attacking the *Fischbeinecorsette*, the whalebone corset that imprisoned the female figure, and she seems to have helped to bring about its demise. Her wide circle of friends included Max Reinhardt, who produced scenes from *A Midsummer Night's Dream* in the deer meadow behind the house, and Albert Einstein, who would pay visits to the Muthesius family from his home in nearby Potsdam.

It was, then, not just any dull bourgeois family but a lively, gifted, artistic and creative household that Auden entered in October 1928. For his part the young Englishman made a strong impression, not uniformly favourable. The youngest son, Ekhart (1904–89), who was only a couple of years older than Auden, often talked about him in his later years. Ekhart's first wife, Miette (born in 1899 and now living in England), can still recall going to dinner at the Muthesius home, meeting Auden, and finding him 'excessively dirty' and 'utterly revolting'. She remembers, too, that the family knew about his sexual preferences and were tolerant of them.

Auden lived there for no more than a couple of months. That the family, as he claimed, insisted on speaking English to him is perfectly consistent with their known Anglophilia, but it has the flavour of an official justification intended for public consumption and was surely not the whole truth. Their splendid house is in one of the most attractive parts of the city, but far from convenient for anyone wishing to savour the pleasures, and especially the night-time pleasures, of downtown Berlin. To reach the Muthesius home involved a longish ride on the S-Bahn, whose timetable would have put an unwelcome limitation on nocturnal adventures. Anna Muthesius's broadmindedness, moreover, might have stopped short at welcoming into her beautiful home her young guest's gleanings from the scruffier boy-bars. Hence the move to Furbringerstrasse, much nearer the heart of the city, where the distance from number 8, the house in which Auden took a room, to the Cosy Corner bar in Zollenstrasse was just seventy paces.

MAGNUS HIRSCHFELD

Chapter 1 has described how, in November 1929, Isherwood travelled to Berlin to begin a period of residence that would last for more than three years and would be brought to an end only by the irresistible pressures of public events. On his first morning in Berlin he knocked on the door of an apartment in one of the tall dignified houses in In den Zelten, in order to enlist the help of his only English-speaking contact. A room was found for him, the establishment being under the care of a sister of Dr Magnus Hirschfeld, whose Institute for Sexology (Institut für Sexual-Wissenschaft) was next door. The Institute was a remarkable place, but not as remarkable as its founder and director, to whom Isherwood devotes several pages in *Christopher and his Kind* and who has come to be regarded, with good reason, as the founding father, saint and martyr of the gay rights movement in Germany, if not worldwide.

Born in Kolberg on the Baltic in 1868, Hirschfeld was one of eight children of a German-Jewish physician who contributed articles on political and social issues to local newspapers. Beginning as a student of literature and philology in Breslau, the young Magnus soon turned to medicine – without, however, completely forsaking his literary interests – and pursued his studies in Strasbourg, Berlin and Munich. After graduating he moved to Paris, met Max Nordau and became deeply interested in Zionism. At this period, during which he worked as a journalist, he seems still to have been wavering between medicine and literature as a career. His subsequent life as doctor, scientific researcher, author and activist was to integrate the two fields with considerable thoroughness and success.

After a couple of years of general practice in Magdeburg, Hirschfeld went to Berlin and became for a time a specialist in nature-cure methods. But his interest in problems of sexuality, and his eagerness to engage in polemic, manifested themselves as early as 1896 with the publication, prudently pseudonymous, of a pamphlet titled 'Sappho und Socrates' and subtitled, with a challenging refusal to prevaricate, 'Wie erklärt sich die Liebe der Männer und Frauen zu Personen des eigenen Geschlechts?' ('How can the love of men and women for those of their own sex be explained?'). As one of his biographers, Charlotte Wolff, has made clear, the pamphlet's origins were dramatically circumstantial and its publication was decisive in determining the future direction of Hirschfeld's considerable energies:

> An officer had shot himself through the head on the eve of his marriage. He had been Hirschfeld's patient for some time before his death, and the day after he died Hirschfeld received a letter from him telling him the whole tragic story which led to his suicide. He called his homosexuality a 'curse' against human nature and the law. He felt unable to marry because of his 'abnormal' desires. He asked Hirschfeld to publish his story as it might help the German people to get a clearer idea about homosexuality.... (p. 33)

One is reminded of the Woolwich cadet whose suicide was one of the precipitating causes of A. E. Housman's poetry, and, as with Housman, Hirschfeld's awareness of his own sexual nature, and perhaps even a sense of how easily he might have shared the dead man's fate lent extra strength to his pity and indignation.

Characteristically, these emotions produced practical results, for Hirschfeld was a tireless activist as well as a vigorous polemicist. In

the following year, with two friends, he set up the Wissenschaf-
tlich-humanitäre Komitee (Scientific-humanitarian Committee) to
work for reform of the laws relating to homosexual behaviour,
and in particular the notorious Paragraph 175 of the penal code
which made homosexual acts punishable with a prison sentence.
Although social life in the capital was reasonably tolerant of homosexuals, Prussia as a whole had a long tradition of homophobia:
until 1794 the law provided for the burning at the stake of con-
victed offenders, and sentences of imprisonment followed by ban-
ishment for life were possible until 1837. In nineteenth-century
Germany, the liberalism of Bavaria was the exception rather than
the rule, and in Prussia Paragraph 143 (the basis, 20 years later, for
Paragraph 175) came into force in 1851, providing for a sentence of
imprisonment for homosexuality and bestiality alike.

From this time on, Hirschfeld's efforts to promote understanding
and tolerance of homosexuals, and to change laws and practices
that discriminated against them, were unremitting, indeed lifelong,
and were conducted on many fronts. While continuing to practise
as a physician he was also a medical and anthropological
researcher, a prolific writer of books and pamphlets, the organiser
of institutes, committees and congresses, and a lecturer throughout
Germany and abroad.

In a society in which homophobia was still widespread, he displayed an impressive courage as well as extraordinary energy.
Unsurprisingly, controversy, opposition and eventual persecution
followed. In December 1903, in a pre-Kinsey attempt to chart and
quantify the sexual orientation of sections of the male population,
he circulated a questionnaire to 3,000 students in a Berlin technical
college and to 5,000 metalworkers whom he had recently
addressed on the subject of homosexuality. The results were perhaps not entirely predictable. The metalworkers took it in good
part and responded willingly, but some of the students took
offence and complained; prosecution followed, and Hirschfeld
had to pay a fine and costs. It was the beginning of a thirty-years'
war between the sexologist and the forces of reaction – what E. M.
Forster calls 'the armies of the benighted' – that would end in
violence, bloodshed and exile.

Meanwhile, Hirschfeld was earning a considerable reputation
throughout Germany and internationally as an expert on sexuality,
especially homosexuality, and found himself making happier
courtroom appearances as an expert witness. Perhaps the most

remarkable of these occasions was his testifying in 1907 on behalf of Maximilian Harden, a German-Jewish journalist who was the defendant in a libel action brought by General von Moltke, the military commandant of Berlin. Harden had published in the previous year a satirical article exposing the homosexual relationship of Moltke (known to his friends as Tütü) and Philipp Eulenberg, a prominent diplomat who was rumoured to be simultaneously conducting an affair with the Kaiser himself. In Harden's article, Eulenberg is referred to as 'Sweetie' (he was known to have a passion for chocolates, and 'sweet' was also a slang term for a homosexual) and the Kaiser as 'Darling'.

In a fascinating essay James D. Steakley has shown that this trial was one of a series of five that, together with a number of courts martial, 'rocked' Imperial Germany between 1907 and 1909. Steakley suggests that what became known as the Eulenberg trials performed a comparable function in Germany to that performed in England by the Wilde trials of 1895, for both events 'dramatically accelerated the emergence of the modern homosexual identity by stimulating and structuring public perceptions of sexual normalcy and abnormalcy'. The social shockwaves of the Eulenberg affair were, however, much more extensive, involving as it did a large number of highly placed figures in military and civilian life and even adding fuel to rumours about the Kaiser's sexual proclivities. (He was known, for instance, to be addicted to leisurely cruises in all-male company.) In a much wider context, it has also been argued that reactions to these scandals led to a shift in German policy that generated increasingly militaristic attitudes and eventually contributed to the outbreak of the Great War.

In the Moltke *v.* Harden hearings in October 1907, Hirschfeld was the last witness to be called, and his expert opinion that, whatever his conduct may have been, Moltke displayed signs of a feminine nature (for example, in his sensitivity to the arts) no doubt contributed to Harden's acquittal. Hirschfeld himself was depicted in numerous cartoons of the period and, as Steakley observes, is shown there as 'a Jewish stereotype'. Contemporary cartoons, incidentally, were often capable of startling frankness in their satirical commentary on public personalities: in November 1907, for example, a Stuttgart paper published, under the title 'Military Innovations', one that was accompanied by the following dialogue: 'Since when is an about-face order given for inspection?' 'At your service, captain – reporting that the division is being inspected by

Count Hohenau today'. Hohenau, commander of the Garde du Corps, was related to the Kaiser, and the cartoon shows a line of young soldiers, their trousers stretched tight over chubby buttocks, awaiting their commanding officer's close and critical scrutiny.

Much later, Hirschfeld appeared for the defence in the less celebrated but still widely publicised trial of Adolf Koch, one of the apostles of the *Freikörperkultur* or nudist movement in the 1920s. Koch, a gymnastics instructor in a working-class area of Berlin, had been in the habit of instructing his pupils to take their classes in the nude with the worthy motive of encouraging better posture and cleanliness, and was soon charged with the corruption of minors.

In 1905 Hirschfeld addressed a Berlin audience one thousand strong on Paragraph 175 – one of numerous lectures and public meetings that over the years took him to many parts of Germany and to Britain, America, Japan and elsewhere. In August 1913 he was in London for a meeting of the International Congress of Physicians organised by the British Medical Association, and lectured (with the aid of slides from his research collection) on homosexuality, androgyny, hermaphroditism and transvestism, his message being the infinite variety of sexual instincts and behaviour, different forms of sexuality shading into one another rather than representing polarities or sharply defined categories.

The stream of books and other writings continued, the list of his publications including, among much else, *Berlin's Drittes Geschlecht* (*Berlin's Third Sex*, 1904), an account of homosexual life in the city at all social levels; *Die Transvestiten* (1910); and *Die Homosexualität des Mannes und des Weibes* (*Homosexuality in Men and Women*, 1914), this last running to over a thousand pages and being based on 10,000 case histories drawn from many countries. He also founded in 1907 the *Zeitschrift für Sexualwissenschaft*, the first journal to be devoted to the scientific study of sex.

As a compiler and classifier of data relating to subjects that had hardly received any serious scientific attention previously, Hirschfeld was the Darwin of sexology. He also engaged in laboratory work, investigating the vexed question of the physical basis of homosexuality, for instance, through the study of cells from the testes of homosexuals and heterosexuals. Other colleagues pursued their investigations in a similar direction, one, for instance, removing testes and ovaries from various mammals and substituting organs from the other sex (he apparently produced by this means, among other phenomena, a lesbian goat). The underlying conviction seems to have been that homosexuality is produced by a combination of genetic and hormonal factors, and not at all by environmental factors such as the parent–child relationship.

It has recently been argued that this pioneering work had a significant influence on debates on gay identity in the 1960s and 1970s. Moreover, not only does modern sexological research owe a debt to Hirschfeld (who was acknowledged by Kinsey), but certain recent developments in genetics and endocrinology continue along lines similar to those he laid down. A distinguished German endocrinologist has been reported as paying the pithy tribute that 'Hirschfeld is my grandfather'. Hirschfeld's concept of a biologically determined third or intermediate sex, which seemed so old-fashioned as long as environmental factors were considered to be of prime importance, has in recent years taken on a new life.

Richard Plant, however, has suggested that the theories pursued so zealously by Hirschfeld may have led him in unintended directions:

> Like many turn-of-the-century psychiatrists, he wanted legal punishment to be replaced by treatment of patients who deserved to be pitied and helped rather than censured and ignored. He followed the conventions of his time when he sought the key to homosexuality by measuring the circumference of male pelvises and chests in an attempt to define a physiologically recognisable 'third sex'. Only after the Nazis had turned his lifework into ashes did he concede that, on the one hand, he had failed to prove that homosexuals were characterised by distinct and measurable biological and physiological qualities and that, on the other hand, he had unwittingly deepened popular prejudices by endowing male homosexuals with 'feminine' characteristics. This had only served to confirm the prevailing assumption that because homosexuals were 'not really men' they were therefore inferior. (pp. 33–4)

A further extension of this argument is that by trying to show that homosexuality sprang from physical origins, Hirschfeld was making his enemies a present of the argument that it was a morbid condition that could be cured by physical means. Although he has been the subject of two biographies (one in English and one, very recently, in German) it seems that Hirschfeld's contribution to the scientific study of the origins of homosexuality still awaits proper assessment.

His 'Scientific-Humanitarian Committee' moved to In den Zelten in 1912; then, in 1919, he moved to another house (number 10) in the same street, where he established his Institute for Sexual Science. Apart from being the home of Hirschfeld, his secretary and lover Karl Giese and the rest of his staff, this handsome house accommodated a research and teaching institute, a library, museum and archive, a lecture hall and a clinic for those seeking advice on sexual matters, including abortion and birth control, and treatment for venereal diseases. The rich paid through the nose, but the poor were seen for nothing, and the clinic was an instant success, with 1,800 consultations in the first year. Lectures and guided tours were open to the public and free. These were the premises that Isherwood was introduced to by Auden: Hirschfeld, Giese and their colleagues were not only the young Englishman's neighbours but his fellow members in a remarkable community.

One of the most outstanding of Hirschfeld's staff of doctors was Max Hodann, whose career was in several ways representative. A successful Berlin physician and a Communist, he worked for six years at the clinic for sexual problems in the Institute and was well known in Germany for his publications on sex education. Going into exile in England, he was sufficiently respected there for an English translation of his *History of Modern Morals* to be issued by a London publisher in 1937, and was also connected for a time with Dora Russell's progressive school at Beacon Hill.

During the 1920s the Institute became one of the sights of Berlin for visitors who had a genuine sympathy with its aims or were simply curious to see a collection ranging from photographs of transvestites to Japanese dildos. It has been said that 'it was as well known in Germany...as Erwin Piscator's theater or the Bauhaus architects'. One of the many distinguished foreign visitors was André Gide, whose haughty inspection Isherwood witnessed and later described.

In the confused and violent post-Versailles world, and with the rise of Nazism, Hirschfeld, as a Jew and a homosexual, found himself the target of verbal abuse and worse: his lectures were invaded by rowdies, and on more than one occasion he was physically attacked. In Munich in 1920 he was knocked unconscious and severely injured. Returning indomitably to the same city to give another lecture in the following year, he was, as Isherwood recounts, 'beaten up again; this time, his skull was fractured and he was left for dead'.

Apparently unstoppable, however, he had more and more ambitious plans to promulgate the ideas he believed in, and his finest hour may well have been in September 1921, when he organised the highly successful First Congress for Sexual Reform. One result of the Congress was the foundation of the World League for Sexual Reform, which in its heyday had a membership of 130,000. He carried on working, speaking and writing throughout the 1920s, though more time was spent out of Germany, with a visit to America and a world tour that included Japan, China and India. Wherever he travelled he continued indefatigably to collect data on sexual customs.

Four other international congresses were organised – successively in Copenhagen (1928), London (1929), Vienna (1930) and Brno (1932) – before the Nazis put a stop to the Institute's activities. The London congress immediately preceded Isherwood's taking up residence at the Institute, so that it must still have been a topic of eager conversation in his early days in the In den Zelten household. Hirschfeld collaborated with Dora Russell, Norman Haire and others in England, and they in turn sought to enlist the support of other liberal-minded writers and intellectuals including H. G. Wells, Arnold Bennett, the Woolfs, J. M. Keynes, Goldsworthy Lowes Dickinson and Bertrand Russell.

Hirschfeld's efforts to change the law, which had begun in the 1890s, showed no sign of flagging in the 1920s, but contemporary history was not on his side. One serious setback was the trial in 1924 of a homosexual serial murderer who had operated on an epic scale. This was the sensational Haarman case, which inflamed popular prejudice and created a climate in which reform seemed less likely. Fritz Haarman, a Hanover petty criminal and police informer, was discovered to have murdered a very large number (one figure given was 147) of destitute boys he had picked up in the city, which was notorious for prostitutes and hustlers. The case included elements of sadism, vampirism and cannibalism; the last of these practices had not been confined to the accused, since the flesh of some of the victims had reportedly been minced and sold as horsemeat for human consumption. Predictably, the case provided headline news for several months, and Hirschfeld did himself and his cause no good by appearing as an expert witness at the trial. The wave of panic and homophobia produced by the

Haarman case, and the association of homosexuality in the public mind not just with criminality but with peculiarly horrific forms of psychopathic behaviour, must have cancelled out much of what had been achieved by years of pamphleteering and speech-making.

A little earlier, Hirschfeld had not only become associated with but had actually appeared in the controversial film *Anders als die Andern* (*Different from the Rest*, 1919), to be referred to later. Its producer and director, Richard Oswald, had approached him with the suggestion that he should cooperate in the making of a film on the subject of homosexuality: 'It should be a work of art, presented as a personal documentary in the framework of scientific knowledge.' Hirschfeld was enthusiastic and secured the official blessing of his Committee, and the project went ahead, his idealism not foreseeing the bitter opposition the public treatment of such a subject would arouse. It seems that Hirschfeld made an appearance in several other films, including one, *Gesetze der Liebe* (*Laws of Love*, 1927), that receives a mention in Isherwood's *Goodbye to Berlin*.

It was at the end of the same decade that Hirschfeld came closest to success in bringing about a reform in the law. In 1929 a parliamentary committee had voted in favour of putting before the Reichstag a bill to abolish Paragraph 175. The Nazi opposition to the proposal took the form of a personal attack on Hirschfeld and an outrageous distortion of his beliefs ('The Jews are forever trying to propagandize sexual relations between siblings, men and animals, and men and men'). But the timing could hardly have been less fortunate from Hirschfeld's point of view, for European repercussions to the Wall Street Crash produced an economic crisis in which social legislation had to be shelved. In the elections at the end of that year the Nazis obtained 107 seats in the Reichstag and the road to reform was closed.

By that date Isherwood had arrived in Berlin, the point at which this account of Hirschfeld began. By the time the young Englishman was shown the curious contents of the Institute, it was the beginning of the end for Hirschfeld's work in Germany. Nazi policy towards Jews and homosexuals had already become dramatically and tragically evident, and Hirschfeld had been identified as a prime target for persecution.

When the Nazis came to power they quickly took an interest in the Institute, which was searched by the Gestapo for records that might refer to party members. In February 1933, three weeks after Hitler had become Chancellor, gay rights organisations were banned, and soon afterwards Hirschfeld's chief administrator, Kurt Hiller, who was also Jewish, was sent to a concentration camp. On 6 May the Institute, which had been subjected to a barrage of abusive Nazi propaganda, was invaded by a mob of around one hundred hooligans. Isherwood rather puzzlingly refers to them as 'students', though elsewhere they have been described as Nazi stormtroopers. Whether students or stormtroopers, they smashed everything in sight and carried off Hirschfeld's lifetime collection of books and archives, which were publicly consigned to the flames a few days later – the notorious *Bücherbrennung* or burning of the books. Isherwood witnessed the conflagration and 'said "shame"; but not loudly'. Exactly one week after the destruction of the Institute, as if responding to a signal, he left Berlin.

For uncharacteristically prudential reasons, Hirschfeld himself had been spending more and more time abroad. Leaving for an extended lecture-tour at the end of 1930, very shortly after Isherwood's own departure from the In den Zelten house, he never returned to Germany and did not witness the looting of his home or the destruction of his research collections. After 1933, the physicians who worked with him, most of whom were Jewish, also left Germany. The building itself, vandalised in 1933 and later taken over by the Nazis for their own purposes, was seriously damaged by Allied bombs in 1943; a photograph taken a decade later shows it still a ruin awaiting demolition.

Dying but indomitable, the exiled Hirschfeld tried in vain to re-establish his Institute in Paris. The visitors' book has survived from his brief final residence in France and indicates that he received a stream of callers interested in his work. He died in Nice on his 67th birthday, 14 May 1935. He left money to Karl Giese to help re-establish the Institute, but the bequest was caught up in a tangle of legal problems: as an exile, Giese was unable to produce the proofs of identity demanded by French law and the money was never paid over. Giese lived for a time in extreme poverty and committed suicide in 1938. As for the famous collection, much of it must have been destroyed when the Institute was invaded and ransacked, but parts were certainly taken out of Germany and later disappeared. There are intriguing but perhaps groundless rumours that Hirschfeld's collection of pornography is in the hands of a French collector who prefers to remain anonymous.

The account of Hirschfeld and the Institute in *Christopher and his Kind* recognises the heroism while making the most of the eccentricity. Shown round the Institute's museum, with its instruments for sado-masochistic practices, its special footwear for the delectation of fetishists and its collection of photographs that ranged from famous homosexual couples (Oscar Wilde and Lord Alfred Douglas etc.) to 'the sexual organs of quasi-hermaphrodites', he finds himself giggling with embarrassment. Hirschfeld himself seemed to Isherwood to resemble (and photographs confirm his impression) a music-hall caricature of an elderly German intellectual. And yet he was not only admirable but lovable – the young Isherwood 'loved Hirschfeld... the silly solemn old professor with his doggy moustache, thick peering spectacles and clumsy German-Jewish boots' – and one of the 'heroic leaders of his tribe' (p. 20).

During his year's residence in In den Zelten Isherwood had many opportunities to inspect the museum and to show it to visitors, but the occasion on which he giggled with embarrassment may have been the very first day of his first visit to Berlin. For, as Auden's journal makes clear, the two of them visited 'the Hirschfeld museum' together, and a brief reference to this visit is the very first item in the record Auden made of his friend's time in Berlin: 'We waited with elderly ladies and adhesive trouser boys. Why was this so obscene? H's boy (Karl Giese) was very earnest and bourgeois yet I felt he was nice....' (The boys' provocatively tight trousers would have been all the more noticeable in contrast to the prevailing fashion in England for loose trousers or 'bags'.) The priority given to this visit on Isherwood's programme suggests not only that Auden had some familiarity already with the Hirschfeld ménage, no doubt through Francis Turville-Petre, but also that he regarded it as one of the sights of the city.

Isherwood's memories, almost half a century later, of the Institute and its founder are not in a vein of high seriousness, but it is difficult to believe that, at the time, he could not also have been aware of the menace in the air and the personal anxiety of those concerned. There is, incidentally, one tiny but interesting example of unconscious autobiographical unreliability in Isherwood's references to Hirschfeld's sister Francisca as acting as housekeeper. Francisca, a talented woman who published children's books, had died in 1928 and Isherwood cannot possibly have known her, but her brother Magnus was devoted to her and must often have spoken of her – and so her name came to be substituted in Isherwood's memory for that of another sister, Teresa, who did run the house and must have come to know him well. Teresa was later deported and murdered by the Nazis.

Hirschfeld's was, in its unorthodox and sometimes eccentric way, a heroic life, the eccentricity proceeding from the single-minded pursuit of ideals not widely shared. There is an engaging solemn dottiness about some of his attempts to spread sexual enlightenment: there survives, for example, a pamphlet on the treatment of impotence that includes diagrams bearing a strong resemblance to a central heating system designed by Heath Robinson but intended to illustrate the cooperation of mind and body in the erection process. At the same time, however, his earnest confrontation with issues and human problems that most of his contemporaries preferred to leave undiscussed commands respect and admiration. In his breathlessly encyclopaedic *British Writers of the Thirties*, Valentine Cunningham performs the feat of rubbishing both Hirschfeld and Isherwood in a single sentence: 'Ordinary readers of *Mr Norris* and *Goodbye to Berlin* weren't informed, of course, that Isherwood had travelled to Berlin specifically for permissive sex with boys, nor that he had naturally fetched up in lodgings next door to Hirschfeld's notorious sex-clinic – that black museum of sado-masochistic gear, hospice for sexual freaks, mecca of homosexuals' (p. 394). I have argued earlier that Isherwood's claim, in his too eagerly confessional old age, concerning his motives for going to Berlin should not be taken literally. As for the summary judgement on Hirschfeld, the present account has perhaps suggested the extent of its intolerant failure to recognise his courage, sincerity and genuine scientific and humanitarian concerns.

As an investigator of human sexuality and a propagandist for enlightened and tolerant views, he has a place in history beside Havelock Ellis, Edward Carpenter and others. (In his biography of Havelock Ellis, Vincent Brome suggests that Ellis's work was 'derivative from Hirschfeld' in its discussion of transvestism and other topics.) In legislative terms, all his enormous labours and all his courage and initiative did not succeed in achieving a great deal during his lifetime. There were repeated set-backs that would have daunted a less energetic and single-minded man, and these came partly as a result of historical accidents and unlucky timing, but also partly perhaps as a result of his idealism, his willingness to embrace any worthy cause regardless of political expediency or simple discretion, and his inability to take into account the ruthlessness of the opposition. His long-term influence, however, though hardly measurable, must have been considerable, and Isherwood and others can hardly have failed to sense at times that they were close to a man who was likely to make an important contribution to the modification of human perceptions.

Today, it is a bronze bust of Hirschfeld that surveys the tiny crowded library of the Freunde eines Schwulen Museums in Berlin, a gay organisation situated in a less fashionable area of Berlin than In den Zelten, and one whose cramped premises, reached by a superannuated lift after crossing a scruffy courtyard, contrast strikingly with the marble halls of the Institute. How the latter was financed, so lavishly and so long, remains a bit of a mystery. Although Hirschfeld himself had bought the house (and later made it over to the Institute), and although many of his staff worked only for their keep and pocket money, the running costs must have been considerable, and it seems likely that wealthy homosexuals in Germany and elsewhere made generous but anonymous contributions.

There is, too, in present-day Berlin a Magnus Hirschfeld Gesellschaft (Research Institute) which since 1982 has made efforts, in the heroic and idealistic spirit of Hirschfeld himself, both to continue his work in sexological research and to conduct and publish historical research on Hirschfeld and his times. The plan of re-establishing an institute on the lines of his own and under the aegis of a German university has not so far succeeded, but the Society issues a newsletter twice a year and has published a series of books that includes reprints of Hirschfeld's own writings. Largely through its efforts, on 6 July 1994 – the 75th anniversary of the opening of Hirschfeld's Institute – a memorial to Hirschfeld was unveiled on a spot not far from its original site.

Sixty years after his death, therefore, Hirschfeld is something more than an eccentric or distasteful footnote to cultural history or a caricaturist's German professor in the pages of *Christopher and his Kind*. The motto he chose for his Institute was 'Per scientiam ad justitiam' ('Through science to justice'), and its nineteenth-century optimism and idealism were tragically contradicted by history and by his own last days. In many ways a nineteenth-century figure, he was gifted (or, some might feel, cursed) with an unfading vision of a world that might be very different from the fear-haunted and guilt-ridden one he knew. For all the touches of eccentricity, even absurdity – and at moments, not least in Isherwood's account, he seems to resemble a shambling figure of farce played by Walter Matthau – Hirschfeld's heroism commands our respect and he has a place in the history of the struggle against intolerance and inhumanity.

FRANCIS TURVILLE-PETRE

When Isherwood knocked on the door of that apartment in In den Zelten in November 1929, the result was dramatic. The door flew open and a figure appeared, 'tousled, furious, one hand clutching the folds of his crimson silk robe. Instantly, he started screaming in German.' The screaming over, the door was slammed in his face. This was his introduction to Francis Turville-Petre, more conveniently known in the boy-bars as Der Franni.

Francis, sleepy and hungover, had mistaken his English visitor, youthful and short of stature, for a light-fingered rent-boy who had been thrown out the previous night, but the misunderstanding was soon cleared up. He occupied a couple of rooms in the apartment, situated in the building next door to Dr Hirschfeld's Institute, and arrangements were quickly made for Isherwood to move into another of the rooms, which happened to be vacant. During the next few weeks Francis became his guide to the bars of the working-class district of Hallesches Tor. It was very much the lower end of the market to which these two upper-class Englishmen made their way, and someone who spoke German and knew his way around (as Francis certainly did) was an advantage when it came to finding the small, backstreet bars that, as Isherwood explains, depended for their business on a regular clientele rather than on catching the eye of passing tourists.

According to *Christopher and his Kind* the two of them 'got along well together', and there is a vivid passage describing their nocturnal excursions, 'like traders who had entered a jungle'. If Hirschfeld, filling notebooks with facts, was the Darwin of the Berlin sexual underworld, Isherwood and his mentor Turville-Petre were two aristocratic ivory-traders, out to exploit the natives with a handful of glass beads. Isherwood also put Francis into *Down There on a Visit*, and there was evidently something about him that made writers instinctively scent copy. (He makes other guest appearances, as we shall see shortly, in one of Olivia Manning's novels and elsewhere.) Furthermore, he was incorporated, as 'The

Fronny', into Auden and Isherwood's private mythology. As Isherwood notes, 'The name appears in several of Wystan's poems, and the Fronny character is present, though unnamed, in the published version of *The Dance of Death*.' As already mentioned, Auden's play *The Fronny* survives only in a very fragmentary state.

The period the unsaintly Francis and his disciple Christopher spent together as traders, or hunters, in the jungle of Hallesches Tor can have lasted no more than a few weeks, for quite early in 1930 both men left Berlin, though Isherwood soon returned to the apartment and, all told, spent nearly a year there. It was much longer before Francis, an incurable wanderer, was back in Berlin. But their time together must surely have constituted for Isherwood a period not quite of initiation – for the first visit to Berlin earlier in 1929 had been that – but of more exhaustive exploration of what life (especially low-life) in Berlin had to offer, and a necessary prologue to the more settled lifestyle for which he later opted. It is difficult, too, not to believe that Francis must have impressed him as something between a role-model and a solemn warning, for their backgrounds were very similar and Francis's present way of life offered Isherwood a glimpse into one of his own possible futures. Since he had more money than Isherwood, whose private income was at that time precarious, the freedom Francis enjoyed may also have made him an object of envy. He was under no necessity, as Isherwood seems to have been, to visit bourgeois households in the socially ambiguous capacity of a private tutor and to give English lessons for a few marks an hour, or to worry whether Uncle Henry's next cheque would be forthcoming.

Francis Turville-Petre was born in 1901, the son and heir of Oswald Turville-Petre of Bosworth Hall, near Lutterworth in Leicestershire. Oswald, who married in his late thirties and was nearly forty when his first-born appeared, had been born Oswald Petre, had inherited the estate at the age of 27 from his cousin, Sir Francis Fortescue-Turville, and had added the 'Turville' to his own surname. He was a country gentleman, a soldier and a devout Catholic descended from an old Catholic family. He had gone to school at Woburn Park, near Weybridge in Surrey, a short-lived educational establishment run by a relative, Monsignor Petre, who later became the 13th Baron Petre and the first Catholic priest since the Reformation to take his seat in the House of Lords. From school – unusually for a Catholic at that time – he had proceeded to Christ Church, Oxford. In due course he became Lord of the Manor of

Husbands Bosworth, a Justice of the Peace and High Sheriff of Leicestershire, and served in the Great War with the Northants Yeomanry – yet another of the fathers who were away at the war during their sons' adolescence.

Oswald married Margaret Cave, 13 years younger than himself, and she bore him, in fairly rapid succession, two sons and three daughters. (The younger son, Gabriel, became a distinguished Icelandic scholar and an Oxford professor.) A drawing of Oswald shows him to have had the family face, long and narrow and tending to become deeply lined with the passing of time, that Francis also inherited.

Though he was born in London, where his family had taken a house for the winter, it was at Bosworth Hall that Francis spent much of his childhood, since the family was accustomed to pass half the year there and the other half at Whitley Abbey near Coventry, the home of his maternal grandparents. Bosworth Hall is on the edge of the village of Husbands Bosworth, through which traffic now thunders on its way to and from the M1 motorway six miles distant. In the early years of the century, though, it must have been a very tranquil spot. The park contains, a short walk from the small country house and its outbuildings, a Roman Catholic chapel, built in 1873 and still used for services and attracting a large and far-flung congregation. Pevsner informs us that the main part of the house was built in 1792, while other portions go back to the sixteenth or seventeenth century. Francis's early years were passed on the nursery floor at the top of the house, where the rapidly growing family was cared for by a nurse, a nurserymaid and in due course a governess. On reaching the age of five or six each child was allowed to pass through the door leading to the corridor at the end of which was the schoolroom, a spacious room with windows overlooking the park.

At seven he was sent to a Catholic preparatory school at Eastbourne, where he seems to have been very unhappy, and from there he proceeded in 1914 to the Oratory School, founded by Cardinal Newman in 1859 and in Francis's time still situated in the Hagley Road, Birmingham, next to the house of the Oratory Fathers. During these years, family holidays were spent at Lyme Regis, where Francis hunted enthusiastically for fossils in the cliffs. There were scientific talents in his mother's family: his uncle Charles Cave had erected a 'thunder-house' in his garden to monitor seismic disturbances. When he was about 12 Francis found a fine specimen belonging to an ichthyosaurus and was persuaded, or perhaps directed, to present it to the local museum. It was on one of these holidays that the three girls went on a picnic with an old lady who sent them to fill the tea-kettle at the brook and boiled it, or did not quite boil it, over a fire of sticks. The girls all fell ill with typhoid, and Gwenda, a year younger than Francis, was expected to die, a Home Office official actually being summoned to the house so that special permission could be granted for the burial to take place beside the private chapel. The civil servant, however, had a wasted journey, for Gwenda recovered and lived to be over 90.

Scraping and prising fossils out of the Dorset cliffs was early evidence of a passion on Francis's part for unburying the past, and at school the same passion manifested itself in a marked enthusiasm for archaeology. By a stroke of luck he was in exactly the right place for a specialised taste of this kind to receive encouragement. For the Oratory School was under the fairly new and highly charismatic headship of Father Edward Pereira (1866–1939), a brilliant talent-spotter who took pains to foster his pupils' individual interests, however unconventional. Francis was actually taught Egyptian by the science master, Daniel Arkell (who also lectured at Birmingham University); one of his contemporaries, George Bowring, who died in 1992, remembered this curious fact to the end of his life, observing justly that it was 'an unusual knowledge in a Physics and Chemistry master'. It seems likely that Francis was better served by Father Pereira and the Oratory School than if he had been sent to a more ancient and more celebrated establishment.

The historian of the school, A. J. Cornwell, has said of Father Pereira: 'I have discussed him with Oratorian nonagenarians, octogenarians and septuagenarians. Their impressions, contributed independently, leave one in no doubt that his influence was paramount, far-reaching and eternal. An interval of fifty or sixty years fails to dim the impact; the picture of him is as if they had only recently left school.'

Pereira's whole life had been closely associated with the school. He had himself been a pupil there at a time when Newman's influence was still potent, became a priest and an Oratory Father, went back to the school as a master and became head, having evidently been groomed for the succession, on the death of the incumbent in 1911. Belonging on his father's side to a wealthy

Portuguese family of tobacco importers (he eventually died of lung cancer), he was no intellectual and did not have a degree, his education having been at the Scots College in Rome, and his natural gifts displaying themselves most notably on the cricket field (he had played for Warwickshire against the Australians). More to the point, he seems to have been free from convictions, not unknown among other public school headmasters, as to the mould into which those in his care should be fitted, and Francis was the beneficiary of his wise and tactful tolerance of the educationally unorthodox.

Francis's time at the Oratory corresponded almost precisely to the years of the Great War. In the two generations before 1918 fewer than a thousand boys had passed through the school, and of those between the ages of 18 and 50 some 500 were still alive in 1914. Of that number nearly 400 served in the war; 71 were killed and 73 wounded. In a small school with a patriotic tradition and an emphasis on character-building, the war, and in particular the service given and sacrifices made by old boys, must have become during those years an inescapable part of the emotional atmosphere of daily life. For Francis, as for Christopher Isherwood, the burden of the Past must have lain heavy and the prospect of escape from it have proved irresistibly tempting.

It was a school of no more than seventy or eighty boys, and under a head less tolerant of individual tastes the atmosphere could have been stifling. Francis did well there, became a prefect, and won prizes for religious instruction, Latin prose composition and history. When he left he was awarded the Senior Norfolk Prize, the gift of the Duke of Norfolk, bestowed only on outstanding candidates, and worth £50 (a large sum in 1919) in books. His youngest sister, Alethea, remembers him at this time as a handsome boy with dark hair, and recalls the day when he came home from school with the first gramophone they had seen or heard and danced a tango with the governess.

He took a year off before going up to Oxford, probably spending at least some part of it in Palestine – for his sense of vocation, it seems, was already strong. So it was not until the Michaelmas Term of 1920 that Francis matriculated at Exeter College, Oxford, his father being described in the college records as 'landowner'. Father Pereira's encouragement of his archaeological leanings had been effective enough to make Francis disregard the family connection with Christ Church (to which his younger brother followed his father in due course) in favour of a less famous college where his specialised interests could be better catered for. One of the fellows and tutors of Exeter was Dr Robert Marett, by training a classicist but by this time University Reader in Social Anthropology and a prolific writer on primitive religion and other subjects. (There is probably no significance in the fact that, as a young man, Marett had studied philosophy at Berlin University.) E. E. Evans-Pritchard, who later became a famous and widely influential social anthropologist, came to the college from an Anglican vicarage one year after Francis.

The record of Francis's Oxford years is scanty, and neither his Catholicism nor (more predictably) his homosexuality forms part of it. The Catholic Chaplain at the time was Monsignor ('Mugger') Barnes, though he was soon to be succeeded by the more celebrated Ronald Knox. 'Sligger' Urquhart (why did university priests have names that make them sound like prizefighters?), who had become the first Catholic don at Oxford since the time of James II, was still at Balliol and used to take reading parties of Catholic undergraduates to his chalet in the Alps. But I have found no evidence that Francis moved in these circles, and it seems likely that the faith in which he had been so carefully brought up was no longer a central element in his life.

Academically, his Oxford career was remarkably undistinguished. Having done well at school, he nevertheless elected to read for a pass degree – an unusual step that was taken at that time by only about one in fifty undergraduates at the college. It meant that he was required to study a group of subjects instead of concentrating on one for honours, and his reason for taking this curious step seems clear: it enabled him to study anthropology, which was not available as an honours subject. Like A. E. Housman, whose Oxford career was even less distinguished, he seems to have been motivated by a mixture of wilfulness and intellectual passion to neglect his prescribed studies in favour of his consuming interests. In his second year he failed a Divinity examination but was successful at the second attempt, and eventually secured his BA in 1925.

He had, however, discovered his vocation, the archaeology of the Middle East, and at some stage, probably between school and Oxford, had already spent a year at the British School of Archaeology in Jerusalem as well as going to the Middle East during at least one of his summer vacations. The next stage in his chosen profession came rapidly and was dramatic, even sensational. In 1920 the study of Palestinian prehistory was, according to William Foxwell Albright's *The Archaeology of Palestine*, 'wholly undeveloped'. Francis had started surveying a site in Galilee in 1923, having probably had his attention directed to it by Marett. Two years later he 'excavated in two caves above the sea of Galilee and discovered the first stratified deposits in Palestine, in one of which he found the first remains of prehistoric man' (Albright, p. 37). The principal find was 'part of a typical Neanderthal skull'.

The skull was brought to England and examined by Sir Arthur Keith, a physical anthropologist, at the Royal College of Surgeons. Keith confirmed the general view that it was Neanderthal, but it is now believed to be much older and a significant find in relationship to one of the main issues of present-day prehistoric archaeology, the emergence of *homo sapiens*. Another historian has dated the 'systematic pursuit of prehistoric archaeology' in this area to Francis Turville-Petre's 1925 excavations: it was the first human fossil to be found in the Near East, and according to Jean Perrot, the discovery of what came to be called the Galilee Skull 'at once attracted the attention of prehistorians, and in subsequent years prehistoric studies developed on such a scale that Palestine soon became one of the principal centres of prehistoric archaeology outside Western Europe' (p. 130).

The finding of the skull aroused popular as well as professional interest, and *The Times* published reports and photographs, including one of Francis in the cave where he had discovered it. His Oxford college was not, however, much impressed by this precocious celebrity, and his record card there bears the curt and dismissive note 'Anthropologising in Palestine and journalistic fame – 1925'.

While still in his twenties, Francis had thus, at a single stroke, earned a significant and permanent place in the history of Middle Eastern archaeology. He lectured to the British Association for the Advancement of Science and published in 1927 *Researches in Prehistoric Galilee, 1925–1926*. The preface, by the Director of the British School of Archaeology in Jerusalem, states that 'the local operations were placed under the direct charge of Mr Turville-Petre, who, while still at Oxford, had made a special study of the Stone Age, and had, during a previous season (1923), made a preliminary exploration of the area.' Francis's own account, though couched in appropriately academic language, conveys something of the excitement of the brilliant hunch that paid off: 'The present writer...decided to make the hills bordering the plains of Gene- sereth the centre of his researches, and to devote particular atten- tion to caves.' He was gifted with a good eye for a site, and one he identified but never worked on was later excavated by Japanese archaeologists.

It was, then, a giant stride at the beginning of the career of a young man who had only recently left Oxford, but that career soon afterwards came mysteriously to a halt. Francis flashes across the sky of prehistoric archaeology like a rocket, and it was only a couple of years after the publication of his book that Isherwood knocked on his door in Berlin and found him a willing and expert guide to the boy-bars, devoting his full-time energies to drink and dissipation. He resumed his work briefly in 1931, when he spent three months in the Kebara Caves at Mount Carmel, seven miles south of Haifa. There he made some significant finds, and more work was later done by others on the same site, but it was his last dig. Thereafter his professional life came to an end – though this may not have been entirely by his own choice, for there is reason to believe that his scandalous reputation led to the blocking of later attempts to dig in Greece. There is a touching moment in *Christo- pher and his Kind* (p. 26) when Isherwood observes that Francis 'wasn't really interested in Germany.... He never felt truly at home, he said, except in the countries of the Eastern Mediterran- ean'. And Isherwood recalls rare moments of sobriety when Fran- cis's conversation would reveal a profound knowledge of prehistoric Greece: 'He spoke of it often, with a quiet understated passion which Christopher found curiously moving. It was as if part of his mind dwelt continually in that world' (p. 26).

How can a career so brief, so brilliant, so bizarre in its aftermath, be accounted for? The passion for archaeology, and the choice of Palestine, are perhaps beyond explanation: it may have been (that favourite locution of the biographer at his wits' end) some lesson on the Old Testament given by Father Pereira that had ignited his interest, perhaps just the prettily coloured maps that relieve the black-and-white monotony of a schoolboy's Bible. What is obvious is that Middle Eastern archaeology took the son and heir of the strict Catholic squire away from his home, his family, his country and his religion to another land, an alien culture. He was to spend the rest of his life as an expatriate, living in Germany and Greece, and dying in Egypt.

Sex and drink obtained an early hold on him, and when he went to Berlin it was primarily to obtain treatment for syphilis at the Hirschfeld clinic. When he worked on the Kebara site in 1931, one of his colleagues was Mrs Charlotte Augusta Baines, a Catholic lady of about sixty, who is said to have cast a disapproving eye on the empty whisky bottles that were tossed out of Francis's tent and the Arab boys who crawled into it. (One story relates that he deposited a considerable cache of them – bottles, not boys – in the caves for future archaeologists to unearth and ponder on.) Reading Isherwood's account, it is easy to form a mental picture of a middle-aged man who had the confirmed habits and unmistakable lineaments produced by long years of dissipation, while references to him as 'The Fronny' seem to come from cheeky schoolboys guying one of their elders. Some biographers seem to have caught this infection, Jonathan Fryer, for instance, referring to Francis as 'much worn by years of debauchery...his aura of decay' (1993, p. 76). The truth is that when Isherwood met him Francis was only a few years out of Oxford, was still only 28, and was thus only three years older than Isherwood himself.

The period between Francis's brilliant archaeological debut and his appearance before the bemused and newly arrived Isherwood is obscure, and exactly when, in the course of his roaming life, he moved to Berlin is unknown. Early in 1928, however, and well before either Auden or Isherwood made their home in the city, the name of 'Francis Turville-Petre, London' appears on printed material issued from 10 In den Zelten by the World League for Sexual Reform. He is named there as a member of the *Gründungs-ausschuss* (foundation committee) of the League, along with Havelock Ellis, Norman Haire and others. This seems to argue that Francis was in Berlin by that time, almost two years before he opened the door to Isherwood, and was taking an active interest in Hirschfeld's campaigns. This is confirmed by another document indicating that on 28 December 1928, after Auden's arrival in the city but still nearly a year before the encounter that Isherwood described so long afterwards, he was elected to one of the committees of the Institute. He continued to participate in its affairs, for an advertisement for a lecture series on sexology given there in the spring of 1930 – that is, a few months *after* Isherwood's encounter – includes him as one of the speakers, his subject being 'sexual ethnology'. (According to *Christopher and his Kind* Francis had left Berlin early in the year, and if Isherwood's memory was reliable must have returned at this time.) This picture of the lecturer and committee member, the trained social anthropologist who has turned his attention to human sexual behaviour, does not quite fit with Isherwood's graphic portrait of a man far advanced in dissipation, and the suspicion arises that the garish colours in which Francis's behaviour is depicted may have been heightened by the novelist-autobiographer to match that crimson silk robe.

Certainly he was one of the delegates attending the League's congress held in Copenhagen in 1928, for he appears in two group photographs taken on that occasion. In one of them, taken outside the city's town hall, he can be clearly seen: erect, dapper, dark-suited, bespectacled, bow-tied, buttonholed, he seems the very model of the well turned out upper-class Englishman, and, in appearance at least, much closer to Bertie Wooster than to the raffish figure whom Isherwood encountered in the following year (or at any rate described long afterwards). Mysteriously, though, his name disappears from later lists of notabilities who lent their support to the League, such as that accompanying the invitations to the London congress issued in the spring of 1929. One can only guess at the reasons for the withdrawal of his name: some quarrel, on personal or ideological grounds, with Hirschfeld or one of his associates, perhaps.

After that first meeting, as we have seen, Francis and Christopher were together for a few weeks until Francis left Berlin 'for warmer southern lands'. His next appearance in *Christopher and his Kind* is in the spring of 1932, when he returned to Berlin full of good resolutions and urged Isherwood to share his new lifestyle. Together they went to Mohrin, where Stephen Spender joined them for a time. But Francis's resolutions were soon broken and he was going off to Berlin for long weekends.

The following year, when Isherwood decided to leave Germany, he was invited by Francis to join him on the Greek island of St Nicholas, where he was living in primitive conditions. He had bought land there and had plans to build a house and resume his archaeological work. These plans came to nothing: though his achievements are on a much less heroic scale, Francis belonged to the same tradition of the brilliant, hunch-pursuing maverick scholar as Heinrich Schliemann, and like Schliemann he incurred the disapproval of the academic establishment.

Francis met Isherwood in Athens on 20 May and accompanied him to St Nicholas; later Spender, and possibly also Auden, visited him there. The journey, and Isherwood's hot and uncomfortable sojourn on St Nicholas which lasted until 6 September, are described at length in *Christopher and his Kind*. The island remained Francis's base for some years, and he stayed there after the outbreak of war and until the Germans bombed it. He was then put, unwillingly, on the last boat for Alexandria – the previous boat had sunk with the loss of all on board – and made his way to Cairo. In her book *Cairo in the War*, Artemis Cooper has given a vivid account of the scramble to escape from Greece at this time: 'People jostled to get a passage on any ship willing to make the journey, while the Luftwaffe kept up their constant bombing on the capital's port at Piraeus...' (p. 77).

A little earlier, in February 1938, there had been a last meeting with Isherwood and Auden, when they were on their way to China, at which time Francis seems to have been in Egypt. Apparently by arrangement, he went to Port Said to greet them when they disembarked: 'He assured them that Port Said, which they had been told was the sex capital of the world, was in fact deadly dull, and he took them instead to the Pyramids, which they in turn found uninteresting, though the Sphinx impressed them with what Auden called its "huge hurt face" '. The well-known photograph of Isherwood and Auden setting off for China shows two young men smilingly eager for experience, but Francis, though belonging to their own generation, sounds old and weary, and had in fact little more than three years left to live. He died in Cairo on 16 August 1941 of peritonitis; with a final lordly refusal to do the sensible and obvious thing, he had not permitted his friends to take him to hospital as no Greek hospital was available.

He is buried in the English cemetery in Cairo, and there is a memorial window dedicated to him in the chapel at Bosworth Hall. By a curious chance he outlived his father by exactly two months and thus inherited the estate whose responsibilities he had so resolutely shunned. During his years of wandering he had kept in touch with his family and often visited his old home (the last visit was in 1939). But he seems to have made it quite clear that he was a visitor whose chosen way of life was entirely different from that of the country squirearchy into which he had been born. He would sometimes bring friends from London, where he kept a flat in Russell Square, and their camp behaviour, transferred from the West End to sedate rural surroundings, is still remembered. One of them, taken for a walk in the park, was so terrified by an encounter with a cow that he had to be gently led to a place of safety. A more sober guest at Bosworth Hall was Karl Giese, Magnus Hirschfeld's partner, who went there after the 1929 London conference. On these visits, it seems, Francis would talk 'obsessively' about his homosexuality, as if to underline his firm refusal to accept, under any circumstances, the role of Catholic English gentleman, manly, philoprogenitive and devoted to the public service, that had been assigned to him. In this firm rejection of a prescribed role, and substitution of one he knew to be startlingly unconventional, he had much in common with Isherwood.

Francis's numerous appearances in Auden's work have already been briefly mentioned. Isherwood, too, wrote about him extensively, and from a much longer perspective of time, in both *Christopher and his Kind* and *Down There on a Visit*. Francis was also put to good use by two other writers in, respectively, an autobiography and a novel. Xan Fielding, a friend of Francis, describes in *Hide and Seek* (1954) how, in late September 1939, he made his way to St Nicholas and stayed there for almost a year:

> Apart from an occasional visitor from Athens and a staff of half a dozen peasant boys, Francis was the only person I saw for the whole of the first winter of the war and for most of the following summer; and he was the last man to censure me for following my natural inclination. Certainly he had followed his. At the age of thirty, after laying the foundations of a brilliant career with his discovery of the Galilee Skull, he had abandoned anthropology because he found the profession interfered too much with his private life, and had come to retire in Greece. His pretext for settling on a deserted island was to excavate a mound on the mainland directly opposite; but it was easier to think of his premature retirement as a gesture of defiance, for the site ten years later was still untouched.

This account of Francis's desertion of his profession may be less than fair, since there is evidence that his genuine efforts to dig in Greece were frustrated by fellow scholars who disapproved of the undignified way in which earlier expeditions had been conducted. Fielding continues:

> Inevitably, I suppose, he had earned a reputation for eccentricity. His appearance was unconventional: long straight Red-Indian

hair framed a sad sallow face so lined that it was impossible to guess its owner's age; below it an emaciated body, always clothed in bright colours, stretched six feet down to an almost freakishly small pair of sandalled feet. His habits, too, were out of the ordinary; he would get up every day at sunset and sit down to a luncheon which had been ordered for three o'clock in the afternoon – a mere formality in any case, for he never ate anything at meal times but lived on brandy and dry bread supplemented by a weekly cup of Bovril. Those who did not know him well might have thought he despised the world. They would have been wrong – it was only public opinion he scorned. Any misanthropic tendency he might have had was checked by a tolerance of human foibles that was almost Armenian in its integrity.   (p. 15)

Francis's entirely natural and unaffected eccentricity, like the furrowed and crumpled face, oddly anticipates the later years of Auden.

Wartime Cairo had some qualifications as an appropriate setting for Francis's last days. It has been said that 'everybody you have ever heard of was [in Cairo] at one time or another during the war', and the different elements combined to make it a hotbed (no dead metaphor in this instance) of sexual intrigue and licence. Olivia Manning, whose husband worked for the British Council, had earlier known Francis in Greece and later put him into her novel *The Battle Lost and Won* (1978), the second volume of her 'Levant Trilogy', where he makes an appearance as 'Humphrey Taupin, the archaeologist'.

[Taupin] had been a famous name around the cafés in Athens. When he was very young, on his first dig, he had come upon a stone sarcophagus that contained a death-mask of beaten gold. The mask, thought to be of a king of Corinth, was in the museum, and Harriet had seen it there. This find, that for some would have been the beginning, was for him the end. She could imagine that such an achievement at twenty might leave one wondering what to do for the next fifty years. Anyway, confounded by his own success, he had retired to the most remote of the Sporades...   (pp. 151–2).

Like Francis, Taupin had escaped 'when the Germans came' and made his way to Cairo, full of British refugees and, with its

wartime romances, like 'a bureau of sexual exchange'. When Harriet shakes his hand: 'She took it but not willingly. She had heard
that he had been cured of syphilis, but perhaps he was not cured.
Feeling his hand in hers, dry and fragile, like the skeleton of a small
bird, she remembered the courteous crusader who took the hand of
a leper and became a leper himself. When Taupin's hand slipped
away, she felt she, too, was at risk' (p. 152). The sense of physical
revulsion is striking, especially when one recalls that Francis was
only forty when he died.

Both Fielding and Manning touch on the mystery of Francis's
tragically aborted career, but Manning's diagnosis of him as one
'confounded by his own success' does not quite carry conviction.
The rebellion and refusal to conform affected every area of his life,
including his dress and his eating habits, and it would surely have
been even more extraordinary if he had followed up his early
success by pursuing an academic career and returning to Oxford
in the fullness of time as Professor of Archaeology. Ultimately there
seems to have been, beneath the surface of aristocratic indifference
to the opinions of others, something wilful and even self-
destructive in his nature. Early fame was quickly followed by
withdrawal from the world, and in his later years on St Nicholas
he seems to have been for much of the time virtually a recluse.

His background – the country house, the military father away at
the war, the education at a minor public school and an ancient
university – was so close to Isherwood's that the latter must very
early in their acquaintance have sensed that the slightly older man's
chosen way of life offered a fearful temptation, to yield to which
would be ultimately fatal for one who wanted to be a writer. In the
event Francis provided him with admirable copy but proved a negative role-model. As already noted, in *Christopher and his Kind* Isherwood makes a point of insisting that, while Francis remained half the
night in the bars, haggling with prospective bedfellows as he had
once haggled with camel-drivers, he himself went home early in
order to be fresh 'to get on with his novel' the next morning.

As for Francis, the haggling with hustlers became almost an end
in itself, an occupation as well as a hobby, and perhaps the most
revealing sentences in all that Isherwood wrote about him are the
following:

Actually, Francis didn't care who he finished up with: he wasn't
much interested in making love. What did fascinate him – and

what began, more and more, to fascinate Christopher, looking at it through Francis's eyes, was the boys' world, their slang, their quarrels, their jokes, their outrageous unserious demands, their girls, their thefts, their encounters with the police.   (pp. 28–9)

In his latter days, tall and cadaverous and looking twice his age, bored with love, with sex, with travel, with friendship, even with food, Francis is like a figure in a morality play, a dreadful warning against the perils of hedonism. Only, almost automatically, the reconnoitring eye and the interrogating voice continued to function.

On Isherwood's part, fascination with 'the boys' world', though real enough, did not bear much fruit in his published writings: the Berlin stories are too discreet, too evasive, too readily disposed to encode and displace, to make much use of what must have been wonderfully colourful material, both comic and sad. It was a world that must surely have been extensively and minutely depicted in his lost diaries and might have received attention in his ambitious, abandoned fictional project, *The Lost*. In Francis's case, it looks as though his eye for a promising site, his curiosity about (and intellectual satisfaction in uncovering) the ways of an alien people, had been transferred from the dusty hills of Palestine to the gritty streets of Berlin, and he was finding an outlet for his exceptional and neglected gifts as the anthropologist of the rent-bars.

JOHN LAYARD

Layard's name appears on the first page of Isherwood's *Christopher and his Kind*, and, much earlier, and thinly disguised, as 'Barnard', he had made an appearance in the autobiography *Lions and Shadows*. In the latter Isherwood had claimed that the desire to meet Layard was his principal motive for going to Berlin, but the candour of riper years compelled him to admit that in making this claim he was 'avoiding the truth'. He had, however, received enthusiastic reports from Auden about this strange Englishman, resident in Berlin, and there is no doubt that Layard was a charismatic personality who over a period of several months had a close relationship with Auden and whose ideas had a permanent influence on his thinking.

Isherwood too became friends with Layard and later admitted that he had learned a great deal from him. In *Christopher and his*

Kind (p. 13) he recalls his first impressions of Layard when they met in Berlin – his 'X-ray eyes, his mocking amusement, his stunning frankness....' This impression was reinforced when Layard practised on him some of his white magic. Isherwood had on his left shoulder-blade a patch of hair, growing on an old acne scar, of which he was irrationally ashamed. Layard explained that this was a manifestation of instinct in contrast to the control and repression represented by the hairless right shoulder-blade. In other words, the hair was not a flaw but a good thing, and to clinch his argument he kissed the part in question. Either the explanation or the kiss was efficacious in curing Isherwood of his embarrassment. Later he introduced Layard to his mother in England, and even she seems to have been impressed, referring to him in her diary as 'very striking and unusual'.

Born in 1891, Layard had gone to Bedales, the famous and at that time very unconventional co-educational boarding school in Hampshire, and then to King's College, Cambridge, where he had read French and German. Graduating in 1913, he had travelled in the following year to Melanesia as an assistant to the well-known Cambridge anthropologist and psychologist William Rivers, but on returning home he suffered a nervous breakdown so severe as to produce acute physical symptoms that made him unable to walk. (The official college record of the time, which gives for him a fashionable London address, notes that since his return from the Pacific he had 'suffered from ill-health'.) He became a patient of the American psychotherapist Homer Lane, who was living and working in England, and not only recovered the use of his legs but became a passionate convert to Lane's unorthodox doctrines, which were duly transmitted to Auden and, through Auden, to Isherwood.

Lane had been born in 1876, the son of a railway worker and a strict Baptist mother, and had run away from home at 14. He did a variety of jobs for short periods, married young and discovered that the advent of his first child made him keenly interested in education. After a teacher training course in Boston he taught for a time in a prison, then taught manual work in a school in Detroit, where he also established a club for delinquent boys and ran 'summer playgrounds' to keep working-class children off the streets during school holidays. His next job was as superintendent of a boys' home, a task he accepted on condition that the home was moved into the country, where the boys could be employed on farm work.

He was obviously a man of exceptional energy and vision, and one who quickly became the subject of anecdote if not legend. When the farmhouse burned down, he broke a wrist in rescuing one of the boys but

> spent the night finding sleeping accommodation for the boys and driving them to neighbouring farmhouses, paying no attention to his broken wrist until the afternoon of the next day. The doctor who at last set it told him that he would now never have the proper use of it again. As a fact, it healed completely in record time. Again and again Lane overcame physical disability by the constructive power with which he set himself to any creative work on hand.   (*Talks to Parents and Teachers*, p. 7)

The exercise of healing power sets the pattern for much of Lane's later work as a therapist, while the defiance of orthodox opinion contains the seeds of his later clashes with authority and his eventual downfall.

The rebuilt home was named the Ford Republic and run on democratic lines, and Lane's work there brought him considerable celebrity and made him much in demand as a lecturer. He paid more than one visit to England and in 1912 settled there as superintendent of the Little Commonwealth, a self-governing reformatory school in Dorset that was soon closed after a scandal and a Home Office inquiry. The details are obscure, but it seems likely that Lane's unconventional methods made him the victim of official suspicion, intolerance and persecution. He remained in England, however, giving lectures on education and working as a consulting psychologist in London – the capacity in which he treated Layard. Again, however, his indifference to conventional standards led to disaster. He had, perhaps innocently but certainly unwisely, accepted a substantial loan from a rich woman patient, and when her family complained to the police his office was raided and such suspicious items as pornographic pictures and contraceptives were allegedly discovered there. He was arrested on a technicality under the Aliens Act (he had not notified a change of address) and was sent to Brixton prison, tried and deported. Settling in France, he quickly died of typhoid and pneumonia in 1925. The temptation to diagnose also a broken heart is strong.

It was a remarkable career, both heroic and quixotic, and its end is little short of tragic: the spectacle of the British establishment ganging up on the unqualified foreign crank, and the readiness with which unorthodox (though evidently effective) styles of therapy were associated with sexual irregularities, is unedifying. But Lane's influence did not cease with his death, and his little book *Talks to Parents and Teachers*, constructed by his disciples from his lectures and notes and published posthumously in 1928, became a bestseller. Layard, whose treatment was still under way at the time of Lane's downfall and death, was seriously disturbed by those events and regarded the healer's disappearance as an act of personal betrayal. He had, however, thoroughly absorbed Lane's ideas, and when, after leaving England and seeking psychiatric help in Vienna, he moved to Berlin with the same purpose, he was ready to pass on the good news to willing converts.

He had settled in Berlin in 1926 and, soon after Auden's arrival in the autumn of 1928, telephoned him at the suggestion of a mutual friend, David Ayerst. Auden visited Layard and at that first meeting they spent several hours talking – so many hours, indeed, that it was too late for Auden to return home to his lodgings with the Muthesius family in a distant suburb, and he spent the night in Layard's flat. What happened that night is far from clear. Layard was bisexual and was immediately and strongly attracted to Auden, falling for him (as he later said in his fragmentary autobiography) 'like a ninepin'. Some considerable time afterwards Auden wrote in his journal that at their early meetings Layard had made a great impression on him and 'his exposition of Lane has made a difference to me.... Going to bed with him at first though was a mistake which lasts. I feel guilty about it.'

Auden did not begin to keep the journal until the following spring, and in common with many of his journal entries, the wording of this one is rather obscure at a crucial point: does 'at first' mean 'at our first meeting' or 'at an early stage of our friendship' (e.g. at their second or third meeting), or simply 'too soon'? Layard's own account states quite unambiguously that Auden rejected his sexual advances on that first occasion, remarking by way of explanation and excuse that he had ' "a boy named Pieps" '. Layard may, of course, have had his own reasons for autobiographical reticence.

The long conversations about Lane, however, had more far-reaching effects than what happened, or did not happen, in bed, and Humphrey Carpenter's conclusion that the older man made a 'tremendous impression' on Auden seems fully justified. Layard's own beliefs had by this time developed well beyond those of his healer and master, and seem to blend ideas derived from Rousseau, Blake, Wordsworth, Froebel, Freud, Lawrence, Grod- deck and no doubt others. The conviction expressed in Blake's epigram 'Sooner murder an infant in its cradle than nurse unacted desires' was developed into a full-blown theory of the evil effects of repression, especially in relation to the psychosomatic origins of disease. Physical illness was the result of psychic or moral disorder, and by a neat stroke each malady was appropriate to its cause, so that (as one of Auden's poems declares) the liar suffers from quinsy and (as another demonstrates at greater length) the sexually unfulfilled woman develops cancer. The great attrac- tion of this doctrine, of course, was that it authorised and indeed enjoined as a solemn duty the kind of acting out of desires in defiance of society and its conventions that Auden was in any case drawn to. Not to behave according to one's inner nature – the God, or good, within one – was to ask for trouble. It is obvious that Auden found these ideas intellectually exciting as well as personally convenient; they were not quickly cast off and have a prominent place in his early writings. Speaking of the develop- ment of his ideas in his *Letter to Lord Byron*, he remarks that 'Part came from Lane, and part from D. H. Lawrence;/ Gide, though I didn't know it then, gave part...', but makes no reference to Layard as the pimp or midwife of his intellectual love-affair with Lane.

During the months following their first meeting, Auden and Layard saw a good deal of each other, but the sexual and emotional elements quickly faded from their relationship – though perhaps more rapidly on Auden's side than on Layard's. Not only was Layard, now in his late thirties, an elder-brother- and almost a father-figure, but he must have been too much of Auden's own nation and class to be sexually stimulating at a period when Auden's sexual tastes seem to have run to brawny working-class foreigners. As time passed, moreover, the older man's charisma wore thin, perhaps because his own serious instability became more apparent. There are hints of discord in Auden's journal entries at this time: 'When J[ohn] disagrees with me he says "You're so young." But if I suggest to him that he is old, he is hurt.' There is evidence, too, that Layard, a man of private means and without career, vocation or occupation, was jealous of Auden's creative powers ('he hates my writing').

One of the earliest entries in Auden's journal catches the flavour of their relationship in the spring of 1929. Though still close, it did not prevent Auden from readily becoming bored and irritated by Layard's depressive state:

> Rather intimate with John. "I kept hoping you'd come and see me during the last two days" "O dear I was just longing to come" "But I never said anything to put you off coming?" "Yes you did. You said you wanted to work in the morning." Presently. "You've just got to get well. You're much too good a person to be like this." I was vilely insincere, because I don't care a hoot. I am ashamed of my laziness and so tell everyone how hard I work, and dislike them if they are lazy....

'Rather intimate' has been substituted for the deleted phrase 'I kissed'. By this stage, while fully recognising the contribution Layard has made to his own development, Auden is ready to admit, if only to his journal, that he no longer has any feelings for the older man. Layard was still, however, a sufficiently interesting figure for Isherwood to be taken to see him very soon after his arrival, an occasion on which, inevitably, Layard talked about Lane. The visit does not seem to have been repeated during Isherwood's time in Berlin.

Layard's mental health, meanwhile, was going from bad to worse. Both grieved and aggrieved by Lane's death, he had transferred his devotion to one of Lane's other patients, a young Italian woman, Etta da Viti, who was now living in Paris. Though he declared his love for her, however, she gave him no encouragement. A woman friend of Layard's from England, Margaret Gardiner, concerned at the news of his state, visited him in Berlin at Eastertime and, confronted with his suicide threats, heroically set off for Paris to find Etta in the hope of persuading her to come to Berlin. The Italian girl could not be found, however, and Margaret had to return to England.

With Auden's help, Margaret had moved Layard from his sordid lodgings into a hotel, but this did little or nothing for his state of mind, which was greatly worsened by the news of Margaret's failure. Nor was the situation helped by Layard's inability to rise to the occasion when Auden lent him his new boyfriend, Gerhart, for the night – though here again the two accounts differ (Gerhart, regrettably, does not seem to have kept a journal or written an autobiography). Auden's journal entry for 2 April, as already described, shows that he talked enthusiastically to Layard about Gerhart in the strong conviction that Layard would want to share him. Layard's retrospective account, on the other hand, says that he 'made up my mind to do the dirty on Wystan . . . . I knew this was a complete betrayal . . . ' In other words Auden laid claim to a generous gesture that might help to cheer up his friend, while Layard claims he took the initiative and seduced the boy behind his friend's back. In this instance one is perhaps more inclined to believe Auden's account, in any case much nearer the event, than the self-dramatising later one.

Auden had all along taken the strictly logical view that if Layard wanted to kill himself he should be allowed to get on with it: to do so would, after all, be no more than to act in the spirit of his belief in the essential rightness of one's inner impulses. What was to be done if the inner impulses of a friend urged a rescue operation was not quite clear. But soon Auden was to be forced into action when the situation took a genuinely dramatic turn. The day after his abortive attempt to enjoy Gerhart, Layard stuck a revolver in his mouth and pulled the trigger. A little earlier in the day, perhaps only a very short time before this deed was done, Auden had been with him, had found him entertaining thoughts of suicide, and had encouraged him to proceed. Auden had found himself quite unresponsive alike to Layard's kiss and to his tears, and soon left him alone and returned to his lodgings.

The method of self-destruction selected by Layard is not, it would seem, one that can be confidently counted on to fail, but it did: the revolver must have been pointed upwards, phallus-like, when it was fired, for the bullet made its way through the nasal passages and found a home in Layard's skull without doing serious damage to the brain. The wonders were not over, however, for on regaining consciousness Layard decided to call on Auden and ask him to finish the job he had so badly bungled. He crawled into a taxi, drove to his friend's lodgings, and climbed several flights of stairs, meeting on the way a couple of boys who seem also to have been heading for Auden's room. One of them helped him to Auden's door while the other went ahead to announce his arrival.

Layard's autobiography states that he had every confidence that Auden would comply with his wishes 'out of friendship', but

Auden declined and instead bundled him into another taxi and took him, through a snow-storm, to a hospital. In Auden's journal the events of this extraordinary day are recounted, with ostentatious brevity and detachment, in a few lines; his strongest feelings on being confronted with the injured man seem to have been of physical revulsion, and it was on the next day that he made the lightning decision to go to Hamburg with Gerhart.

Yet again there is a disparity between the versions given by the two principal actors in this drama. Layard's reproduction of the dialogue that allegedly took place when he appeared in Auden's room – ' "Wystan, I've done it.... But it hasn't killed me. Please finish me off – here's the pistol and ammunition".... "I'm terribly sorry, I know you want this, but I can't do it, because I might be hanged if I did...." ' – need be taken no more seriously than any other conversations reproduced after an interval of many years. But he also states quite unequivocally that he had 'never talked' to Auden about suicide, and this is clearly contradicted by Auden's journal, which there is no reason to disbelieve on this point.

An odd footnote to Layard's suicide attempt is provided by an anecdote recounted in Jonathan Fryer's 1992 biography of Isherwood. It seems that in 1926 and well before his Berlin period, Isherwood in a fit of depression also contemplated suicide, bought a pistol, and sought the advice of a friend as to the most efficacious method: 'He recommended sticking the gun into his mouth, and pointing it upwards towards the brain to inflict maximum damage' (p. 59). The unanswerable questions fairly leap at one: whether, if it actually happened, Auden knew of this and passed on to Layard the advice given by Isherwood's friend; whether Isherwood mentioned it to anyone before Layard's attempt, and, if not, whether the truth is that he incorporated Layard's experience as a heroic episode in the story of his own life, just as he incorporated a fictionalised version of it into *The Memorial*.

Layard's suicide attempt had taken place on 3 April, and when Auden returned to Berlin from Hamburg on the 6th he found that Layard's mother had arrived and they went to the hospital together. A few days later Mrs Layard called on him to discuss her son's future: her notion was that all would be well if he could contrive to fall in love with a nice girl, and Auden judged this a shrewd view of the situation. She also talked about Layard's childhood, and Auden recorded some of her remarks in his journal: ' "John was a model little boy until he was five. Almost too good.

Devoted to me. Too devoted according to these modern psycholo-gical ideas."' To this no doubt accurate diagnosis Auden adds: 'John tells me that when he was at school there was love (girls) and holy love (mother).' It was, of course, a subject in which Auden, another mother's boy, had a strong personal interest.

Later Auden took Gerhart to see Layard in hospital. On this occasion Auden's principal emotion was anxiety lest Gerhart should let slip the fact that they had gone off to Hamburg the day after Layard shot himself, while Gerhart's was distaste for the sight of physical weakness. The young sailor was convinced that Layard would die and, in an unusual flight of eloquence, declared that he would not sleep with him for a hundred marks. He could hardly have made his point more strongly. Gerhart's indifference seems to have acted as a reproach to Auden, who was fully aware of his own lack of response, and indeed his con-duct throughout this whole sorry affair is not easy to account for. As a doctor's son he might well have become accustomed to the idea of physical suffering in others, but he seems, on the evidence of the journal, to have taken pains to stress his total lack of horror or even concern. Layard's friendship had by now become some-thing of a burden to him, and Layard's withdrawal from the arena of his life in Berlin would not have been unwelcome, but this hardly seems enough to explain his behaviour. Perhaps the solu-tion is to be found in his all-consuming infatuation with Gerhart, then at its apogee.

Contrary to Gerhart's prediction, Layard made an excellent and surprisingly rapid recovery, and by 23 April was fit enough not only to accompany Auden to the Cosy Corner but to celebrate Shakespeare's birthday by going off, at Auden's suggestion, with one of the boys. Once again, however, his evening was not a great success, and the next morning he called on Auden to recount how he had got drunk and had collapsed in the lavatory so that, embarrassingly enough, the landlady had had to be summoned to show the boy out. He joined Auden and Isherwood in the Harz Mountains for a few days in July. Soon afterwards, like Auden, Layard left Berlin and returned to England. They remained friends, and Layard eventually married and found a career as a Jungian analyst. During the war he flourished briefly as an author, produ-cing a long-delayed account of his anthropological work (*Stone Men of Malekula: Vao*, 1942) as well as *The Lady of the Hare: Being a Study in the Healing Power of Dreams* in 1944.

Despite the turbulent emotions it involved, mainly on Layard's side, the real importance of their relationship is intellectual. Auden did not hesitate to communicate his enthusiasm for the doctrines expounded by Layard to others – notably to Isherwood, who must have heard about them during Auden's Christmas visit to England in 1928 and who met Layard when he went to Berlin in the spring of 1930. The revolver was fired only six days after Isherwood's departure, and it is conceivable that sexual jealousy experienced when Layard saw the two younger men together may have conspired with his sexual failure with Gerhart to precipitate his happily incompetent attempt to act – quite consistently with his own beliefs – upon his self-destructive impulse.

GERALD HAMILTON

Like Francis Turville-Petre, Gerald Frank Hamilton Souter, better known as Gerald Hamilton, seems to have offered himself almost importunately as literary copy; unlike Francis, however, he was always ready to take up the offer himself. Part of his special appeal for Isherwood may have been his knack of fictionalising his own life and rewriting his own past – colourful enough, it might have been thought, without further embellishment – in the terms of a romantic novelist (which, among much else, he was). Charlatan and trickster though he must be judged to have been, his conversational and literary escapades on the frontiers of autobiography and fiction must have formed a source of fascination to a writer who had made that border-territory his own special field of operations. In due course Hamilton not only provided the central figure in *Mr Norris Changes Trains* and some vivid pages in *Christopher and his Kind* but himself wrote of his life in Berlin and his relationship with Isherwood and others in a couple of autobiographical volumes. The first of these, *Mr Norris and I*, contains a brief but very interesting prologue by Isherwood.

Born in Shanghai of Irish parentage in 1889, he was 15 years older than Isherwood. His career, which had taken him to many parts of the world, was that of con man and fixer: as Isherwood says in *Christopher and his Kind*,

If you wanted to sell a stolen painting to a collector who didn't mind enjoying it in private, to smuggle arms into a foreign country, to steal a contract away from a rival firm, to be decorated with a medal of honour which you had done nothing to deserve, to get your criminal dossier extracted from the archives, then Gerald was delighted to try to help you, and he quite often succeeded. (p. 63)

His method was bribery, and for his pains he not only took a 'commission' but was also apt to run up a hefty expenses account. For his tastes were extravagant, and as a result he was chronically short of funds.

Over the years, Hamilton had served several prison sentences: two in England (one for gross indecency with a male person, the other for unpatriotic activities during the Great War), others on the Continent (there had been some unpleasantness in Italy over a pearl necklace). He had also published, pseudonymously, a homosexual novel titled *Desert Dreamers* (1914). But when Isherwood met him in the winter of 1930–1 Hamilton was passing through a rare period of respectable employment. Living in Frankfurt for a time, where an obliging contact found him work as a broadcaster, he had noticed that it was not easy to buy *The Times* in that major German city. He drew this fact to the attention of the London headquarters of the newspaper, and the outcome was his appointment as sales representative of *The Times* for Germany. His discharge of these duties obviously gave satisfaction, since a year later he was asked to open an office in Berlin, where he made his home in the Derflingerstrasse.

Hamilton's later reflections on his appointment are of interest. His curriculum vitae, if he ever had one, must have been colourful rather than confidence-inspiring if it was not entirely a work of fiction, but his dignified employers in Printing House Square seemed entirely uninterested in his past, and as he remarks blandly in *Mr Norris and I*, 'This serves to show with what ease anybody can to-day obtain a responsible position, no matter what his past life may have been'. He adds, more severely, that getting such a job so easily 'is only another illustration of the vast scale of hypocrisy upon which the standards of our civilisation really depend' (p. 122). His subsequent friendship with Guy Burgess provided him with a more sensational example of the phenomenon that provoked these moral reflections, and there cannot be much doubt that Hamilton's family connections, accent and social manner opened doors to him that his criminal record might have encouraged people to leave carefully locked.

Later *The Times* sacked him, the reason he himself gave being his involvement with the Communists in Germany. But before this time, in the winter of 1930-1, he had met Isherwood, who seems instantly to have spotted his fictional potential. Referring to the description of Mr Norris in the opening lines of *Mr Norris Changes Trains*, Isherwood later said that Hamilton and Norris were 'identical'. That description is strikingly detailed and vivid:

> My first impression was that the stranger's eyes were of an unusually light blue.... Startled and innocently naughty, they...were the eyes of a schoolboy surprised in the act of breaking one of the rules....
> His smile had great charm....
> His hands were white, small and beautifully manicured....
> He had a large blunt fleshy nose and a chin which seemed to have slipped sideways. It was like a broken concertina.... Above his ripe red cheeks, his forehead was sculpturally white, like marble. A queerly cut fringe of dark grey hair lay across it, compact, thick and heavy. After a moment's examination, I realized, with extreme interest, that he was wearing a wig.

(I give the description here as quoted, very selectively and with incomplete indications of omissions, in *Christopher and his Kind*.) If the 'extreme interest' was also Isherwood's reaction to his actual scrutiny of Hamilton, he may have had an intuition that the wig furnished a ready-made symbol for a basically dishonest personality.

In the course of time Isherwood introduced Hamilton to Auden, Spender and other friends, including E. M. Forster and Benjamin Britten. There was a notable gathering in 1935 when Isherwood and Heinz, Forster and his policeman-lover Bob Buckingham, Spender, Brian Howard, Klaus Mann and Hamilton all found themselves in Amsterdam at the same time. Hamilton himself was not short of friends, sometimes of a distinctly grander variety, and his memoirs are punctuated by frequent name-dropping. We can safely assume that his conversation was not dissimilar, and if the name in question had a scandalous or lurid reputation that was no deterrent. In the autobiographical *The Way It Was With Me*, published near the end of his life and repeating much material that had appeared earlier, he states that he first met Isherwood 'under the auspices of Alesteir [*sic*] Crowley' and thereafter saw him 'almost daily'

(p. 44). Whatever 'auspices' may mean, this seems to imply that Crowley effected the introduction, though Brian Finney's account is that Hamilton 'introduced Isherwood and Spender . . . to Aleister Crowley' (p. 86). Finney's version is presumably based upon an anecdote in Hamilton's earlier *Mr Norris and I*, which recounts a visit to Crowley 'with an English friend, Christopher Isherwood, whom I was seeing very often in Berlin at that time' (p. 126). Probably it does not much matter who introduced whom, but the discrepancy and the confusion are revealing: Hamilton is a most unreliable autobiographer and, after giving so many accounts of his own past to different people on different occasions, quite likely did not himself know what had really happened.

If the name to be dropped was royal or aristocratic, so much the better, and the following is, though sounding close to self-parody, representative: 'The late Tsar Ferdinand of Bulgaria, whose guest I was twice at Sofia when he was on the throne, and a third time at Coburg for the so-called Coburg wedding in October 1932, had been good enough to confer several decorations on me . . .' (*Mr Norris and I*, p. 39). The beauty of such claims, which seem to belong to the pre-1914 world of Saki's short stories, was that no one was likely to be in a position either to verify or contradict them. Probably, however, no one cared about doing so, for Hamilton's forte was that of the brilliantly entertaining dinner-guest, the Oscar Wilde of his time and place (for Isherwood and his friends he was 'enchantingly "period"'), and his outstanding charm and urbanity do not seem to have been in question. He would (the Wildean touch again) dress up to the nines even for some commonplace social occasion, and, as Isherwood says, would 'make you feel you were at a banquet' if the only fare available was scrambled eggs and *vin ordinaire*. Something of his camp stylishness and wit comes over in his writings, which, though diffuse and repetitive, can also be witty and self-mocking. Recounting (more than once) an anecdote about calling one day at the Nollendorfstrasse *pension* and being invited by Jean Ross to come and talk to her while she took her bath, he remarks: 'I have often maintained that I am the last of the Puritans, but have never found anybody yet to believe me' (*Mr Norris and I*, p. 44). In the same straight-faced spirit he can correct the rumour that he made 'a bid for peace' during the Second World War through the medium of the Papal Nuncio – it was, he insists, actually through 'the late Duke of Bedford' (conveniently late, one suspects) – and anyway, he adds primly, there is no Papal Nuncio in England, only an Apostolic

Delegate. The technique of mendacity is not often displayed with such brilliance. He adds that his plan to escape to Ireland disguised as a nun was frustrated by his arrest 'before I had even got my coif in place' (pp. 38–9).

Given Isherwood's habit of drawing heavily on his real-life 'originals' while retaining the freedom to depart from them when he chose, we are bound to wonder about the nature of Hamilton's relationship to the character who was in some sense 'based' on him. Both he and Isherwood have in fact made explicit comments on this point, though well-advised scepticism towards the teller of a tale ought in this case to be extended to his model. Introducing *Mr Norris and I*, Isherwood began by saying that when he was asked whether Mr Norris was 'based on' Hamilton, 'Sometimes I answer "No" to this question, sometimes "Yes" – according to my mood and the suspected motives of the questioner. Neither answer is more than partially true'. He goes on to stress the fact that the fictional character and the 'old friend' who has written the book he is introducing differ in a number of respects:

> Just imagine poor Gerald trying to participate in the impossibly melodramatic plots of Mr. Norris and his fellow-conspirators! His prudent and fastidious nature would shrink in horror from such irresponsible antics. Just imagine Mr. Norris daring to substitute himself as host at one of Gerald's inimitable lunches! His attempts at conversation would expose him instantly as a puppet who had lost his ventriloquist.

This may well have been true, and truly meant, but one has a sense that, for entirely understandable and honourable reasons, Isherwood was concerned to play down the resemblance during Hamilton's lifetime. Certainly the account of Hamilton's personality given in *Christopher and his Kind*, written after Hamilton's death, is markedly different in tone:

> Good old, bad old Gerald! ...
> Gerald didn't look evil, but, beneath his amiable surface, he was an icy cynic. He took it for ganted that everybody would grab and cheat if he dared. His cynicism made him astonishingly hostile towards people of whom he was taking some advantage; at unguarded moments, he would speak of them with brutal contempt....
>   (pp. 61, 63)

This suggests that the fictional portrait softened the hard edges of the real adventurer, making comic and endearing what was actually rather unpleasant and sinister. For Mr Norris is a terrible bungler, lacking the nerve and the *savoir-faire* that seem to have characterised Hamilton. The most important discrepancy, however, is frankly admitted in *Christopher and his Kind*: the homosexuality that was 'the most enduring bond' between them is not bestowed on Mr Norris except in innuendoes so discreet that some readers have missed them entirely. As we shall see in the later discussion of the novel, there is a radical ambiguity, evasiveness and unsatisfactoriness about the depiction of Norris's sexual nature. This had no counterpart in Hamilton's own life, as Isherwood very well knew.

Hamilton himself took kindly to the celebrity that the novel bestowed upon him, and lived up to and exploited his transformation into a picaresque hero. He even published in the *Spectator* (4 November 1955) a letter from 'Mr Norris' to his creator, in which the supposed writer refers to himself as 'your poor friend Arthur Norris'. This was, of course, no more than following Isherwood's own example in creating a fictional character called Christopher. His book *Mr Norris and I*, though it deals with a great many topics other than his friendship with Isherwood, bears a title that exploits the literary labours of the man who had, as he said near the end of his life, 'now been a friend of mine for nearly forty years'.

The latter phrase appears in his autobiographical volume of 1969, which reproduces an article he published in *Punch* on 17 November 1954 with the Wildean title 'The Importance of not being Norris'. The ostensible purpose of this was to deny the stories of him as a model for Norris:

> I do not know how the rumour got around. Christopher Isherwood always said that It was a composite character, and although many of my *obiter dicta* were put into the mouth of Mr Norris, I must once and for all decline to admit any closer resemblance, much as I admire the enchanting hero of so successful a novel. The rumour started when I lived in the same pension as Isherwood did in pre-Hitler Berlin.... (p. 37)

(Elsewhere, incidentally, Hamilton denies ever living in Fräulein Thurau's *pension* and cheekily, or perhaps innocently, attributes the incorrect report to Isherwood.) A few pages later, however, he is 'ready to admit... that there is much of me in the character of Mr Norris (not, I hasten to say, in the sex life of that worthy), in his manner of speech, his reluctance to face the issue, that would fit a description of me at that very distant Berlin period' (p. 40). One can only conclude that when it suited him Hamilton was quite prepared to admit, or claim, that 'Mr Norris, c'est moi'.

Ultimately, though, it would be foolish to look for consistency in one who was by nature and vocation incorrigibly deceptive and unreliable. Isherwood's final verdict on him in *Christopher and his Kind* is clear-eyed and even-handed, but in reaching an estimation of his 'misdeeds' and finding them after all 'tiresome rather than amusing' he to some extent returns to his earlier non-judgemental manner. Perhaps Hamilton offered a valuable lesson to a writer of fiction as one whose character seemed to have no stability: just when we think we have made up our minds about him, some piece of evidence turns up – for instance, his substantial and perfectly genuine efforts on behalf of various charities and campaigns for social reform – that compels us to readjust the picture.

A Vicar of Bray on a European scale, Hamilton was variously a Communist, a Catholic convert, and whatever else it suited him for the time being to be. Forster wrote to Isherwood on 28 February 1944 saying that he had declined to see Hamilton again after hearing that he was 'violently anti-Semite', but added: 'I ought to examine his depths for myself, since I got amusement out of his shallows in the continental days. Occasionally, when I have been where perhaps I shouldn't, I have been conscious of him through the reek'. Hamilton's depths might have turned out to be terrible to contemplate, but his shallows undoubtedly added to the gaiety of nations, and in portraying Mr Norris Isherwood remained cautiously close to the surface.

Two details from the post-Berlin years show Hamilton as a continuing source of innocent merriment. In 1937 Isherwood, who should have known better but was obviously at his wits' end over the safety of his lover, paid him a thousand pounds to arrange for a Mexican passport to be supplied to Heinz, who would be conscripted if he returned to Germany and for whom Isherwood was anxious to secure some suitable citizenship. The money was accepted but the passport never materialised. And it was a nice touch that, according to Jonathan Fryer (1992, p. 82), Hamilton's 'ultimate coup was to sit as a model for part of a memorial statue to Winston Churchill, who was of similar bulk'. Joe Orton, one feels, might have made something out of this, just as Waugh or Firbank might have made something of Hamilton's life and adventures. But then it seemed to be Isherwood's fate, or instinct, to be drawn to characters well qualified to sit as life models.

4

The Other Camera – Aspects of Weimar Cinema

Though Auden's involvement with the cinema was less intense and sustained than Isherwood's, his journal makes it clear that he was in the habit of frequently dropping into a 'kino' during his residence in Germany. Almost the first entry in the journal records that he went with John Layard to the cinema (where both, for unexplained reasons, were sick). As we have seen already, he took Gerhart there during the visit to Hamburg, an occasion on which Gerhart's girl friend completed an uneasy threesome, and it had been his failure to gain admission to the house that was showing May's *Asphalt* that had led to his first meeting with Gerhart. Humphrey Carpenter has noted that Auden 'greatly admired contemporary German cinema', and like Isherwood he was later to be professionally associated with the medium.

As for Isherwood, he seems to have had a lifelong love affair with the cinema. 'I had always been fascinated by films,' he confesses in his early autobiography, *Lions and Shadows*, and he admitted to an interviewer in the 1970s that he had 'an enormous passion for film'. In Berlin he was in the right place, at the right time, to witness some of the most exciting contemporary developments in that medium. He would have had access there to a cinematic art both more experimental and more outspoken than its British or American counterparts, and it would have been strange if his profound interest in a non-literary narrative medium had not had some influence on his writing.

By his own account he saw his first film at the age of 12 – that would have been in 1916 – and by the time he was an undergraduate was already a confirmed film fan. According to his biographer Brian Finney, at one stage he was going to the cinema several times a week as well as reading at least three film magazines weekly. *Lions and Shadows*, in its account of the manifold distractions from serious study, contains a vivid sentence evoking the atmosphere of a film show in the 1920s: 'There were the flicks with the films which were, even in those days, not silent, because the audience supplied the popping of champagne corks, the puffing of trains, the sound of horses' hooves and the kisses' (p. 64). At Cambridge he joined the recently established Film Club, and according to Jonathan Fryer, when Edward Upward laughed at his 'indiscriminate love of the movies', Isherwood explained it in terms of 'a fascination for the outward appearance of people'. It was a remark that could subsequently have formed an article of his creed as a writer, and is confirmed by another passage in *Lions and Shadows*:

I was, and still am, endlessly interested in the outward appearance of people – their facial expressions, their gestures, their walk, their nervous tricks, their infinitely various ways of eating a sausage, opening a paper parcel, lighting a cigarette. The cinema puts people under a microscope: you can stare at them, you can examine them as though they were insects. True, the behaviour you see on the screen isn't natural behaviour; it is acting, and often very bad acting, too. But the acting has always a certain relation to ordinary life; and, after a short while, to an *habitué* like myself, it is as little of an annoyance as Elizabethan handwriting is to the expert in old documents. Viewed from this standpoint, the stupidest film may be full of astonishing revelations about the tempo and dynamics of everyday life: you see how actions look in relation to each other; how much space they occupy and how much time. Just as it is easier to remember a face if you imagine its two-dimensional reflection in a mirror; so, if you are a novelist and want to watch your scene taking place visibly before you, it is simplest to project it on to an imaginary screen. A practised cinema-goer will be able to do this quite easily.   (pp. 85–6)

This acknowledged fascination with the visible details of the 'everyday', like the voyeuristic stance, applies as much to the novelist as to the cinema-goer. It is not surprising, therefore, that photographic and cinematic terms offer themselves naturally when Isherwood's writing is being discussed – a tendency encouraged by Isherwood himself. In *Lions and Shadows* he compares the episodic structure of some of his fiction to 'an album of snapshots', though (as Finney observes) he might equally well have made the comparison with cinematic 'takes'.

During his Cambridge period he not only watched films but had aspirations, never to be realised, to direct them. He was also, briefly and unmemorably, a film actor. At the Film Club he heard a talk by George Pearson (1875–1973), one of the leading British producers and directors of the period, took up Pearson's invitation to visit his studios in London, and spent a day, 'dressed up as a midshipman', as a paid extra on the set, though when the film was shown he was not to be seen. After quitting Cambridge with panache and ignominy, he applied, unsuccessfully, for jobs in two British film studios. Not long afterwards he conceived a long-distance passion for the child star, Jackie Coogan (born 1914), who had become famous as a result of his appearance in Chaplin's *The Kid* (1920). Isherwood claimed to have seen him in *Oliver Twist* (1922) seven times. His ironic self-awareness, already well established at this early date, is revealed in a letter to Upward written early in 1923, in which, admitting his addiction to the infant Coogan, he comments that 'I think paederastia is the lowest state of the human soul and the Film Industry the nadir of Commercial Prostitution'.

In Berlin he continued to indulge his enthusiasm for what the generation would have called the silver screen, and in his Californian old age would recall with pleasure the films, stars and directors he had long ago admired, many of whom – Fritz Lang, G. W. Pabst, Louise Brooks, Werner Krauss, Conrad Veidt, Peter Lorre and others – had by then taken their place in the histories of cinema. During the Berlin years, references to cinema visits in the company of Auden and Spender are on record. In Spender's *The Temple*, the character (William) based on Isherwood applauds the cinematic riches on offer in the city: ' "There are terrific Russian movies by the producers of films like *Ten Days That Shook the World*, *Potemkin*, *Earth*, *Mother*, *Menschenarsenal*, *Turkish*. There are also marvellous German movies by directors such as Pabst. *M* is hair-raising and *Kameradschaft* stupendous" ' (p. 192).

It was in fact with Spender that Isherwood saw Pabst's now classic *Kameradschaft* when it appeared in 1931. As he relates in *Christopher and his Kind*, 'when the tunnel caved in and the miners were trapped, he had thought: "That makes Virginia Woolf look pretty silly." ' With his boyfriend Bubi, as he recounts in the same volume, he saw Pudovkin's *Storm over Asia* and Wedekind's *Pandora's Box*, and at some stage he saw the 1926 silent version of Henrik Galeen's *Der Student von Prag* (*The Student of Prague*), starring Conrad Veidt and Werner Krauss. The last of these became a particular favourite. One of Isherwood's early viewings of *Der Student von Prag* was in Auden's company, and when they came to collaborate on a play, *The Enemies of a Bishop*, one of the characters was based, according to Isherwood, on a figure in the film.

In the Berlin stories, some of his characters are cinema-goers: '"Let's go to the cinema,"' says Christopher to Sally Bowles, and in the 'Landauers' section of *Goodbye to Berlin* Natalia asks Christopher whether he has seen René Clair's 1930 film *Sous les toits de Paris*. After he had left Germany, Isherwood was to write a novel, *Prater Violet* (1946), about the making of a film, to work in the Hollywood film industry and to win international fame through the screen versions of his Berlin stories. In an interview published in 1961 he stated that he 'had my first training in writing movies before I even wrote *The Last of Mr Norris* (the American title of *Mr Norris Changes Trains*)', and that 'what the movies taught me was visualisation'.

The camera with which the narrator of one of those stories famously identifies himself could thus even more appropriately have been a movie camera, and both Isherwood and Auden seem to have embraced what has since become an accepted part of the cultural world of young intellectuals: in a generation in which a traditional literary or 'high' culture was still dominant, they were representatives of a broadening of tastes and sympathies to include popular culture and the mass media. Possibly, though, they were not all that exceptional in their time, for a contemporary of Auden's is on record as having referred starchily to 'the gramophonic, cinematographic life of the Oxford set'.

This made it as natural for them to refer to a cinematic as to a literary text in their everyday discourse, and probably they were the first generation to do so. Thus, writing to Naomi Mitchison in 1932 and describing Ottershaw College, where he wished (in vain) to find employment, Auden described it as 'the buggers dream; a cross between Mädchen in Uniform and The Castle' – Leontine Sagan's lesbian film of the previous year coming as readily to mind as Kafka's novel published six years earlier. In a similar way, it occurs naturally to Isherwood, recalling the youthful Stephen Spender in his autobiography, to say that he 'illuminated you like an expressionist producer, with the crudest and most eccentric of spot-lights'. Yet again, in analysing his own youthful behaviour in *Christopher and his Kind* (p. 48), he suggests that he possessed 'a remarkable power of dramatising his predicament at any given moment, so that you experienced it *as though you were watching a film* in which you yourself had a part' (italics added). On the same page he refers to his own characteristic youthful habit of holding the hands 'extended, slightly apart from the body' as 'unconsciously copied ... from the pose of a fighter in a western movie who is just about to draw his guns'.

Isherwood's first experience of working for the film industry (if we set aside his brief inglorious undergraduate acting career mentioned above) came after he had left Berlin but before the writing of his Berlin novels. In October 1933, through the not quite disinterested agency of Jean Ross, he was hired by Gaumont-British Studios to work on a film called *Little Friend*, directed by Berthold Viertel. Viertel, an Austrian Jew, had moved from Vienna to Hollywood but had been invited to England to make three films for Gaumont-British. He was sufficiently impressed by what he read of *The Memorial*, and perhaps also by Isherwood's command of German, to offer him a job that kept him intensively occupied during that winter. Viertel was a friend of Greta Garbo, as Isherwood himself in later years became, and this contact, at one remove, with the magic world of Hollywood must have been exhilarating.

Later Viertel appeared as Friedrich Bergmann in Isherwood's short novel *Prater Violet*, a work for which its author had a high regard. (He told Denis Hart in 1961 that he considered it superior to his other early novels: 'I think it penetrated the character more', whereas 'I feel a certain coldness, an aloofness, in my attitude to the other characters.') But a more immediate by-product of the several months Isherwood spent working on the writing and shooting of *Little Friend* was a radical change in his conception of literary style and technique. As he told a lecture audience in 1975, working in a film studio 'You have suddenly the most tremendous sense of immediacy, from being a kind of introvert, shut up in this room, you're terrifically extroverted.... I think this had a lasting effect on me, starting with *Mr Norris....* I took to hearing much more clearly what the speeches would sound like that people said' (quoted by Finney, p. 105). It is probably no exaggeration to claim, as Finney does, that this experience 'permanently affected his writing'. Certainly there is a marked and lasting shift in style and technique as one turns from the first two published novels, in which the hand (or Woolf's paw) of Modernism lies heavy, to the books that followed.

Isherwood's time in Berlin came near the end of the finest period in the history of the German cinema. It is a period that has recently received a considerable amount of attention, and Patrice Petro's feminist account of Weimar culture with special reference to the evidence of its films opens with the declaration that 'It would be difficult to name any other period or nation in film history that has sustained such elaborate and sophisticated analysis as the Weimar cinema'. The eruption of creative energy (much of it drained away in the latter half of the period through emigration), in the context of a society that fluctuated between permissiveness and censorship in a rapidly changing social and economic climate, has indeed proved seductive to cultural historians, and for 'elaborate and sophistic- ated' one must sometimes regretfully substitute 'self-indulgent and silly'. It is true, nevertheless, that many of the films of the period that are still remembered seem to dramatise one aspect or another of a society in crisis – and this whether they are overtly didactic and propagandist (as many are) or not.

At the same time it is as well to remember that the films dis- cussed by historians of the cinema constitute only a tiny proportion of what was a very large output, and even the dedicated cinema- goer of the period would have been much less aware than we are of the emphases and tendencies that any present-day account is likely to delineate. As Lotte H. Eisner points out in *The Haunted Screen*, 'the films nowadays denoted as German classics were in their day exceptional, and swamped by the spate of commercial films' (p. 309).

Thus, in the period that immediately followed the Armistice, there was an overwhelming and entirely understandable appetite for escapist cinema in the form of costume dramas such as Ernst Lubitsch's *Carmen* (1917) and *Madame Dubarry* (1919). Simultan- eously, however, with the brief lifting of film censorship in 1918 came a vogue for a very different kind of film: one that undertook the exploration of the social implications of sexual 'problems' such as prostitution or homosexuality. Ostensibly educational, these productions could also provide an acceptable variety of soft porno- graphy. The brief postwar vogue for what came to be known as *Aufklärungs Filme* (instructive or enlightening films) was not entirely without precedent in Germany, for in 1917 Richard Oswald's *Es Werde Licht* (*Let There Be Light*) had dealt with the subject of syphilis, while 1919 saw the release of the same director's *Prostitution* as well as the most celebrated example of this genre, *Anders Als die Andern* (*Different from the Others*), which is usually cited as the first film to deal extensively with homosexuality.

It tells the story of a famous violinist who is blackmailed, ruined and driven to suicide following a homosexual encounter, and is based on a real-life tragedy, that of the violinst Paul Körner. Its moral (to which Vito Rosso devotes an interesting page in his study of homosexuality in the cinema, *The Celluloid Closet*) is that similar tragedies will occur unless the law criminalising homosexual behaviour is changed. Magnus Hirschfeld's appearance in the film has already been mentioned. Although, inevitably in its period, the acting and direction now seem to be afflicted by a painful slow-motion hamminess, the film still possesses a certain crude power. But the church, the press and the conservative public were outraged at the sympathetic and even romantic treatment of such a distasteful and politically explosive theme, bitter controversy ensued, and despite Hirschfeld's best efforts the film was banned in August 1920. When it was re-released in the more tolerant climate of seven years later, it was in an expurgated form in which Hirschfeld's part had disappeared.

The leading role in *Anders Als die Andern* is played by Conrad Veidt, whose career, both curious and paradigmatic, deserves the passing tribute of summary mention. He is now more readily remembered for his association with several other widely discussed films of the silent German cinema, and especially his haunting and spidery portrayal of the wide-eyed somnambulist, clad in skin-tight black, stalking the rooftops in high-wire, high camp style in *Das Cabinett des Dr Caligari* (also 1919). And it is his early career in Germany rather than his subsequent years in Hollywood that has now made him something of a gay icon. At any rate he has in recent years received a good deal of attention, including an impressive exhibition at a Berlin gay museum in 1993 to commemorate the centenary of his birth.

Isherwood spotted Veidt's iconic quality at a Christmas all-male costume ball he attended a few weeks after arriving in Berlin: at least it emerges in his much later account in *Christopher and his Kind*, where he describes Veidt's 'dazzling' presence among the drag queens and other exotics (Isherwood himself went dressed, very convincingly and not unrevealingly, as a working-class hustler): 'The great film star sat apart at his own table, impeccable in evening tails. He watched the dancing benevolently through his monocle as he sipped champagne and smoked a cigarette in a long holder. He seemed a supernatural figure, the guardian god of these festivities, who was graciously manifesting himself to his devotees.'

Trained in the Max Reinhardt Theatre School, Veidt had begun as a stage actor but turned to the films in 1916 and made unforgettable appearances in *Caligari* and *Der Student von Prag* (1926); less memorably, he also starred in some of the popular costume dramas of the epoch, playing Nelson in *Lady Hamilton* (1921) as well as Cesare Borgia, Paganini and Rasputin in subsequent productions. Quitting Germany in the early 1930s, he spent some years in England, appearing in Alexander Korda's *The Thief of Baghdad* as well as in *Rome Express* and *Jew Süss* (this latter based on Feuchtwanger's 1925 novel), and playing opposite Vivien Leigh in *Dark Journey*. Veidt became a British citizen in 1939 but in the following year emigrated a second time, to Hollywood, where he specialised in playing Nazi officers until a heart attack killed him on a California golf-course in 1943. It was a long journey, from the anxiety-ridden homosexual of *Anders Als die Andern* to the suave German officer of *Casablanca*, and a reminder of how far the cinema had come, and what it had foregone, in a quarter of a century.

The problem with films like *Anders Als die Andern* is that the motives behind them could be, and have been, readily and even wilfully misunderstood. A curiously hostile account of this chapter in the history of the postwar German cinema is given in Siegfried Kracauer's standard work *From Caligari to Hitler: A Psychological History of the German Film*. Kracauer writes:

When, immediately after the war, the Council of People's Representatives abolished censorship – a measure revealing that government's confused ideas about revolutionary exigencies – the effect was not a transformation of the screen into a political platform, but a sudden increase of films which pretended to be concerned with sexual enlightenment. Now that they had nothing to fear from official supervision, they all indulged in a copious depiction of sexual debaucheries. Refreshed by the atmosphere of freedom, Richard Oswald felt in so creative a mood that he ... made a film called PROSTITUTION. Scores of similar products swarmed out under such alluring titles as VON RANDE DES SUMPFES (FROM THE VERGE OF THE SWAMP), FRAUEN, DIE DER ABGRUND VERSCHLINGT (WOMEN

ENGULFED BY THE ABYSS), VERLORENE TÖCHTE (LOST DAUGHTERS), HYÄNEN DER LUST (HYENAS OF LUST), and so forth. One of them, GELÜBDE DER KEUCHHEIT (VOW OF CHASTITY) intermingled pictures detailing the love affairs of a Catholic priest with shots of devotees reciting the rosary for the sake of the priest's soul. Two other films, significantly entitled AUS EINES MANNES MÄDCHENJAHREN (A MAN'S GIRLHOOD) and ANDERS ALS DIE ANDERN (DIFFERENT FROM THE OTHERS), dwelt upon homosexual propensities; they capitalised on the noisy resonance of Dr. Magnus Hirschfeld's campaign against Paragraph 175 of the penal code which exacted punishment for certain abnormal sex practices.

This indiscrimate lumping together, in a respected scholarly work, of high motives and commercial opportunism is, to say the least, unedifying and unworthy.

In any case their period of flowering in the immediate postwar years was very brief. David Shipman has said that such films 'would have been unthinkable in any other national cinema at the time', and they soon became officially unthinkable in Germany, for the censorship was reintroduced in 1920 and the harsh realism of social propaganda yielded to entirely different styles. *Caligari* belongs to the opening phase of a period of Expressionism in the German cinema that lasted until Murnau's *Der Letzte Mann* (literally *The Last Man*, but usually known as *The Last Laugh*) in 1924. According to Roger Manvell and Heinrich Fraenkel's history of the German cinema, *Caligari* was anticipated by Martin's *Von Morgens bis Mitternacht* (*From Morning to Midnight*) earlier in the same year. (Isherwood was surely recalling *Caligari* when, years later in Hollywood, he was working on the script of a film based on James Hilton's novel *Rage of Heaven* and suggested the addition of a prologue in which a doctor explained that the protagonist had spent a period in a lunatic asylum.)

'Expressionism' is not a very precise term in this context – as Manvell and Fraenkel observe, it 'became a generic term for many different forms of experiment and protest against convention' – but the significant point is that such films engaged in an exploration of psychological rather than social and legal problems. It has been said of the early 1920s in Germany that 'no films of the time attempted to come to terms with postwar social reality', and this is the one factor shared by the Expressionist classics and the forgotten romantic or nationalistic costume dramas.

Perhaps we should not be surprised that, in an era of crisis, when traumatic defeat and revolution were followed by political and economic instability and mass unemployment, the last thing cinema-goers demanded was films holding up a mirror to current issues. Lotte Eisner, however, has detected darker forces than consumer demand at work, and has suggested that post-Versailles Germany 'seemed impregnated by an overwhelming sense of fatalism which was transformed into a violent art'. Certainly a film such as *Caligari* can still move and shock not only by its physical violence and its lurid images but by its invocation of a world in which ordinary values and even the sense of everyday reality are called into question.

The stabilisation of the German currency at the end of 1924 encouraged American companies to buy cinemas in Germany and to show therein a large proportion of Hollywood films, a policy that soon led to the introduction of a quota system that required every imported film shown to be matched by a German production. This, combined with the rapidly growing prosperity of the second half of the decade, produced a general expansion of the cinema industry. In 1927 Germany produced 241 feature films, compared with America's 743, France's 74, and Britain's 44. By 1929 there were 5,078 cinemas in Germany, compared with 3,731 in 1920, and German film-making continued on a larger scale than that of any other European country.

Almost as soon as recovery was perceived, the cinema began to confront the issues it had eschewed during the period of crisis. Thus a film such as Pabst's *Die Freudlose Gasse* (*Joyless Streets*, 1925) depicts in painfully harsh terms the sufferings of a time that had only just begun to pass away. This remarkable film set a fashion for social-problem cinema that came to be known as the *Neue Sachlichkeit* (New Objectivity) and has its counterpart in contemporary painting – though again it is as well to stress that any map we now draw of the cinema of the period might look very strange to a surviving cinema-goer with a good memory, for the available menu was large and varied.

Die Freudlose Gasse is interesting in a number of ways, including the fact that it is Greta Garbo's only German film. It belongs to a minor tradition of 'street' films and was preceded by Karl Grune's *Die Strasse* (*The Street*) of 1923. Such productions, according to

Eisner, epitomise 'the Germanic visions of the street and the obsession with dimly lit staircases and corridors'. Literary precedents and analogues for such stories of the lives of the denizens of a poverty-stricken neighbourhood are not difficult to find and go back a long way: in English one thinks, for instance, of the mainly London-based slum fiction of the turn of the century such as Arthur Morrison's *Tales of Mean Streets* (1894), Somerset Maugham's unexpected first novel *Liza of Lambeth* (1897) and Jack London's powerful *The People of the Abyss* (1903). Without being firmly situated within this literary-cinematic genre, Isherwood's *Goodbye to Berlin* shares some of its characteristics, though in a form that is sanitised and somewhat sentimentalised, at once more ironic and less committed.

That such films present, as Eisner points out, a specifically *Germanic* vision becomes clear by comparison with Anglo-American productions of the interwar period. *Die Freudlose Gasse* belongs to the same year as *The Gold Rush*, but the tramps, waifs and blind girls of Chaplin's great period seem cosily sentimentalised beside the brutal realism of the German production. Chaplin knew about poverty from firsthand experience, as the early portion of his autobiography makes clear. Therein, perhaps, lies a clue, for the account, from the standpoint of great wealth and fame, of a childhood that at times approached the edge of destitution has some Dickensian touches, and the Dickens tradition of viewing the poor as endearing or funny (when they are not squalid or criminal) dies very hard and is in fact still very much alive in, for example, a good deal of television enjoyed by middle-class audiences today.

A little later, a British film such as that based on Walter Greenwood's stark novel *Love on the Dole* displays a similar sanitising, even more grossly apparent in the marketing during the Depression of the Lancashire mill-girl Gracie Fields. It may be revealing that one of her most popular films, *Sing As We Go* (1934), was scripted by J. B. Priestley, a middle-brow novelist of the Dickensian tradition. Priestley also knew about poverty, at least as a conscientious observer, for his *English Journey*, which appeared in the same year as *Sing As We Go*, offers a still graphic account of unemployment and hardship in the north of England during these terrible years; the book owes something to Cobbett and in turn influenced Orwell's *The Road to Wigan Pier*. One of 'Our Gracie's' best-known songs (one has difficulty in thinking of the heroine of *Die Freudlose Gasse* as 'Our Greta') celebrated the solidarity and warmth of working-class life: '... don't ever wander / Away from the alley and me.' It is a very different vision of the mean streets of a slum neighbourhood from that given by Pabst's film, and perhaps this is saying no more than that the best German cinema did not readily capitulate, as Anglo-American productions usually did, to the commercial pressures of audience demand for escapism and comforting illusion.

Though set in Vienna, *Die Freudlose Gasse* clearly reflects very recent German experience. It depicts the gradual ruin of middle-class families by runaway inflation: dearly held values and even common decencies are abandoned in the face of the daily struggle to survive on the most primitive level of satisfying hunger, and the daughter (a leading role played by the 20-year-old Garbo) is driven to prostitution. Its stars included Werner Krauss, Asta Neilsen and the popular cabaret artist Valeska Gent (who plays the madame of a brothel), but its uncompromising realism led to its being banned in England and being shown only in heavily expurgated versions in France, Italy and elsewhere.

Near the beginning of the film there occurs an extraordinary scene in a butcher's shop – an almost inevitable locale, for in a starving world the butcher (played by Krauss) is the all-powerful tyrant. For hours women have been queuing in the freezing streets to await his pleasure and thankfully receive whatever he may condescend to sell them. When the virginal middle-class girl (played by Garbo) enters, there is a highly charged atmosphere of sexuality: Beauty and the Beast in a grimly contemporary, post-Freudian setting. The butcher is physically gross and obviously brutal as well as lustful; he smokes the largest cigar anyone has ever seen, and though there are times when a cigar is just a cigar this is not one of them. He is also accompanied by a fierce dog that competes with the intimidated customers for the offerings of raw flesh. At one point the butcher slices a piece of meat off a carcase and thrusts it, unwrapped, at the young girl; when she shrinks away from taking the piece of flesh into her hand – and for a startling moment one is aware that it is not just butcher's meat that she is being invited to grasp – he tosses it at the dog. As Paul Coates says of *Der Blaue Engel* five years later, it is all blatantly Freudian; it also underlines the dependence of the silent cinema, at least when it was trying to say anything significant, on a symbolism that could not easily avoid paying the price of heavy-handedness for its undeniably telling effects.

Pabst's subsequent films include *Die Büchse von Pandora* (*Pandora's Box*, also known as *Lulu*, 1928), in which the American actress Louise Brooks plays the prostitute. This was first shown in Berlin in February 1929, while Auden was living in the city. Apparently Pabst had plans to turn his attention next to the Heinrich Mann novel that became in other hands the basis of *Der Blaue Engel*, and Coates has speculated that the 'male masochism of these films is that of a self-consciously disadvantaged Germany'. Perhaps so, though I shall argue when we turn to *Der Blaue Engel* that other readings are possible. First, however, it will be as well to outline other developments in German cinema in the second half of the 1920s.

It was, in the cinema as well as in other respects, a decade of contrasts and dislocations. As already noted, the immediate postwar period witnessed both romantic and escapist costume dramas and treatments of social problems unmatched for candour anywhere in the world at that time, while the next few years saw the brief vogue of Expressionism succeeded by the social-problem cinema of the *Neue Sachlichkeit*. Dreyer's *Michael* (1924), for instance, had continued the minor tradition of films dealing with homosexuality, a theme again in evidence in Wilhelm Dieterle's *Geschlecht in Fessen* (1928). Dieterle went to Hollywood in 1929 and directed some classic 'biopics' or biographical films. One of these, *Dr Ehrlich's Magic Bullet* (1940), is notable for contriving, within the commercial and censorial context of Hollywood, to handle the story of the search by a German-Jewish scientist (played by Edward G. Robinson) for a cure for syphilis. The opening scene, in which a young patient commits suicide after his condition is diagnosed, has in its melodrama, its lighting and its solemn didacticism a strong flavour of the German cinema of the 1920s.

Some of the preoccupations of *Die Freudlose Gasse* recur in the 1929 film *Mutter Krauses Fahrt ins Gluck* (*Mother Kraus's Journey to Happiness*), directed by Phil Jutzi. Set in the slums of Berlin, it portrays the downfall of a respectable family under the pressure of circumstances as the daughter is seduced, the son arrested for debt and the mother finds 'happiness' in suicide. Such treatments of the life of the poor, including the new poor, contrast jarringly with the apolitical nonchalance of Auden's bourgeois boast about 'going to live in a slum' and Isherwood's brief spell with the family of 'Otto', whose living conditions are presented without indignation or even concern in 'The Nowaks'. Washing in the kitchen sink and peeing in a bucket may have charms provided they are under-taken voluntarily and for a strictly limited period.

By this point – the year of Jutzi's film being also one in which both Auden and Isherwood were in Berlin – the brief boom had been succeeded by the depression following the collapse of the world's stock markets. It was natural, therefore, that concern with contemporary issues should carry over into early sound films such as Pabst's *Die Dreigroschenoper* (*The Threepenny Opera*, based on Brecht and Weill's theatrical success of 1929), Leontine Sagan's *Mädchen in Uniform* (*Girls in Uniform*), Fritz Lang's *M* and Pabst's *Kameradschaft* (*Comradeship*), all belonging to 1931.

Before the end of the 1920s, however, restrictions on the freedom of the cinema were becoming more acute. From about 1927 the Nazi influence was being felt both positively and negatively, through greater emphasis on propaganda films and also through organised demonstrations against those films deemed to be ideo-logically unsound. Attempts to prevent the showing of Pabst's powerful anti-war film *Westfront 1918* (1930), based on Remarque's novel, were not successful, but its American counterpart of the same year, Milestone's *All Quiet on the Western Front*, was banned after an organised riot outside the cinema. The foundation in 1929 of the Deutsche Liga für Unabhängigen Filme (German League for Independent Films) was an attempt to counteract these increasing pressures, but Hitler's rise to power and the Nazi victory in the 1933 elections were closely followed by the establishment of the Reichsfilmkammer as a branch of the Kulturkammer (Ministry of Propaganda) responsible for controlling the film industry and exploiting its propaganda potential. Goebbels had long been interested in the medium of cinema and had grasped the simple but not always obvious truth that propaganda disguised as entertainment may be more effective than straight propaganda. The subsequent work of Leni Riefenstahl in particular was to demonstrate that it was possible for political and aesthetic concerns to coexist.

Before 1933, the left-wing resistance to National Socialist pres-sures had resulted in a number of films intended to counteract the cinematic glorification of nationalism, militarism and war. Pabst, Piscator and others had set up the Volksverbund für Filmkunst (People's Alliance for Cinematic Art) with this end in view. Slatan Dudow's *Kühle Wampe* (1932; shown in America as *Whither Ger-many?*), for instance, had financial support from the Communists and was subjected to drastic censorship at home and abroad – so much so that no unmutilated copy appears to survive.

Before the end of the 1920s, the large-scale emigration of some of the German cinema's best talents had begun. Indeed, Lubitsch had made his first Hollywood film as early as 1923. Soon the seepage turned to a flood as directors like Leni and Murnau and stars like Emil Jannings and Pola Negri, as well as Conrad Veidt and Marlene Dietrich, headed west. With an impressively professional sense of timing, Dietrich actually left Germany on the evening of the first showing of her first great success, *Der Blaue Engel*, in Berlin on 1 April 1930, going straight from the cinema to catch the night train. This film, and this star's appearance in it, have become so firmly established as icons of late Weimar culture that it and she demand, or will at any rate receive, more extended discussion. It was by no means, as is sometimes supposed, Dietrich's first film but her nineteenth, the list starting with *Der Kleine Napoleon* (*The Little Napoleon*) in 1922; she had in fact appeared in the first German feature film to use sound, *Ich küsse ihre Hand, Madame* (*I kiss your hand, Madame*) in 1929.

She had been performing in Berlin theatres from 1921, and contemporary recordings of some of her vocal performances in otherwise forgotten revues of the 1920s reveal a voice that took some time to settle down: at first conventionally light, it only later assumed the husky and sexually ambiguous depth that was to become one of her trademarks. To listen to some of these songs is to observe her androgynous image in the process of creating itself, and it was perhaps in *Der Blaue Engel* that that image and voice first defined and proclaimed their identity. Certainly in the 1928 revue *Es liegt in der Luft* the voice, while instantly recognisable, is still relatively light and feminine, but in some of the songs in the film of less than two years later there is a marked contrast, even competition, between two identities. To take the most familiar example, in both the English and the German versions of 'Falling in Love Again' the middle section is sung in a deeper, more masculine and aggressive voice – that of a seductress who intends to remain firmly in control – than the opening section, so that one has the curious impression of Dietrich singing a duet with herself. (The text of the German version, 'Ich bin von Kopf bis Fuss auf Liebe eingestellt', incidentally, conveys an almost obsessive quality of infatuation that is weakened in the more traditionally romantic English translation.)

Der Blaue Engel is not superficially of its time and place, though certainly so at a deeper level. It is based on Heinrich Mann's novel of 1905, *Professor Unrath*, which attacks bourgeois hypocrisy, but the action of the film, set in some unspecified seaport such as Hamburg or Lübeck, is quite explicitly moved to the second half of the 1920s. Its director, Josef von Sternberg, had been born plain Sternberg in Vienna and had been a painter and student of art before he turned to films. As a teenager he emigrated to America and in Hollywood had risen to be a director, making his first sound film (*Thunderbolt*) there, and returning briefly to Europe in order to direct *Der Blaue Engel*. Later he was to say, in an interview for BBC Television in 1966, that the influences upon his work as director, 'if there are any', were not from other film-makers but 'from literature and painting and other arts which I then incorporate into a film'.

Filming began on 4 November 1929 and was completed on 22 January 1930, each scene being shot twice, with German and English dialogue. Dietrich had problems with English pronunciation: in the lines 'Men cluster to me / Like moths around a flame', it seems that the word 'moths', difficult for a German speaker, kept coming out as 'moss'. (There may be some exaggeration in the story that it took her two days to get it right.) Emil Jannings, the famous star apparently upstaged by the virtual newcomer (though his performance is in the event a brilliant one), made himself extraordinarily difficult, and von Sternberg later declared that he 'would not do another film with him were he the last remaining actor on earth'. Dietrich tells us in her autobiography that Jannings 'hated the whole world, himself included.... this psychopathic star performer.... von Sternberg even whipped him when Jannings asked him to'. Even without a whip, von Sternberg was a tyrannical director who regarded himself as virtual and exclusive 'author' of the films he made, and his own autobiographical musings include the comment on Dietrich (also implicitly a comment on himself) that 'Despite her melancholy, she was well dressed and believed herself to be beautiful, though until this was radically altered by me she had been photographed to look like a female impersonator'.

There was, then, no shortage of drama and temperament on and off the set of this film of sadism, humiliation and human disintegration, and already some of its curious features have become apparent: a German classic shot also in an English version, with a non-German director and two stars about to leave Germany. It is indeed a film that seems compounded of ambiguities and equivocations, many of them belonging to Dietrich herself, the woman of legendary beauty whom at least one unsympathetic observer could claim to mistake for a female impersonator.

Von Sternberg's snide and self-serving observations apart, the history and legend of Dietrich have always been beset by ambiguity and paradox. It is, of all the possible choices, her face and no other that looks out from the frontispiece of the first volume of Paul Roen's *High Camp: A Gay Guide to Camp and Cult Films*. More, however, than any other of the group of international female stars who (for reasons not always entirely obvious) have been adopted as gay icons – Marilyn Monroe, Judy Garland, Maria Callas and the rest – Dietrich's public personality has always been unstable, one image dissolving Orlando-fashion into its antithesis. Appearing often as the incarnation of a voluptuous and exaggerated femininity, with her high cheek-boned, flawless-complexioned beauty and her timelessly slim figure sheathed in satin or swaddled in furs, she at other times discarded all this in favour of male attire. According to her autobiography she made a conscious choice of 'top hats and worker's caps' as part of her costume. One photographic record of her career shows on adjacent pages a goddess almost buried beneath a heap of white furs that must have sent wildlife statistics tumbling, and a woman who could easily be mistaken for a lesbian novelist in a man's suit, collar and tie, and who, without actually doing so, conveys a strong impression of having an Eton crop and smoking a pipe. It is said that when she arrived in Paris in 1933 wearing a man's polo coat, pearl-grey suit and beret, she was warned by the police that this outfit rendered her liable to arrest and prosecution; the advice was ignored. Her sartorial image in the 1930s was largely the creation of the gay designer Travis Banton, with whom she had a complex relationship. And it was an image that did not quickly fade: a whole generation after the end of the Weimar Republic, she was still appearing in top hat and trousers for a Las Vegas engagement.

But perhaps the most famous of all the innumerable Dietrich images is one of the earliest: that of Lola Lola (spiritual mother, one guesses, of the Lolita or young Lola created by another ex-Berliner), in black stockings and top hat, a mythological creature, half Circe, half ringmaster. For her role in *Der Blaue Engel* precisely utilises the wiles of the seductress to attain the kind of power traditionally regarded as masculine if not patriarchal. In creating for herself this persona she was drawing on a German, and specifically a Weimar, social and sexual tradition in which transvestism was a recognised mode of behaviour. It is no doubt significant that the comparable cultural phenomenon in Britain has almost always operated within a comic, even farcical context of stage or screen illusion, from the cross-dressed heroine of Shakespearean comedy to *Charley's Aunt*, the pantomime dame and her contemporary successors, the mass-audience female impersonator and the drag queen of the commercialised gay scene.

In her study of lesbianism in the cinema, *Vampires and Violets*, Andrea Weiss has shown that the early cinema's use of cross-dressing and gender-reversal for comic purposes was significantly modified in the late 1920s (the period of the controversy in England over *The Well of Loneliness*), when lesbianism began to be depicted in a more serious and sympathetic light. *Der Blaue Engel*, as it happens, falls exactly between two of the key texts that Weiss invokes to support this thesis, *The Wild Party*, a Hollywood film of 1929, and *Mädchen in Uniform*, made in Germany in 1931, both of which contain key scenes involving cross-dressing. In *Mädchen in Uniform*, for instance, set in a girls' boarding school, Manuela is still wearing the male costume she has adopted for the school play when she makes her declaration of lesbian love. Both films, according to Weiss, were 'informed by their directors' direct association with lesbian communities (in Berlin and Hollywood, respectively)'.

Even earlier, Pabst's 1928 film *Die Büchse der Pandora* presented a heroine (Lulu) who has been described as 'the aggressive suitor of other women, the ruthless, perverted competitor of the male suitor'. While Lola Lola, unlike the Lulu whose name so closely resembles her own, is not depicted as the 'suitor of other women', there is no doubt about her unfeminine aggression and ruthlessness and love of power. As Weiss relates, the making of Pabst's film was not without its problems:

According to Louise Brooks's memoirs, Belgian actress Alice Roberts as Countess Geschwitz 'was prepared to go no further than repression in mannish suits'. When she arrived on the set and was instructed to dance a seductive tango with Lulu, she responded with outrage. Pabst averted an emotional explosion by convincing her that she would be seducing him, not Louise Brooks: 'Both in two-shots and in her close-ups photographed over my shoulder, she cheated her look past me to Mr. Pabst, who was making love to her off camera. Out of the funny complexity of this design Mr. Pabst extracted his tense portrait of sterile lesbian passion.' (p. 22)

The unintended result of this stratagem was that in the finished film the Countess appears to be intent on seducing the female spectator. In Britain and America, however, this hazard was avoided by the censors' deletion of the entire scene.

Characteristic though it was of Weimar Berlin in general and the late Weimar cinema in particular, Dietrich's sexual evasiveness persisted long after she had quitted her homeland and Weimar had passed into history. In broader terms, her subsequent life perpetuated the pattern of ambiguity and paradox. Refusing to return to Germany, she made Paris her last home but insisted on being buried in Berlin. In contrast to many European émigrés who found their way to Hollywood, the unmistakable foreignness of her English accent, an essential part of her stock-in-trade, made her German origins seem never very far away. Her well-publicised private life embraced a series of lovers of both sexes, though throughout her career in divorce-happy Hollywood she remained (as *The Times* obituarist put it in a phrase of lapidary tact) 'distantly married' to her husband.

As Andrea Weiss shrewdly observes, while the Hollywood image-makers 'went to great lengths to keep the star's image open to erotic contemplation by both men and women', a hint of lesbianism could be titillating and therefore permissible (as a comparable hint of gay identity presumably could not) – though targeted less at lesbian audiences than at male voyeurism. The Paramount publicity machine's description of the Dietrich-von Sternberg film *Morocco* (1930) as presenting 'the woman all women want to see' seems, though, to offer a carefully phrased hint that 'normal' women might be excited by the carryings-on of a less conventional member of their sex. At the same time the invitation is extended without any real threat to the sanctity of the American home, for to see is not to be.

And in any case *Morocco*, quite unlike *Der Blaue Engel*, only flirts with unconventionality on the road to a thoroughly orthodox and undisturbing conclusion. For a modern viewer the film's most memorable moment occurs in an early scene, when Dietrich, in male evening dress from head to foot, having finished singing a song ('What am I bid for my apples?') rich in sexual innuendo, climbs over a barrier and leans forward to kiss a female member of her audience on the mouth. This momentary but startling reversion to European manners – Hollywood's unthinkable being Berlin's commonplace – appears to have been improvised by the star and tolerated by the director. Even earlier, the entertainer Amy Jolly, played by Dietrich, has shown herself to be a thoroughly independent woman when she tears up the visiting card given her by a rich male admirer who has gallantly offered her help. So far, so like that only very slightly earlier entertainer, Lola Lola. Even after she has come under the spell of the handsome, square-jawed legionnaire (played by Gary Cooper), Amy can still speak out for her sex, murmuring breathily that '"There is a Foreign Legion of women..."'. Eventually, though, love conquers all, including Amy's refusal to conform to conventional expectations of feminine roles, and in a final image that contrives to be both haunting and ludicrous she discards her high-heeled shoes to stumble across the desert sand with the other camp-followers in the wake of the marching soldiers, tugging a reluctant goat that she has borrowed for purely symbolic purposes.

Such a chicken-heartedly compromised ending is all very different from the ruthless, even contemptuous survivalism, the woman's victory in the struggle for power, at the end of *Der Blaue Engel*. We cannot help reflecting that Lola Lola would not have kicked off her high heels for such a purpose – would not have capitulated to the implied reproach when Amy, seeing the camp-followers for the first time, is told that they are the women who care for their men. From the Berlin of 1929 to the Hollywood of 1930 turned out to be a giant stride in the direction of conformity to an industry whose moral code, especially where the position of women was concerned, had hardly developed beyond the nineteenth century.

Sartorially, the heroine of *Morocco* moves in the direction of renouncing an aggressively male for a winningly female attire. Von Sternberg's direction again makes interesting use of unobtrusive but symbolic patterns of visual detail, tiny echoes and cross-references, and an essay could be written (perhaps has been written) on the use of headgear in this film. Amy's early gestures with her top hat, for instance, are later appropriated by the legionnaire, Tom, in respect of his own picturesque head-dress. Another nice touch is Amy's treatment of two texts: the stranger's card is torn to pieces, but the message scrawled by Tom on her mirror preserved.

J. C. Suares's recent *Hollywood Drag* documents a remarkable sweep of male and female impersonation in the American cinema and includes not only the predictables (Brooks and Garbo among them, as well as Dietrich) but a few surprises, including Rod Steiger and Boris Karloff. It comes as no surprise, however, that whereas the female impersonators are almost exclusively in a context of farce (Stan Laurel, Lou Costello, Harpo and Chico Marx, Jerry Lewis) or sophisticated comedy (Cary Grant, Jack Lemmon, Tony Curtis), male impersonation does not rule out seriousness. Garbo's *Queen Christina*, which Suares calls 'the most famous role reversal ever committed to film', is neither unique nor the earliest example. Very shortly before playing Lulu for Pabst, Louise Brooks had appeared in a Hollywood film, William Wellman's *Beggars of Life* (1928), which concerns a girl who murders her father after he has tried to rape her and then disguises herself as a male in order to find refuge among a group of down-and-outs. This was not, however, to be Dietrich's kind of role, and Suares suggests that her male impersonation in *Morocco* was innovative in two ways: not only did she reject the Brooks/Garbo vein of soulful and suffering woman-as-man, substituting for it a provocative and relished exploitation of the idea of cross-dressing, but she carried it over into her off-screen life. To relate this behaviour pattern to the life-styles of Weimar Berlin in which she had begun her career makes no excessive demands on imagination or credulity.

Historically speaking, the emergence of a distinctive lesbian identity in the western world around the turn of the century corresponds closely to the increased demand by women for polit-ical power and social freedom, and the central action of *Der Blaue Engel* – the assumption of power by the female and the consequent reduction of the male to ignominious helplessness – has obvious political as well as psychoanalytical implications. In general terms Petro has identified 'three different types of male figures in the Weimar cinema that exhibit an unstable masculine identity': the 'impotent, self-punishing and frequently sadistic male who projects his sense of powerlessness onto a female figure with whom he comes to identify', the 'passive and homosexual male', and the 'passive and eroticized male who elicits the desiring gaze of a textually inscribed female spectator' (pp. 155–8). *Der Blaue Engel* belongs to the first of these categories, as *Anders als die Andern* and *Die Büchse von Pandora* belong respectively to the other two. Jannings plays the bachelor schoolmaster, the tyrant of the classroom, who (for palpably if unconsciously mixed motives) pursues his boys into the local bars after school in his zeal for their moral welfare. The plot is one of tragic, or tragicomic, *peripeteia*, whereby the situation is reversed and the tyrant becomes helpless in the hands of a woman.

In a brilliant analysis of the *mise-en-scène* of this film, Carole Zucker has shown how its first half is 'divided mainly between two sets', Professor Rath's classroom and the Blue Angel cabaret, representing two morally and physically contrasting worlds. The classroom is bare and orderly to the point of rigidity: the straight lines of small desks that accommodate, far from comfortably, the sexually mature young men who are Rath's students, and the much larger desk behind which Rath sits, imply a hierarchical power system mirroring that of an entire society. Hierarchy, and the respect automatically accorded to status and title (especially by women towards men), are indeed evident from the outset, for the first words spoken in the film are the landlady's summoning of Rath to breakfast with the formal title 'Herr Professor'. It is characteristic of the film's subtle cross-references that the phrase is later repeated, no longer respectfuly but ironically and mockingly, by Lola when she announces breakfast after their first night together.

The order of the classroom, overthrown when the students riot and Rath quits the school, reflects the tyrannical conventions of an outmoded authoritarian society clinging to power and, on an individual level, the repression of natural sexual drives. In contrast the riotous life of the cabaret, on both sides of the footlights, and behind the scenes no less than on stage, draws sustenance from a much wider range of human instincts and emotions. A familiar parallel from a much earlier generation is in the schoolroom/circus antithesis of Dickens's *Hard Times*, where the opposite of a ramshackle, hand-to-mouth disorder is a stultifying and repressive power system. Ultimately, though, Dickens's horror of *moral* disorder, as well as the strict limits of contemporary tolerance, makes his circus a much tamer place, more sentimentally conceived, than the Blue Angel cabaret.

Rath himself is, visually and dramatically, a survivor from an imperial past that has faded into history – though new regimes, of course, have a habit of retaining such survivors in positions of power. His costume of cape, top hat and walking stick is that of the nineteenth century; his ritualistic nose-blowing before beginning the lesson (the straight lines of the handkerchief he holds up

reproducing those of the blackboard behind him), and his fastidious, even obsessive habits of arranging the objects on his desk
and making entries in his notebook, reveal a mind initially imprisoned in unvarying custom.

Earlier, breakfasting in his lodgings, he has observed the corpse
of a songbird lying at the bottom of its cage: one of the film's
blatant symbols, this prefigures his replacement of the dead creature by another songbird who refuses to remain in a cage and who
in due course reverses the roles and turns him into a grotesque
bird, crowing hideously and laying eggs for the entertainment of a
noisy audience that includes his former colleagues and students. At
the beginning, though, he can afford a moment of sentimentality
over the tiny corpse, immediately dispelled when the landlady
briskly consigns it to the stove. For this is a harsh world, indifferent
to the sufferings of others, as Rath will discover; and in any case
feeling is not his strong suit: teaching his class *Hamlet* (the story of
another scholar reduced to antic behaviour), he puts the main
emphasis on the correct pronunciation of the English definite article.

The transformation of the pedant into the clown comes about
through his excursion from the classroom into the alien world of
the Blue Angel, where, as Zucker has shown, 'the order of the
classroom is inverted'. In the cabaret, disorder rules, and the
straight lines and rigid hierarchies are replaced by a turbulent,
swirling world: the scenes in which Dietrich appears are crowded
with diversely costumed figures, doors are constantly opened and
closed, snatches of music and of the noise of an unruly, ribald
audience are heard.

It is also a world disturbingly indifferent to status, and Lola soon
has the professor scrabbling under the table for something she has
dropped – a casual but deft reversal of their roles (for he belongs to
an older generation as well as being her superior in gender and
status), and a foreshadowing of the way she will use her sexuality
to bring about his abasement. In the subsequent scene in which he
bemusedly watches her mounting the stairs, she is again consciously placing him literally and symbolically at her feet, and
this in fact becomes one of the recurrent motifs of the film. Later,
for instance, he picks up from the floor the pictures of her that he
will try to sell to the audience; he kneels to help her put on
her stockings; and when she insists, near the end, that he go on
stage as a clown, she is again standing on the stairs above him. In

the all-male classroom he has firmly closed the window to exclude the noises of the outside world in the form of a schoolgirls' singing lesson, but that world, including its sexuality and its music, invades and dominates his life until, having entered it as an outsider still asserting his status, he finds himself a despised and powerless part of it.

The film, still compelling after nearly seventy years, clearly has something to say about both sexuality and society, and about the relationship between the two. Rath represents a discredited pre-1914 *Kultur* that is clinging to power in the new Germany but whose days are numbered; the unrepressed (or only temporarily repressed) sexuality of his students, who escape to the Blue Angel after school, belongs to a younger generation unwilling to accept the values of its elders; and Lola embodies a powerful and morally nihilistic sexuality that wholly rejects the conventions and repressions of the past, just as so much in Weimar culture, from architecture and theatre to popular songs and satirical cartoons, defined itself along new lines.

As already suggested, though, Lola is not simply a vamp or *femme fatale* but an androgynous figure who usurps male power by calling into question hard-and-fast distinctions between the sexes. In Kenneth Tynan's phrase, revived by at least one of Dietrich's obituarists, Lola, like Dietrich herself, represents 'sex without gender'. Even after her migration to the very different and less tolerant social and cinematic world of Hollywood, the star's androgyny remained: brought there as a rival to Garbo, she seems to have set herself to outbid the strong flavour of sexual ambiguity in Garbo's screen persona – most evident in *Queen Christina*, where the Queen kisses her lady-in-waiting on the mouth even more unmistakably than Dietrich had done three years earlier in *Morocco*.

In a *Guardian* obituary (7 May 1992), Clancy Sigal wrote that Dietrich's art was not only 'blazingly erotic' but 'sexually ambiguous', and pointed out that – apparently paradoxically – this image solidified after she reached Hollywood:

The six American pictures she did for Sternberg set once and for all the faintly transvestite stereotype that drag queens henceforth loved to imitate: the smirking wide mouth, veiled eyes, angular cheekbones lighted to accentuate her dramatic gauntness. Above all, the deliberate suggestion emphasised by the tailored suits

and slacks of mannishness, lesbianism and shocking sexual inde-
terminacy.

What seems worth adding is that this 'sexual baroque', though to
some extent motivated by the wish to shock the timid public
morality of Hollywood, was a natural development from the first
collaboration of director and star on *Der Blaue Engel*. When they
travelled across the Atlantic, the power struggles, sexual indeterm-
inacy and sado-masochism of that great film were carried in their
luggage. The later Dietrich, even after she turned from cinema to
theatre and cabaret, retained the Sternberg legacy of which the
foundations had been laid in Berlin, and Sigal rightly adds that 'it
is no insult to [Dietrich's] memory to recall that she never willingly
departed from the perverse, sado-masochistic femme fatale that he
had made out of her'.

In *Morocco*, as we have seen, Dietrich appears in male evening
dress and top hat, and even the seductive Destry insists on having
the same as the boys in the back room and is at least the equal of
any man. (The latter role has some interesting points of similarity
to that of Lola; Hollywood in the 1930s was not, however, capable
of the uncompromising ending of the German film, resorting
instead to the nineteenth-century convention of having the fallen
woman square her account with respectable society by making a
good death.) It was a period in which Hollywood films at their
most popular were likely to depict gender without sex in the cause
of family entertainment: Fred Astaire and Ginger Rogers, like their
less talented but immensely popular contemporaries Jeanette Mac-
donald and Nelson Eddy, pursue their romantic love affairs while
irretrievably encased in faultless costumes that at times completely
cover the body save for the face.

In the Astaire-Rogers vehicle *Top Hat* (1935), though there is,
interestingly, some outrageously camp behaviour on the part of
the lesser characters (notably Edward Everett Horton), a single kiss
from the hero generates panic in the heroine; that the smooth-
cheeked Astaire, singing with such joyful excitement of putting
on his top hat, white tie and tails, should ever doff them to climb
into bed lies beyond our powers of imagining. But Dietrich
remained – in a context that became ever more censorious after
the 1934 Motion Picture Code forbade any reference to homosexuality in the cinema – a dissenter and a vigorously surviving representative of the Weimar tradition of sexual ambiguity.

In her *In the Realm of Pleasure*, Gaylyn Studlar has written of Dietrich that she 'is frequently mentioned as an actress whose screen presence raises questions about women's representation in Hollywood cinema. She has also acquired her own cult following of male and female, straight and gay admirers.' Studlar concludes that 'The diverse nature of this group suggests that many possible paths of pleasure can be charted across Dietrich as a signifying star image, and across von Sternberg's films as star vehicles.' This multiplicity of 'paths of pleasure' is a concept transplanted from Weimar Germany, and one that stubbornly took root in an environment that for long proved hostile or at best half-hearted.

Dietrich's post-Weimar career and personality, then, challenged convention in ways that were far from alien to the Berlin she had left behind and that found many other outlets, from Grosz's satirical drawings to Isherwood's fiction. And if *Die Blaue Engel* itself has a moral, it is that the power of human sexuality can find unexpected and disturbing modes of expressing itself: a truth to which so much in Weimar life and art lent support. The film thus becomes not just an individual masterpiece but an icon of its time and place – though, as often happens with icons, what it came to stand for was rather different from what it actually is.

Francis Bacon said of his own adolescent sojourn in the city that 'by way of education I found myself in the atmosphere of the Blue Angel', yet this kind of shorthand allusion serves somewhat to misrepresent a film that seems to teach that the wages of lust is folly, humiliation, disgrace and death. Compared with what could be readily seen in the bars and cabarets and even on the streets of Berlin at this time, it is even a rather decorous film: after seducing him, Lola makes an honest man of the Professor by marrying him (economic considerations, needless to say, entering into her decision), and even when she is at her most professionally titillating, the patrons of the Blue Angel are permitted to see no more than a few inches of bare flesh. Ultimately the film is ironic rather than pornographic, offering warning rather than stimulation: when, after the Professor's death, it concludes with Lola singing 'Falling in love again', the message is that, whatever love may be, it is something far removed from what was celebrated under that label by the Romantic poets. This scepticism, involving a rejection of the past, is very much in the Weimar spirit. At the same time, a more immediate past is recognised and suffers retribution, and in the extraordinary scene in which Rath, the victim of crowd-sadism,

is subjected to cruel physical humiliation, he is the representative
of an entire generation, the one that had taken Germany into war
and defeat.

5

Writing about Berlin

Isherwood is a co-dedicatee of Auden's *Collected Poems*, a fact that may justify a brief digression on dedications. The sense of a group – living together or in close contact, sharing ideas and journeys and books and even beds and lovers, and collaborating on literary enterprises, much in the manner of the English Romantic poets (some of whom also headed for Germany): all this is powerfully reinforced by photographic images. It is significant that two of the most important general studies of the 1930s, those by Valentine Cunningham and Samuel Hynes, both carry on their covers portraits of the Auden-Isherwood-Spender trio. But their habit of mutual dedication equally exemplifies the sense and solidarity of the group. Auden's 1930 *Poems* was dedicated to Isherwood, the collected edition of Isherwood's Berlin stories to Auden, the original version of Spender's *The Temple* to both of them. Just a little outside this small circle are such figures as Cecil Day-Lewis (dedicatee of Auden's *Paid on Both Sides*) and Benjamin Britten (dedicatee of *On the Frontier*).

The first poem in the *Collected Poems* is dated December 1927, less than a year before Auden went to Berlin. Very recently, however, Katharine Bucknell's magnificent edition (1994) of Auden's juvenilia has made it strikingly clear that this was far from being a beginning: Auden, who had decided at the age of 15 that he wanted to be a poet instead of a mining engineer, had been writing with extraordinary talent, energy and dedication as a schoolboy and undergraduate, and over two hundred poems survive from the period preceding his departure for Germany.

He took with him to Berlin, as we have seen, an unfinished play and resumed work on it soon after his arrival. But his time there was also fertile in short poems, and although his early poetic style characteristically involves a high level of abstraction, generalisation and myth-making, occasional traces of Berlin scenes, characters and ideas may also be found in his work at this period, including poems not written, or not completed, until after he had left the city. A good example here is the fine poem in four sections titled '1929' and written between April and October of that year. German friends (Kurt Groote and Gerhart Meyer) are mentioned by name, other friends (John Layard perhaps among them) less precisely referred to, and the tense atmosphere of the times is evoked in a few urgent phrases ('anxiety at nights', 'proletariat against police'). Though not free from the inflated rhetoric and sophomoric attitudinising that mar some of Auden's earlier work – and a portentous line like 'It is time for the destruction of error' challenges the reader to devise a disrespectful retort – it is, taken overall, both a remarkably accomplished technical performance and a poem showing control, insight and even wisdom.

Some of the other poems of this period may loosely be described as political, including one, 'Let History Be My Judge', written when Auden had been in Berlin for only a few weeks. Implied in this laconic and sardonic dramatic monologue is the story of a failed *coup d'état*, and the atmosphere seems to be compounded of turbulent Central European politics in the postwar period and a schoolboy or undergraduate fantasy world of adventure that owes something to the fictional school of John Buchan and is a recurring feature of Auden's early work, both poetic and dramatic.

A poem written towards the end of the Berlin period, 'Sentries against inner and outer', on the other hand, begins with the vocabulary of military aggression ('sentries', 'enemy', 'raid') but turns out to be a love poem, and it seems likely that Auden's romantic experiences during this year, and in a broader sense his heightened awareness of love and sexuality in himself and others, provided the impetus for a number of love poems. If so, it was a development that had far-reaching consequences, for he is surely one of the great love poets in English. Though perhaps a truth not yet universally acknowledged, this claim received a sudden and unexpected boost in 1994 when the reading aloud of one of his poems in the film *Four Weddings and a Funeral* had the extraordinary effect of placing prominently on bookstore counters piles of hastily produced pamphlets of his love poems.

One of the poems in this category, 'This Loved One', is about Isherwood's feelings for Bubi, and since it was apparently written in March 1929 must register Auden's response to a very early stage of that infatuation. Coolly enigmatic in the manner of much of the verse Auden wrote at this time, it resorts at one point to the favourite metaphor of the frontier, the challenge to decisive action in contrast to hedonism and emotionalism:

> Before this last one
> Was much to be done,
> Frontiers to cross....

One of the best-known of Auden's 1929 poems, 'Sir, no man's enemy', was written in October, after he had left Berlin, but bears the impress, in its prayer for 'power and light', of a mind liberated by its period of absence from England as well as, more specifically, expressing his enthusiasm for the doctrines of Layard. In the exuberant 'Which of you, waking early', written in the same month, are lines that, though placed in an English setting, could have been based on observations made in Berlin:

> As a boy lately come up from country to town
> Returns for the day to his village in expensive shoes,
> Standing scornful in a ring of old companions
> Amazes them with new expressions, with strange hints ....

Such boys, and such reactions to temporary affluence, must have been a familiar sight in the Berlin bars.

Auden's brief return to Berlin in the summer of 1930 produced an unexpected result in the shape of six poems written in German, apparently soon after his return, and sent to Isherwood. Linguistically they are not above reproach: according to David Constantine, there are 'at least half a dozen major grammatical errors... in every poem'. Auden evidently spoke and wrote German as Wilde's Algernon played the piano, not accurately but with great feeling. These verses are, however, of great interest as an exile's view of the Paradise of which he has too briefly been permitted to call himself an inhabitant. Five of the six are sonnets, and not far behind them are those of Shakespeare, a copy of which Auden had carried with him on at least one occasion on his German travels. As Constantine clearly shows, the 'financial and commercial imagery' of Shakespeare's love poems finds a modern equivalent in Auden's 'sense of love as a commodity'. 'Lacrimae Rerum', for instance, contains the line 'Weil ich kein Geld hab', komm ich nicht im Frage' ('Since I've no money you'll not want to bother with me'); another declares '...wenn ein olle Herr hat Dich gekusst / Geh mit; ich habe nichts hezahlt...'('That gentleman who is kissing you, go with him; I have paid for nothing'). The fifth in the series agonises 'Weiss aber nicht was jezt dein

Körper macht' ('Don't know, though, what your body is up to just now').

The sombre mood of these five poems is unexpected and may of course have been unrepresentative of Auden's life in general at this time, though it is not inconsistent with his earlier statement that he was 'homesick' for Berlin after his year there had come to an end. Away from the city, David Constantine suggests, Auden 'remembers Berlin life without illusion. He wants to get back there for the sex, but he knows very well what these remembered relationships are like: mercenary'. It is surely, however, a very personal melancholy and disillusion: his anatomising of the commercial sex of the rent-bars is not, even (or especially) in his Scottish exile, a matter of moral disgust or indignation but an expression of loneliness and frustration and, ultimately perhaps, a craving for love at any price. At the same time his unillusioned sense of the commercial basis of the Berlin sexual scene is perfectly consistent with his deep and unsatisfied longing for a stable relationship based on mutual affection and respect. There may, too, have been some grain of consolation in the Shakespearean precedent: to be creatively unhappy in such distinguished company must almost have made the whole wretched business worthwhile.

The exception to the sad rule in this group of poems in bad German is the sixth, 'Chorale'. This is a jaunty, Brechtian lyric that has none of the self-pity and sense of deprivation of its companions. It celebrates, instead, the joys of the flesh and obscenely enumerates the physical attributes of the boy who awaits him in Berlin and the activities they have shared: 'Der ist ein schöne Junge / Er wohnt jezt in Berlin....' ('There is a handsome boy, he lives in Berlin right now....'). To this boy (unidentifiable, if he ever existed as a single individual) he hopes to return in four months' time. The specified period would have brought him to the Christmas holidays and temporary release from bondage at Larchfield Academy; but the plan, if it was a plan, came to nothing. A cheeky note suggests that the poem should be sung 'To the Passion Chorale tune'; it could certainly have been a witty cabaret song, a form that Auden later practised with success.

Auden's enthusiasm for the popular brand of educational and self-help psychology purveyed by Homer Lane and John Layard, and especially for the attractive but facile connections it made between psychic and bodily ills, is reflected in many of his early poems, though its fullest expression has to wait until 1937 and the grim ballad 'Miss Gee'. He wrote a large number of what John Whitehead characterises as 'comic epigrams, some of them bawdy': two-, three- or four-line squibs that in their laconic, dogmatic, uncompromising specificity owe something to Blake's prose 'proverbs'. For instance,

> If a whore shocks you
> Then she will pox you

and

> Love your cock
> Stand a shock
> Hate your cock
> Soon a crock.

Some of these (though neither of those quoted above) found a place in a bouquet of a dozen titled 'Shorts' and included in *Collected Shorter Poems*.

Auden's short verse-and-prose 'charade', *Paid on Both Sides*, occupied him during the summer after he left Oxford, and the first draft accompanied him to Berlin that autumn. He worked at a second version, conflating old and new material, during November and December, and on the last day of 1928 sent the finished work to T. S. Eliot, editor of the London magazine *Criterion*. Eliot judged it 'quite a brilliant piece of work', published it in his magazine, and took modest pride in talent-spotting the young author.

Among other changes, the pre-Berlin version seems to have been modified by giving German names to some of the characters and also reflects Auden's absorption of the Lane-Layard doctrines. As Humphrey Carpenter has shown (p. 93), Auden himself described the piece as 'A parable of English Middle Class (professional) family life, 1907–29', these being the dates of his own birth and the charade's completion. As an attempt to exorcise his own background, it inevitably brings to mind Isherwood's first two published novels.

Another 'charade', *The Enemies of a Bishop*, was the joint work of Auden and Isherwood, though its origins lay in an idea of Auden's for a play titled *The Reformatory*. Auden seems to have begun to think about it in April 1929, very soon after Isherwood's visit, and the two of them worked on it together during the early part of the summer and finished it when they were together in London in the autumn. Its full title was *The Enemies of a Bishop, or Die When I Say When: A Morality in Four Acts*, but its original title had been *Where is Fronny?* – the reference being, of course, to Francis Turville-Petre. This rejected title is only one of a number of personal and private allusions in a work that, for all its claim to belong to the public world of the theatre, has a very strong flavour of the in-group.

The surname of the hero, Robert Bicknell, is that of Auden's mother before her marriage, while Robert's brother Augustus has one of the names of Auden's father. The two boys who escape from a reformatory and enter a middle-class world, one of them disguised as a girl, surely owe something to the ethos of the Cosy Corner and its denizens. One of the other characters is a pederast, another is based on a character in the film *Der Student von Prag*, and the Bishop himself is based on Homer Lane. Auden introduced one of his favourite lead mines, and Isherwood contributed characters who owed much to the fantasy world he and Upward had created together. It is, in other words, a gallimaufry of references, often obscure or coded, to the authors' private lives, and it comes as something of a surprise to learn that they had it professionally typed, presumably in the hope of getting it produced.

The play is dedicated to Bubi and Otto: memories of the weeks spent at Rötehutte must have been still fresh when it was written, and Otto, as it turned out, was actually an escapee from a reformatory. Isherwood's admission that the play is 'full of private jokes' is not one that need be quarrelled with, and Humphrey Carpenter's summing-up of it as 'a hotpotch of fine verse and schoolboy foolery' (p. 106) seems fair. In its introduction of extravagant characters and incidents into conventional settings such as a grand hotel, it looks forward to the anarchic world of Joe Orton, though Orton's pace, economy and wit are sadly lacking. What it does offer is strong confirmation of the closeness of Auden and Isherwood's relationship at this time and their shared exhilaration at what they had found in Berlin.

Of Auden's more private writings during this period, few letters survive. The so-called Berlin journal remains unpublished, though plans are afoot for its eventual appearance in full. What Auden would have thought of its publication can only be surmised: in one of his verse aphorisms he declares himself willing to forgive gossip columnists but expresses his scorn for literary biographers who try to justify their pryings by claiming 'it's for scholarship's sake'. On the other hand, unlike Isherwood, he carefully preserved this early diary, evidently reread it from time to time, and must have realised that it might outlive him and pass into the public domain. There may, moreover, be a sense in which almost any diarist ultimately desires a reader, whether an intimate or a stranger. Virginia Woolf's short story 'The Legacy', about a woman who achieves 'publication' by bequeathing her private diaries to her husband, perhaps dramatises an impulse that Woolf was not the only one to feel.

The worn and fragile manuscript designated as Auden's Berlin journal is in fact a number of different things: a commonplace book (he copied down with approval, for instance, a phrase from D. H. Lawrence's 'Mother and Daughter', 'The silky puppy-like sexuality of the English'), a poetical notebook (with many Lane-and-Layard-inspired squibs), and a record of notes and aphorisms mainly on psychological topics, as well as a kind of diary for the spring and summer of 1929. It is easier to say what kind of diary it is not than what it is. For the most part it certainly does not appear to be a daily record of events written within hours of their occurrence. As suggested in Chapter 1, there is clear evidence that much of it was written retrospectively, and after 26 May there is not even the pretence of regular entries, a long section headed with the date 12 June summarising what has happened in the previous two and a half weeks.

There is considerable stylistic unevenness, some of the writing being laconic or telegraphic to the point of obscurity, other parts blossoming into fully developed narratives, descriptions or arguments that at times achieve real eloquence. A phrase like 'adhesive trouser boys' (used of some of those in the waiting-room at Hirschfeld's Institute), for instance, has the flavour of a private allusion, an aid to memory rather than an attempt to communicate an idea to a reader, whereas the description of Gerhart's 'electrical' power or the analysis of the difference between Auden and his brother show a more consciously literary shaping. There is much use of dialogue, as if to catch the distinctive tone of a particular moment, and even more self-analysis: at one point Auden describes himself actually inspecting his own body in the mirror, but in a sense he is engaged in a continuous inspection of his own mind and heart.

One of the most curious features of the 'journal' is the use of headings strongly reminiscent of the captions used in the silent cinema. What seems to be an account of Isherwood's first full day in Berlin is headed 'Saturday getting tight', and later come 'Intervening period of Margaret and sex expectation', 'Meeting Gerhart and John's attempted suicide', 'The Dutchman and the Tour'. Again, the implication is of a writer less concerned with recording daily happenings than with discerning the phases into which his life has fallen, the shape and pattern of recent experience. This is consistent with what seems, after all, to have been the main purpose of this brief and almost unique spell of diarising: to reach a fuller and truer understanding of himself. Repeatedly some trivial incident or conversation is followed by an analysis, sometimes quite lengthy, of the underlying issue – infatuation, or jealousy, or infidelity, or falling out of love. For all the close and detailed observation of his friends and lovers and of certain aspects of life in Berlin, one's strongest sense is of a young man intent on watching himself, trying to understand his own emotions and to come to terms with his own nature.

In August 1930, a year after he had ceased to be a resident of Berlin but only a short time after his two-week holiday there, Auden told his brother that he was 'writing another play'. A couple of months later, with the play nearly finished, he assured Naomi Mitchison that it represented 'the best I can do just now'. Before the end of the year he had sent it to T. S. Eliot at Faber & Faber, but it never achieved publication and the manuscript subsequently disappeared. This play was *The Fronny* – again named after Francis Turville-Petre, who may well have been a subject of conversation between Auden and Isherwood during that June visit.

The medium is, again, a mixture of verse and prose, and the action seems to have concerned the quest for The Fronny after he had quitted England. After moving through scenes depicting different aspects of contemporary society, it concludes with The Fronny making his will and dying. His list of bequests in particular seems to have been full of private jokes, and as a drama for the stage it seems unlikely that *The Fronny* represented much of an advance on *The Enemies of a Bishop*. But the continuing fascination with Turville-Petre, and his incorporation into a myth by both Auden and Isherwood, is striking.

Auden's three major dramatic collaborations with Isherwood – *The Dog Beneath the Skin* (1935), *The Ascent of F6* (1936), *On the Frontier* (1928) – belong to a post-Berlin phase of their relationship, but a couple of general points are worth making. The preoccupation with frontiers, most obvious in the title of the second of these plays, is pervasive: the challenging mountain F6, for instance, stands 'exactly on the frontier line', and in *On the Frontier* itself Dr Thorvald reflects that 'Perhaps "country" and "frontier" are old-fashioned words that don't mean anything now'. A frontier is both a barrier, a restraint on freedom of movement, and an invitation or challenge to step across into a new world, and it seems likely that residence in Germany, where the frontiers drawn by the Versailles Treaty were still of passionate concern, added contemporary force to what may have originated as a more personal metaphor. In *The Ascent of F6*, the excitement of crossing frontiers and confronting the unknown is combined with an outsider's view of England and its decline to a second-class power, and again these kinds of aware-ness may owe something to the time spent in Berlin.

At the same time the preoccupation with frontiers links these works of the second half of the decade with Auden's poems of a few years earlier. Samuel Hynes has suggested, though, that the concept had in the meantime undergone a significant shift: in the earlier poems, 'the frontier was always a place up ahead, beyond which was a New Country. But now, in 1938, he was *on* the frontier...' (*The Auden Generation*, p. 308).

Isherwood's first published novel, *All the Conspirators*, had appeared in 1928, the year before he moved to Berlin. When he arrived there towards the end of 1929 he had with him the third draft of its successor, *The Memorial*, which he was to characterise in *Lions and Shadows* as 'an epic disguised as a drawing-room comedy' and to describe there as 'about war: not the War itself but the effect of the idea of "War" on my generation' (pp. 297, 296). He con-tinued to work at this novel during 1930, but though it was fin-ished by the end of that year it suffered multiple rejections and did not appear until 17 February 1932. Though pre-Berlin in its origins, therefore, *The Memorial* is a Berlin novel in the sense that it was largely composed there in the form in which we have it. With limited exceptions, however, it is not a novel that makes use of very recent experience: Isherwood, who had devoted *All the Conspirators* to the demolition of the Edwardian family, was still occupied in getting the past out of his system rather than exploiting the present. As it turned out, he was not to put the present to literary use until it had become the past. Later, with not much exaggeration, he was to describe himself as a historical novelist; as he told W. J. Weatherby in 1960, his writing 'always has to be about a few years ago with a gap between my subject and the present'.

So far as *The Memorial* is concerned, the main exceptions to this rule are to be found in the opening section, in Chapter 5 of which the hero, Edward Blake, finds himself in Berlin in 1928. With the Tiergarten behind him and the bright lights of the Sieges Allee stretching before him, he is placed in a specific spot in the city that Isherwood had come to know while the book was still in progress. Later in the same chapter Edward attempts suicide in a manner that closely resembles the attempt made by John Layard. This event had of course taken place before Isherwood's arrival, but Auden's account of it had evidently been sufficiently graphic for him to scent copy. He uses the incident again in *Lions and Shadows* (p. 196), this time applied ironically and self-mockingly to the narrator, and Spender uses it in *The Temple* (pp. 20–1), putting the story into the mouth of the Isherwood character, who is (of all things) thinking of using it in a novel. Layard was certainly in no position to complain that his sensational performance had gone unnoticed.

The final pages of *The Memorial* show the protagonist again in Berlin, his room 'overlooking the trees and the black canal and the trams clanging round the great cold fountain in the Lützowplatz'. There he receives a visit from a hustler, Franz (the name, with a slight variation of spelling, of one of the boys frequently mentioned in Auden's Berlin diary), and they talk of his suicide attempt and of the war. Franz too now has a scar, caused by a stray machine-gun bullet fired by the police through the windows of his sister's house, though his response to the question whether he is a Communist is a scornful negative. The two men remain suspended between the past and the future, their own relationship incomplete and perhaps impossible, in a manner that may owe something to the ending of Forster's *A Passage to India*.

Soon after the appearance of *The Memorial* in February 1932, Isherwood wrote to John Lehmann outlining his programme of literary projects. He was, he told Lehmann, already at work on 'an autobiographical book...about my education' (that is, an early draft of *Lions and Shadows*), and would soon be starting 'a book about Berlin, which will probably be a novel in diary form and semi-political' (quoted by Fryer, 1993, p. 86). After that he would write another autobiographical work, and perhaps a travel book. Later in life he was to write both, but nothing came of these latter plans, or ideas, for a very long time. The 'book about Berlin', however, was *The Lost*, never completed but in a sense the ancestor or Ur-text of the published Berlin novels.

Isherwood's Berlin experiences are extensively exploited in *Mr Norris Changes Trains* (1935) and *Goodbye to Berlin* (1939). (The 'Sally Bowles' section of the latter had been published separately in 1937.) The second of these in particular is historical fiction in that, published six years after Isherwood's departure from the city, it deals with a world that must at the time of publication already have seemed remote. An odd feature of these two works is that, whereas one might have expected the later one to have begun where *Mr Norris* left off and to have continued Isherwood's Berlin chronicle into a further phase of contemporary history, the two books actually traverse roughly the same period of time. Dependent as he was, however, upon firsthand experience recorded in his diaries rather than upon research or invention, he really had no choice. In *Mr Norris* the account of public events had already been taken almost up to the point at which he himself had left Berlin, and there was nothing left but to go back to the beginning and start again with a largely different group of characters and a different structuring principle.

The action of *Mr Norris Changes Trains* (retitled for American publication as *The Last of Mr Norris*) opens towards the end of 1929, very close to the date at which Isherwood had arrived in Berlin – and opens with the Isherwood-like figure of the narrator, William Bradshaw (Isherwood's own second and third Christian names), arriving in Berlin by train. (The same journey is described on the closing pages of the autobiographical *Lions and Shadows*, published three years later, so that in a curious and paradoxical way the earlier book starts where the later one was to leave off.) The narrative of *Mr Norris* thereafter is straightforwardly chronological: at the beginning of Chapter 3 it is 'a few days after Christmas', Bradshaw then meets Norris to celebrate New Year's Eve, and most of the subsequent chapters begin with some reference to time.

For this is a novel constructed with close attention to an unfolding public history as well as to a plausible framework of fictional events. In Chapter 5 it is 'towards the end of April [1930]', and three chapters later it is 'the beginning of March [1932]', with specific allusions to the campaign for the presidential elections held on 13 March. In Chapter 9 the narrator returns to England for an extended period, spending four months in the country after being in London, so that it is 'the beginning of October' before he is back in Berlin. Isherwood himself had been in England during the same summer, though for a shorter period, from early August to the end of September, and one senses that Bradshaw's absence is a convenient device for absolving his creator from depicting events in Germany during that period. Chapter 11 begins in 'the first week in November' and continues 'early in December'. By the final chapter (16), it is 'early in March [1933], after the elections...', these being the Reichstag elections on the 5th of the month that gave the Nazis a large majority.

In the closing pages, events follow each other quickly, mirroring both the rapidity of change after the Nazis came to power and the hugger-mugger quality of Isherwood's own last weeks in Berlin. It was perhaps for this reason that he described his novel, not altogether justly, as 'a sort of glorified shocker', and compared it to the work of Graham Greene. Bradshaw's young friend Otto reappears with the news that he has been hunted down and has narrowly escaped arrest by the Nazis 'two days after the Reichstag fire' – that is, on 1 March; he has then been on the run for a fortnight, so that it is now mid-March. 'Three weeks later' – that is, fictionally speaking, in early April – Bradshaw returns to England. Isherwood had gone there on 5 April, but his brief return to Berlin in May before finally leaving for Greece has no counterpart in the fiction and would have served no useful purpose there. Now immovably established in England, Bradshaw receives news during May that Norris is in Mexico City, and later messages come in rapid succession from California, Costa Rica and Peru. But by now both the novel and the reality on which it is so closely based have left Berlin behind.

In both of the Berlin novels private lives are invaded and transformed by public events, in accordance with standard practice in the historical novel – a generalisation equally true, for instance, of a nineteenth-century classic such as Dickens's *A Tale of Two Cities*. But Isherwood's is a tale of one city, with virtually no attempt to set events in Germany against the background of a quieter, less obviously threatened life elsewhere. And whereas Dickens makes an event such as the storming of the Bastille or the lynching of an enemy of the people the occasion for a rhetorical and emotional set-piece, Isherwood plays down the drama of contemporary happenings: the landmarks of history are scaled down so that, subjectively perceived, they take their place with the banalities of everyday life. The influence of Forster may again be detected here, and specifically what Isherwood admiringly referred to as his 'tea-tabling', the technique of conveying through domestic fiction a sense of momentous issues. Although Isherwood had by now left Modernism behind, there is perhaps also a trace of the Woolfian subduing of events of all kinds to the vagaries of an individual consciousness indifferent to accepted hierarchies of significance.

Chapter 16 of *Mr Norris*, for instance, opens with a reference to the weather, 'suddenly mild and warm', in early March 1933:

> 'Hitler's weather,' said the porter's wife; and her son remarked jokingly that we ought to be grateful to van der Lubbe, because the burning of the Reichstag had melted the snow. 'Such a nice-looking boy,' observed Frl. Schroeder, with a sigh. 'However could he go and do a dreadful thing like that?' The porter's wife snorted.

The mediation of sinister and momentous happenings through the gossip of the politically ignorant and innocent reduces everything to the same level – a strategy belonging to diaries rather than history books – and the outrageous Nazi plot becomes material for a boy's joke and a sentimental woman's pity for the scapegoat. These reductions, however, belong to the world of the novel's action, not that of the narrator or the reader, who are privy to the ironic and tragicomic discrepancies.

In the paragraph that follows, Isherwood's prose artfully juxtaposes the national and the local: in the Nollendorfplatz 'people were sitting out of doors before the café in their overcoats, reading about the coup d'état in Bavaria'; 'An ice-cream shop was open. Uniformed Nazis strode hither and thither, with serious, set faces, as though on weighty errands' – and the past tense of the distanced narrator is briefly nullified as we share the experience of living through a moment of history in which the ice-cream is for some as important as the Nazis. Hynes has argued that one of the themes of *Mr Norris* is the disappearance of the private life under tyranny:

> Bradshaw knows no public figures, and has no public existence, being only a poor foreigner; but that private world is gradually invaded by the public world.... As public violence increases, the private life recedes, and the private man is drawn

out of his closed world, into the streets.... [By the end of the novel] the public drama of Germany has been acted out to a tragic conclusion: in Berlin there is no private life left to be lived.

(*The Auden Generation*, p. 178)

The passage from the novel's final chapter cited above, however, suggests that private lives can absorb and digest a version of public events (not necessarily, of course, an authentic one), reducing public figures and their actions to the level of their own limited experience. In the Berlin novels it is Fräulein Schroeder, with her endless curiosity about the private lives of others, who is a unifying figure, and in his introduction to the 1975 reissue of the novels Isherwood praises her as a survivor and as 'the most genuine Berliner of them all':

Only Frl. Schroeder could boast that she had lived in the same flat on the same street since the pre-war days of Wilhelm II, through the war and the defeat and the Republic and the inflation. Only she was fated to remain there throughout the Third Reich, to witness its fiery end and the arrival of the Russians....

Another kind of levelling process can be found in Chapter 8, where Olga, a 'woman of numerous occupations', is described: 'she was a procuress, a cocaine-seller and a receiver of stolen goods; she also let lodgings, took in washing and, when in the mood, did exquisite fancy needle-work'. In the social and moral chaos of 'those bankrupt days', it is clear, needlework and cocaine, laundry and prostitution, no longer belong to different worlds.

The novel's central character, Arthur Norris, though an outsider and a kind of picaresque anti-hero, embodies this confusion. He has been seen by Brian Finney as a representative figure in more ways than one:

His self-centred hedonism in fact parallels the attitudes of the Berlin population at large during the final years of the Weimar Republic. His sexual masochism is like their political self-abasement. His distortion of language to conceal the truth from Bradshaw and everyone else is paralleled by the debasement of linguistic meaning by the politicians and the press as the political confrontation between the right and the left heightens. And like them he is made to pay for his abandonment of responsibility by the escalating intrusion of public affairs into his private life.

(pp. 115–16)

Persuasive though this view of Norris is, it presents two problems. It leaves out of account the fact that Norris is a comic figure: even at the end, his 'paying for' his shortcomings takes the form of a farcical scamper from one uncongenial hiding-place to another. And in its emphasis on representativeness it does not do justice to the individuation, even the wild eccentricity, of a character whom we know to have been based on a real-life original.

Whatever it may have been intended to express about Weimar society at large, the ambiguity of Norris's sexual orientation parallels his political and financial deviousness while at the same time handily insuring Isherwood against the personal and professional risk of being suspected of creating a homosexual protagonist. A passage in Chapter 4 summarising Norris's early life indicates that he came of age in the 1890s, so that he may be supposed to be in his fifties, perhaps sixty, when Bradshaw meets him. This makes him considerably senior to his prototype Gerald Hamilton, born in 1889, and much closer to Isherwood's father's generation. In the postwar world Norris remains a Nineties Decadent: one who has in his youth ' "learnt the meaning of the word 'luxury' " ', who has an interest in the Wilde circle and passes off a Wilde epigram as his own, who boasts of his library of erotica and his Swinburnian collection of whips, and who in the age of Eliot and Pound admires the work of the poetaster William Watson – still alive in the early 1930s, but, like Norris, a relic of the 1890s, when his most popular volumes appeared. His espousing of 1890s aestheticism, moreover, places Norris conveniently above or beyond morality, and his criteria for commercial or political action are less a matter of truth and justice than of self-gratification and self-serving.

With his wig, his cosmetics, his camp locutions (' "my dear boy" ') and his high-pitched giggling and tittering, he seems at moments like an unmistakable portrait of an ageing but still effervescent 'queen', and Isherwood from time to time comes close to allowing himself to say as much unambiguously: sitting at his dressing-table in a 'delicate mauve wrap', Norris invites Bradshaw to ' "Come and talk to me while I powder my nose," ' and even the guileless Fräulein Schroeder is moved to comment on his silk underwear (' "More like a lady than a gentleman" '). Yet Isherwood deliberately blurs this portrait or caricature by occasional references to more socially acceptable forms of dissipation: Norris's inheritance has 'disappeared with magic speed into the mouths of horses and the stockings of ballet girls', and his only current form of sexual activity seems to consist of masochistic sessions at the hands of Fräulein Anni (he even makes it plain that ' "some equally charming young lady" ' would be quite acceptable).

On the subject of Norris's sexual ambiguity, then, Isherwood is himself ambiguous. There was nothing ambiguous about the homosexuality of his model, Gerald Hamilton, but Finney's reference to 'Hamilton's fictive heterosexual counterpart' (p. 85) seems to bypass a real problem. Nor can Isherwood's stance quite be accounted for by talking about androgyny or bisexuality, though the title metaphor of changing trains may conceivably be, among other things, a discreet gesture in this direction. Muddying the waters was an effective way of preventing publishers, reviewers and readers from looking into the depths and being startled by what they saw there, and this prudence – which might less charitably, and perhaps unfairly, be called failure of nerve – is characteristic and pervasive in Isherwood's early work. It is evident, for instance, in a curious non sequitur in the closing pages of *Goodbye to Berlin*, where the desperate plight of civilians during the closing stages of the Great War is recalled: 'Everybody sold what they had to sell – themselves included. A boy of fourteen... peddled cocaine between school hours, in the street'. What is interesting here is that the candour promised by 'themselves included' simply evaporates between the two short sentences. Isherwood knew more than most about boys who sold themselves, but was unprepared to come clean.

In the end, though, Norris is not just a louche expatriate who might have been equally at home on Norman Douglas's Capri: like Bradshaw, he is drawn out of his 'closed world' (in Hynes's phrase) by the force of public events. Until nearly halfway through the book, these events impinge only marginally on the action of the novel. In Chapter 7, a quarrel between two young Germans over a girl is the occasion for a minor coup by the rapidly developing Nazi propaganda machine: the men are enemies, 'both political and private', and the occasion of the quarrel is Anni's appearance with Otto's rival 'in a Nazi *Lokal* [pub] on the Kreuzberg'. In the Nazi newspapers, Otto's drunken attempt to fight his rival appears as ' "an unprovoked and cowardly attack on a National-Socialist *Lokal* by ten armed communists..." '. It is the lives of these three minor characters that are foregrounded, the satirical reference to Nazi propaganda and the Nazis' invasion of social life being still held at a distance – which is no doubt, after all, how most residents of Berlin would have treated such a matter at this time.

By the next chapter, however, the restrictions on personal freedom ('Each week there were new emergency decrees...') and the outbreaks of violence have suddenly moved into the foreground:

> Berlin was in a state of civil war. Hate exploded suddenly, without warning, out of nowhere....In the middle of a crowded street a young man would be attacked, stripped, thrashed and left bleeding on the pavement; in fifteen seconds it was all over and the assailants had disappeared. Otto got a gash over the eye with a razor in a battle on a fair-ground near the Cöpernickerstrasse....

The sudden specificity of the last sentence quoted brings us back to the immediate world of Bradshaw's daily experience, but it is now the generalisation that is given precedence, and the paragraph that follows is a miniature essay, somewhat in the manner of George Orwell, on the corruption of language and mass culture (popular songs and cinema) under a tyranny. At the beginning of Chapter 9, when Bradshaw returns from England and goes by taxi from the station to his lodgings, the presence of uniformed Nazis in the streets is unmistakable: the new regime has now invaded the small stage of Isherwood's fiction.

And yet Bradshaw remains, as Isherwood himself had been, an outsider, conscious of the menace in the air of the city he has made his home but free, after all, to quit it at a moment's notice whenever he chooses. Towards Germans and his own compatriots alike, Bradshaw's feelings are always more or less detached: he is never shown forming the kind of passionate attachment that Isherwood felt for certain German youths, and again this may have originated in a necessary or at least an irresistible prudence. Isherwood is an autobiographical novelist, but only up to a point: the confessional impulse is always under firm control. In the penultimate chapter it is made quite explicit that, despite the interest Bradshaw finds in Norris's personality and behaviour, he has no intention of ever crossing the frontier that separates an acquaintance from an intimate friend: 'Here we were, as so often before, at the edge of that delicate, almost invisible line which divided our two worlds. We should never cross it now.'

The age difference partly accounts for this, and Norris may be seen as an alternative father, as disreputable and unreliable as 'real' English fathers of the Edwardian middle class (like Isherwood's own) were conventional and dependable. Though the passage appears to lay the blame at Norris's door, however, the real reason for the failure to develop a closer relationship is surely Bradshaw's refusal to become involved. It is the same trait that makes him partially withdraw his spontaneous reaction of horror and pity to the news of the homosexual Kuno's death – ' "Poor devil" ' – by adding 'apologetically' that he ' "knew him slightly" '. (Kuno's name, incidentally, may have been intended to recall that of one of the highly placed figures in the notorious Eulenberg affair, General Kuno Count von Moltke, the military commandant of Berlin.) Standing up to be counted was not the strong point of Bradshaw or, at this stage, his creator. And the bantering tone in which the novel ends – a tone curiously at odds with the picture of Norris fleeing, not altogether successfully, for his life – seems to affirm once and for all the refusal to be involved in the life or destiny of other people. A sense of his own failure to speak out or come clean may have been one of the reasons why, in later life, Isherwood tended to disparage his Berlin stories.

Isherwood's narrative technique mirrors this detachment, or caginess, by eschewing psychological analysis in favour of a largely dramatic mode of presentation replete with the equivalent of stage directions. Characters blush, frown, shrug their shoulders, sweat with embarrassment, sink heavily into chairs, look away or up ('like a spaniel that is going to be whipped') or at their finger-nails ('with dismay'): the fictional text is often very close to a play script or (more pertinently) a film script. *Goodbye to Berlin* has on its first page (though not, as is often supposed, in its first sentence) the only phrase of Isherwood's that everyone knows and the only prose quotation of his to find its way into the *Oxford Dictionary of Quotations*: 'I am a camera'. The words that follow make it clear that it is not a movie camera that is in question, though this might have made the analogy closer.

Yet a close analogy it can never be, and the famous dictum turns out to be a confidence trick that would not have disgraced Mr Norris himself. For the famous 'camera' is not quite the tightly fitting symbol of sharply accurate but wholly detached observation that it has often been taken to be. Even if, as Isherwood stipulates, it has its 'shutter open, quite passive, recording, not thinking', somebody has had to point the camera in one direction or another, and the words that immediately follow – 'Recording the man shaving at the window opposite and the woman in the kimono washing her hair' – imply a rigorous selection of details, and details of details, from the vast unsorted mass or mess of visual stimuli in the surrounding world. Language, after all, can never simply 'record', and any pretence to this effect is naive or duplicitous. As for the final sentence of the paragraph, 'Some day, all this will have to be developed, carefully printed, fixed', the reference is presumably to the processing by which memory becomes art, but there is scope here too for a selectivity and distortion, even for a wholesale reordering of the past, just as the developing of a negative involves decisions and judgements that affect the end product. As Gore Vidal has pointed out, though Isherwood 'became famous' with this four-word statement, he is not really a naturalistic writer, a 'recorder of surfaces'. He must be judged in this instance to have been as evasive about the nature of his art as he is about Norris's or Bradshaw's sexuality.

Understandably, writers tend to become impatient with such of their own dicta as are turned into clichés, and in two interviews he gave in the 1970s, Isherwood discouraged emphasis on this familiar phrase and also on his own identification with the fictional character or characters who bear his name. Insisting in 1972 that far too much prominence had been given to 'I am a camera', he explained that what he was trying to do was to 'describe my mood at that particular moment. Obviously the description does not fit Christopher Isherwood in many of the other sections [of *Goodbye to Berlin*]'. There is perhaps scope for misunderstanding here as to which Christopher Isherwood is being referred to.

Another statement five years later is less ambiguous:

'You see, "Christopher Isherwood" in the early books wasn't *me* at all. He was a device used to tell the story in the first person. If he had been a person, and he had announced that he was homosexual, he would have upstaged everyone else. The reader would be constantly wondering what he would do next. So he had to shut up, push the other characters into dialogue, and so on.

But 'wasn't *me* at all' is hard to swallow, and this statement is obviously intended to get Isherwood off a double hook: the reader is discouraged from taking the stories as autobiographical (though they are certainly that to a significant extent), and what we may feel like regarding as evasiveness is given an aesthetic justification. The problem with the second of these points is that the evasiveness over matters of sexual orientation or conduct is by no means limited to the narrator. And in any case it is surely disingenuous of Isherwood to insist that the Christopher figure is not himself 'at all' when he has made that character a young upper-class English-man, with a public school and Cambridge education, who is teaching English in Berlin and has published a book called *All the Conspirators*. Similarly unconvincing is the implication that only technical considerations inhibited him from making the character's homosexuality explicit. It is as well to be prepared, therefore, for some degree of evasiveness, even of inconsistency, in the handling of this protagonist-narrator who is also, if only up to a point, a portrait of the artist.

Disingenuity and evasiveness apart, it has of course often been argued (by, for instance, Jeffrey Meyers in his *Homosexuality in Literature 1890–1930*) that reticence, suppression and ambiguity, whether or not they are morally reprehensible, may be a source of artistic strength. Certainly the marked inferiority of, say, For-ster's *Maurice* to his less explicit fiction implies that speaking out, whatever marks for moral courage it may earn, can result in a diminution of literary power and a thinness of literary texture. There is, indeed, a very striking contrast between the force and richness of some of the masterpieces of suppression that Meyers discusses (by, among others, Mann, Proust, Conrad and Lawrence) and the depressing banality of much contemporary gay fiction, which seems unable to steer a course between the hard rock of crude pornography and the softer one of maudlin sentimentality. The act of throwing off one's chains does not, as some have sup-posed, automatically provide a valid literary objective. Isherwood's fiction, even as late as *A Single Man* (1964), which many regard as his best novel, remains doggedly reticent, though by the 1960s greater explicitness would surely not have involved very serious risks, commercial or personal. His fiction includes no *Maurice*, and certainly nothing like the self-indulgent stories that appear in For-ster's posthumous volume *The Life to Come*: perhaps he had learned from *Maurice* (despite his early enthusiasm for it) that reticence

pays. The eleventh-hour outspokenness of *Christopher and his Kind*
looks like an attempt to atone for a lifetime of watching his step.

Possibly, however, the real justification for the virtual exclusion
of sexual politics from the Berlin stories is that they are concerned
with a wider and more tragic politics, that of a Germany reeling
from one war to the next. Isherwood himself made this point, even
if rather elliptically, when he was interviewed by Arthur Bell for a
gay magazine in 1972 after the publication of *Kathleen and Frank*.
Asked, in the context of a discussion of his role in gay liberation
activities, whether the Berlin books were 'political stories', he
replied: 'Yes. They certainly have strong political overtones; that's
true. But not of that kind [i.e. sexual politics] because that wasn't
the current concern.'

The time-scheme of *Goodbye to Berlin* begins in the autumn of
1930, almost exactly the point at which William Plomer went to the
city and found there (as he wrote 45 years later) a 'feverish atmosphere' in which

> Acute political and economic uncertainty and tension were not
> concealed by the flashy up-to-dateness of life in the centre of the
> city. Naked ambition and naked despair were both conspicuous.
> Two strong currents, often intermingling in a puzzling way,
> especially puzzling to someone unfamiliar with the German
> character, were earnestness and cynicism. And resentment was
> visibly gaining over disillusionment.
>
> (*The Autobiography of William Plomer*, pp. 273–4)

Translating these abstractions into the daily experience of ordinary
people, Isherwood takes something like this account as the agenda
for his book, though he is in no rush to bring political and economic
issues to the surface. In the opening section, Fräulein Schroeder, her
home and her lodgers are introduced: one lodger is a barman,
another a prostitute, and it is clear that both derive their living
from the city's considerable influx of foreign visitors, whether tourists or business men, for his bar is visited by Dutchmen and one of
her best regular customers is a Japanese. Fräulein Schroeder herself
is a representative figure of her generation, a bourgeoise whose
independent income has been annihilated by postwar inflation and
whose standard of living has dramatically dropped.

Covering as it does the same historical ground as *Mr Norris*,
Goodbye to Berlin adopts an entirely different, episodic technique,

its six sections dealing with separate individuals or groups of characters in a variety of socially and topographically contrasting settings in and outside Berlin. The introductory note to the first edition describes the book as a 'short loosely-connected sequence of diaries and sketches' and recalls that its origins lay in the 'huge episodic novel of pre-Hitler Berlin' that was to have been titled *The Lost*. The 'Berlin Diary' that provides the first and last sections (dated a little more than two years apart) serves as a frame for what amounts to a sequence of linked stories, the three longest ('Sally Bowles', 'The Nowaks' and 'The Landauers') being almost of novella length. The opening and closing passages, and many that lie between, are written in the present tense, the traditional mode of lyric poetry and dramatic soliloquy rather than prose fiction, and the effect is not so much that of a diary as of a running commentary on a scene that lies before the narrator's eyes.

The book makes extensive use of autobiographical material, but, as usual, what is more interesting is the divergences between the fiction and the knowable facts. Some of these divergences follow naturally from the reordering to which real experience, so often untidy, repetitive and long-winded, must be subjected in the process of being turned into narrative, but as in *Mr Norris*, the author's self-censorship also involves him in strategies of concealment and displacement. In 'Sally Bowles' – the most familiar, though in itself one of the least interesting parts of the book – Christopher's relationship to Sally is never clearly defined. It is instructive, too, to see how subsequent theatrical transmogrifications of this story, seizing on this vagueness, move in the direction of making Christopher unblushingly heterosexual, the musical stage in particular being less tolerant of ambiguity, or nonconformity, than fiction. Little wonder that Isherwood told an interviewer, Denis Hart, in 1961 that he had become 'fairly tired of the Berlin material by now'. A production one would like to have seen is a musical based on the Berlin stories in which Isherwood collaborated with Auden and Kallman, and Marilyn Monroe played Sally Bowles; nothing, however, came of this intriguing idea.

'"I'm glad you're not in love with me, because, somehow, I couldn't possibly be in love with you,"' Sally tells Christopher, and the reader inclined to do so is left to ponder the significance of that 'somehow'. In *Christopher and his Kind* (p. 53) Isherwood comments that it 'may be taken to suggest that Sally knows instinctively that Christopher is homosexual – or it may not', the different responses presumably reflecting the sexual sensibilities of the reader. This is confirmed by Isherwood's reply to an interviewer, Tony Russo, in 1977, when asked whether he felt there was 'a certain gay sensibility' in his early work; he considered that 'anybody who really had any sensibility of that kind could tell at a single glance', not only in the Berlin stories but in the two novels that precede them.

It is clear, though, that other characters in 'Sally Bowles' see them as potential lovers, and Fräulein Schroeder is 'rather shocked' at Christopher's easy acceptance of Sally's affair with another man. Near the end Christopher wonders 'whether I hadn't, all this time, in my own peculiar way, been in love with Sally myself', but the reflection is not pursued and there is a thinly coded saving clause in the reference to his 'own peculiar way'. They are together constantly, but the relationship remains not only chaste but curiously distant and even indifferent, so that Sally's abrupt disappearance at the end of the story causes no pangs for either narrator or reader. That disappearance, complete and unredeemed, departs from the biographical facts of the case, since Isherwood and Jean Ross remained friends until the time of her death.

Sally owes something to the nineteenth-century tradition of the *femme fatale* that remained alive and kicking in Weimar popular culture, but as a sister of Lulu or Lola Lola she seems strikingly vulnerable and almost insipid, her outrageousness willed rather than springing from deep within her nature. But then Christopher, though sharing the same profession, is no Professor Rath. Rejecting the society and the morality that have produced and shaped him, he nevertheless hesitates to commit himself to an alternative. Had Isherwood possessed the courage or foolhardiness to write it, a section of *Goodbye to Berlin* that depicted the Cosy Corner as a rival establishment to the Blue Angel would have been worth having. But then no English publisher, in the decade that began with the furore over James Hanley's realistic but totally non-pornographic *Boy* (1931), would have touched such material.

Like Isherwood himself, Sally has come to Berlin to escape the constraints of a conventional family, and to some extent she acts as a reflector of late Weimar social and sexual mores. In this moral fable of the limitations of hedonism, politics are marginalised: one or two contemporary events, such as the failure of a bank, are briefly mentioned, but they remain peripheral and domesticated ('"The milkman says we'll have civil war in a fortnight!"'). In the most serious passage of the story, though, the detachment of these expatriates is suddenly perceived as soul-destroying: 'Perhaps in the Middle Ages people felt like this, when they believed themselves to have sold their souls to the Devil.... Yes, I said to myself, I've done it, now. I am lost' – the last word recalling the origins of this book in the unwritten panoramic novel thus named.

In 'On Ruegen Island', dated 'Summer 1931', the manipulation of the autobiographical basis is more palpable. This story utilises memories of the experiences of the two summers Isherwood spent in the Baltic resort, especially of the summer of 1931, when Auden and Spender as well as the youth referred to as 'Otto' were his companions. Isherwood had met the real Otto in Berlin and had known him for more than a year before taking him to Ruegen, but the fictional 'Christopher' meets 'Otto' by chance on the island and only subsequently sees him in Berlin. Auden and Spender have no counterparts in the fiction, but a character named Peter is introduced who has much in common with Isherwood, so that the latter's actual characteristics may be seen as being divided between the innocuous Christopher (more readily identified, of course, with the author) and the weaker, more problematic Peter. (Hugh David's suggestion that Peter is based on Spender does not carry conviction and is explicitly denied by Isherwood in *Christopher and his Kind* (p. 40).)

There is something a little perfunctory about the disguise bestowed on Peter, who was at Oxford (instead of Cambridge) and has lost his mother (instead of his father) but who comes from a social background resembling Isherwood's own and whose feelings for the youth are similarly compounded of lust, sentimental affection, and anger and jealousy at his cupidity, disloyalty and heterosexual philandering. Peter is unconvincing as a character, and the expository section that summarises his early life is clumsily done, reading like a synopsis for a *Bildungsroman*, but he enables 'Christopher' to be presented as coolly in control of the situation and fully detached from Peter's humiliating entanglement. 'Very much taken up' with the novel he is writing, he spends a lot of time alone, taking long walks and observing the other man's turbulent emotions with mild and noncommittal interest.

Since Isherwood's feelings for the real Otto have been tactfully displaced onto Peter, it was open to the author not only to identify but to analyse the nature of Peter's feelings for the youth. That would perhaps be expecting too much, however, from a writer who hoped to be published and sold, and it would certainly be expecting too much from Isherwood at this stage. Although it is clear that Peter and Otto share a room, and that Peter waits up late for him, gives him money and is tormented by jealousy, their relationship is never made clear, and the reader is left with the sense of something missing. (Much later Auden was to complain, not unjustly, to Isherwood about a similar hiatus in his novel *The World in the Evening*: ' "We have to know who was fucking whom. And you never make that clear in the book". ') The riskiest statement in the whole story is the narrator's observation that 'It is quite natural for Peter often to feel bored with Otto – they have scarcely a single interest in common – but Peter, *for sentimental reasons*, will never admit that this is so' (italics added). Isherwood no doubt knew a good deal at firsthand about both the boredom and the sentimentality that such a relationship could entail, but any further discussion of this emotional dilemma is blocked, promising though such an exploration might in literary terms have been.

In the next section of *Goodbye to Berlin*, 'The Nowaks', he moves a little, though only a little, closer to candour and confession. Back in Berlin, and with Peter returned to England, Christopher now develops a relationship with Otto and moves as a lodger into his home in a slum tenement. Isherwood had, as we have seen, done the same, quite briefly, in October 1930 – but that was before, not after, the first summer at Ruegen. In *Christopher and his Kind* (pp. 44–5) he describes this postdating of the fictional event by about one year as a 'falsification' but gives two reasons for it. One is technical – that it was important to introduce the major characters associated with Fräulein Schroeder's establishment before the relatively unimportant Nowaks – but the second is more interesting: 'since "Isherwood" is not overtly homosexual, he has to be given another reason for knowing Otto and another motive for going to live with his family'. He adds that the decline in the value of sterling following the British government's abandoning of the gold standard in September 1931 provides his fictional protagonist with 'a respectable motive for going to live with the Nowaks: he becomes their lodger because he is poor, not because he wants to share a bedroom with Otto'. This again demands a fictional ordering of events that is chronologically different from their autobiographical counterparts. Isherwood, furthermore, had quitted the tenement in Simeonstrasse after a month or so, whereas the fiction involves a longer stay, the story moving from 'clammy autumn weather' to a period 'after Christmas'.

In 'The Nowaks', then, Christopher is shown as sleeping with Otto because sharing beds is a normal way of life in the slums, but not as 'sleeping with' him in the euphemistic sense which usually denotes the opposite. The real Isherwood had never been so hard up that he had to live in such conditions, nor was he driven into the leaky tenement by any Orwellian urge to discover how the poor lived. He was there because he had yielded to Otto's persuasions, and even in the story there are hints that the more sophisticated or more cynical reader might respond to: for instance, Otto receives money from a Dutchman for unspecified services. (Was Isherwood perhaps recalling Auden's Dutch friend Dan, about whom he must have heard?)

The narrative ice gets even thinner when Isherwood describes the Alexander Casino, identified as 'a cellar *lokal*' at the end of the street. This is clearly, though not explicitly, a rent-bar and quite possibly based on the Cosy Corner. The narrator is taken there by Otto but recalls visiting it a year earlier during Saturday night tours of the city dives (just as Isherwood, almost a year before moving in with Otto's family, had been introduced to the boy-bars by Francis Turville-Petre). Boys are sitting around waiting, some in 'sweaters and leather jackets', one in shorts and an open-necked shirt (sartorial details paralleled in the description of the Cosy Corner in *Christopher and his Kind*); an elderly bourgeois is sitting in earnest conversation with a boy who from time to time lays his hand on the man's knee; at weekends foreign visitors invade the place, the Englishmen talking 'in loud, high, excited voices'. There cannot be much doubt as to the nature of the business transacted in this establishment, but the text contains nothing explicit. When the police raid the place they are looking for 'wanted criminals or escaped reformatory boys' (the latter phrase perhaps forming a discreet memorial to Auden's Otto Küsel). Christopher becomes a regular but seems to content himself with sitting and observing the scene. Perhaps, though, he is not always just an observer, for later, for obscure reasons, he worries about 'an unpleasant and mysterious rash' that 'might be due to Frau Nowak's cooking, or worse'.

One is reminded a little of the scenes in certain Victorian novels that, daring by the standards of their day, are yet worded with sufficient evasiveness not to bring a blush to the cheek of virgins of either sex or any age. In 'The Nowaks' sexuality remains a subtext until very near the end. There is then, however, a curious epilogue that seems almost irrelevant until it becomes clear that the narrator's homoeroticism has been displaced onto the dying women in the sanatorium who crave sexual satisfaction as an assurance that, for just a little longer, they are still alive. The real Otto's mother had actually been sent to a sanatorium, and this had evidently prompted Isherwood's departure from the crowded Simeonstrasse tenement, but the scrap of actuality is transformed and elaborated in the fiction – a nice instance of Isherwood's waste not, want not policy towards actual experience.

The sanatorium scene has a quality of brutality at odds with the normally relaxed tone of the book. One patient recalls with relish how her husband (' "such a great strong man" ') used to thrash her; another describes salaciously how Erika, ' "such an innocent girl until she came here" ', has now been sexually initiated by the other women and takes a doll (' "a little mannikin" ') to bed every night ' "because she says she must have a man in her bed!" ' The sexuality displaced onto these women is of a violent and morbid kind, suggesting the extent of the repression that the main part of the story has involved.

That repression comes close to failure once or twice, notably in the descriptions of Otto. With limited intellectual equipment, and viewed entirely from the outside, the youth can only be presented as a healthy animal with a strong instinct for self-preservation: when first glimpsed by Peter in 'On Ruegen Island' he is turning somersaults on the beach, and then exploits the stranger's interest by the time-honoured gambit of asking for a light. Thereafter, like a very model of contemporary *Naktkultur*, he expresses himself by physical, especially athletic, feats as much as by speech. (Compare the behaviour of the hustler in the final scene of *The Memorial*, whose form of greeting is to perform 'three rapid handsprings on the back of the sofa'.) There is in particular a scene in 'The Nowaks' describing Otto's habit of remaining in the room and stripping after bringing Christopher breakfast in bed, to 'do exercises, shadow-box or stand on his head'. He is, as the for once not-so-detached narrator observes, 'so animally alive, his naked brown body so sleek with health'. The frequent emphasis on Otto's taste for running after girls is not an entirely adequate counterweight to such revelatory moments.

In the Nowaks' Berlin slum, and even on Ruegen Island, politics invades private lives. Otto's brother Lothar joins the National

Socialists and even Otto expresses a preference for ' "a communist revolution" ', while their mother longs for a return to ' "the good old times" ' of the Kaiser. On the beaches of Ruegen, sandcastles fly the swastika. But it is in 'The Landauers', which immediately follows 'The Nowaks', that politics moves closer to the foreground, and in a more menacing shape than flags on sandcastles and young men dressing up in uniform.

The two central characters in this episode (not counting the Christopher-narrator) are both Jewish and both based quite closely on real-life prototypes. The model for Natalia Landauer, the daughter of the wealthy and cultured owner of a large Berlin department store, was Gisa Soloweitschik, a Jewish girl whom Spender had met on a skiing holiday in Switzerland when he was at Oxford and she was 17. Later they met again in Berlin, whither Spender had come to join her, and he introduced her to Isherwood. The two Englishmen would go often to Sunday lunch with Gisa's family at their Wilmersdorf flat; in the story the Landauers also live in Wilmersdorf, and Christopher goes there for lunch, but there is no figure in the story corresponding to Spender. Gisa was a student of art history who left Berlin in 1933 for France and there married a nephew of André Gide; Natalia too goes to Paris to study art and eventually settles there.

There are several other points of correspondence between Isherwood's story and the account of Gisa given in Spender's *World within World*. Gisa's family, according to Spender, 'called Christopher Shakespeare and me Byron', and the conversation at the Landauers' turns to Byron as well as (more riskily) Oscar Wilde; both girls, in the autobiography and the fiction, speak breathlessly of their enthusiasm for art and music; Gisa had 'an Oriental sense of untouchability' and 'could not drink from a glass if anyone else had drunk from it', while Natalia is fastidiously unwillingly to share a coffee-spoon with Christopher. What one cannot be sure of, naturally, is how far Spender's portrait of Gisa, some twenty years after the event, may have been derived from his friend's story rather than his own uncorrupted memories, though the chances are that Isherwood's version bears in any case a close resemblance to actuality.

Natalia's cousin, the young businessman Bernhard, is more loosely based on another of Isherwood's friends from the Jewish community of Berlin, Wilfrid Israel. Wilfrid, like Bernhard, worked for a department store owned by his family. Five years older than

Isherwood, he had an English mother (Bernhard speaks 'beautiful English') and was actually a British subject, born in England. After fleeing from Nazi persecution he lived in England and helped with the resettlement of refugees, but in June 1943 was killed when a civil aircraft flying from Lisbon to London was shot down by German fighters over the Bay of Biscay. (One of the other victims of the crash was the film star Leslie Howard.) At the end of Isherwood's story Bernhard dies mysteriously, presumably murdered by the Nazis, but at a date more than ten years earlier than Wilfrid, and Isherwood later admitted that this dating, demanded by the timeframe of the book and its 1933 terminus, was 'unconvincing' (*Christopher and his Kind*, p. 60).

Bernhard's sexuality is the subject of hints and implications: he lives in 'a quiet street not far from the Tiergarten' (as Isherwood had done when he first came to Berlin), quite alone; he is wearing 'a beautifully embroidered kimono' when Christopher visits him, and has a habit of resting his hand on the other man's shoulder. He also owns a luxurious villa 'on the shores of the Wannsee' somewhat resembling the Muthesius home where Auden had lived and which he may well have described to Isherwood. Near the end of the story, as the atmosphere in Berlin grows more tense, an oddly equivocal little conversation follows Christopher's announcement to Bernhard that he is going to England. Bernhard proposes that they should go to China together, leaving Berlin that very evening: Christopher treats it as a joke, but enters for the moment into the spirit of this fantasy, only adding with narratorial hindsight:

> Perhaps I am slow at jokes. At any rate, it took me nearly eighteen months to see the point of this one – to recognize it as Bernhard's last, most daring and most cynical experiment upon us both. For now I am certain – absolutely convinced – that his offer was perfectly serious.

The arresting word here is 'daring', which seems to mean that Christopher was being invited to 'come out' to his friend and to enter into a romantic relationship with Bernhard.

If so, it was a test that he failed, though a homoerotic subtext gives a meaning to the friendship between the two men that otherwise seems curiously lacking. In *Christopher and his Kind* (p. 59) Isherwood states: 'I believe Christopher suspected that Wilfrid was a severely repressed homosexual', and he adds that the novel

seemed to imply that Bernhard was concealing 'a romantic attachment to "Isherwood"'. These hints he found, with hindsight,
'offensive', and he was uncomfortable to reflect that Wilfrid had
read the book. He also notes (p. 56) that Spender's account of
Wilfrid in *World within World* differs radically in some respects
from his own.

'The Landauers' picks up a detail mentioned in the opening
section of the book – that one of Christopher's pupils is a Jewish
girl, Hippi Bernstein – and makes the increasingly hazardous situation of the prosperous Jewish business community the central issue
of the story. In that earlier passage, the Nazi threat still seems
'quite unreal': 'Hippi never worries about the future. Like everyone
else in Berlin, she refers continually to the political situation, but
only briefly, with a conventional melancholy, as when one speaks
of religion.' Even her father is dismissive towards the signs of the
times:

> 'You can go in the tram,' said Herr Bernstein. 'I will not have
> them throwing stones at my beautiful car.'
>   'And suppose they throw stones at me?' asked Frau Bernstein
> goodhumouredly.
>   'Ach, what does that matter? If they throw stones at you, I will
> buy you a sticking-plaster for your head. It will cost me only five
> groschen. But if they throw stones at my car, it will cost me
> perhaps five hundred marks.'

By a later stage in *Goodbye to Berlin* daily life has been invaded by
political events that cannot be turned aside with a jest, and 'The
Landauers', unlike any of the preceding stories, opens in an atmosphere of contemporary violence: 'One night in October 1930, about
a month after the Elections, there was a big row on the Leipziger-
strasse. Gangs of Nazi roughs turned out to demonstrate against
the Jews....' It is still, however, only 1930, and after this opening
politics recedes until the last dozen pages. Nevertheless, the essential keynote has been struck.

Towards the end of the story, there is a sudden access of political
awareness: at a party given by Bernhard at his Wannsee villa,
many of the guests are 'talking politics in low, serious voices', for
it is the night of the August 1931 referendum and there is a sense
that this may be 'the last night of an epoch'. Time passes quickly
during these final pages of the story, and after an interval of eight

months the overthrow of the government seems even more immin-
ent: as Christopher says to Bernhard, '"And what do you think
will happen in Germany now? . . . Is there going to be a Nazi putsch
or a communist revolution?"' A few pages later there are references to events in the early months of 1933: to Hitler becoming
Chancellor (30 January), the Reichstag fire (27 February), the boycott of Jewish businesses (1 April), and the narrator's departure 'for
the last time' – closely coinciding, as in *Mr Norris*, with Isherwood's
own.

The concluding section of *Goodbye to Berlin* offers not sequential
narrative but a series of vignettes drawn from Isherwood's last
winter in Berlin, and here he comes closer than ever before –
though still not very close – to candour concerning his own sexuality and lifestyle. With a friend he goes on a tour of what are
noncommittally referred to as 'the dives' but which are plainly gay,
lesbian and transvestite bars:

> It was to be in the nature of a farewell visit, for the Police have
> begun to take a great interest in these places. They are frequently
> raided, and the names of their clients are written down. There is
> even talk of a general Berlin clean-up.

There is an unusually vivid snapshot of the grotesque glitz of
contemporary Berlin nightlife ('a young man in a spangled crino-
line and jewelled breast-caps' painfully does the splits), its outrageousness magnified through the eyes of an American tourist:

> 'Say,' he asked Fritz, 'what's on here?'
> 'Men dressed as women,' Fritz grinned.
> The little American simply couldn't believe it. 'Men dressed as
> *women*? As *women* hey? Do you mean they're *queer*?'
> 'Eventually we're all queer,' drawled Fritz solemnly . . . .
> 'You *queer*, too, hey?' demanded the little American, turning
> suddenly on me.
> 'Yes,' I said, 'very queer indeed.'

The moment of confession, or proclamation, passes – or is, rather,
brushed aside with an ironic and ambiguous jest – but it has been a
close shave, and there is another nasty moment for Christopher a
few pages later when, on a visit to a reformatory, he is suddenly
overcome by guilt and shame at the sight of the boys: 'I seemed, at

that moment, to have become the sole representative of their gaolers, of Capitalist Society. I wondered if any of them had actually been arrested in the Alexander Casino, and, if so, whether they recognised me.'

Again, there is a hidden logic beneath the non sequitur: having been the exploiter of these boys (or boys like them), whose sexual services he was rich enough to purchase, he is now alarmed by the possibility of betrayal and exposure. But the alarm must be Isherwood's, not that of his fictional namesake who has apparently done nothing more than sit and watch the proceedings at the Alexander Casino. Again, as so often in the early writings, we have a sense of a 'wobbling' between invention and confession – of an indiscreet subtext speaking almost, though not quite, loudly enough to be heard. The appearance of these passages very near the end of the Berlin stories (the word 'queer' appears for the first time on page 562 of the omnibus edition) suggests a last-minute, barely repressed confessional impulse that, as it turned out, had to wait almost another forty years before it was fully articulated in *Christopher and his Kind*.

The guilt-feeling evident in the closing pages of *Goodbye to Berlin*, most obviously in the somewhat implausible visit to the reformatory, is interestingly glossed in the introduction Isherwood wrote for Gerald Hamilton's *Mr Norris and I* (the essay was later included in the volume titled *Exhumations*). He writes there that

What repels me now about *Mr Norris* is its heartlessness. It is a heartless fairy story about a real city in which human beings were suffering the miseries of political violence and near-starvation. The 'wickedness' of Berlin's night-life was of a most pitiful kind: the kisses and embraces, as always, had price-tags attached to them, but here the prices were drastically reduced in the cut-throat competition of an overcrowded market.... The only genuine monster was the young foreigner who passed gaily through these scenes of desolation, misinterpreting them to suit his childish fantasy. This I later began to understand – which is why my second book about Berlin is at least somewhat better than my first.

That the comparative judgement is exclusively moral rather than aesthetic is a natural corollary of the intensely personal nature of these works.

Almost thirty years after he left Berlin, Isherwood put one of his Berlin acquaintances to fictional use in *Down There on a Visit* (1962), the 'Ambrose' section of which has as its protagonist a character closely modelled on Francis Turville-Petre. This story thus serves as a kind of pendant to the Berlin novels. Or perhaps a postscript: for 'Ambrose' opens in May 1933 with the narrator leaving Berlin, and the main action derives from Isherwood's far from blissful period of residence on Francis's Greek island. It was, however, to be another 15 years before Francis's Berlin days received their fullest and frankest commemoration in *Christopher and his Kind*.

At first glance this latter book appears to be the long-delayed second instalment of an unfinished autobiographical work, though on closer examination it turns out to be something rather different. *Lions and Shadows* (1938) had been subtitled 'An Education in the Twenties', had begun with the narrator's schooldays and had ended with him leaving London for Berlin on 14 March 1929, exactly as Isherwood had done. But the preface contains a warning that the work is 'not, in the ordinary journalistic sense of the word, an autobiography;...it is not even entirely "true"', and the reader is urged to 'Read it as a novel'. Though figures readily recognisable as Auden, Upward and others make an appearance, most of the names are fictitious and 'a novelist's licence' has been used in recounting incidents. Its subject, Isherwood claims, is 'the education of a novelist': what is in question is representativeness rather than uniqueness. Hence there is no special virtue in truth-telling, and this is a convenient arrangement in more ways than one. As Sir Philip Sidney said of the poet, Isherwood cannot be blamed for falsifying because he is entering into no contract to tell things as they were, and this also grants him a licence for evasiveness. Published between *Mr Norris* and *Goodbye to Berlin*, *Lions and Shadows* shares their reluctance to come clean, and in fact the gap in Isherwood's practice between fiction and autobiography is so nearly invisible that the validity of these traditional generic labels is called into question by the one as much as by the other.

Characteristically evasive is the account of the sexuality of the young Auden (Weston in *Lions and Shadows*):

Weston's own attitude to sex, in its simplicity and utter lack of inhibition, fairly took my breath away. He was no Don Juan: he didn't run round hunting for his pleasures. But he took what came to him with a matter-of-factness and an appetite as hearty

as that which he showed when sitting down to dinner. I don't
think that, even in those days, he exaggerated much: certainly,
his manner of describing these adventures bore all the marks of
truth. I found his shameless prosaic anecdotes only too hard to
forget, as I lay restlessly awake at night, listening to the waves,
alone in my single bed.
                                                          (p. 195)

Little or nothing here, perhaps, is untrue (though 'no Don Juan'
may have been intended to point the reader in the wrong direction): what is missing is the central fact of Auden's homosexuality
and his influence on Isherwood as lover, mentor, trailblazer and
role-model.

Almost forty years later, *Christopher and his Kind* (1977) opens
with the words 'There is a book called *Lions and Shadows....*' The
warnings and recommendations of that earlier book's preface are
recalled: that work of his youth is 'not truly autobiographical' and
'should be read as if it were a novel' (an injunction that is, in
practice, not easy to obey). The new book, however, will be quite
different, 'as frank and factual as I can make it, especially as far as I
myself am concerned'. Given this resolve, it was obviously an
option for Isherwood to rewrite his earlier book in a spirit of
new-found candour. What he does, however, is to begin where
Lions and Shadows leaves off, with his first visit to Berlin. The earlier
book had covered the years 1921 to 1929; the second covers 1929 to
1939, and about two-fifths of it are devoted to the Berlin years. It
was, of course, a phase of his life that provided plenty to be frank
and factual about.

Christopher and his Kind is not subtitled 'An Education in the
Thirties' but, superficially at least, the heavy hand of the *Bildungsroman* tradition lies upon it. Adrift in Berlin, the hero encounters
colourful figures like Layard and Turville-Petre, explores the city's
day-life and night-life, and finds himself pulled between two sexual worlds: that of Hirschfeld's Institute, where homosexuality is
treated with sympathy and scientific tolerance and daily life is
decorous and respectable, and that of the Cosy Corner and the
other boy-bars, raffish, intensely exciting, exploitative and at least
semi-criminal. Karl Giese, representing the former, and Francis
Turville-Petre, his guide to the latter, offer him two contrasting
models of homosexual lifestyles, the domestic and the cruising,
and the urgent, though largely unspoken, question is which
one (if either) can both grant personal fulfilment and sustain his

vocation as a novelist. In the event he effects a compromise: the bars give him material to write about, but the disciplined world of the Institute defines the conditions in which the writing can be done.

None of this is very far away from the kind of nineteenth-century autobiography that describes the narrator's struggles with religious doubt or some other burning contemporary issue. What Christian faith or its rejection were to Newman or Gosse, homosexuality was to Isherwood. But as we turn over the pages of *Christopher and his Kind* it becomes clear that there is another theme to which this narrative of early experiences is subservient: the book becomes an inquiry into the nature of memory, the processes by which experience is turned into art, and the very possibility of autobiographical writing as conventionally understood. And inevitably these concerns raise doubts about the initial promise that the book will be 'frank and factual' and about the attainability of this objective. For if it turns out that the truth about the past is irrecoverable, what is such a promise worth?

On one level the book exposes, ridicules and repudiates the author's own earlier attempts to mythologise the past. A self-confessed myth-maker, Isherwood now presents himself as coming clean about his earlier autobiographical statements in the same spirit as that in which he has recently come out as a homosexual. A good example of this is in connection with the destruction of the diary he kept in Berlin:

> Christopher's declared reason for burning his Berlin diary was unconvincing. He used to tell his friends that he had destroyed his real Past because he preferred the simplified, more creditable, more exciting fictitious Past which he had created to take its place. This fictitious Past, he said, was the Past he wanted to 'remember'. Now that I am writing about Christopher's real Past, I sadly miss the lost diary and have no patience with this arty talk. (p. 37)

There is no reason, however, why we should find the new stance more credible than the old one: myth-making may be habit-forming, and if there were formerly motives for falsifying the past, there may be different motives for doing so again. In any case, recovering the past is more easily said than done: however firm the resolve, the task may be simply impossible, and

Isherwood is surely naive or disingenuous in claiming that the existence of the diary would enable him to tell the truth. For the diary itself can only have been a version of the truth, selective, sometimes unconsciously or wilfully distorted, as artful a compound of lights (or lions) and shadows as an Expressionist film. He is more honest when he admits that he cannot really remember Jean Ross because the original image has been obscured by too many actresses playing Sally Bowles.

The detached, ironic, sometimes cynical tone of *Christopher and his Kind* nourishes the illusion of truth-telling, as does the careful nomenclatorial distinction between his past and present selves (respectively 'Christopher' and 'I'). Among the self-created myths that undergo an apparently scrupulous process of dismantling is that of his first Berlin lover, 'Bubi', as The German Boy (see p. 42 above). But if there was self-delusion in the past, there may now be an overstating or oversimplifying of the case for the sake of literary effect, and neither account may succeed in conveying the genuine flavour of a relationship that was clearly of considerable intensity and duration. There is perhaps something suspicious in Isherwood's deft exchanging of one simple version of events for another, and more honesty in the young Auden's recognition, in his scribbled journal, of the complexity and contradictoriness of his feelings for Gerhart.

It is true that Isherwood is ready enough to admit that the Berlin stories misrepresented actuality for aesthetic or other reasons. As already noted, he was never so poor that he was compelled to live in a slum, and he spent a month with Otto's family for sexual rather than economic reasons, though he found it tactful in the story based on this episode of his life to adduce the more respectable motive. The description of Otto, he acknowledges, is inaccurate in its reference to his 'spindly, immature legs': there was nothing wrong with the real Otto's limbs, far from it, but the homoeroticism of the passage was nearing danger point and a little dust needed to be thrown in the reader's eyes. Even in a much later book, *Down There on a Visit*, there is some misrepresentation in the portrait of Francis Turville-Petre as 'Ambrose', though Isherwood himself maintained that all he says is true except for three sentences. Despite this reassurance, among so many confessions and corrections of the record one is bound to wonder how much has gone consciously or unconsciously unconfessed. True confessions, excellent in principle, may be next to impossible in practice.

In an earlier chapter I have questioned the belatedly acknowledged 'genuine' reason given for going to live in Berlin ('Berlin
meant Boys'), which perhaps does little more than replace one
myth, handy enough in its generation, by another more appropriate to an age of tolerance, enlightenment or authorised exhibition-
ism. But in the most significant passage in this connection, and one
of the most striking in the whole book, Isherwood comes close to
recognising that his homosexuality may itself be part of his personal myth. Asserting his right to 'live according to my nature', he
nevertheless admits that even if his nature were different he would
still have to fight those he saw as his enemies (the Others of his
undergraduate myth-making, shared with Upward) and would
adopt sexual nonconformity as a mode of protest: 'If boys didn't
exist, I should have to invent them' (p. 17). He turned to homosexuality, that is, as some others of his class and generation turned
to Roman Catholicism or left-wing politics, as a mode of protest.
His rebuttal of the charge of 'repressed heterosexuality' amounts to
no more than a reminder that his sexual inclinations have not
changed with the passing of time – a point at which one recalls
that myths can be of sufficient power and permanence to be indis-
tinguishable in their effects from the truth.

The promised 'frank and factual' book – the book that could not
have been written, and certainly could not have been published,
forty years earlier – does not quite materialise in *Christopher and his
Kind* for the very good reason that such a promise embodies an
impossible ideal. Franker and more factual as well as funnier and
more graphic than *Lions and Shadows* it certainly is, though it has
the advantage of dealing with a more colourful phase of the
author's life, and a book about late Weimar Berlin that was as
pussy-footed as *Lions and Shadows* is difficult to imagine.

Ultimately, however, it does not matter a great deal whether the
promise is fulfilled or not: the biographers can be relied on sooner
or later to fill in the gaps and correct the false impressions. What is
significant in the pages that follow that opening statement is the
deep interest in the relationship between autobiography and fiction, and the concessions and compromises to which both are
subject. It is an interest that ensures a continuity between Isherwood's practice of these two genres, much closer together in his
case than is customary: so much so, indeed, that a new taxonomy
of genres, more subtle and flexible than the existing one, seems
called for.

Epilogue:

GOODBYE TO BERLIN

After the war a publisher invited Isherwood to spend six months in the city and to write a book about it. He refused the invitation, partly because he was too busy with other projects, partly because such an idea seemed 'terribly willed'. One suspects, though, that, as with Kipling declining to revisit India, some deeper motive was involved: the ruins of the city he had known in its heyday might have turned out to be an irresistible metaphor for the loss of his own youth. Two postwar visits to Europe failed to include Germany in their itinerary, but at last in 1952 he spent a short time in Berlin and revisited the now famous house in Nollendorfstrasse. His old landlady, Fräulein Thurau, cognisant of her own literary celebrity, greeted him rapturously, and in later years Isherwood would mimic for the benefit of his friends her exclamations of joy at their unexpected reunion. Once she had calmed down, she gave him news of Otto, who was prospering in the postwar world of shortages and black markets, and he called on Heinz, now married with a child.

In his own later years, Auden was back in Berlin on several occasions for short periods and did not entirely escape reminders of the personal as well as the public past. On one occasion he was startled by the vision of a former boyfriend who had turned into the fattest man he had ever seen ('he should have been in a circus'), and was made wistful by the reflection that 'the city of my youth has now gone'. In 1945 he was (somewhat improbably) sent to Berlin by the Morale Division of the United States Strategic Bombing Survey with the rank equivalent to major, the team of which he was a member being charged with investigating the effects of bombing on the German population. Twenty years further on, in 1964–5, he spent six months there as a Ford Foundation writer-in-residence. This latter visit was not a success: after thirty years, both he and Berlin had changed too much. It was during this stay that he kept a diary, the only one he is known to have kept apart from that which belongs to his period of residence in 1929. Re-reading the earlier diary at that time, as he is known to

210

have done, must have induced an overpowering sense of then and now.

For both of these writers, Berlin had constituted a short but crucial chapter in their experience. It must be said, though, that to link their names, as this book has constantly done, is to risk giving a misleading impression of long-term personal intimacy and literary parity. Their gifts and achievements were after all of a very different order: beside the creative energy, the formidable intellect and the profound originality of Auden, Isherwood's talent, though distinctive, seems narrow and low-pulsed. There is a case for regarding Auden as the greatest British poet of the mid-century, while Isherwood remains a minor novelist and autobiographer who was shrewd enough to recognise his own strengths and limitations at a fairly early stage. It is the difference between a stream and a geyser, or between a great waterfall and a backyard swimming pool – which is not necessarily to say a word against streams or swimming pools. It must also be said that they were unequal in the direct use they made of their Berlin experiences. Almost inevitably, the novelist and autobiographer exploited them more fully and obviously than the poet.

Still, the significance of the time the young Auden spent in Berlin ought not to be undervalued. Without the experience, at a particular stage, of that extraordinary place, so much in the future lives and work of both Auden and Isherwood might have been different. Auden spent a relatively short time there but did so when he was, in more ways than one, standing at the crossroads. He came to recognise his own sexual identity, rejecting the notion he had brought with him of his homosexuality as a passing phase, an entertaining sidetrip from the well-marked route to heterosexual love and marriage. Perhaps more importantly for his work, he also had there his first experiences of intense sexual passion and his first yearnings for a stable and mutual relationship. His Berlin journal offers compelling and moving evidence of his intellectual and emotional strivings to understand himself and others: in the words of one of his own poems, the appeal he made to Berlin was to tell him the truth about love. It was in Berlin, too, that he first became seriously aware of politics. Though he initially, for reasons beyond his control, returned to England, Berlin seems also to have given him a taste for the life of the exile that was to be satisfied by his later residence in America, Austria and elsewhere. Without the nine or ten months spent there, the rest of his life might have been very different – and might have beens, though fruitless for the subject, may be profitable for the student of biography.

Isherwood told W. J. Weatherby in a 1960 interview, ' "I write fundamentally about foreigners, about exiles, about oddballs, the excluded and so forth..." '. His own lifestyle was to remain that of the permanent voluntary exile, but he was to continue over many years, and almost to the end of his days, to draw on his Berlin experiences for literary copy. At the same time the transmogrifications of his work into stage and screen entertainments, like the books by or about Mr Norris and Sally Bowles in which he had no hand, gave those experiences and writings an autonomous life, so that *Goodbye to Berlin* has become, like *Hamlet* or *Frankenstein*, not only a work of literature but the starting point for a metaliterature or mythology.

Bibliography

WORKS BY AUDEN AND ISHERWOOD

W. H. Auden

Juvenilia: Poems 1922–28, ed. Katherine Bucknell, London, 1994
Collected Poems, ed. Edward Mendelson, London, 1976
Berlin Journal (unpublished: Berg Collection, New York Public Library)

Christopher Isherwood

The Memorial (1932)
Mr Norris Changes Trains (1935)
Lions and Shadows (1938)
Goodbye to Berlin (1939)
Prater Violet (1945)
The Condor and the Cows (1949)
Down There on a Visit (1962)
Exhumations (1966)
Kathleen and Frank (1971)
Christopher and his Kind 1929–1939 (1977)

W. H. Auden and Christopher Isherwood

The Dog Beneath the Skin (1935)
The Ascent of F6 (1936)
On the Frontier (1938)

OTHER WORKS

Albright, William Foxwell, *The Archaeology of Palestine*, Harmondsworth, 1963.
Alexander, Peter F., *William Plomer: A Biography*, Oxford, 1989.
Bell, Arthur, 'An Interview with Christopher Isherwood', *Fag Rag*, Summer 1973.
Bell, Arthur, 'Christopher Isherwood: No Parades', *New York Times Book Review*, 25 March 1973, pp. 10, 12.
Boyd, Brian, *Vladimir Nabokov: The Russian Years*, London, 1990.
Brome, Vincent, *Havelock Ellis, Philosopher of Sex: A Biography*, London, 1979.

Bullock, Alan, *Hitler: A Study in Tyranny*, London, 1964.

Carpenter, Humphrey, *W. H. Auden: A Biography*, London, 1981.

Coates, Paul, *The Gorgon's Gaze: German Cinema, Expressionism, and the Image of Horror*, Cambridge, 1990.

Constantine, David, 'The German Auden: Six Early Poems', in W. H. Auden *'The Map of All My Youth': Early Works Friends and Influences* (Auden Studies I) ed. Katherine Bucknell and Nicholas Jenkins, Oxford, 1990, pp. 1–15.

Cooper, Artemis, *Cairo in the War*, London, 1989.

Cunningham, Valentine, *British Writers of the Thirties*, Oxford, 1989.

David, Hugh, *Stephen Spender: A Portrait with Background*, London, 1992.

Douglas, Don, 'Christopher Isherwood Speaks Out', *Gay Scene*, V, 9, February 1975.

Eisner, Lotte H., *The Haunted Screen*, London, 1969.

Farnan, Dorothy J., *Auden in Love*, London, 1984.

Farson, Daniel, *The Gilded Gutter: The Life of Francis Bacon*, London, 1993.

Fielding, Xan, *Hide and Seek*, London, 1954.

Finney, Brian, *Christopher Isherwood*, London, 1979.

Forster, E. M., *Selected Letters: Volume 2, 1921–1970*, eds Mary Lago and P.N. Furbank, London, 1985.

Fowler, Marian, *The Way She Looks Tonight: Five Women of Style*, New York, 1996. (Includes a section on Marlene Dietrich.)

Friedrich, Thomas, *Berlin: A Photographic Portrait of the Weimar Years 1918–1933*, London, 1991.

Fryer, Jonathan, *Eye of the Camera: A Life of Christopher Isherwood*, London, 1993.

Fryer, Jonathan, *Isherwood*, New York, 1978.

Gardiner, Margaret, 'Auden: A Memoir', *New Review*, 3 (July 1976), pp. 9–19.

Gay, Peter, *Weimar Culture: The Outsider as Insider*, London, 1968.

Geherin, David J., 'An Interview with Christopher Isherwood', *Journal of Narrative Technique*, 2 (September 1972), pp. 143–58.

Green, Henry, *Pack My Bag: A Self-Portrait*, Oxford, 1986.

Green, Martin, *Children of the Sun: A Narrative of 'Decadence' in England after 1918*, London, 1977.

Hamilton, Gerald, *Mr Norris and I: An Autobiographical Sketch*, London, 1956.

Hamilton, Gerald, *The Way It Was With Me*, London, 1969.

Hart, Denis, 'Here on a Visit' (interview with Isherwood), *The Guardian*, 22 September 1961.

Heilbrun, Carolyn G., 'Christopher Isherwood: An Interview', *Twentieth Century Literature*, 22 (October 1976), pp. 253–63.

Hillier, Bevis, *Young Betjeman*, London, 1988.

Hollis, Christopher, *In the Twenties*, London, 1976.

Hynes, Samuel, *The Auden Generation: Literature and Politics in the 1930s*, London, 1976.

Kane, Martin, *Weimar Germany and the Limits of Political Art*, London, 1987.

Kracauer, Siegfried, *From Caligari to Hitler: A Psychological History of the German Film*, Princeton, NJ, 1947.

Lane, Homer, *Talks to Parents and Teachers*, London, 1928.

Lehmann, John, *Christopher Isherwood: A Personal Memoir*, London, 1987.

Lehmann, John, *In the Purely Pagan Sense*, London, 1985.

Lehmann, John, *The Whispering Gallery*, London, 1955.

McAlmon, Robert, *Being Geniuses Together 1920–1930*, New York, 1968; rev. edn, 1984.

McAlmon, Robert, *Distinguished Air: Grim Fairy Tales*, Paris, 1925.

Mackay, John Henry, *The Hustler (Der Puppenjunge)*, trans. Hubert Kennedy, Boston, Mass., 1985.

Mann, Klaus, *The Pious Dance (Der Fromme Tanz)*, trans. Laurence Senelick, London, 1988.

Mann, Klaus, *The Turning-Point: Thirty-Five Years in this Century*, New York, 1984 (originally published 1942).

Manning, Olivia, *The Battle Lost and Won*, London, 1978.

Manvell, Roger and Heinrich Fraenkel, *The German Cinema*, London, 1971.

Meyers, Jeffrey, *Homosexuality and Literature 1890–1930*, London, 1987.

Mitchison, Naomi, *You May Well Ask: A Memoir 1920–1940*, London, 1979.

Osborne, Charles, 'Berlin in the Twenties: Conversations with Otto Klemperer and Lotte Lenya', *London Magazine*, 1 (May 1961), p. 49.

Osborne, Charles, *W. H. Auden: The Life of a Poet*, London, 1980.

Perrot, Jean, *Syria-Palestine I: From the Origins to the Bronze Age* (Archaelogia Mundi series), Geneva, 1979.

Petro, Patrice, *Joyless Streets: Women and Melodramatic Representation in Weimar Germany*, Princeton, NJ, 1989.

Plant, Richard, *The Pink Triangle: The Nazi War against Homosexuals*, New York, 1986.

Plomer, William, *Autobiography*, 1975.

Read, Anthony and David Fisher, *Berlin: The Biography of a City*, 1994.

Riley, Thomas A., *John Henry Mackay*, New York, 1972.

Roberts, Susan, *The Magician of the Golden Dawn: The Story of Aleister Crowley*, Chicago, 1978.

Russo, Tony, 'Christopher Isherwood' (interview), *Christopher Street*, I, 9, March 1977.

Sawyer-Laucanno, Christopher, *An Invisible Spectator: A Biography of Paul Bowles*, London, 1989.

Scobie, W. I., 'Christopher Isherwood Interview', *The Advocate* (Los Angeles), No. 179 (17 December 1975), pp. 6–8.

Scobie, W. I., 'The Youth that was "I": A Conversation in Santa Monica with Christopher Isherwood', *London Magazine*, 17 (April–May 1977), pp. 23–32.

Shipman, David, *The Story of Cinema*, Vol. I, London, 1982.

Shirer, William, *The Rise and Fall of the Third Reich*, London, 1960.

Sinclair, Andrew, *Francis Bacon: His Life and Violent Times*, London, 1993.

Spender, Stephen, *Journals 1939–1983*, ed. John Goldsmith, London, 1985.

Spender, Stephen, *Letters to Christopher*, ed. Lee Bartlett, Santa Barbara, Calif., 1980.

Spender, Stephen, *The Temple*, London, 1988.

Spender, Stephen, *World within World*, London, 1951.

Steakley, James D., 'Iconography of a Scandal: Political Cartoons and the Eulenberg Affair in Wilhelmine Germany', in Martin Duberman et al. (eds), *Hidden from History: Reclaiming the Gay and Lesbian Past*, London, 1989.

Steakley, J. D., *The Homosexual Emancipation Movement in Germany*, New York, 1975.

Sternberg, Josef von, *Fun in a Chinese Laundry*, New York, 1965.

Suares, J. C., *Hollywood Drag*, Charlottesville, Va., 1994.

Upward, Edward, 'Remembering the earlier Auden', *Adam International Review* (1973–4), pp. 17–22.

Vidal, Gore, 'Christopher Isherwood's Kind', *Pink Triangle and Yellow Star*, London, 1982.

Vogel, Bruno, *Alf*, trans. Samuel B. Johnson, London, 1992.

Völker, Klaus, *Brecht: A Biography*, trans. John Nowell, London, 1979.

Von Eckardt, Wolf and Sander L. Gilman, *Bertolt Brecht's Berlin: A Scrapbook of the Twenties*, New York, 1975.

Weatherby, W. I., 'Christopher Isherwood', *The Guardian*, 17 November 1960.

Weiss, Andrea, *Vampires and Violets: Lesbians in the Cinema*, London, 1992.

Whitehead, John, 'Auden: An Early Poetical Notebook', *London Magazine*, 5 (May 1965), pp. 85–93.

Willett, John, *The New Sobriety 1917–1933: Art and Politics in the Weimar Period*, London, 1978.

Willett, John, *The Theatre of the Weimar Republic*, New York, 1988.

Willett, John, *The Weimar Years: A Culture Cut Short*, London, 1984.

Wolff, Charlotte, *Magnus Hirschfeld: A Portrait of a Pioneer in Sexology*, London, 1986.

Zucker, Carole, *The Idea of the Image: Josef von Sternberg's Dietrich Films*, London and Toronto, 1988.

Index

Index